HANGING MARY

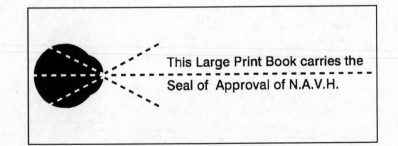

This Large Print Book carries the
Seal of Approval of N.A.V.H.

Hanging Mary

Susan Higginbotham

THORNDIKE PRESS
A part of Gale, Cengage Learning

GALE
CENGAGE Learning®

Farmington Hills, Mich • San Francisco • New York • Waterville, Maine
Meriden, Conn • Mason, Ohio • Chicago

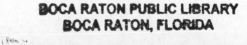

GALE
CENGAGE Learning

LIBRARY OF CONGRESS CATALOGING-IN-PUBLICATION DATA

Names: Higginbotham, Susan, author.
Title: Hanging Mary / by Susan Higginbotham.
Description: Large print edition. | Waterville, Maine : Thorndike Press, 2016. | © 2016 | Series: Thorndike Press large print basic | Includes bibliographical references.
Identifiers: LCCN 2016003895| ISBN 9781410489517 (hardcover) | ISBN 1410489515 (hardcover)
Subjects: LCSH: Booth, John Wilkes, 1838-1865—Friends and associates—Fiction. | Lincoln, Abraham, 1809-1865—Assassination—Fiction. | Conspiracies—Fiction. | Washington (D.C.)—History—Civil War, 1861-1865—Fiction. | Large type books. | GSAFD: Historical fiction. | Suspense fiction. | Biographical fiction.
Classification: LCC PS3608.I364 H36 2016b | DDC 813/.6—dc23
LC record available at http://lccn.loc.gov/2016003895

Published in 2016 by arrangement with Sourcebooks, Inc.

Printed in Mexico
1 2 3 4 5 6 7 20 19 18 17 16

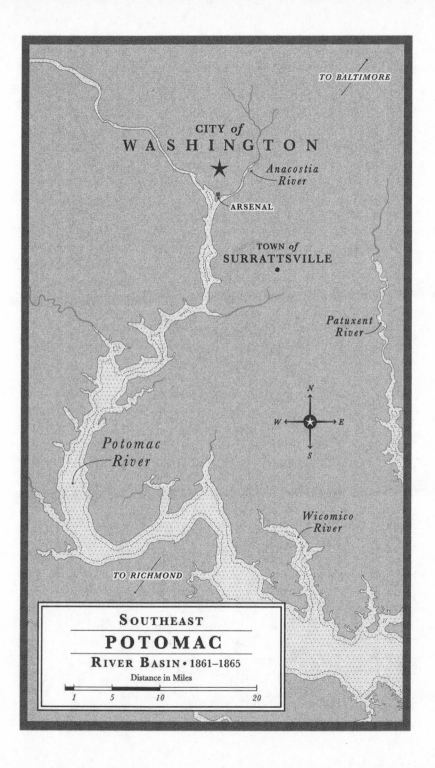

TO BALTIMORE

CITY of
WASHINGTON

★

Anacostia
River

ARSENAL

TOWN of
SURRATTSVILLE

•

Patuxent
River

N

W ←✦→ E

S

Potomac
River

Wicomico
River

TO RICHMOND

SOUTHEAST
POTOMAC
RIVER BASIN • 1861–1865
Distance in Miles

1   5   10   20

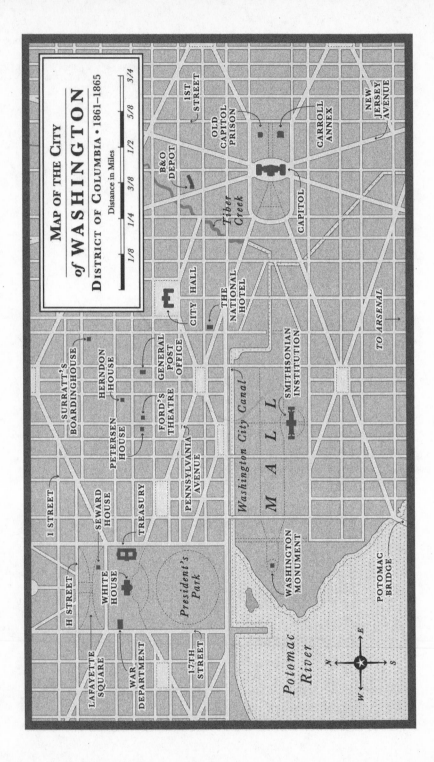

MAP OF THE CITY
of WASHINGTON
DISTRICT OF COLUMBIA · 1861–1865
Distance in Miles

1/8   1/4   3/8   1/2   5/8   3/4

1ST STREET
OLD CAPITOL PRISON
CARROLL ANNEX
NEW JERSEY AVENUE
B&O DEPOT
Tiber Creek
CAPITOL
CITY HALL
THE NATIONAL HOTEL
TO ARSENAL
SMITHSONIAN INSTITUTION
SURRATT'S BOARDINGHOUSE
HERNDON HOUSE
GENERAL POST OFFICE
PETERSEN HOUSE
FORD'S THEATRE
Washington City Canal
M A L L
PENNSYLVANIA AVENUE
I STREET
SEWARD HOUSE
TREASURY
WASHINGTON MONUMENT
President's Park
H STREET
WHITE HOUSE
LAFAYETTE SQUARE
WAR DEPARTMENT
17TH STREET
Potomac River
POTOMAC BRIDGE

N E S W

■ ■ ■ ■

Part I

■ ■ ■

"I wish you knew Ma, I know you would like her."
— John Surratt, writing to his cousin

"This young woman is a plain unassuming girl."
— W. P. Wood, superintendent, Old Capitol Prison

1
MARY SURRATT
AUGUST 1864

There were two things for which I could thank my late husband: buying our house in Washington, and dying.

It was in 1862 when my husband left this world, but two years later I still woke sometimes, trembling, before I remembered I was perfectly free. No more drunken rages to endure. No more finding my husband facedown on the floorboards. No cuffs to the head, which to John's credit did not come that often, but of which I always lived in dread. I could lie in bed and stretch out comfortably, knowing no brute was going to soil the sheets or violate my body.

A drunken man is seldom careful with his money, and John was no exception: though he was fairly prosperous when I married him (it was, I must admit, one of his attractions), he made bad decisions, the worst of which was to build the tavern and bar I continued to run after his death. How I hated the place! It brought John to his ruin, I sincerely believed, because as a naturally taciturn man, he had to drink harder than ever to make himself jovial to his customers. Worst, it left him in debt, which I still owed — his parting gift to me. For two years, my children and I struggled to maintain this folly of his, and with the prospect that Maryland would soon adopt a new constitution that would free our three slaves, we could expect only to struggle harder.

But John made one investment that brought in a steady income: a handsome house on H Street in Washington, about fifteen miles from this sleepy crossroads in southern Maryland. For years, it had been rented to a reliable tenant — until, one sweltering August day, I received a letter. Poor health was obliging my tenant to move to the country, and he would not be renewing the lease. So atop of everything else, we would have to find a new tenant, one who might or might not be dependable. Bad news — until I sat back and pondered the situation more thoroughly.

This was my chance to start a new life.

"The tenant in Washington is not renewing his lease," I told my son and my daughter as we sat down to our dinner that evening.

"After praying about the matter, I have come up with an idea I hope will suit us all. Instead of leasing our house in Washington, we move into it ourselves. If we lease this place, and take in boarders at H Street, we can live much less expensively than we are living now, and we can pay off some of those wretched debts."

"Boarders?" Anna wrinkled her nose.

"We must, my dear. Even if we did not need the income, it would be foolish to waste all of that space. And what is wrong with taking in a few quiet, well-behaved people in the city when we already take our chances with anyone who passes through here?"

"That is a point. And there will be shops, and concerts, and the theater . . . I like the idea, Ma."

"And we can walk to church as well. You, Johnny?"

"Suits me fine. And I might even have a boarder for us: my friend Mr. Weichmann. He's got a government job now, so he can pay, and I know he's not happy with his present lodgings. Too far from his job, and too large and lonely, he says." Johnny looked sidelong at his older sister. "And no pretty girls."

"Johnny! If he is to come to live with us,

11

you mustn't encourage that sort of thing. I won't abide it. But when can we move, Ma? I will need a new dress for the theater. It won't do to walk around in rags, or we will never attract a good class of boarder."

"Don't pack yet, child. We must first lease this place. And we have to get the Washington house fixed up as well." In truth, I was scarcely less excited than Anna and was already settling in my mind which furniture to take to Washington and which to leave here.

The last of the evening tipplers had weaved away from the bar and Anna had gone to bed when Johnny knocked at my door. "Ma, you're going to rent the place to someone on our side, aren't you?"

"Most certainly."

War is men's business, I had always believed, but on the day Lincoln was inaugurated, my oldest son, Isaac, rushed off to Texas and later joined the Confederate army, so it drew me in. It drew me in another way as well: my husband — who, like most people in this part of southern Maryland, sympathized with the South — allowed the tavern to become a stop for those making the dangerous journey across the Potomac River into Virginia, running the blockade between North and South with goods, mail, and money. I had no choice in the matter, of course, but had I been consulted, I no doubt would have agreed. How could I do otherwise, with a son fighting for the Confederacy? So after my husband died, I saw no reason to alter the tavern's status as a safe haven — especially as my Johnny had been aiding the Confederacy too, since he left school after my husband's death, first by using the post office in our tavern as a drop for those wishing to send mail to the South, then, once the Union took his postmaster position away from him for disloyalty, as a courier himself.

"I have been thinking, Johnny, that a tenant may not be necessary. Should you want to run the place on your own —"

Johnny shook his head. "I'm tired of peeling drunks off the floor, Ma, and I can serve the Confederacy a lot better if I don't have this place to worry about. No, as a matter of fact, I was thinking when I was tending bar tonight that I know a man who might be perfect, a Mr. Lloyd. He's in Washington now, but he stops here whenever business brings him through Prince George's County, and I know he's been hankering for a country life, if he can find something to do."

"And he is a Southern man?"

"Yes — and even better, he's a man who minds his own business."

2
NORA
AUGUST 1864 TO OCTOBER 1864

"I don't like my present lodgings, Father."

My father looked around at my room, which was large and comfortably furnished. It was not cool — no place could be so in Washington City in late August — but a shade tree rendered it at least tolerable. "Why not, child? The Misses Donovan are sweet ladies."

"They are sweet *old* ladies. We do nothing besides drink tea and go to Mass. If I go outside, I have to go with their servant, Clarence, and he is almost as old a lady as they are."

"Child —"

"Well, it is true. 'Miss Nora, the misses won't like you going on this street. There is a saloon here!' There's a saloon on every street in Washington, Father. I might as well be a prisoner."

"Surely you exaggerate, my dear."

"There's nothing to read here, either."

"Why, they have a library full of books."

"Dreary books. Dull books. Nothing but essays and history and religious works, because the misses consider novels unsuitable reading for impressionable young ladies." I frowned. "Well, that's not entirely true; they do have *Clarissa,* which I have read. Twice. It's very sad."

"What about the piano? Don't they let you play upon it?"

"Yes, but it's out of tune. They can't hear it well enough to know the difference. When I asked them if they could engage a tuner, they acted as if I were trying to turn the place into the Canterbury music hall." I sighed theatrically. "I might as well enter a convent, Father. This dreariness is insupportable."

My father sighed as well.

My mother had died when I was quite small, and my father, having loved my mother dearly and not caring to remarry, had sent me away for my education. The schools I attended were not the sort of places depicted by Mr. Dickens or Miss Charlotte Brontë (whose novels I devoured), but well-run, quiet establishments where I learned to write an elegant hand, play the piano, and speak tolerable French. In such a manner, I had passed a happy, if somewhat

16

monotonous, existence in tranquil surroundings until this June, when at age nineteen, I had reached the point where there was very little that could be taught to me (or so I thought), and so I came home.

Father was a messenger and a collector for the Metropolitan Bank and had been so for decades. He had once left his position due to ill health, but his superiors missed him so sorely, and he missed them so sorely, that they begged him to resume his duties, which he did, with a rise in salary as his reward. He probably could have afforded to lease a small house, with me keeping it, when I left school. But he worked long hours and sometimes had to go out of town on business, and Washington City was not the quiet town it had been when he came there in the 1830s. The war had brought in people from everywhere and every walk of life, and Father feared that, home alone, I might fall into unsuitable company. So he had placed me to board with the Misses Donovan, just a few blocks away from his own lodgings.

"You are truly unhappy here, child?"

"I do like the ladies, Father," I replied truthfully. "But they are old maids, and if I stay here much longer, I will turn into one

17

myself. I can just feel myself growing old here."

"I will consult with Peter, then. Perhaps he will know of a suitable lodging."

I suppressed a groan. There were two sorts of men my father admired — learned men and men of religion — and my older brother, Peter, an aspiring priest who had taken a teaching job at the soon-to-be-opened Boston College, had the happy distinction of falling into both categories. For the past few years, Father had been in the habit of consulting him about any business involving the family, which, since my older sister, Hannah, was a cloistered nun, generally meant my business. As Peter had often told Father that I was overindulged, I could imagine only with the greatest trepidation what sort of lodging, short of a convent, he would consider suitable. I knew better than to argue, however, although I felt that Father hardly needed Peter's advice. It was true that he had no more than a charity school education and that he felt this keenly, but he could read anything put in front of him and wrote a beautiful hand. He could add and subtract long figures in his head while others — Peter included — were scratching their pens on papers and frowning over their errors.

Weeks passed, and I was resigning myself to staying with the Misses Donovan and getting used to their untuned piano when, in late September, Father came to see me again, this time with Peter — come all the way from Boston to see to my affairs — at his side. "Peter has found an ideal situation for you, Nora. A widow, Mrs. Surratt, is moving to Washington from the country and will be taking in boarders at her house on H Street. She is a very respectable lady."

A respectable widow sounded to me little better than an old maid, but I nodded politely.

"She has been keeping a tavern and bar in Surrattsville, in Prince George's County in Maryland," my brother informed my father. I noticed Peter was prematurely balding — unlike Father, who at age sixty-four still had a full head of gray hair.

"A bar?" Father, who had never been a drinking man, frowned.

"Her husband ran the bar, and it was necessary for her to continue with that line of business in order to live. She has long wished to give it up, she told Father Wiget, and move to Washington, but it was not until recently, when the tenant here failed to renew his lease, that this became a realistic possibility."

19

My father's expression lightened. "She knows Father Wiget, then?" As well as being the priest at St. Aloysius, he was the president of Gonzaga College, where Peter had been both a pupil and a teacher.

"Yes. She has known him for many years, and her sons were at his school of St. Thomas Manor before it closed."

I perked up. Mrs. Surratt had sons?

"She has had a difficult life, Father Wiget tells me. Her husband was adopted by a family of substance and inherited a handsome estate, but he was a poor businessman and a heavy drinker and squandered much of his holdings, and the war did the rest. They have only the tavern and the house in Washington." My brother glanced at me. "Nora, I have spoken rather freely. I hope that if you do go to live with Mrs. Surratt, you will treat what I have said as matters of confidence."

"Yes," I said. In truth, I had been too busy wondering about Mrs. Surratt's sons — Two? Three? More? Handsome? — to care about her difficult life.

"Are her sons much about the house?" Father asked.

"The elder is serving with the Confederate army — coming from where they do, that is to be expected, though — and the younger

20

helps his mother with her affairs. Father Wiget sees the younger one occasionally when business takes him to Washington and knows him to be of good character. But what makes this situation ideal — and, I believe, more congenial for Nora than her present one — is that Mrs. Surratt has a daughter, an accomplished young lady of twenty-one. She will therefore have a suitable companion."

"It sounds ideal," said Father. "I knew that you would come up with something."

Peter nodded modestly.

"Of course, I must meet this lady and satisfy myself that Nora will be safe in her care, but I am sure that is merely a formality. Is she living here now?"

"No, her business necessitates her staying in Surrattsville for a while longer, but her daughter will be moving here to set up the house."

"Then if Nora is agreeable" — I nodded — "we will drive over there on Saturday afternoon and introduce ourselves."

Two days later, we made our trip to the country. Father, who did not keep his own equipment, had rented a rather smart buggy for the occasion. It was a beautiful September day, neither too hot nor too chilly, and I felt very pleased with myself as, clad in my

21

newest striped gown and the brand-new bonnet I had convinced Father I needed for the occasion, I settled into the buggy. Still, I could not help wishing I had a fine young suitor beside me instead of my father. We drove through the streets of Washington to the Navy Yard Bridge, after which we passed into the countryside. "Let me give you the advice I have always given you, child: speak little about the war in these parts — anywhere, really, but especially in these parts. Feeling is very strong here against the Union."

"I know that, Father."

"A reminder can't go amiss."

Although the war had been raging for over three years, I had never succeeded in finding out my father's true sympathies, so diligently did he follow the rule he had set for himself and me. I had come to suspect he, in fact, had no sympathy for either side: that his allegiance lay solely with Washington City, where he arrived over twenty-five years ago as a poor Irishman and where he had married, fathered six children, and buried my mother and my three baby sisters. His work brought him into every street and alleyway of the city; there was simply no address he could not find. If a building had been torn down over the past two decades, he could tell you where it had stood and what had replaced it. Few people in the city did not know him at least by sight, and there had to be a truly raging snowstorm to keep him from performing his duties. His affection for the city extended even to its miserable summer heat, in which he took an almost proprietary pride.

In good time we arrived at the crossroads of Surrattsville, so named because the Surratts had once operated the local post office out of their tavern, which, along with its outbuildings, was the only habitation I could see in the immediate vicinity. Being accustomed to town life, I understood why the family was so eager to leave this quiet place.

As a colored servant took charge of our horse and buggy, Mrs. Surratt came outside to greet us. "This is the young lady Father Wiget recommended to me?"

"Yes, ma'am. This is my daughter, Miss Honora Fitzpatrick. We call her Nora."

I stood by silently as my father and Mrs. Surratt eyed each other. It was clear they each approved. Clad in gray half mourning, Mrs. Surratt looked to be in her early forties. She was tall, with dark brown hair, and her figure was of substantial, though not fat, proportions. As for my father, with his

23

gray hair and his erect figure, and with his faint Irish lilt, his presence was a courtly one. Had he not been aghast at the idea of replacing my late mother, he could have remarried six times over.

Father explained to Mrs. Surratt what a modest and innocent young woman I was, presumably, I suppose, to assure her that I would not be attempting to sneak men into the house or to do any of the other untoward things that more adventurous boarders than I evidently managed. It was all quite true — I was modest and innocent — but he made me sound like such a dull creature, it was disheartening to hear it all. Fortunately, there was not much to say about this subject, and the conversation soon turned to Mrs. Surratt, who assured Father that her boardinghouse would be a perfect repository for my virtue. Only well-behaved young men would be allowed to board, anyone with liquor in his rooms would be turned out immediately, and I would be sharing a room with either Mrs. Surratt herself or her daughter, Anna (an equally respectable and virtuous creature), depending on how many boarders were in residence. It went without saying that I would be expected to attend Mass with the family regularly; as a matter of fact, Mrs. Surratt stated, the ease of walking to church from the H Street house had been one of the chief advantages of removing to the city.

Soon, my father and Mrs. Surratt were discussing terms. The price — thirty-five dollars per month — seemed reasonable to me, although my existence had been too sheltered for me to be much cognizant of such things. After Father expressed his satisfaction with the terms, Mrs. Surratt turned to me with a smile. "The bargain needs only your consent, Miss Fitzpatrick. Would you like to stay in my house?"

"Yes," I said without hesitation. Mrs. Surratt and I had barely exchanged two words, but I liked her face, and I liked the fact that she had put the final decision in my hands.

So two weeks later, after Miss Surratt, who had been visiting friends in Baltimore on the day I met her mother, removed to the Washington house, I walked to my new lodgings, having shamefacedly bade goodbye to the Misses Donovan, who sobbed over me like they would a beloved granddaughter. To heap further guilt upon my shoulders, they would not hear of my paying someone to carry my trunk for me but sent Clarence with me to push it in a wheelbarrow.

"Them poor old ladies will miss you awfully, Miss Nora," he said as he puffed along at my side. "They thought the whole world of you."

I shifted the cat basket I held from arm to arm as a faint hissing emitted from it. "I will miss them too, Clarence, but I wanted a companion of my own age, and I promised them that I would come over for tea once a week."

"I do hope so, Miss Nora. It'll break their old hearts not to see you again. Old ladies getting up there, they set a lot of store by such things, you know. Why, they was going to buy you a nice little cake for your birthday."

My twentieth birthday was a few days away. "I'll visit next week. I promise."

I had issued several such assurances by the time we arrived at our destination, a gray brick house on H Street between Sixth and Seventh. It was tidy and well kept, though not as nice as that of the Misses Donovan, who took boarders more for the company than because of any actual need. Clarence could not resist a derisory sniff as he walked up the steps and knocked at the door leading to the parlor story of the house.

An auburn-haired young lady, tall like Mrs. Surratt but otherwise not bearing a strong family resemblance to her, answered. "Miss Fitzpatrick, I suppose? Bring your trunk in here. This is where we will be sleeping for now."

Clarence carried my trunk down the hall to a large bedroom at the back of the house. It was sparely furnished with a view of the alley, and I could not help but compare it to my comfortable, chintz-filled quarters at the Misses Donovan's home. "It will be nicer once I buy a few more things," Miss Surratt assured me. "I have but just come to town and brought only what was absolutely necessary from the country." She looked ruefully out the window. "Nothing to be done about the alley, I fear."

"Of course," I said. I turned to say my good-bye to Clarence, who clearly shared my misgivings about my new quarters. "Thank you, and I will visit in a few days, I promise."

"We'll all be looking for you, Miss Nora." He bent close to my ear. "Don't forget: there's always a home for you with the ladies."

"What did he say?" Miss Surratt asked as Clarence shut the door behind him.

"Oh, he just wished me well."

An indignant mew came from my basket. "I see you've brought a cat."

27

"Your mother said he would be fine." I set the basket down and opened it. Mr. Rochester leaped out, glaring at his new surroundings.

"Oh yes, we could use a mouser. Come into the parlor."

Our bedroom opened into that room, which Mr. Rochester had already found. As he perched by a window and surveyed H Street, his tail flipping majestically, I asked Miss Surratt, "Are there any other boarders here?"

"Not yet. Mr. Weichmann — a dreadful friend of my brother's — will be coming, I think, and Ma wants to put a family with him on the third floor. So there's no point in us staying up there and then having to move out. There are bedrooms up in the attic where we can sleep once Ma comes, if there's space."

I nodded amicably, for years of boarding, at school and in homes, had made me flexible. "I'm sure it will suit."

"You don't have an accent."

"Should I?"

"Well, you're Irish. Didn't your family come here because of the famine? But, of course, you must have been a little child at the time."

I shook my head. "I was born right here

in Washington City. Father has been in America since the twenties. He helped some of his kinsmen leave during the famine, though."

"Where does your father live? Swampoodle?"

She spoke of Washington's crowded and poor Irish neighborhood. I stiffened. "Certainly not," I said. "Father boards on Twelfth Street. I don't know anyone who lives in Swampoodle, nor would I care to."

"Well, you needn't get your Ir— get annoyed, I mean. I am sorry."

As this sounded sincere enough, and I was going to have to share a bed with her, I nodded and began to put my things away in the drawer Miss Surratt indicated. I noticed with pleasure that my clothing was as good a quality as hers, if not better. As Father had always lived well within his means and was no longer charged with the keep of my brother or my sister, he gave me a generous allowance. To change the subject, I said, "Your mother mentioned your brothers. Will they be living here?"

"My younger brother, John, comes and goes from our house in Surrattsville. You'll meet him soon, I imagine." She gave me a look. "My older brother, Isaac, is fighting for the Confederacy."

"God keep him safe," I said politely.

"Which side are you on?"

Though I inclined toward the North, I remembered my father's advice. "I have friends and family caught up on both sides," I said vaguely. "I just hope it ends soon."

"Do you have a sweetheart?"

This was ostensibly a safer topic than Swampoodle or the war, but it was a rather irritating one. "No," I admitted. The truth was, like Jane Eyre, I was plain and little, and Washington City was woefully short of Mr. Rochesters in human form. I'd never had a beau, nor had I even had a young man give me more than a passing glance. "And you?"

"I thought I had one, but he is serving as a doctor in Richmond. You can imagine, with all the young ladies acting as nurses, and all of them and their mothers inviting him to dine, there's not much time for me."

"You're very pretty. I'm sure you're well rid of the faithless wretch."

"Why, thank you." Miss Surratt held out her hand. "Call me Anna, Miss Fitzpatrick."

"And you may call me Nora. Not Honora. Only the nuns at school called me Honora."

"It's good to have someone else in the house, Nora. We have some distant relations — Mr. and Mrs. Kirby, living just a few blocks from here — but he's busy with his work, and she's busy with her children, so they're not very diverting. I've hardly had a chance to see the city."

"I'll show it to you. We're close to everything. The shops, the theaters — we're just blocks from Ford's Theatre. I've been there several times."

"I've never been there," Anna admitted.

"It's a lovely theater. We must go together." I could not resist what I said next. "Why, I saw John Wilkes Booth play there."

Anna stared at me. "Him?"

If you had put a young lady from New Orleans, a young lady from Boston, a young lady from Richmond, a young lady from Cleveland, a young lady from Baltimore, and a young lady from Washington together, the one thing they would have agreed upon, before they scratched one another's eyes out, was that John Wilkes Booth was one of the handsomest men in America. Any woman worthy of her sex, and I was no exception, could rhapsodize for hours upon his curling black hair, his soulful black eyes, his beautiful skin, and his fine physique — even those women who hadn't actually had the privilege of seeing him in person. I was indeed among the lucky ones, for the previous year, he had played at Ford's Theatre, and since I had been at school in Georgetown at the time, I had plagued my father until he agreed to take me. As the play had been *Richard III,* Mr. Booth's looks had not shone to their best advantage, since he was forced by the role to assume a hunchback and to scowl a great deal. Even so, I had had to repress a smile when Lady Anne informed Richard that he was a foul toad. I had gone to bed that night thoroughly convinced such a lovely man could not possibly have killed his nephews, although of course the play said he did.

Just the memory made me sigh. "I did see him, and he was wonderful. Did you know that he now spends much of his time in Washington? We might get to glimpse him in the street sometime."

Anna's eyes widened. "That," she breathed, "would be absolutely divine."

3
MARY

"Anna writes that she and Miss Fitzpatrick are having a splendid time furnishing the house," I told my son, waving a letter on top of a stack handed to me by Mr. Robey, our pro-Union neighbor who replaced Johnny when he was removed as postmaster and who seemed perpetually disappointed he had not yet detected any suspicious correspondence coming to our house. "I do hope that she is being prudent. Miss Fitzpatrick seems a sweet young woman, but it's plain that she's her old father's darling, and she didn't look the sort to economize."

"Is she pretty, Miss Fitzpatrick?"

"She's pleasant looking."

"That faint praise says volumes, Ma."

"She has a pretty figure, a great quantity of dark brown hair, and nice brown eyes."

Johnny shrugged and wrapped his blanket more tightly around him. The previous month he'd fallen deathly ill with influenza,

33

and for a while I feared I would lose him, the son who had always been the closest to me. He was delirious for two terrible long days, and I sat beside him and mopped his forehead and listened to him rave. Touchingly, he ranted not about the war or about his courier activities, but about a young lady from the neighborhood on whom, completely unbeknownst to me, he had set his heart before she went off to stay with relatives elsewhere. It broke my heart to see my boy's own heart broken, but when he came to himself, he would say nothing about the young lady, save to grudgingly admit she might have done well enough for him. Just a few days later, before he should have, he set off for Washington on one of the journeys about which he said so little, and when he returned, he promptly had a relapse and had to take to his bed again. But he was well enough now for us to discuss things that needed to be discussed, which did not happen to be Miss Fitzpatrick's looks.

"Johnny, when you are well, you must find some sort of work. You barely escaped the draft this time."

"Don't I know it. But I could still get drafted, even if I had work."

"Yes, but you could buy yourself out of it.

But it is more than that. You need something steady."

"I'm hardly idling, Ma. Were it not for this illness, I would not be sitting here. I'd be carrying messages."

"And not earning a cent from it."

"Only perhaps the thanks of a grateful nation someday."

"That's commendable, but it's not putting bread on the table. And it's putting your very life in danger." I touched him on the shoulder. Johnny had never carried any extra weight on him, and now he felt painfully bony. "Isaac could be dead for all I know, and last month I feared I had lost you as well."

"They've never come close to catching me, Ma, and if they did, it'd be a spell of imprisonment, that's all. Most likely."

This addendum did not fill me with confidence.

"It's important work, Ma. I can't just walk away from it. And if I did, I would fall under suspicion from the people I've been helping. Then where would I be?"

There was enough sense in this to make me sigh.

"Anyway, maybe the election will make this all moot."

"You know full well there's not much hope

of that. McClellan doesn't stand a chance since Atlanta fell."

"A man can dream." My son shook the blanket off his shoulders and rose. "I'm going out."

"Where? You are in no fit state to travel."

"I'll not go far. I just need to get out of here."

And away from my nagging, I thought guiltily. But Johnny, with his naturally kind temperament, would never dream of saying so.

Johnny went only to Washington and returned in two days, looking healthier and bearing good news: Mr. Weichmann had decided to board with us and would be moving in on the first of November. The girls, with the house to themselves, had been acting like a pair of society ladies, looking up all of their old schoolmates in the area (of which Miss Fitzpatrick in particular seemed to have an abundance) and inviting a different set over for afternoon tea each day. They had found a used pianoforte at a reasonable price, and it now graced the front parlor. Johnny assured me they had not beggared us, however, and Mr. Weichmann, who came by to look at his prospective lodgings, found them very homey and appealing. Johnny had made a few inquiries about employment — preferably a job where he could combine the commercial and the clandestine, as he put it. I did not know how easy it would be to come by such a situation, but at least he was making an effort, and as we had a small farm, along with the tavern, and had to attend to the crop there, it was just as well he had no regular employment at present.

In the meantime, as it would not do to have Mr. Weichmann living with Anna and Miss Fitzpatrick without my presence, I packed my things.

We set off on a crisp November day in a wagon, loaded only with my favorite chair, my bedstead, my clothing, and a few other necessities, as Mr. Lloyd was leasing the tavern furnished. Johnny glanced back as we left the crossroads. "Armpit of the universe," he said. "I can't wait until I can leave this behind for good."

"Why, you used to sigh after this place when you were in school. I remember your letters."

"That was before I discovered other places, Ma."

"Washington City?"

"New York. Montreal."

"When have you been to those places?"

37

"A few months ago, for work, or what I call work anyway. I'd like to go to Europe one day. That reminds me, Ma, of something I should have asked before. Will my friends be welcome at H Street?"

"When have your friends ever not been welcome?" Then I realized his meaning. "Friends of the South? Of course, provided that they don't turn out the paying boarders. And we must be careful around Mr. Weichmann and Miss Fitzpatrick."

"Miss Fitzpatrick's harmless. If she gives a thought to the war, and I'm not sure she does, it's for the South. She seems to know half the Irish in Washington City, and the draft riots up in New York ought to tell you what *they* think of the war."

"Miss Fitzpatrick is of rather a different class. But no, I don't think she troubles her head much with North or South, from what Anna writes. But Mr. Weichmann? Didn't you say he works for the War Department now?"

"Yes, but that could prove useful. I tell you, he's a Southern man at heart."

"Well, you do know him very well, I suppose."

"It's not just that. I've become adept at detecting such things. One has to be. Sat beside a man on the stage a few weeks back, and he tried to get me to talk secesh with him. I wouldn't do it. I pretended to be a dolt who cared for nothing but horses and hunting. Later I learned that he was a government agent. He said all of the right things, yet something about him had made me doubt him all along."

"A government agent?"

"Oh, they're always sniffing around southern Maryland, Ma. Nothing new there."

"Then I am even more glad we are leaving the tavern." Since removing Johnny from his postmaster position the year before, the government appeared to have been leaving us well alone, but one never knew . . .

The roads were dry, so we made good time to Washington. As we turned onto H Street, I looked around me with pleasure. Washington was not a terribly attractive town, it had to be said — pigs strolled around as freely as the humans there, and there was plenty of garbage to keep them well fed — but this was one of its better streets, and the farther into the city we drove, the more substantial and well-kept the houses appeared.

As our cart pulled up by the house, Mr. Weichmann appeared, carrying a handful of books. He was on the whole a good-looking young man, though his slightly chubby face spoiled the effect a little. Johnny, having kept in touch with him since having to leave school to help me with the tavern, brought him on a visit to our place a couple of years before. At the time, Mr. Weichmann was thinking of entering the priesthood, though the way his eyes rested upon my stately daughter made me wonder if this was his true calling.

"What timing!" Johnny called. "You travel light."

"My trunk's already here. This is the last of my things."

Anna and Miss Fitzpatrick came out on the stairs to greet us. I had not seen Anna look so well dressed since she left school; her dress was newly trimmed, and she was wearing a pair of earrings that in the country she donned only for special occasions. "Here's Ma, to save you girls from certain ravishment at the hands of Weichmann," Johnny called up the stairs.

"Really, Johnny," Anna and I chorused while Miss Fitzpatrick giggled and Mr. Weichmann blushed.

Well before Election Day came around, I was settled into my new lodgings. Mr. Weichmann was everything one could wish for in a boarder — quiet, polite, and temperate, neither too solitary nor too social — and Miss Fitzpatrick was sweet tempered and quite willing to lend Anna a hand with the housekeeping. I just wished I had one more of each of them.

Johnny, back at the tavern tending to the crops, was a year too young to vote, but Mr. Weichmann, who was twenty-two, went to Philadelphia to cast his ballot and returned to Washington that evening. As we sat in the parlor, I thought of the last presidential election, when my husband was alive and our tavern was the local polling place. Not a single soul had cast a ballot for President Lincoln, my husband announced as he tallied the vote — a quick task, and one for which he had commendably remained sober.

"Whom did you vote for, Mr. Weichmann?" Anna asked.

"Now, Anna," I said. "Mr. Weichmann need not tell us that." I was curious to hear the answer myself, however.

"I voted for the man I thought would serve the country best," Mr. Weichmann said.

"I hope President Lincoln is defeated," Anna put in. "He is a hideous man."

"Father saw him once. He said he has very kind eyes."

"Your father sees everyone, Miss Fitz-patrick."

"Indeed, he does. There's hardly a soul in Washington he doesn't know, at least by sight. But he only glimpsed the president riding to his summer place." Miss Fitz-patrick put her chin on her hand and sighed. "It is such a pity to live in the capital city and have to find out the election results in the morning, just as if we were in Kansas or something. I wish we could stand out by the White House and wait. If we had an escort, we could go."

This was such a naked appeal to Mr. Weichmann, I could not help but smile and wonder how many such sad-eyed petitions Mr. Fitzpatrick had heard over the years. Fortunately, Mr. Weichmann reacted as desired. "I can escort you there, if you like — and Miss Surratt too, if she wishes."

"Oh, would you please, Mr. Weichmann?"

"I'll go," Anna said. "Even though I won't be able to endure it if that creature wins."

"Which he probably will," I warned her.

"It will be a long wait, perhaps, and it is a miserable night," Mr. Weichmann added.

"We'll wrap up well," Miss Fitzpatrick promised. "Mrs. Surratt, won't you come? It will be lonely sitting here all by yourself."

Touched, I said, "I would be delighted to."

So, bundled up and carrying umbrellas that knocked against one another as we made our way down the muddy street, we headed under Mr. Weichmann's protection to the White House, in front of which a crowd of white and black, male and female, had already gathered. The club rooms and the hotels, Mr. Weichmann told us, were the best places to await news, but they were not suitable places for ladies to linger.

Even where we stood, however, news arrived regularly in the form of men, some more sober than others, who came to yell out the latest returns. Most were in favor of President Lincoln, which invariably met with a chorus of "Huzzah!" By the fifth or sixth time, however, even Miss Fitzpatrick was so caught up in the excitement so as to cheer with the rest. "I wish Mr. Surratt were here," she said apologetically, stamping her boots to keep her feet warm. "How sad to be away when there is so much excitement in Washington."

As the night wore on and it became clear the president's reelection was assured, we were preparing to go home when a group of men, bearing the Pennsylvania flag, pushed their way through the crowd and began to sing:

Yes we'll rally 'round the flag, boys, we'll
    rally once again,
Shouting the battle cry of freedom,
We will rally from the hillside, we'll gather
    from the plain,
Shouting the battle cry of freedom!
The Union forever! Hurrah, boys, hurrah!
Down with the traitors, up with the stars;
While we rally 'round the flag, boys, rally
    once again,
Shouting the battle cry of freedom!

"There is a Southern version of this song too," Anna hissed. "Johnny taught it to me."

"For goodness' sake, child, don't sing it here."

"I'll hum it," Anna decided.

When the Pennsylvanians stopped singing and Anna humming, the former began yelling for the president to appear — which, presently, he did, leaning his head out the window as the crowd yelled and Miss Fitzpatrick gave a yelp of delight.

"Hideous!" muttered Anna.

"Oh, hush, you'll get us cast into prison," Miss Fitzpatrick said good-naturedly. "He looks kind, just as Father said. Don't you think so, Mrs. Surratt?"

"I can't make out his features," I admitted. "My vision is not like it used to be."

We fell silent as the president began speaking. "I am thankful to God for the approval of the people, but, while deeply grateful for this mark of their confidence in me, if I know my heart, my gratitude is free from any taint of personal triumph. I do not impugn the motives of anyone opposed to me. It is no pleasure to me to triumph over anyone. But I give thanks to the Almighty for this evidence of the people's resolution to stand by free government and the rights of humanity."

"The rights of darkies," Anna muttered and turned away, her nose in the air, leaving us no choice but to follow her. "Four more years of that man," she said as we walked home, pressing close to Mr. Weichmann as drunkards wove too close to us. "Can I bear it?"

"A lot can happen in four years, Miss Surratt," Mr. Weichmann said.

Anna sniffed as Mr. Weichmann angled his umbrella more protectively over her head. "No need to state the obvious, sir."

4
Nora

DECEMBER 1864

On Christmas Eve, we in the boardinghouse all had plans to go our separate ways — Mr. Weichmann to take the train to Philadelphia to see his family, me to accompany my father to Baltimore to visit my sister and some family friends, the Surratts to spend Christmas at their new home without us boarders underfoot. But first, we sat down for breakfast.

The men, who shared a bedroom, were the last to arrive. They had gone out last night, Mr. Weichmann to buy some presents for his sisters and Mr. Surratt to offer him his invaluable advice, as he put it, and had stayed out until past their usual hour. Mr. Surratt yawned as he sat down. "Ma, you didn't wait up for us last night."

"Should I have? I trusted that Mr. Weichmann would keep you out of trouble."

"If you had, I would have told you whom I met."

46

"So now you can tell all of us," Anna said.

"As I was planning to. But you must guess. Whom do you think Weichmann and I met in the street?"

"The president?"

"Old Abe? Who cares? No, try again."

"Mrs. Sprague?" Anna suggested, naming Kate Chase, the recently married daughter of the even more recently appointed chief justice of the Supreme Court. One of the most beautiful women in Washington, and now one of the richest, her wedding to the governor of Rhode Island had been the talk of the town last year.

"No, those dainty slippers would never touch the mud, although I'd much rather meet her on the street than Old Abe any day. You try, Miss Fitzpatrick."

I shrugged. There were so many important people in Washington one might glimpse. "John Wilkes Booth," I said idly.

"Why, how did you guess?"

I dropped my fork. "Him?"

"Yes. Mr. Weichmann and I were by Odd Fellows Hall when we saw Dr. Mudd from Bryantown. You probably know Dr. Mudd from when you were at school there, Anna."

"I do. He treated one of my classmates when she fell sick. But what's Dr. Mudd to me? I want to hear about Mr. Booth."

47

"Well, to get to the Booth, you must step through the Mudd. Dr. Mudd hailed us and introduced his companion — who, if you're clever, you might deduce was Mr. Booth."

"I thought his name was Mr. Boone at first," Mr. Weichmann admitted.

"Oh, Mr. Weichmann." Anna sighed. "You are such a stick."

"How does he look close up?" I asked.

"I'm not a connoisseur of men's looks, Miss Fitzpatrick, but I think most would call him very handsome. Perhaps more so in person than onstage, since there's not the gaslight or the makeup to intrude."

I gazed raptly into space.

Anna leaned forward. "So what happened next? Did you continue on?"

"Goodness, no, Sister! It gets better. Mr. Booth invited the three of us to his rooms at the National Hotel, and we sat and had milk punch —"

"And smoked cigars," Anna said. "I smell them on you and Mr. Weichmann."

"Yes, well, we men like our cigars, you know. If you wish to marry, you will have to learn to tolerate them or else die an old maid. Anyway, we drank our milk punch, smoked our fiendish cigars, and talked awhile. Afterward, we went on to Dr. Mudd's rooms at Pennsylvania House — he

48

came to town to see some relatives — and talked some more. And that is it, except that Mr. Booth has promised to call upon us here sometime."

"Truly?"

"So he said. Mind you, he didn't say precisely when."

"We shall have to keep the place spotless at all times, Ma," Anna said. "Thank goodness the furniture in the parlor is new — I couldn't bear to see Mr. Booth sitting here in shabby surroundings."

"He travels a great deal and must stay in all sorts of places," I said. "Perhaps he will be willing to make some allowances."

"Nay, Miss Fitzpatrick, that will not do. We must be in readiness to receive him at any possible moment, and the house must be in a state of nearly palatial splendor." Mr. Surratt studied his egg thoughtfully. "Perhaps we should not serve any meals here, lest the smell of cooking offend him."

"Johnny, stop tormenting the young ladies," Mrs. Surratt said. "This is a perfectly respectable house, and a clean one too, if I must say so myself, and there is no reason Mr. Booth, if he comes, should not be pleased. He will not, of course, be expecting a grand house."

"Well, I might have added a staircase or

two in my description of it, and a bay window. Is it too late to bring a builder over?"

A few hours later, Father came for me in a hack, and we took the train to Baltimore, where my brother, Peter, was supposed to have arrived from Boston the day before. Sure enough, he was waiting at the station for us.

I repressed a sigh as we stepped off the train. I loved my brother, but beside him and my father's great pride in him, I felt frivolous and insignificant, especially as I could think of nothing I was likely to do that would make Father shine the same proud look upon me, except perhaps to marry someone very much like Peter.

As we sat down to tea at our hotel, Peter pulled a journal from his valise. "The *National Quarterly Review* did a little piece about Holy Cross, where I was last year, and I am mentioned in it," he said modestly and handed it to Father.

My father plucked a pair of spectacles from his pocket — accoutrements he normally used with the utmost reluctance — and began to scan the pages. " 'Professor Fitzpatrick has always an appropriate suggestion to make when the student seems to get confused, which scarcely ever fails to restore his presence of mind.' Why, Son, you have impressed this writer very much."

"He was taken with the institution as a whole, not just me, Father."

"Still, he singled you out for notice. I shall read the rest when I retire tonight."

"I would like to read it too before you leave."

"Of course. What have you been doing, Nora?"

I was relieved to be able to report, "I have been going to one of the hospitals and reading to the convalescent soldiers. I have so much free time on my hands, and I felt that I should be doing something to help them."

My brother gave me a rare grin. "I hope you allow them something besides Charlotte Brontë, Nora. She is not to all tastes."

"I do read from others," I said in an injured tone. "I read *Pickwick* the other day. The men thought my Sam Weller was excellent."

"Whatever you read to them, I am glad you are doing it," Father said.

"I don't think Mrs. Surratt entirely approves," I admitted. "With her sympathies —"

Peter, who was the only abolitionist I knew in person, snorted. "She may as well

51

resign herself to the inevitable. The Confederacy is in its death throes, and it is high time."

"Peter," my father said, "remember where you are. We are not in Massachusetts."

"We are in the Union, and as a Union man, I shall speak as freely as I please." But he did add, "Out of respect for you, Father, I will speak quietly while I am here in Baltimore."

I had not enjoyed seeing my father reprove my brother as much as I had expected. To lighten the mood, I said, "Mr. John Surratt met a new acquaintance yesterday, and you'll never guess who. John Wilkes Booth, the actor."

Both my brother and my father gratified me by turning astonished faces toward me. "Why, I would have hardly thought that Mr. Surratt traveled in theatrical circles," Father said.

"He met him through Dr. Mudd, a physician in the country. Mr. Booth even invited Mr. Surratt and the other gentlemen to his lodgings at the National Hotel. He might even pay a call at Mrs. Surratt's."

"He may have simply said he would call, without having meant to keep his word," Peter said gently. "A man like that surely has more fashionable company with which to occupy himself."

"Nora and I saw him play last year," Father said. "He is a marvelous actor. Have you seen him, Peter?"

"No. Only his brother Edwin in Boston. I should hardly say 'only,' though, for he is as gifted an actor as I've ever seen."

"I believe that John Wilkes Booth is every bit as talented as his brother," I said proprietarily. "And I believe that he will not be so ungentlemanly as to make an engagement to come see Mr. Surratt at his home and not keep it."

"You could well be right," Father said. He cleared his throat. "If he does keep his word, you must be on guard that he doesn't pay you and Miss Surratt improper attentions. He is — how should I put this? — a man of the world."

"Oh, Father." I giggled. "I won't let him seduce me." Though I was thrilled beyond description at the possibility that someone thought he might try, even if that someone was only my father.

Father gave me a stern look, and I sat up straighter and sipped my tea.

"I am certain she is in good hands with Mrs. Surratt," Peter said kindly. "Despite her regrettable proclivity for the Confederacy."

Having finished our tea, we returned to our rooms to prepare for Mass. I was heading into the small chamber where my bed was when Father stopped me. "I have had a letter from Mrs. Surratt about you."

I winced. I had never been in genuine trouble at school — I did not bully other students, or cheat, lie, steal, or sneak out to meet young men — but I did rather like to have things my own way, and I had been known to answer back. On several occasions, my headmistresses had sent notes home, and it had been agreed at both St. Joseph's and the Visitation Academy at Frederick that I might be happier elsewhere. "What did she say?" I said in a small voice.

"She said that you are a delightful companion to her and Anna and that she could not be better pleased with having you in her house. I am proud of you, Nora. You have grown up into a fine young woman."

I blinked back tears. "Thank you, Father."

Father opened the larger of his bags. "I have something for you — besides your Christmas present. I thought you might want to wear it to church."

He handed me a soft bundle. I gasped as I untied it. Inside the wrapping was a Kashmir shawl, full enough to cover my entire gown. I had shawls, of course, but none so large, so soft, or so beautiful as this one. "Father, it's wonderful."

"I bought it a couple of months ago when I traveled to New York. I was saving it for a special occasion." My father smiled and pinched my cheek. "I found one."

I arranged the heavy shawl until it hugged me from my shoulders to my ankles. But as we headed out in the chilly Baltimore night, it was not the warm shawl that made me glow from the inside out. It was my father's compliment, prompted by Mrs. Surratt's kind letter.

From that night on, I would love Mrs. Surratt as I would a mother.

5
MARY
DECEMBER 1864

With Mr. Weichmann and Miss Fitzpatrick safely bound for their respective destinations and Anna fussing over the cooking, I took the opportunity to catch Johnny alone. He was leaning against a partly open window, smoking a cigar — the reason, I surmised, for the open window. "Sorry, Ma. Last of the day, I promise. So what do you think of my new acquaintance?"

"As I haven't met him yet, I presently think nothing about him."

"Ah, come. Wouldn't he make a good husband for Anna? Although she might have some competition there with Miss Fitzpatrick. I've never seen her so excited."

"I'm not looking to match my daughter with an actor."

"Not even a rich one? They say he makes a handsome sum. But it might be wise not to get Anna's hopes up, anyway. He has his eye on a senator's daughter."

"You certainly did learn a lot about Mr. Booth in a short time."

"He's a very personable man. It was almost like meeting an old friend."

I began to wonder who was more stage-struck, the young ladies or Johnny. "How did Mr. Booth meet Dr. Mudd?"

"The same way I did." Johnny flicked the remnant of his cigar expertly out onto H Street and closed the window.

"You mean that Mr. Booth is a Southern man?"

"You have hit the nail on the head and pulverized it, Ma. Yes, he is, and a quite passionate one. He wants something from me in connection with that business. I'm not sure what yet. I shall find out when we meet after Christmas."

I shook my head. As much as it pained me to think it, the South was crumbling, the city of Savannah having been President Lincoln's Christmas present this year. Johnny was expending all of his youth and energy on a lost cause.

"Now, Ma, don't look so glum! I know what you are thinking, and I'm going to offer you some Christmas cheer. I am employed, at a salary of fifty dollars per month. I will start work at Adams Express Company next Tuesday."

"Truly, Johnny?"

"Truly. I wrote to offer my services with 'a ready hand and a willing heart' — a pretty turn of phrase, I thought, and so did the agent there, for he offered me a position upon receipt of the letter."

"You could not have given me a better Christmas present, Johnny." The truth was, I did not have nearly enough boarders and had resorted to advertising for them, whereas I once hoped to acquire them strictly through the recommendations of mutual acquaintances. My very breath seemed to come easier with the news that Johnny would be bringing in a steady income. I had no doubt he would flourish in his job, for he had always done well when he applied himself. Perhaps — although the thought was a guilty one — he would even give up his clandestine activities. Surely having to worry about one son being felled by a Yankee bullet was enough for a mother.

6
NORA
JANUARY 1865

The New Year came in quietly and, I thought, promisingly. There was an end to the war in sight, and although I knew that end wasn't the one Mrs. Surratt and her children were hoping for, they and everyone else would surely be better off when peace prevailed. In the meantime, I stayed busy with my convalescents — we were working through *David Copperfield* — and Anna occasionally lent a hand with the piano lessons at the nearby Visitation school for girls. Mr. Weichmann was still employed at the War Department, and Mr. Surratt seemed to enjoy his new job at Adams Express — at least, he said he had no complaints. As for Mrs. Surratt, she had a new boarder, a ten-year-old girl named Mary Apollonia Dean, who attended school nearby and who had not been happy at her previous lodgings.

That was the state of affairs one evening in early January when Anna and I sat side by side on the piano bench, singing a duet. I was not particularly musical — my older sister, the nun, had inherited all of the family talent in this direction — but I did enjoy singing, and no one had been known to cringe when I lifted my voice in song. Anna, on the other hand, played and sang beautifully, to the point where she could have earned her living working in a music hall, had it been respectable. So she and I were happily warbling away when the parlor door opened. As Mr. Surratt was expected any moment, we paid it no mind and carried on until we finished with a great flourish.

"Bravo!" said a voice of pure velvet. "Well played, ladies!"

Anna and I turned and found ourselves face-to-face with John Wilkes Booth. If I looked half as foolish as Anna, and I daresay I looked far more foolish, the two of us must have resembled a pair of gaping idiots. And how we were dressed! We weren't in curl papers, fortunately, but I had my oldest shawl flung carelessly around my shoulders, and Anna's fair hair was twisted up in a ragged knot. Neither of us would have wanted to meet a lady friend in such a condition, much less this epitome of male beauty.

For Mr. Booth was every bit as splendid

as I could have imagined. To my surprise, he was not tall, but of medium height. I quickly decided tallness was an overrated trait in men, especially since I myself was short. In every other aspect, however, he was even finer than he appeared in his photographs, which could be purchased at any studio in Washington. His black hair fell in soft curls, framing a face that was lit up by deep brown eyes that I, to this day, dare not demean with any further description, lest it be inadequate. His clothing, a study in black and white, was simply yet exquisitely cut, and showed off his fine physique without at all seeming to do so.

He was, in short, sheer perfection.

"Now that we have finished our concert, introductions are in order," Mr. Surratt said. "Mr. Booth, my mother, Mrs. Mary Surratt. And at the pi-an-ny, Miss Anna Surratt, and our lodger, Miss Nora Fitzpatrick." Mr. Surratt grinned wickedly at us. "And last, but certainly not least, our newest lodger, Miss Mary Apollonia Dean, who is very insistent on using all three names, you'll find."

"That's a very long name," Mr. Booth said gravely. "It rather wears out the tongue. What say we call you Miss Apples?"

Miss Dean, who clearly had not the slightest idea who Mr. Booth was, giggled. "That would be all right."

"Hark!" Mr. Surratt turned at the sound of feet on the staircase. "Here comes Weichmann. You are now in the presence of the entire Surratt household."

Mr. Weichmann, who generally read in his room at about this time, entered at the sound of his name. "Mr. Booth," he said with an emphasis on the surname, "how good to see you again."

Mr. Booth held out his hand. "You are just in time, Mr. Weichmann, to join my petition."

"Petition?"

"To have Miss Surratt and Miss Fitzpatrick perform another song for us. I was unfortunate enough to catch only the last few minutes of their final piece."

Anna beamed. "We would be honored, Mr. Booth." She riffled through some sheets of music. "How about this, Nora?"

I nodded without even seeing the piece she indicated.

We squeezed together on the bench and began to play. Anna had chosen a piece where she could shine, which was reasonable, I supposed, as she was the more talented and the daughter of the house to boot. It was just as well, because I flubbed my first few notes before my instinct took over and allowed me to get through the rest creditably.

"Beautiful!" Mr. Booth clapped. "Have either of you had professional training?"

Although he had considerately addressed his question to both of us, I knew Anna was its true object, so I stayed silent as she replied, "No, indeed, only at school."

"She won several medals at school," Mrs. Surratt added proudly.

"And do you sing these duets every night?"

"Nearly so," I said, startling myself to find my voice sounding so normal, as if I was speaking to any ordinary person.

"Well, it is charming. You will think me foolish for running on so upon the point, but living as I do in hotels and associating mainly with fellow bachelors, I so seldom encounter family scenes such as this, except when I visit my own people, and they are scattered now."

I mustered the courage to make another contribution to the conversation. "I believe you have a large family, Mr. Booth?"

"Indeed, I do. You know of my brother Edwin, of course, and Junius is making a name for himself on the stage as well. Joseph lives out West and is carrying mail, the last I heard — not an easy task in San Francisco, he tells me! I confess to being closer to my sisters than my brothers. Asia is the prettiest and the most outgoing; she is the most like me, they say. Rosalie is rather shy, but a very good sort of girl. She is the best of all of us. And of course there is our mother. She makes her home with Edwin now."

"Does she have a favorite, Mr. Booth?" Anna asked archly.

"Anna!" Mrs. Surratt said, more amused than reproving. "No mother admits to such things."

"No, she does not mention it, as you say, Mrs. Surratt, but I believe my brothers and sisters, if pressed, would say that I was the favorite." Mr. Booth bestowed a smile upon us. "They would probably be right, I fear, for I certainly was the most petted growing up, I believe. I could hardly be expected to object, though."

We laughed.

"But enough about me. Your son tells me, Mrs. Surratt, that he has a brother fighting for the South."

"I have not heard anything about him, good or ill, for several years," Mrs. Surratt said sadly.

"I hope you will hear good of him, and

soon. And you, Miss Fitzpatrick? Do you have kinsmen fighting?"

I felt myself flush with pleasure. Men seldom remembered my name, or at best remembered it only partially and called me Miss Fitzgerald. Some of the patients at the hospital, even one who rather liked me, still called me by the latter name; with all the misery they had seen, it seemed petty to correct them. "Not close ones, sir. My father is employed by a bank here in town, and my brother teaches. He wants to become a priest."

"Miss Fitzpatrick's sister is a nun," added Anna, rather too precipitously.

"Do you have plans to enter a convent?"

I put my chin up. "Certainly not."

"Well, good," Mr. Booth said. "I have every respect for those good women, but it is a life that one should enter only if one embraces it wholeheartedly, I should think." He turned to Miss Dean. "You, Miss Apples?"

"Only some cousins," Miss Dean said, "and I don't like them anyway."

"Well, that is a comfortable way of looking at it," Mr. Booth said. He grinned, showing teeth I need hardly say were perfect, and turned his attention to Mrs. Surratt. "Mrs. Surratt, I have been enjoying the company of your son very much over the last few weeks. I sought an introduction to him in the purely selfish hope that he could smooth out a business transaction for me, but I found his company so amusing, we have become friends."

Mrs. Surratt glowed with motherly pride. "Business with Dr. Mudd, sir?"

"Yes. I grew up in Maryland, in the country and in Baltimore, and I have been considering buying some property in Charles County for a country retreat. Dr. Mudd owns land that would be ideal for my purpose. But, alas, he is proving to be intractable as to price, in spite of Mr. Surratt's efforts. I am prepared to be reasonable, but he really is demanding too much. I must live, after all, and he would leave me absolutely land poor. But it is such pretty country. I hope he will relent."

We all clucked our tongues sympathetically at Mr. Booth's sad predicament. "I hope he sees reason, Mr. Booth," Anna said. "I should think that with the war, and times so hard, he would be happy to sell. I'm sure your offer is perfectly fair."

"I wonder if he's waiting until the war ends, so he can sell at a higher price," I said darkly. "A detestable man."

"I may have to replace you as my agent

for the negotiations, John," Mr. Booth said solemnly. "The young ladies plainly surpass you as an advocate."

At that moment, my cat wandered in. He was a white cat, greatly prone to shedding, and I knew from experience he would be drawn as if to a lodestar to Mr. Booth's smart black pantaloons unless I intervened. "Here, Mr. Rochester," I said, gathering him up as he yowled in protest. "Sit with me."

"Mr. Rochester? We have an admirer of Miss Charlotte Brontë here, I see."

"Yes, sir. Have you read her novels?"

"Why, of course. Who hasn't?"

"I haven't," offered Mr. Weichmann. I had forgotten he was in the room.

"Mr. Weichmann believes that novels are frivolous," Anna said.

"That is not true," Mr. Weichmann protested. "You have seen me read Dickens countless times here."

"I really pay little attention to what you read, Mr. Weichmann."

I stole a look at Mr. Booth to see if he was put off by this bickering and was relieved to see he looked amused. Perhaps this too reminded him of home.

Mr. Booth stayed for another hour or so, guiding but never dominating the conversation, always seeing to it that no one was left out. When he rose to leave, he shook the men's hands and kissed the women's. "I hope you will come again," Mrs. Surratt said. "It has been a delightful evening."

"I certainly shall, madam." Mr. Booth flashed a parting smile, leaving Anna and me bedazzled.

7
MARY

"So how did you like our guest?" Johnny asked the evening of Mr. Booth's visit to our house.

"I liked him very much. I was surprised that so famous a man should be so easy and natural. He could have been one of our neighbors from Surrattsville, practically."

"Only much better looking. I'm glad you liked him, Ma, because I have to leave town for a few days on account of his business."

"Leave town? You mean, take leave from your job?"

"Yes."

"But you have been working there only for a short time."

"Twelve days," Johnny said gloomily. "I haven't done the arithmetic for the hours yet. Too depressing."

"Johnny, you can't just take leave from a job you've held only for a couple of weeks! Not without a good reason."

"I have a good reason. I will be escorting you to Surrattsville on business, as your protector."

"Johnny, you know perfectly well I am making no such journey. That is a blatant lie."

"But in a good cause."

"What cause? Mr. Booth's land negotiations with Dr. Mudd? Surely you could write a letter to Dr. Mudd instead of taking leave and losing pay. If you're even allowed leave."

"Ma —" Johnny peeked through the folding doors of the parlor into the bedroom, where little Miss Dean was snoring slightly on her trundle bed. The young ladies had scurried up to one of the attic rooms after Mr. Booth's departure, stars in their eyes. In a low voice he said, "There are no land negotiations. As I thought, Booth wanted my help with something for the Confederacy."

"Courier work?"

"No, although he's done a bit of that himself in his traveling about."

"Then what is it?"

"I can't say. But it is important. Far more important than anything I am doing for the express company."

"More important than earning an honest

living and helping me?"

"It will all turn out for the best. I promise."

The sound of the young ladies descending the stairs put an end to our conversation but not to my misgivings. We left off there. The next afternoon, Johnny came home from work looking dejected. "Old Dunn — my boss — wouldn't give me leave."

"I'm not at all surprised."

"He might relent, though, in the face of a mother's pleading."

"You expect me to go to the office and lie that you are needed to escort me to the country?"

"Yes. Plead — wring your handkerchief — play the poor-widow card to the hilt."

"It is not a card, Johnny. It has been my existence for more than two years now."

"I'm sorry. That was thoughtless. But please, Ma? Trust me, I wouldn't be asking you to do this if it weren't important. I'll be the laughingstock of the office once you turn up. But I can live with that, because it's in the service of a noble cause."

I felt myself beginning to weaken, as I had so often over the years where my youngest child was concerned. He was right: no self-respecting man of his age would want a mother to meddle as he was asking me to,

71

unless he had a good reason.

"It's the only time I'll ask such a favor, Ma."

"Very well."

Johnny embraced me. "Don't act too dignified. Act helpless and wring your handkerchief."

"If I am going to lie for you, at least give me credit for having the sense to do it properly," I snapped.

So the next morning, a couple of hours after Johnny had left for his job, I arrived at Adams Express Company and was nearly knocked down by all the men rushing to and fro as a clerk escorted me to the office of Mr. Charles Dunn, the company's agent in Washington. Johnny's description of him as "Old Dunn" was clearly youthful slang, for Mr. Dunn was only in his thirties, with a sprightly air about him. This changed, however, as soon as I stated my business. "I am afraid I cannot accommodate you, Mrs. Surratt."

"Why not?"

"Look around you, madam. Business is frantic here. I cannot give any of my long-term employees leave at this time, much less a young man who has worked here for a mere two weeks."

I lifted my handkerchief to my eyes. "But

I desperately need him to accompany me, sir."

"I am sorry, madam. It is simply not possible. Have you really no male relation to assist you? A cousin or a brother-in-law perhaps? A neighbor or a clergyman?"

"Had I those alternatives, I would not be troubling you," I said irritably. "I am a newcomer here, sir, and have not made those acquaintances. My male relations are in the country."

"Well, I am sorry, but I simply cannot spare your son, or anyone, at the moment. And I might add that others have asked for leave, under more compelling circumstances, and have been refused as well. Were I to grant your request, I would be justly accused of favoritism. Perhaps you can postpone your business until a less busy time. If not, I am sure there are perfectly respectable drivers who can be hired to take you."

"Then you cannot be persuaded to spare him."

"I cannot. Of course, he is a free man and can go if he pleases, but it will be at the cost of his employment."

"Then good morning, sir." I sniffled into my handkerchief, but Mr. Dunn was completely unmoved.

73

"I know. It didn't work," Johnny said to me as he banged into the house in the evening. "But thank you for trying," he added, clearly as an afterthought.

"Maybe it just wasn't meant to be," I said gently.

"You're right."

"Surely you can help Mr. Booth in some other way, or some other time."

"Some other way, some other time? No, I'll be helping just as I promised. I'm taking French leave from Adams Express."

"Leave a perfectly good job, which you were doing perfectly well, to help a man you barely know in a dying cause? When we need the money you earn so badly? Have you lost your mind?"

"The cause isn't dying!"

"It is, and you know it! But it's not the cause, is it? You just don't want to do an honest day's work! That's it, isn't it? You'd rather be gadding about the countryside. You're no better than your worthless father!"

Miss Fitzpatrick, evidently believing from my raised voice that someone was being murdered in the house, rushed into the

74

parlor. When she saw it was only Johnny who was the target of my wrath, she scurried away.

"Good God, Ma, no wonder Pa drank, with your nagging!" Johnny turned and thumped upstairs to the room he shared with Mr. Weichmann. From the parlor, I heard their unintelligible voices in the room above. When Johnny stomped downstairs, he was holding a carpetbag.

"Johnny, where are you going?"

"Out."

"When will you be back?"

"A week, a month, a year. Maybe never." He did not slam the door but shut it carefully behind him. Somehow, that was far worse.

Mr. Weichmann appeared downstairs a few minutes later. "I'm sorry, Mrs. Surratt. I tried to get him to reconsider."

"I appreciate that, Mr. Weichmann."

"This is very ill-advised of Mr. Surratt. I do not believe Mr. Booth has been a good influence on him at all."

I shook my head bleakly and sank into a chair.

Anna was staying a couple of days with a friend, so it was Miss Fitzpatrick who slipped downstairs and stepped into the role of landlady for the evening, presently calling us to dinner. It was an almost silent one, for even little Miss Dean sensed the dismal mood and did not engage in her usual childish prattle. When it was over, Miss Fitzpatrick said, "Miss Dean, why don't you come upstairs with me? We'll play with your hair."

Though rather plain of face, Miss Fitzpatrick had lovely chestnut hair, which she arranged beautifully. I shot her a grateful look as Miss Dean said, "Oh, yes, miss." So with the girls engaged and Mr. Weichmann taking himself upstairs to his room, I was free to retire to my bedroom behind the parlor and sit in my favorite chair, tears falling down my cheeks as I alternately imagined myself losing this house and Johnny lying dead in the streets of Washington, having encountered some sharp stranger. And did he mean it when he said he would never come back?

There was no sign of Johnny in the morning, of course, and although I considered walking over by Adams Express to see if he had changed his mind and appeared for work, I gave it up as a hopeless task. By early afternoon, I was alone, for Miss Dean was at school, Miss Fitzpatrick was reading to Yankee soldiers, and Mr. Weichmann was at work.

Why could Johnny not be steady like Mr. Weichmann? Or like their friend Mr. Brophy, an old classmate of theirs who had gone to teach at a boys' school in Washington and had already become its principal? Not long before, when Johnny had had him for dinner, I had asked him politely what his future plans were, and I had thought the young man would never stop talking in response. He was not much older than Johnny, yet he was brimming with purpose.

Then I heard the sound of the doorbell — ours surely had to be the loudest in Washington City, which made me think the original owner of the house was slightly deaf. I answered it to find Mr. Booth on the front stairs. "My son is not here," I said coldly.

"I know, Mrs. Surratt. He is away on my business. May I please have a word or two?"

I waved him in, and we took seats in the parlor. "You do not understand, Mr. Booth. I am not well off, and my son has thrown away a respectable position, with an adequate salary. All, he tells me, for your sake."

"I do understand, Mrs. Surratt. I loved my father dearly, and he was a genius on the stage, but he was not . . . not entirely temperate, to put it gently. When he died, he left us with a place in the country she

77

was ill-equipped to run, having been brought up in London, and often, we were hard up. It was not until my brother began doing so well that she began living in the comfort she deserved."

"And that is what a son should be doing, Mr. Booth. Oh, I don't expect Johnny to take care of me; I like to do for myself. But I do expect him to help, at least a little. He knows that." I wiped a tear from my eye. "This war has changed him so much. He is so careless now."

Mr. Booth leaned forward in his chair. "I believe your son told you the nature of my business?"

"Yes, but none of the particulars."

"I would prefer that you not know the particulars, for your own protection. All I can tell you, my dear lady, is this: it is no small matter that I asked John to help me with, and I sought him out because I had information that led me to believe he would be the best man for my purpose. He has fully justified my hopes in him. I regret that he was unable to get leave, and now that I consider the matter, I should have realized that there would be difficulties. I am so used to this actor's peripatetic existence, I forget others do not have the freedom of movement that I do. For this, madam, I am very sorry."

"I can't live by your apologies, sir."

"I know, madam. But consider this: if our plan succeeds, I assure you that John will reap the benefits. He is such a bright young man, Mrs. Surratt, and so devoted to the South. He longs to exercise his gifts and to exercise them for the good of himself and his country."

"Mr. Booth, I do not share your optimism. I fear it is too late. Every day, more bad news arrives."

Mr. Booth shook his head. "I wish I could tell you more; if I did, you would realize that we are not foolish dreamers. Our plan is an audacious one, but a viable one. And with the right men, including your son, it will succeed. I have faith that it will. John has told me you are a woman of faith."

"In the Almighty, yes. I have rather less faith in mankind. Things have not been easy for me these past few years. They are not easy now." I stopped, appalled. Why was I blurting these things to a young man I barely knew?

"Yes, John told me of some of your troubles. Yet think how much you have done. Your children — the two I have met, at any rate — are fine young people; your boarders seem much attached to you. And your support of the South is well-known in the circles where it should be known."

I nodded and stiffened my spine. "I despise self-pity, Mr. Booth, and I should not have given way to it just now. But John and I parted on a sour note, and it has left me melancholy. The truth is, I needed the money from his new job, but it is more than that: I fret about him. He makes light of the risks he runs, but I know they cannot be small."

"I sympathize, my dear lady. My position is not unlike your son's. My mother, whom I love dearly, made me promise that I would not join the army — either army, but of course there is only one army I would join. I kept the promise, and if truth be told, I am probably of more use out of the army than in it, but it has deeply pained me to think of those poor boys suffering so much while I live in such comfort here."

He sighed, and I stared into space. Perhaps I had been too hard on Johnny, underestimating the idealism that lay beneath his boyish love of adventure. He had never given himself up to dissipation or light-minded pursuits, after all. "This plan of yours, Mr. Booth. Should it succeed, will it prolong the war?"

"I believe not, Mrs. Surratt. I believe that it would end it and leave the South independent. And then all of the men can return to their shops, or their farms, or their desks, including your John."

I did not know how to ask my next question. "Is it — is it something of which Johnny would have to repent?"

"No, madam."

"Then when he returns, I will give him my blessing. I will redouble my efforts to get some more families in here. I will get by."

"I would be delighted to tell him that, if I should see him before he sees you." Mr. Booth rose gracefully to his feet. "Mrs. Surratt, I have enjoyed our talk. It is almost as if I am in my own mother's parlor. May I come again, even if John is not present?"

"Of course you may, Mr. Booth."

I saw him to the stoop and watched as he strolled in the direction of the National Hotel. Perhaps it was a bit lonely in that hotel room of his.

A few days later, after nightfall, Mr. Booth returned. "I took the liberty of bringing a companion, Mrs. Surratt."

Johnny stepped out of the shadows. "I'm back, Ma."

"Johnny!" Not caring about the display I

was making in front of Mr. Booth, or indeed for anything but the fact that my son was back, I took him in my arms. "Johnny, please forgive me. I spoke so harshly to you."

"Ma, I was going to say the same to you." There were tears in his eyes. "I'll find another job, I promise."

"No. Do what you have to do for now. There will be time for all that later." I pulled Johnny from the hall into the parlor, where Anna and Miss Fitzpatrick on one team, and Mr. Weichmann and Miss Dean on the other, had been playing charades. "Johnny is home! And Mr. Booth is here to visit too," I added almost as an afterthought.

Miss Fitzpatrick clapped. She, even more so than Anna, had noticed how preoccupied I had been since my argument with Johnny.

Anna said, "Well, at last, Johnny! You had Ma so worried."

"Mere business, my dear."

"Shall we have a song in celebration?" Mr. Booth suggested. "I hope you will oblige us, Miss Surratt."

Anna nodded graciously and settled at the piano. Mr. Weichmann looked on with some irritation as Mr. Booth hastened to lift the lid for her; that was usually his task.

"I'll make some inquiries tomorrow about

getting some more boarders, Ma. First thing."

I nodded. But as Johnny squeezed my hand, and as Mr. Booth and the boarders — even Mr. Weichmann — joined in singing the joyful song that was filling the room, I thought I could not possibly want my house any different than it was tonight.

8
NORA
JANUARY 1865

"Now, you ladies must pledge not to faint when Mr. Booth dies," John Surratt said as our carriage headed toward Grover's Theatre. "Or to hiss the actress playing Juliet."

After Mr. Surratt had walked off his job at the Adams Express Company, Mr. Booth had somehow smoothed matters over with Mrs. Surratt, and in the course of the pleasant evening following the reconciliation of mother and son, he had mentioned he would be playing Romeo at a benefit performance and would any of us care to watch? Of course, Miss Surratt and I cared to watch. Mrs. Surratt would have joined us too, but Miss Dean had come down with a cold, obliging Mrs. Surratt to stay with the child. As a result, our party consisted of Mr. Weichmann, Anna, Mr. Surratt, and me, tidily paired up as if we were about to board Noah's Ark.

I almost wished we had other escorts, such

as my father or Mr. Kirby, a family connection of Mrs. Surratt who lived nearby. I had no objection to John Surratt. He had always been friendly and courteous to me, although I had seen from the moment he laid eyes on me that he had dismissed me as too plain and inconsequential to be an object of his affection — perhaps to the disappointment of his mother, whom I suspected would not have been averse to his courting me. But I had never expected any other reaction, being used to men looking past me, so I was perfectly happy to sit beside Mr. Surratt and focus without guilt on Mr. Booth's magnificence. But poor Mr. Weichmann! His eyes had lit up like a burst of gaslight when the trip to the theater was proposed, and it was clear he thought of the evening as a step forward in his pursuit of Anna, though I didn't share his hopes that it would be a step in the right direction.

"Who is playing Juliet?" Mr. Weichmann inquired.

"Who cares?" said Anna.

"Miss Avonia Jones," I said, giving Anna a look. There was no need to be so rude. "I have heard that she is a fine actress."

Mr. Booth turned out to have procured a box in such a good location that some members of the audience glanced up, thinking we must be people of some importance. No one could mistake any of us for Washington society, but at least we did not look like intruders in our box either. Anna and I wore our prettiest gowns, and the cold weather had enabled me to wear my beautiful new shawl. Mr. Surratt was wearing what appeared to be a new suit of a rather nicer cloth and cut than what I had seen him in thus far. Perhaps he had used his earnings from his short term of employment to refurbish his rather countrified wardrobe.

As we had not arrived with much time to spare, we did not have long to await the appearance of Mr. Booth, who turned out to be a splendid Romeo — not, of course, that I had expected otherwise. During the balcony scene, a cough from the box opposite ours drew my attention from the stage, and I noticed a young lady there was staring at Mr. Booth with as much intensity as Anna was. I saw too that Mr. Booth was returning her attention when he could do so without ignoring his Juliet. "Lady, by yonder blessed moon I vow," he said and gazed directly at her. But this byplay diverted me only for a few moments. When Mercutio and Tybalt lay dead on the stage and the lights came up for intermission, I had been so transported to sixteenth-century Verona that I had to blink for a moment to reorient myself to modern-day Washington City.

It was Anna's voice that brought me out of my Italianate trance. "Mr. Weichmann, I did not appreciate your taking my hand during the fight. I will thank you to refrain in the future."

"The fight was so very realistic, Miss Surratt; I thought you might be alarmed."

"Do I look so silly?"

"Mr. Booth put all of his heart and soul into the fight," I said. "Someone could have easily been hurt."

"Oh, don't be foolish, Nora. The actors are well trained to avoid such things. And even if they weren't, I fail to see how holding my hand would help matters."

I looked at Mr. Weichmann with commiseration. He said with dignity, "Perhaps we should not stay for the pantomime. I am leaving for Baltimore tomorrow, to visit St. Mary's Seminary. I have at last received a letter clearing the way for me to begin my studies for the priesthood, and Father Dubreuil has asked that I meet him to discuss my vocation."

"You're going to Baltimore tomorrow? So am I," said Mr. Surratt. "We can travel together, if you wish. Share a hotel. It will be just like Ma's house, without Ma's cooking."

Poor Mr. Weichmann did not crack a smile. "That would be fine. Why are you going?"

"Oh, business," Mr. Surratt said airily. "We can talk more on the train. But it would be a shame to leave before the pantomime. Mr. Booth has said that we may visit him backstage, and would you want to break Anna's heart, or Miss Fitzpatrick's, by losing this opportunity?"

Anna and I lost no time in protesting that our hearts could not be trifled with in this fashion. Mr. Weichmann sighed and agreed to stay.

This being settled, I turned my attention to the young lady who had been watching Mr. Booth. She had light brown hair that fell in ringlets and was a little older than Anna, I guessed, with a face that was a bit chubby, rather like that of Mrs. Lincoln, whose photograph I had bought at Brady's gallery for my album. Her gown, as much as I could see of it, was of the highest quality, and she wore a many-stranded coral necklace of the sort I had coveted. With her in the box were a stuffy-looking older couple, the gentleman carrying a handkerchief that branded him as the one who had coughed, and another young lady. All were plainly well-to-do. A lawyer's or a doctor's family, I guessed, or perhaps a congressman's.

The play ended in the usual manner, sending Anna and I into floods of tears. We needed the pantomime afterward to compose ourselves so we would look sufficiently presentable to go backstage. None of us had ever been in the working part of a theater before, and we were standing in our box uncertainly, wondering how we might get there, when a man appeared and said, "Mr. Booth's people? Follow me."

Mr. Booth had changed into his street attire by the time we arrived in his dressing room. When Anna and I in our hoops went inside, it proved too small to accommodate Mr. Surratt and Mr. Weichmann, who stood in the doorway.

"Your acting was marvelous, Mr. Booth," Anna said. "It was truly heartfelt."

"I am glad to hear that, Miss Surratt, as it has been some time since I have acted the role." He smiled wistfully. "But it probably helped that my own Juliet was in the audience tonight."

"The young lady you were acting at?"

Mr. Booth quirked an eyebrow. "So you spotted that, Miss Fitzpatrick. Well done!

You should have been a theater critic, for you miss nothing. Yes, that is my Juliet. I hope she was as observant as you, Miss Fitzpatrick."

"I never saw her take her eyes off you, sir. Of course, I was attending to the play most of the time, not to her. Were those her parents and sister? Do they approve?"

"Yes, they were, and I heartily doubt that they approve. She is Miss Lucy Hale — the daughter of Senator Hale from New Hampshire. Needless to say, an actor is not their first choice of a husband for her."

I clucked my tongue sympathetically. Flattering as it was to have Mr. Booth's undivided attention, I wished someone else would contribute to the conversation. Mr. Weichmann had been sunk in gloom ever since Anna rebuffed his attempt at handholding, and I did not dare turn to see the expression on Anna's face after Mr. Booth had revealed this romance. Mr. Surratt was lost in admiration of some dancers who strolled by showing a generous amount of ankle, arm, and bosom. "I am sure all will come right in the end," I said lamely. "After all, this is Washington City, not Verona."

Mr. Booth chuckled. "Well said, Miss Fitzpatrick. Now, shall I give you a tour of the theater? It shall be an abbreviated one, as everyone will be wanting to lock up and go home, but there are a few things I can show you."

For a good half hour, Mr. Booth led us around, showing us all of the wonders that went into creating the magic of the theater. He had a friendly word for everybody he passed, from his leading lady to the scruffiest of stagehands, and I had the distinct impression they would have kept the place open another hour if he had asked them to do so. When he led us to the exit, he said, "Mr. Surratt, Mr. Weichmann, why don't we have a drink together after you take the ladies home? I confess I am restless tonight and not ready for my bed."

I expected Mr. Weichmann to demur, owing to his trip to Baltimore, but he said firmly, "I would be happy to," even before Mr. Surratt could accept on his own behalf.

"Why didn't you tell me about that woman?" Anna demanded as we braided our hair that evening in our front attic room. It was practically the only thing she had said to me since we had seen Mr. Booth in his dressing room.

I had no need to ask what woman. Instead, I said mildly, "I didn't know anything about her until Mr. Booth mentioned her."

"You said he was acting at her and that she was staring at him."

"Well, all women stare at him. And I thought it might just be some sort of acting trick, his gazing at one person in the audience like that."

"What did she look like?"

"Pleasant. Pretty, I suppose, but nothing really out of the ordinary. A little plump. She was very well dressed, though. Of course, she would be so, being a senator's daughter."

"Is she prettier than I am?"

"No. I think you're far prettier," I said truthfully. "But sometimes it's not the only thing men care about."

Like many very pretty girls I had encountered over the years, Anna looked completely taken aback by this idea. Then she nodded. "Money," she said glumly. "Of course. Money and social position. That's what I don't have that she has."

"I didn't mean —"

"My father was a drunkard — oh, even I know that now — and my mother keeps a boardinghouse. Why should I have ever thought that someone like Mr. Booth could have ever wanted me?"

I wrapped my arm around Anna. "He's known her longer. I'm sure that's it. Maybe it might have been different if he had met you first. And he does like you, Anna. He invited you backstage and gave you tickets. I'm sure he doesn't do those things for everyone."

"He does those things because of whatever business Johnny is handling for him. He pays me no more attention than he does you, and you know it. We'll both die as old maids."

Although I could have taken offense at this, now was not the time. "Anyway, you heard him; her parents don't approve of her seeing an actor. Maybe he'll give up on her." Although privately, I doubted I would like Mr. Booth nearly as well if he dropped Miss Hale simply because of that.

"Maybe she'll die of consumption."

"She didn't look at all consumptive."

Anna flipped her braid behind her neck angrily. "Let's go to bed."

I was sleeping quite soundly when I heard a commotion in the street, followed by a banging at the front door. I opened the dormer window and looked about. Standing on the porch, barely visible in the moonlight, were two shapes, one of which, upon hearing the window open, yelled, "Mother! Anna! Miss Fitzpatrick! Miss Dean!"

"Miss Anyone!"

I made my way downstairs. By the time I reached the parlor hall, Mr. Surratt and Mr. Weichmann had opened the door and were weaving their way inside, Mr. Surratt holding a key aloft in triumph. "Found it!"

"He found the key," Mr. Weichmann said, "the material key, the object itself. But he did not find the key to our existence." Mr. Weichmann jabbed a finger in the air and nearly lost his balance, staggering into Mr. Surratt, who did not absorb the impact well.

I glared at the men and tried to guess who was more intoxicated. My money would have been on Mr. Weichmann, although Mr. Surratt could certainly have made it a fair contest. "You're drunk," I pointed out.

"Miss Fitzpatrick speaks with the voice of Delphi," said Mr. Weichmann.

"A veritable oracle," Mr. Surratt agreed. "Oh, good evening, Ma."

Mrs. Surratt had come out of her bedroom and was regarding the men with a steely eye. "What is this about?"

"Renunciation," said Mr. Weichmann, flopping down on a chair and displacing Mr. Rochester, who mewed in protest and stalked away. "I have renounced the fair Miss Surratt, Mr. Booth has renounced the fair Miss Hale, and Mr. Surratt has renounced — what did you renounce, John?"

"Renunciation. I renounced renunciation."

"I see," Mrs. Surratt said. "Go upstairs, you two, and go to bed."

"But we must have a song first. Miss Fitzpatrick, play us a song."

"I will not."

"Then we'll sing anyway. One, two, three! 'I wish I was in the land of cotton' — sing, Weichmann."

" 'Old times there are not forgotten —' "

" 'Look away, look away, look away, Dixie land!' "

"Upstairs!" said Mrs. Surratt. "Now!" She picked up the poker. "Or I shall take this to you. Go!"

The men obeyed, their slow progress up the stairs marked by the thump of their boots and by a version of "Dixie" my maiden ears had not heard before, and which I hoped never to hear again. At last their bedroom door banged open, then shut. I squeezed Mrs. Surratt's hand. "They went out with Mr. Booth, ma'am."

"So I gathered." Mrs. Surratt yawned. "Go to bed, Nora. Thank you for letting the young fools in."

She kissed my cheek, and I made my way to bed, puzzled. Knowing what I did about her husband, I had thought Mrs. Surratt would have been quite upset about this little spree, but she seemed to be taking it in stride. Perhaps she'd have been more perturbed if their drinking companion had been other than Mr. Booth.

Anna yawned as I crawled back into bed. "What was all that racket?"

"Just a musical interlude," I told her. "Go back to sleep."

The next morning, Mr. Weichmann and Mr. Surratt left the house for the railway station — or, I should say, slunk out of the house, looking as if the small carpetbag each held bore the weight of the world inside it. To spite them, Mrs. Surratt had made their favorite breakfast, which neither of them could touch. Having eaten heartily myself, I packed a basket full of the leftover biscuits and went to the hospital to visit my soldiers.

I would occasionally play a game of cards with a patient, but usually I read to them or wrote letters home for them. Many of the men had been here for weeks, even months, and I had settled into sort of a routine. Captain Patterson worried a great deal about his farm and would dictate letters about its proper handling that went on for pages, though I personally thought he probably underestimated Mrs. Patterson's ability. Private Murphy liked to assure his mother he was being well fed, and he also never failed to add a postscript for her to give his dog a pat for him ("and a bone," I sometimes added). Private Morgan was terrified his sweetheart might take up with someone else and could not be persuaded by me, nor by Private Murphy (who occupied the bed next to his and regarded himself as an expert on affairs of the heart), that instead of dissuading the young lady by issuing her admonitions to this effect, he might be putting ideas into her head. Private Cohen preferred the *Evening Star;* Lieutenant Green preferred the *Daily National Intelligencer.* Private Biddle wanted only the Bible to be read to him; Private Armstrong preferred the penny dreadfuls, which Private Biddle said a lady should not be reading. There was a Dickens contingent and a Trollope contingent, and alas, not a Brontë contingent at all. But I tried my best to please them all, because I had learned early on that some of them would never leave this place alive.

I had a favorite patient, however: Private Flanagan. It had taken me two visits to begin to understand him, so thick was his New York accent, though he claimed he talked perfectly normally and it was I, with my Washington drawl, who was incomprehensible. He liked me to read only amusing things to him, which he said were made even more amusing by my accent.

Private Flanagan had lost his right arm — or, as he pointed out, he hadn't lost it, since he knew perfectly well where he had last had it. It was, he said, at least a good excuse for not having to write long letters.

Because he was my favorite, I usually saved Private Flanagan for last. On this day, when I settled at his bedside, he grumbled, "I thought you'd never stop jawing with those others."

"I'm sorry. They need company too."

Private Flanagan harrumphed.

"Well, shall I read to you?"

"Nothing else to do to pass the time."

This was completely unlike Private Flanagan, but as it was not at all unusual for the men to have their snappish days when they were in pain, I shrugged it off and began to read from *The Pickwick Papers*. I had barely gotten through the Christmas at Dingley Dell when Private Flanagan said, "That's enough. I'm tired. You can go."

"Very well," I said. I rose. "Would you like me to leave my book with you? You can read it when you are feeling more yourself."

"No."

"It is light enough that you could hold it — er, one-handed."

"I don't want the damn book, Miss Fitzgerald! Do you understand me?"

"Yes." I turned to go. "And it is Miss Fitz*patrick,* sir. If you are going to be rude, at least make the effort to get my name correct."

"Miss Fitzger— Miss Fitzpatrick. Wait."

I turned — not a quick operation in those hoopy days — to see Private Flanagan stretching out his left arm to me. "Yes?"

"I've been calling you by the wrong name all this time, and you never said a blasted thing. Why?"

"At the time, it seemed so trivial. And I suppose it just never occurred to me to correct you, sir."

"But I thought we were friends. Don't you call your friends by the right name?"

"Well, I hope I do, sir. Perhaps they have never corrected me, though."

Private Flanagan chuckled. "I'm sorry I was a bear today, Miss Fitz*patrick.* You see, I was thinking of what I could do back home with one good arm. There doesn't seem to be a whole lot."

"Oh, I am sure there is something that a man as intelligent as you are can do. Why, I

99

have seen advertisements for the art of left-handed penmanship."

"I'm not well educated, Miss Fitzpatrick. I can shift to read and write, and that's about it. Shanty Irish, that's all I am."

"You are not shanty Irish! You had to earn a living starting young, I suppose, and there is no dishonor in that." I looked at the book in my hand. "I have an idea. What if I helped teach you to read and write better?"

"That's a lot of trouble, miss."

"It is not a lot of trouble. It makes perfect sense. You have plenty of time on your hands" — I grimaced at my mistake — "plenty of time to spare, and learning will help take your mind off your arm."

"I don't know if I can learn at my age."

"Of course you can. That's pure silliness. And you won't have me to read to you forever, you know."

"No, I suppose I won't."

"So shall we commence on Monday?"

Private Flanagan nodded slowly. "Let's try it, miss."

My plan to improve Private Flanagan wasn't completely foolhardy. I'd been quick at school, though I had not always applied myself, and my teachers at Georgetown Visitation had been clever enough to realize that what I might not do if left to my own devices, I would do when others were involved. So I had been set to helping the younger girls with their lessons, and I discovered that, like my brother, I had a certain knack for this — although it was not something I cared to advertise, as to teach school would surely mark me out as an old maid more than I was already. But this was for a good cause.

So between Mr. Booth's visits to our boardinghouse and my planning Private Flanagan's lessons, January slid by quickly. It was nearing its end when, on a day when Mrs. Surratt had gone to the country, Mr. Surratt came home with a guest.

This man could not be more unlike Mr. Surratt's last guest, Mr. Booth. His clothes never seemed to make the acquaintance of a brush, and I suspected he slept in them more often than not. His eyebrows nearly met over a broad nose, and his face, which had an unfortunately froggy shape to it, was half forehead. Worse, he reeked of tobacco. Poor Anna's fine nose was twitching like a rabbit's at the smell, and I felt my eyes begin to water.

Mr. Surratt seemed blithely unaware of the less than happy impression his companion was making. "Mr. Weichmann, ladies, joining us from Maryland this afternoon is my friend George Atzerodt."

"Mr. At— who?" Anna asked.

The man shrugged. "The ladies never can pronounce it," he said cheerfully in a slight German accent. "So just call me Port Tobacco. That's where I live, over in Charles County."

"Port Tobacco," we echoed. He certainly lived up to his name, I thought.

"He'll be staying here awhile," Mr. Surratt said. "Unless, I trust, the attic rooms have all been rented in my absence."

"No," Anna said, clearly with regret, "they have not been. But shouldn't you consult Ma?"

"Of course, but there's no harm in having him stay here in the meantime, is there? Be a good sister and have the girl make up the bed for him."

Anna obeyed with the greatest show of reluctance, although Mr. Atzerodt, looking about the parlor as though in a place of uncommon luxury, appeared oblivious. "Be quick about it," she hissed as Mrs. Surratt's colored servant, Susan, headed upstairs with clean linen. Anna flashed a smile at Port Tobacco. "Would you excuse Miss Fitzpatrick and myself, Mr. At— Mr. Port Tobacco? We must make certain the girl does her work correctly. She's new here."

Port Tobacco — I feel it unnecessary to include the salutation — nodded graciously, and I followed Anna up past the floor where the men slept and up to the attic, where we had been sleeping since Miss Dean's arrival. Susan was quite competently making up the room, a task that hardly required supervision. "We can't sleep up here with him, Nora. We must sleep in Ma's room. He'll murder us. Or ravish us."

"Surely not with your brother sleeping below."

"Maybe not, but he'll smoke his cigar."

"That is certainly bad enough."

We quickly got our things together and carried them downstairs, not without escaping the notice of Mr. Surratt, who called, "Making yourself more comfortable, girls?" Fortunately, he, Mr. Weichmann, and Port Tobacco went upstairs, leaving us the field of the parlor.

"I can't imagine what Johnny wants with that man," Anna said as we settled into bed for the night. We were alone, Miss Dean being home on a visit to her parents. "Surely he can't be involved in that business scheme Johnny's talking about."

"Well, I think Johnny's plans are quite clear."

"What do you mean?"

"Why, he's brought Port Tobacco here to marry you."

Anna slammed me full across the face with her pillow, a classic boarding school move, but having spent much of my own youth at boarding school, I was no mean pillow fighter and was ready with my own goose down to hand. We scampered about the room, shrieking and pummeling each other in a manner that did our respective alma maters proud, until someone banged on the floor above us and Mr. Surratt's voice called, "Ladies! We gentlemen are trying to sleep. Show some womanly consideration and feeling for us, please."

"We will," we chorused dutifully. Then we renewed our match, until the sound of Port Tobacco's contented snoring filled the house.

9
MARY
JANUARY 1865

In late January, my older brother, John Zadock Jenkins — Zadock, as I always called him — sent me a letter telling me our mother was ill. As Mother was at the age where even a minor illness could prove to be her last, I accepted his offer to come to Washington where he had business, to fetch me to Mother's house, just a mile or so from the tavern in Surrattsville.

As usual since the war started, it was a somewhat uneasy drive to Surrattsville. Zadock was that rarest of creatures in Prince George's County — an avowed Unionist in a county where most of the few men who did support the Union kept their opinions very much to themselves. I had never discussed politics with my brother, but then, I had never needed to. I had a son in the Confederate army; Zadock stood guard with his gun under a Union flag to keep Confederate sympathizers from tearing it down. Yet my brother and I were by no means divided completely asunder. To our mother's disgust, he, like me, was a convert to Catholicism. His sons were friendly with Johnny, and his daughters — especially my own favorite, Olivia — had a standing invitation to visit us in Washington. By keeping to safe topics — mostly gossip about our respective churches, to my shame — we passed the time pleasantly enough.

To my relief, when we arrived, my mother was in bed but sitting up, alert and spry. The only sign of illness I could detect was a slight rasp in her voice and an occasional cough. "How is your girl?"

"Anna is well, Mother."

"Caught herself a man yet? No? You best take care that she doesn't turn into an old maid. Set in her ways a little too early, I always thought."

"When the war is over, I have no doubt that she will find a suitable young man."

"Best hope she doesn't take up with one of your tenants. I never liked the idea of your running a boardinghouse, Mary. All sorts of riffraff there."

"My only male tenant at present is a very respectable young man, a former schoolmate of Johnny's, and Anna is not the least bit interested in him."

"There you go, too set in her ways. So how is your Johnny? Working?"

This was still a sore spot with me, despite Mr. Booth's intervention, and Mother knew it only too well. "No, Mother, not at present."

"In my day, young men wanted to work. But I reckon things are different now."

Zadock shot me a look that was a combination of sympathy and mischief, for he and most of Prince George's County knew perfectly well Johnny occupied his time in the service of the Confederacy. "He makes himself useful," I said stiffly.

"Well, are you liking it in Washington with your Catlickers?"

As I had been doing for decades, I counted to ten and pretended my mother had merely mispronounced the word. "I am very glad to be able to attend church regularly again, Mother."

"I still don't understand why you and your brother can tolerate that papist mumbo-jumbo."

My mother was sick and fractious, I reminded myself, though in truth, she was not much different when she was in the peak of health. "I have found great comfort in my religion, Mother. It has helped me through some very difficult times."

"Ah, that's not the only thing I've heard you've found comfort in. Tongues still wag about that priest of yours."

"Surely, Mother, you know that was a pack of lies."

"Maybe. But it was enough to make people talk."

"I cannot help what these foolish people talk about."

"You certainly could have. A lady should never do anything to get herself talked about."

"I did not —" I started to say but gave up the point as a futile one. "Can I get you anything, Mother?"

As I settled for the night in the bed in which I spent my girlhood, I remembered what I hated most about the country: how its quiet forced one to focus on one's thoughts. My mother's words brought back a conversation I had many times with my husband about the man he called "that greasy Italian priest of mine." It was the bone he picked most often when deep in drink: our rumored sin together. "John, how many times must I tell you that was nothing more than idle chatter?"

"Idle chatter, my foot. Why did they send him to Boston? Why were you spending so much time in his company? How many times a day do you damn Catholics need to go to confession anyway?"

"I was not making my confession all of those times."

"So you admit it."

"I admit nothing! Father Finotti was my confessor, but he was also my friend. We enjoyed each other's company. There were so few educated people here at the time —"

"There you go, bringing up your fancy education again! Woman, why don't you just tell everyone I'm not good enough for you? Do it. I dare you. Go down to the tavern and tell everyone there, 'John Surratt is not good enough for me!' Who knows, maybe one of the guests will take you to bed. Maybe you'd like that, now that your dear priest friend is gone."

And yet John had not been entirely wrong, for I had sinned many times with other men, albeit only in my own thoughts. It was the only way I could bear the marital act in the last years of our marriage, on those nights when John, just sober enough to negotiate his way to our bed, would insist on taking me. I had tried other defenses. Sometimes I had begged to be left alone, or even flat-out refused, but at best I would be ignored, at worst slapped or forced to perform acts I could not bear to this day to think about. Two or three times I had gulped a shot of whiskey before going to bed, only to be left with a raging headache the next morning. So finally I had retreated into a world where the hands touching me were gentle and caring, safe in the knowledge that John was too far gone to guess where my thoughts might be. There was no other way I could perform my duty as a wife.

Occasionally in my widowhood, especially on chilly nights such as this, I found myself missing the arms of a loving man. Even the embrace of my husband was once a welcome one, before drink stole him from me. But why should I lie alone when I might remarry? At forty-two, I was not too old to do so. No one had ever asked me, but there were a couple of widowers at church I suspected might be predisposed to that, given a little subtle encouragement.

But then I thought of the risks: my little property being squandered, the man who smiled at me so pleasantly at church being a slave to the bottle at home. No, I would not remarry. These night urges would pass; they always did.

Having scolded me the day before to her heart's content, Mother was genial enough the next morning, and she looked much improved. I could therefore depart for Washington in good conscience. Zadock having business elsewhere, I was waiting for the stage in the parlor of my tavern when my tenant, John Lloyd, shuffled in. There was something all too familiar about his gait, not to mention the odor of his breath. "Afternoon, Mrs. Surratt."

"Good afternoon. How is business?"

"Excellent. Good night!"

"It is barely afternoon, sir."

"Nott'll take care of things. Nott takes care of everything! Good night!" He left the room, and I heard his unsteady progress upstairs.

Reluctantly, I stepped across the hall and into the bar, where Mr. Nott, whom I knew slightly from the neighborhood, stood behind the little counter.

"Is Mr. Lloyd quite well?" I asked him.

"Well enough. You saw him just now?"

"I did."

"Pretty tight, wasn't he? That's the way he is more often than not now. That's why I'm here, I suppose. Someone has to be able to stand up and tend to the customers."

Was every man who stood behind this counter doomed to turn out a drunkard? Not for the first time, I silently praised the

Lord that Johnny was no longer living here, even if he was unemployed and risking his neck for the Confederacy. At least Mr. Nott seemed sober — for now. "How is business?"

"Quite good, ma'am. Mr. Lloyd can afford to stay tight."

The arrival of the stage put our conversation to an end, and none too soon, for I was in no mood to linger here. Perhaps if the boardinghouse did well, I would be able to sell this place.

As I made my way home from the stage's stopping point at Washington's Pennsylvania House, I saw Anna run down the steps to meet me. My first heart-stopping thought was that there was bad news of Isaac. But I barely had time to prepare myself for the worst when Anna said, "Ma, there is a dreadful man at our house, and you must not let him board here."

"Is that all? What a turn you gave me! I thought Isaac was dead." Mr. Weichmann had joined us, and I smiled as he relieved me of my carpetbag. "Thank you, Mr. Weichmann. Now, who is this man?"

"Port Tobacco."

"His name is George Atzerodt," Mr. Weichmann said. "The young ladies call him Port Tobacco."

"It's the name he said we could call him. What does that tell you about him, Ma?"

"Not much at all. Who is he? How did he come here? I have not placed an advertisement in the paper for some weeks."

"Johnny brought him."

"Well, if he is a friend of Johnny's . . ."

"He can't be a friend of Johnny's. Johnny would never have such friends. He must go, Ma. You know I have very strong likes and dislikes, and I strongly dislike this man."

"He's on the unkempt side," Mr. Weichmann said helpfully. "Rough looking, but not rough acting. He seems harmless enough to me."

"And did anyone ask your opinion, Mr. Weichmann?" Anna tugged on my arm. "Come inside, Ma. He was lounging about the parlor like some sort of king of the jungle. Miss Fitzpatrick is terrified of him."

I entered the parlor with trepidation, but all seemed harmless enough. Miss Fitzpatrick, far from exhibiting terror, was trimming a bonnet, and the man I assumed was Mr. Atzerodt was reading the newspaper. He stood when I entered the room. Hardly a barbarian, I had to admit.

But hardly a gentleman either. I could only hope he had not been using his room as a spittoon. Mr. Fitzpatrick, with his im-

113

maculate linen and perfect posture, would be aghast to see his darling in company with such a man, as would Mrs. Dean, a fretful lady who wrote me every other day to inquire about her little daughter's health. And Father Wiget from church had found a couple, Mr. and Mrs. Holohan, in need of respectable lodgings. What would they think if they arrived to see this grimy fellow in the parlor?

No, much as I hated to turn away a paying lodger, Mr. Atzerodt could not stay. My opinion was strengthened a little later at dinner. Even if Mr. Atzerodt had not belched three times, to Anna's consternation and to Miss Fitzpatrick's amusement, his victuals alone would ruin me, for he accepted two helpings of everything and looked somewhat disappointed when no third was forthcoming.

So that evening, when Johnny had returned from that business that occupied so much of his time lately, I said to him, "A word with you in your room, please."

Johnny obediently followed me upstairs. Mr. Atzerodt remained below with Mr. Weichmann — who, oddly enough, seemed to like our new boarder. Perhaps Mr. Atzerodt reminded Mr. Weichmann of one of his German relations. "My instinct tells me you are going to question me about our boarder, Ma," Johnny said.

"Your instinct is correct, Son. Is he a friend of yours?"

"More a business associate."

"What kind of business does he do?"

"In theory, he paints carriages over at Port Tobacco — not the center of the carriage industry, so he's slack of work, as you might guess. In practice, he ferries men across the Potomac. He's quite good at it."

"Including you?"

"Including me. He's saved my neck more than a couple of times. I hope you consider it in the rent."

"Grateful as I am, Johnny, he can't stay here. He is not a gentleman, and the young ladies' parents have a right to expect that the other boarders here will be of their sort. And your sister cannot bear him."

"If Anna was our criteria for accepting boarders, we'd have only you, Miss Fitzpatrick, and perhaps Miss Dean staying here. I'm not sure she'd allow me."

"Anna can be particular, but in this case I believe she has a point. I am sorry, Son. We will give him a day or two to find new lodgings. I am sure he will find something more congenial and less expensive."

"But, Ma, I was going to give Anna the

task of making a gentleman of him. Her Estella to his Magwitch, maybe. Granted, that doesn't quite fit, but it's the best I can do on short notice."

"He must go."

"Am I to break the news? What am I supposed to tell him? He's a sensitive soul under that grime, you know." Johnny's face brightened. "I'll tell him that the servant noticed the liquor in his room when she was making his bed."

"Is there liquor in his room?"

"Of course there is. A man like Mr. Atzerodt needs his lubricants, you know."

"Then I have no scruples about sending him away."

"Well, I'll tell him, Ma. I just hope the news doesn't send him into a consumption. Though come to think of it, he probably already is consumptive."

He turned to go, and I touched his sleeve. "Johnny. If your Port Tobacco friend is running the blockade in Maryland, why is he staying here in Washington?"

Johnny turned and kissed me on the forehead. "Don't trouble yourself with such things, Ma."

10
Nora
FEBRUARY 1865

"My brother-in-law, Mr. Clarke, is playing at Ford's for the next few weeks," Mr. Booth said as he settled into his accustomed chair one chilly February day. I winced, for it was also Mr. Rochester's favorite chair, and he had undoubtedly left a few snow-white hairs on it in revenge for being displaced — and sure enough, Mr. Booth was wearing black pantaloons. "I am certain I can procure some tickets if you would like. From Mr. Ford, mind you, not from Mr. Clarke."

"You don't like him?"

"Indeed no, Miss Surratt. Even if we got on well in the ordinary course of things, which we do not, he is married to my sister, and no man is good enough for her. I suppose you understand that sentiment, John."

"Indeed I don't," said Mr. Surratt, who was leaning on the mantelpiece. "Anna can marry anyone she pleases, and I won't raise an eyebrow. She can even bring home a

Yankee, and I won't care."

"There's no danger in that," Anna said. "I despise the Yankees, and it's a mark of my affection for Miss Fitzpatrick that I put up with her ministering to them."

"She doesn't literally minister to them," Mr. Surratt said. "She doesn't preach sermons to them. Or do you, Miss Fitzpatrick? There may be a whole world of doing on Miss Fitzpatrick's part that we know nothing of. Maybe she performs surgery upon them."

"I just read to them and keep them company," I said. I looked at Mr. Booth, who wore a thoughtful expression. "And write letters for them sometimes. They're perfectly nice men, and it is very hard for them, being ill and far from home. I think there is wrong and right on both sides, but they shouldn't suffer for the wrong."

"I quite agree with you, Miss Fitzpatrick. What do you read to them?"

"Oh, Dickens, of course, and Trollope, and there used to be one man who was fond of Poe, but he was sent home. One man will have nothing but dime novels. It is quite mortifying to buy them for him, but it makes him happy to have a fresh one."

"You must try Shakespeare on them one

day. You do have a volume of Shakespeare, I trust."

"Yes, indeed."

"Then bring it here, if you please, and we shall have an elocution class. I did the same thing with some young ladies at my hotel. All of you shall read for me. It will be great fun."

I hurried into my room and delved into my trunk, where I stored my small collection of books — my tattered copies of Charlotte Brontë's novels, a few volumes of Dickens, and the Shakespeare I had used in school. When I returned with Shakespeare in hand, Mr. Booth gave a courtly bow to Mrs. Surratt. "As the lady of the house, will you go first?"

Mrs. Surratt looked at the book Mr. Booth passed to her and shook her head ruefully. "My eyesight is too poor to read this tiny print by gaslight. I should wear spectacles, but my daughter says I am too young."

"And you are, Ma."

"Then will you oblige us, Miss Surratt?"

Anna flipped through the pages, frowning as she rejected one selection after another. Finally, Mr. Surratt said, "Wilkes, are all of your auditioning actresses this particular?"

"Don't rush me, Johnny. I want to do this properly."

At last, Anna stood. " 'The quality of mercy is not strain'd,' " she began. I had been expecting one of Juliet's speeches, although on further consideration, I could see where this could be rather awkward with Mr. Booth and Mr. Weichmann looking on.

"Very nicely done," Mr. Booth said when Anna had finished addressing Shylock and we all had duly applauded. "I would enunciate a little more, and speak a bit more slowly, but on the whole very creditable. And you, Miss Fitzpatrick?"

"I haven't decided what to read yet."

"Then we will come back to you. John?"

Mr. Surratt clutched his chest. " 'A plague o' both your houses! 'Zounds, a dog, a rat, a mouse, a cat, to scratch a man to death! a braggart, a rogue, a villain, that fights by the book of arithmetic! Why the devil came you between us? I was hurt under your arm.' "

" 'I thought all for the best,' " Mr. Booth said meekly.

" 'Help me into some house, Benvolio, Or I shall faint. A plague o' both your houses! They have made worms' meat of me. I have it, And soundly too. Your houses!' " Mr. Surratt limped into the hall, then swept back in with a bow. "How'd I do, Wilkes? Am I ready to take to the boards?"

120

"You looked rather too cheerful, but on the whole, creditable, very creditable. Of course, Mercutio always steals the show, which is why I am grateful that he leaves me with an entire act to myself. Mr. Weichmann?"

Mr. Weichmann arose, like Mr. Surratt not having need of a book. " 'To be or not to be,' " he intoned grandly, and I could not help but think of Mr. Wopsle in *Great Expectations.* I suspected Anna was having the same difficulty, for she pressed her hand hard against her lips while Mr. Weichmann continued to revolve his fate. " 'Soft you now, the fair Ophelia,' " he concluded, and Anna hissed into my ear, "Not nearly soon enough."

Mr. Booth frowned. "I think we need to see Hamlet thinking as he speaks," he said after a moment or two of consideration. "You have to be Hamlet; you can't simply speak Hamlet. But it is an extraordinarily difficult role, and the critics have never entirely taken to my own performance of it, so who I am to say? Your turn, Miss Fitzpatrick."

"I chose *A Midsummer Night's Dream,*" I said, reluctantly getting to my feet. "I prefer Shakespeare's comedies to his tragedies." I cleared my throat and turned toward Anna:

121

"Puppet? why so? ay, that way goes the
    game.
Now I perceive that she hath made
    compare
Between our statures; she hath urged her
    height;
And with her personage, her tall personage,
Her height, forsooth, she hath prevail'd with
    him.
And are you grown so high in his esteem;
Because I am so dwarfish and so low?
How low am I, thou painted maypole?
    speak;
How low am I? I am not yet so low
But that my nails can reach unto thine
    eyes."

Mr. Booth sputtered.

"Was it that awful?" I asked, sitting down.

"No, no, my dear girl. It was exactly as it
should be — funny. I am not flattering; you
truly have a comedic gift. It is a raw talent
and hardly shows to its best advantage when
you are reading from a book, but it is a real
one. I believe you could act, although I
certainly would not advise you to try to do
so professionally. It is a hard life for a
woman, with unscrupulous men who will
try to take advantage of you. But in private
theatricals, you could shine, especially since

you prefer comedy. There are many would-be Juliets and too few Hermias."

I felt my face glowing in delight as Mr. Booth rose, shrugging as he noticed a few white hairs on his pantaloons. "May I have a word in private, John?"

Mr. Surratt nodded, and he and Mr. Booth went upstairs, leaving a frowning Mr. Weichmann in the parlor with the rest of us. As Anna sat down to the piano, I sat at the desk to write a letter to my sister at her convent in Baltimore. Mr. Surratt had dropped what he was writing there, and as I started to push it out of my way, I saw my name. Naturally, I could not stop myself from reading.

I have just taken a peek in the parlor. Would you like to know what I saw there? Well, Ma was sitting on the sofa; Anna sitting in the corner, dreaming, I expect, of J. W. Booth; Miss Fitzpatrick playing with her favorite cat — a good sign of an old maid — the detested creatures . . .

The impudence! The letter was addressed to Mr. Surratt's cousin, a young lady named Belle Seaman. I had half a mind to try my hand at imitating Mr. Surratt's handwriting, add a postscript proposing marriage to

Miss Seaman, and then mail the letter. That would show the cheeky fellow. Old maid, indeed!

But instead, I pushed the letter aside and began writing to my sister. Mr. Booth had said I had a gift. What did I care for the opinion of Mr. Surratt?

At the hospital a few days later, I found that Private Flanagan looked a little peaked. "I thought I'd be heading back to New York soon," he said, "but I've been sick the last couple of days, and Doc says nothing doing. And I haven't been able to do any schoolwork for you, miss. I'm sorry."

"That's perfectly all right," I said. "I have been thinking: perhaps when you go to New York, my brother might be able to help you continue your schooling. He teaches at Boston College and knows many people in New York."

"Perhaps," Private Flanagan said without much enthusiasm.

I read to Private Flanagan for about a half hour or so — Mr. Booth's praises ringing in my ears all the while. When I had said my good-byes to Private Flanagan and the other soldiers and had turned to go, I heard a rustling behind me. Someone muttered, "Hand it over, Flanagan."

"Miss Fitzpatrick? Flanagan has something for you."

I turned as Private Flanagan clumsily extracted something from underneath his pillow. "Here," he said gruffly. "I'm sorry it's not red."

It was a valentine, woven together from pages of a newspaper — my first valentine in my entire life. "It's the nicest one I've ever seen," I said, blinking back tears. How long had Private Flanagan worked on this?

"I had a little help from the boys here."

"And I saved the newspaper for him," Private Murphy offered.

"I almost didn't give it to you, Miss Fitzpatrick. I thought it might be a little forward."

"It's not forward at all." I carefully slipped it into the book I carried. "I will cherish it always."

When I reached the boardinghouse, I carefully set my gift on the bedroom mantelpiece. Sitting up there among the china plates and figurines and the clock, though, it looked terribly homely. For all the world I wouldn't have Anna, or anyone, laughing at Private Flanagan's effort. So I took my valentine off the mantel and tucked it into my album, and sat smiling at it until Mrs. Surratt called us to dinner.

11
MARY
FEBRUARY 1865

Thanks to Father Wiget's referral, I had new tenants, the Holohans — a polite but rather reserved couple with a daughter in her early teens. With their presence and the rent coming from Mr. Lloyd in Surrattsville, I could at last begin to see my way to ridding myself of some of the debt my husband left me — though it would be a slow process.

"If Weichmann doesn't mind the company, perhaps you can find a lodger to share his room with him," Johnny said early in February.

"Why, where are you going?"

"Europe, maybe."

"Europe? What on earth would you do there, and how would you pay for your passage?"

Johnny shrugged.

"Is it this business of yours with Mr. Booth? Son, I dislike all of this mystery." I touched his forehead. "You seem very restless lately. Are you getting a fever?"

"I'm fine, Ma."

Which, coming from Johnny, could mean he was at death's door. "If there is something on your mind, I hope you know you can confide in me."

"Didn't I do just that? I said I might be going to Europe. How much more confiding can a fellow be?"

"I think you might have left out a few details."

"I don't know all of them myself. It may never come to pass. I should have kept quiet and sprung it on you."

I fixed Johnny with the glare I used to quell him in his childhood. To my surprise, he was still susceptible to it. "It's all tied up with a cotton speculation, Ma. It may come to nothing, or it may make us rich. Mr. Booth is backing it."

"Well, I daresay he can afford to take a risk." I had heard of such schemes, borne of the need of Northern mills for Southern cotton. I did not have a great deal of faith in them, but I could see their appeal for a young man, and they were unlikely to get Johnny shot.

"He can. He's investing in oil as well. He says I may be of help to him there." Johnny grinned. "Who knows, Ma, maybe in a couple of years you can have this place all to yourself. No need to take in boarders."

"I like them; they're good company. But I admit it would be pleasant not to have to depend on them. Just promise me, whatever you do, you will not involve our own property. We can afford no such risks, Son."

"I promise. Now, I am off to meet Mr. Booth."

He strutted away, wearing a new suit of clothes I certainly had not paid for, and I could not help but think he was already walking like a wealthy man.

Johnny was out of town (but not, he assured me, bound for Europe) when, some days later, Mr. Weichmann approached me in the parlor. I was there alone, for the young ladies were at a little party being held by one of their friends from church, the Holohan family was in their rooms (I could hear the rumble of what I had learned to recognize as an argument between husband and wife, but it was not my place to pry), and Miss Dean had retired to her trundle bed for the evening.

"Mrs. Surratt, I am worried about John."

I was fond of Mr. Weichmann, who escorted me every Sunday to church on the days when Johnny was not there to do it (which was most of the time), but Anna's disdain for him must have infected me somehow, for I did not feel the alarm I would have felt if someone else said these words. Perhaps I would have been more unsettled if Mr. Weichmann did not look so very earnest. "Oh, Mr. Weichmann?"

"He is changing, Mrs. Surratt. He is not the same man I knew at school."

"He is grown to man's estate, Mr. Weichmann. It is natural, surely, that he should be changed?"

"But he has changed for the worse." Mr. Weichmann leaned forward, his neat little mustache twitching. "He has become more dissipated."

I trembled, for my greatest dread was that Johnny would turn out like his father. "Is he drinking too much?"

"No."

"Except for that evening with you," I said tartly.

"That was an aberration," Mr. Weichmann said a little sulkily. "No, Mrs. Surratt, I do not mean that he drinks too much, or that he consorts with loose women, or that he gambles. It is not any one or more of these things. It is more of a deterioration in his character. He is more cynical, more careless, less considerate, just looser in general.

He is not the same friend I knew and loved just months before, and I can say why: Mr. Booth."

"Ah." I understood then. In friendship, there is often one who loves more than the other, and in the friendship between Mr. Weichmann and my son, it was poor Mr. Weichmann who played the role of the ardent. And now he was being supplanted by Mr. Booth — and no wonder, for who would stand a chance against him? "You must not take Johnny's actions so much to heart, Mr. Weichmann. I know he is very fond of you, but he is engaged in some business of Mr. Booth's."

"But he is being corrupted by him, Mrs. Surratt. You do not know, perhaps, how dissolute actors can be."

"I have heard such stories, but none so bad about Mr. Booth. He is so well-known that if he behaved badly, it would be notorious. He has conducted himself entirely like a gentleman since he has been here."

"In your presence."

"Has he not acted like a gentleman when he is with you?"

"Yes," Mr. Weichmann acknowledged crossly. "But I still believe he poses a danger to John. Gambling, fast women, fast horses . . . Have you seen how fast John rides?"

"He has always ridden at what I consider a breakneck speed, but you must remember he was brought up in the country, where men are accustomed to ride hard. That, at least, is not due to Mr. Booth's malign influence, only that of Prince George's County." Mr. Weichmann did not smile, so I added, "I do appreciate your concern for Johnny, sir, and I hope you do not think that I am taking it lightly. But I do not share your low opinion of Mr. Booth. I believe he has been a good influence on Johnny. I see a purpose in him that I have not seen before."

"You think so, Mrs. Surratt, truly?"

"I do. Now let us talk about you." I had been neglecting Mr. Weichmann, allowing him to spend his evenings in his room when he should have been enjoying everyone's company in the parlor. "I believe you said that the letter had finally arrived allowing you to study for the priesthood."

"Yes, if all goes as planned, I will begin my studies in the fall."

"Are you certain it is the right path for you? Forgive me if I seem to be prying, but I sometimes wonder if you are prepared to embrace the life of a priest."

Mr. Weichmann's mustache trembled.

"There is no hope for me with your daughter, Mrs. Surratt, if that is what you are alluding to."

"She is not the only young lady in Washington, Mr. Weichmann, and the fact that you even hoped for her makes me wonder if you would truly be happy in the priesthood. Didn't you once say it was more your mother's wish for you than your own? If so, perhaps you and a priest should talk with her. There are other paths a good Catholic might take."

My lodger said with the utmost dignity, "I thank you for your concern, Mrs. Surratt, but the path to the priesthood is a slow one, and I daresay if there are any impediments of that nature, my confessor and I will deal with them."

I supposed after my rebuffing his concerns about Johnny, I deserved this.

A day or so later, Anna, Miss Fitzpatrick, Mr. Weichmann, and I were gathered in the parlor after dinner when the doorbell rang. Mr. Weichmann, always gentlemanly, rose to answer it. "A Mr. Wood wishes to see you, Mrs. Surratt."

"Show him in, please."

Mr. Wood, clad in a black overcoat that had seen better days, entered the room. He was a tall, strongly built man of about Johnny's age, with hair as black as his overcoat and piercing blue eyes. His stern features were handsome, although in an entirely different manner than those of Mr. Booth, and it was obvious their appeal was not universal. Miss Fitzpatrick clutched her cat closer, as if hoping he would transform himself and begin barking, and Anna's face settled into that stony position that was the bane of many a hopeful young male traveler passing through Surrattsville.

"Mrs. Surratt? I came here to see Mr. Surratt. I am told he is not at home." Despite Mr. Wood's imposing physical presence, his voice was almost high-pitched.

"No, sir."

"I have somehow become confused, ma'am. I expected to find him here in Washington. Will he return tomorrow, do you know?"

"No, sir, I do not."

"Then I must have confused my dates. Ma'am, would you allow me to stay the night in his room? I have just enough to pay my train fare back to Baltimore tomorrow, and no more." The young man bent closer to me and dropped his voice. "I am in the same business as Mr. Surratt."

The last sentence decided me, even

though behind Mr. Wood I could see Mr. Weichmann frowning. "You may stay, but as Mr. Weichmann is occupying my son's bed, you will have to lodge in the attic."

"I thank you, ma'am." Mr. Wood hesitated, then cleared his throat. "Perhaps, ma'am, I could get a bite to eat?"

Free meals, free lodging — this young man certainly expected a lot, and how was I to know that he was even a friend of Johnny's? But in some distant city, Johnny might be begging someone else's mother for hospitality. "You certainly can." I turned to Mr. Weichmann. "The girl will be cleaning the kitchen, and the attic room is not ready. Would you be so kind to allow Mr. Wood to eat in your room until the girl can get to the attic?"

Mr. Weichmann, no doubt relieved to hear I was not asking him to share his bed with Mr. Wood, nodded.

Our visitor proved to be a most unsocial creature. As soon as I put together a plate of food for him, he followed Mr. Weichmann upstairs, and when his attic room was ready shortly thereafter, he retired to it immediately, apparently having no desire to mingle with the young ladies as any other young man might. "Perhaps he doesn't like cats," suggested Miss Fitzpatrick. Mr.

Rochester purred smugly.

"Did you find anything out about him, Mr. Weichmann, while he was up in your room?" inquired Anna slyly.

"As a matter of fact, I did. It is, after all, my room. I feel I have the right to know something about who eats there."

"Certainly," said Miss Fitzpatrick, and I thought, not for the first time, that it was a shame Mr. Weichmann had not set his heart on her.

"I asked him where he was from. He said Baltimore."

"Well, we knew that," Anna said.

"I then asked where he was employed. He told me he worked for Mr. Parr, who owned a china shop there."

"He looks like a bull in a china shop," Miss Fitzpatrick said. "What else did you find out?"

"Nothing. He's not very forthcoming at all."

"Well," Anna said, "I just hope he doesn't murder us in our beds."

Mr. Wood did not murder us in our beds but left to catch the early train to Baltimore, his exit observed only by the servant girl. Except for his not being a paying guest, he was an ideal one, for his room was left immaculate.

This was a month for Johnny's friends, for no sooner had Mr. Wood vanished than another appeared in his place. This man, a swarthy gentleman of about thirty named Mr. Howell, was not a stranger, for he had passed through the tavern at Surrattsville on a number of occasions. I had always assumed, without knowing for certain, that he ran the blockade, but his present business, he informed me, was to await the arrival of a young lady whom he planned to escort to New York. She would be here in a few days.

It was no simple matter to elicit this information from Mr. Howell, for while not unfriendly, he was the most evasive of men. In the few years I had known him, he had used no fewer than three first names — Spencer, Augustus, and Gustavus — and I had never succeeded in learning anything about his family. It was all I could do to learn how he liked his eggs prepared. I found myself offering him a second helping of those eggs, for he was rail-thin and coughed a great deal, although of course he said nothing about his state of health. Perhaps he needed to conserve his strength, for once he arrived at the boardinghouse, he never ventured out but spent his days reading and coughing in the parlor and his evenings upstairs with Mr. Weichmann, who seemed rather taken with him.

Late one afternoon as Mr. Howell sat reading in the parlor — he even held the book so as to obscure the title — Miss Fitzpatrick, hearing a horse whinny outside the parlor window, said, "There's Mr. Surratt! In a carriage, and with a lady. Is that your friend, Mr. Howell?"

Mr. Howell looked out the window furtively. "Yes, that's her," he said, as if giving the answer under duress. He opened the window. "Coming! Just let me get my things."

"I would be happy to offer the lady some refreshment before you set out."

"Thank you, but there's no time." He scurried upstairs.

Miss Fitzpatrick looked harder. "Why is she wearing a veil?"

I glanced out the window myself. The lady's spruce gown, smart bonnet, and slender figure suggested youth, but it was impossible to say for sure with the heavy veil, in such strange contrast to her bright clothing. Even odder, and more disturbing, was how close to Johnny she was sitting, even though there was plenty of room in the ample carriage for a couple to leave a decorous space between them. As I chided myself for being too judgmental, for it was a crisp day and the lady might merely be chilly, she drew her arm through his.

Mr. Howell, carpetbag in hand, settled his bill and bade us all farewell. At least he was a paying guest, unlike Mr. Wood. He and Johnny changed places, and as the lady waved good-bye, the buggy rattled off, and Johnny bounded up the stairs to the parlor. "The prodigal son returns yet again," he said, pecking me on the cheek.

"Who is that young woman?"

"Mrs. Slater."

"Mrs. Slater? Where is her husband?"

"Dead, perhaps, or alive, perhaps."

"She is not acting like a woman with a living husband, Son. Nor is she acting like a respectable widow." I remembered Miss Fitzpatrick and Miss Dean. "Nora, could you tell the girl to get some supper for John? Miss Dean, your mother would like very much to have a letter from you."

"You're going to miss a fine lecture," Johnny called out to them as they left the room.

I lowered my voice. "That woman is a hussy, John."

"You've never even met her. You haven't even seen her face."

"And that is another thing. Why does she

138

wear that veil? Is she pockmarked?"

"Assuredly not."

"So you have seen beneath it?"

"She does have to eat occasionally, you know. Ma, simmer down. I'm not her lover."

"I hope you will continue not to be, for she looks exactly the sort of woman who would foist another man's bastard upon you."

"But you haven't even looked at her, Ma. We've established that."

"Women can sense this sort of thing. But who is she? Needless to say, Mr. Howell would say nothing about her, other than that she was female, which I can certainly see for myself."

"Mrs. Slater is a courier, one of the best. Trouble is, it's too dangerous for her to travel alone at some points, so she needs a male companion. She's on her way down to Richmond from our people in Montreal. I met her in New York. Howell will be taking her across the Potomac, courtesy of our friend Port Tobacco."

"I still think she looks like trouble. Where is her husband in all this?"

"Serving in the army — the Confederate army — assuming he hasn't been killed or captured. They're not a happy couple."

"I can't imagine why. Where is she from?"

"Ma, I'm not proposing to marry her! Connecticut, actually, but her family moved to North Carolina, and that's where she met her husband."

Having gone to school in Virginia, I sniffed at the mention of North Carolina, but at the same time felt a sense of relief. A Maryland boy like Johnny would never marry a little chit from North Carolina, should Mrs. Slater lose her apparently inconvenient husband.

"She speaks perfect French and can pass for a native should she ever get caught. Or at least a French Canadian."

"And the veil?"

"You'd wear one too, Ma, if you were carrying the secrets she carries."

12
Nora
MARCH 1865

Private Flanagan, who was expecting to be
released from the hospital within the month
if all went well, had been whiling the hours
away by considering professions a one-
armed man might enter. "I've been thinking
of keeping a grocery," he said a couple of
weeks after Valentine's Day.

"Oh, that might do very well."

"I would need to get my stock in trade,
though, and rent a place. I suppose I'd have
to get a loan."

"You have an honest face and have served
your country bravely. Someone will give you
a loan. Why, my father often travels to New
York on business and knows a number of
men there. I'm sure you could use his
name."

"I'll keep that in mind. I was wondering,
Miss Fitzpatrick . . ."

"What, sir?"

"Nothing."

This was the third time in our conversation this afternoon that Private Flanagan had seemed to be on the verge of asking me something. This was the most progress he had made. "Sir, I know you wish to tell me something. What is it? Is there something I can bring you? You know I will be happy to get you anything that can be had in Washington — that the doctors will allow, of course."

Private Flanagan muttered something.

"I did not understand you."

"I said I would like your picture," Private Flanagan repeated, so quickly that the sentence came out pretty much as one word. "If it's not too bold of me."

It was rather bold in those days, but how could I say no to a sick man? And besides, I did not really want to say no — except I had no recent photographs of myself, save for a very severe picture of myself and the other young ladies of the Georgetown Visitation class of 1864, posed around a harp that towered over all of us. "I'll have to get one taken," I said. "But I will bring it to you straightaway."

So the next day, I put on my best gown, the dusty pink wool with the braided trim, and walked to Gardner's Photographic Gallery on Seventh and D Streets. I wasn't get-

142

ting the photograph made only for Private Flanagan, I reasoned. My family would like one, as would Anna and my other friends. Really, Private Flanagan asking me for a photograph was simply fortuitous. I'd been planning to get one made all along.

To underscore the respectability of this enterprise, I brought a book to use as a prop — not a prayer book, as in the photograph of Mrs. Surratt that sat on the mantelpiece, for I didn't want Private Flanagan to think of me as a matron counting my beads — but a nicely bound copy of *Jane Eyre.* This earned me a bit of teasing from the photographer, who said I must be quite the little bluestocking, but at least he didn't ask if I was posing for my sweetheart.

When I got home, I found I had missed Mr. Booth. This should have pleased Anna, who I had discovered preferred not to have another young lady in the parlor during his visits, but instead I found her scowling. "He talked of that creature," she said.

I had no need to ask who "that creature" might be. She was Miss Hale, whom Anna had come to hate more than the entire Yankee army combined. "What did he say?"

"Their romance is still going on. He sends her fresh flowers every other day. Even when he's not in town. He has an arrangement with the florist."

"A floral arrangement. How apt."

"That's not funny."

"Well, you must admit that it is very romantic. Does he choose different flowers each day? Or does the florist decide, I wonder?"

"Who on earth cares? I was hoping that they would have had a falling-out by now. Maybe about politics. But no, she's even procured him a ticket for the inauguration."

Mr. Booth's political sympathies, of which he never spoke in the parlor, had been the subject of great speculation between Anna and myself. As he was friendly with Mr. Surratt, who everyone knew was no friend of the Union, we assumed Mr. Booth inclined in the same direction. Our opinions from that point diverged: I thought Mr. Booth would take the expected Northern victory in stride. "After all, his brother Edwin is loyal to the Union," I had pointed out. "And he is in love with Miss Hale."

"A man like Mr. Booth cannot be lukewarm about such an important subject," Anna had countered. "If he is a man of Southern feeling, he must be a passionate one."

Following Father's advice, and also knowing the question would be shockingly unladylike, I had never considered taking the simple expedient of simply asking Mr. Booth his opinion. Anna, who had certainly never restrained herself from interrogating poor Mr. Weichmann about his beliefs, was not as daring in the case of Mr. Booth. So the matter had remained unsettled, although upon hearing that Mr. Booth would be attending the inauguration, I was inclined to think I had the better of the argument.

"I hear she is positively bovine," Anna said.

"No, she's not. A little plump."

"Maybe she put on some weight during the winter." Anna ran her hands along the piano keyboard. We were alone in the parlor, everyone else in the boardinghouse being engaged in some activity or the other. "I want to see her."

"Why, for heaven's sake?"

"To get the lay of the land. To see what he sees in her that he sees in no one else."

"Anna, love is very strange."

"What would you know of it?"

Probably as much as she did, and perhaps even more, if one counted Private Flanagan asking for my picture. I decided not to point any of this out. "How are you going to see her? It's not as if you can knock at her family's door and ask for her social calendar."

"Silly, her family stays at the National. I looked in the city directory. So she must dine there. We will spy on her while she dines."

"We?"

"Of course. You don't expect me to go there and eat by myself, do you?"

I could not find any adequate fault with this logic.

We decided that breakfast would be the best time to spot — I refused to use the word *spy* — Miss Hale, as at any other time she might be shopping or doing charitable work or riding her horse or kissing Mr. Booth. So two days later, having concocted a story of going to meet one of Anna's friends, we took ourselves to the cavernous dining room of the National Hotel.

I had a bit of a sentimental attachment to the National Hotel, as my father had worked there for a short time after coming to Washington, before he was hired away by the bank. It was not the finest hotel in Washington — that would be the Willard — but it had its share of distinguished guests, some of whom, like Senator Hale and his family, lived there while in Washington rather than going to the trouble of keeping their own house. Thanks to Father, who had old friends on the staff there, I could walk into the dining room without feeling too much abashed, as I had often eaten there with my family during my school vacations. I could have even probably asked one of the waiters to point out Miss Hale, but I was hardly prepared to explain what a bank messenger's daughter might want with a senator's daughter.

"I might not even recognize Miss Hale," I warned Anna as we settled into our seats, which were fortunately close enough to the door for us to see anyone who came in. It was early, and only a few people had arrived. "I saw her for only a few moments, and I wasn't trying to engrave her features upon my memory."

"You'll know her," Anna said. "She'll be the heftiest woman in the room. Unless Mrs. Lincoln joins us."

I was wrong, though: it wasn't hard to spot Miss Hale at all. Not for the rude reason that Anna assigned, but because she was with her parents and her sister, just as she had been the night of the play. Moreover, although she was in a simpler gown, of course, as befit the time of day, she wore the same coral necklace, which stood out prettily against the gray silk dress.

I kicked Anna to inform of her my sighting. Anna duly glanced at Miss Hale but fortunately had better manners than to stare as the girl and her family made their way to their table, not too far off from ours. "Well?" I asked after the Hales were out of earshot. "What next?"

"We wait for Mr. Booth. Besides, we have a breakfast to eat."

I have neglected to say that the National was not famed for the quality of its breakfasts.

Anna and I plodded on through our meal, making stilted conversation as Miss Hale and her family dined, oblivious to all of the inconvenience they were causing us. Then, just as we had ordered more coffee, Mr. Booth sauntered into the room and headed straight toward the Hales' table. As he bowed to the ladies, I could feel the chill from Mr. and Mrs. Hale emanating through the dining room, but Mr. Booth seemed to take all of this in stride. Leaving the Hales, he roamed about and greeted half a dozen other diners before a look of surprise settled upon his face. He headed straight to our table.

"Why, Miss Surratt, Miss Fitzpatrick! What brings you here?"

I decided Anna could deal with that question. She managed admirably. "I have been in Washington all these months and have never once eaten here," she said. "It is such a Washington institution, I thought I should try it."

"Well, they do a better dinner than breakfast, if truth be told, but who's awake enough to care? Not me, I fear. I have never been an early riser, despite all my dear mother's efforts. May I join you?"

"Why, of course you may."

Anna was so busy attending to Mr. Booth, she could not witness the fine sight of Miss Hale glancing at our table curiously. I would have to gratify her with that information later. In fact, quite a few people were glancing at our table, clearly wondering what Mr. Booth's business was with a tall blond lady and a short dark lady, dressed nicely but hardly in the height of fashion. For their benefit, I tried to look sultry and mysterious, but I probably just looked cross.

Mr. Booth had picked up yesterday's discarded newspaper and, after chatting for a while, began to amuse us by reading the notices from it in his best Shakespearean manner. " 'Serious proposals are invited by the undersigned for supplying the United States Quartermaster's Department with hay,' " he intoned grandly. " 'Corn. Oats.

And straw. The price must be written out in' " — he lifted his arm dramatically and looked skyward — " 'words on the bids.' Now, you try it, Miss Fitzpatrick."

" 'Corn to be put up in good stout sacks of about two bushels each,' " I said in my most dire manner. " 'The hay and straw to be securely baled.' "

"Excellent! Now, you, Miss Surratt."

Anna scanned the front page. " 'Item,' " she read. " 'The chief engineer of the Hartford Fire Company keeps his hydrants thawed out by occasionally throwing steam into them from the steam fire engines.' "

By the time we had worked through the newspaper, the Hales had departed, unnoticed by even Anna. "I must go," Mr. Booth said, rising. "It has been delightful seeing you. No doubt I will be finding some excuse to call within the next few days. After all, I always do. Waiter! Put the ladies' charges on my account, please."

We walked out to Pennsylvania Avenue — or, in Anna's case, floated. "He sat with us and not her," she chortled.

"Her parents weren't very welcoming," I reminded Anna gently.

"But he could have sat with anyone — any lady there — and he chose to sit with us! Even you can't shrug that off, Nora."

150

"Fair enough," I acknowledged.

As this was the day my photograph was to be ready, we walked to the photographer's instead of back to H Street. I studied my picture with considerable relief. I did not look severe, as I had feared, but serious, and my hair, my best feature, had stayed in place. I could present this to Private Flanagan without shame.

Anna, meanwhile, was admiring the array of pictures for sale — President Lincoln, General Grant, Queen Victoria, and some actors and actresses and opera singers. Overshadowing all of them was Mr. Booth's photograph. "I must buy this for my collection," Anna said, opening her purse. "Nora, why don't you buy one too?"

With Mr. Booth visiting as often as he did, it seemed almost redundant to have his picture as well, but I was flush with pocket money, Father having just sent my monthly allowance. Besides, I had been neglecting my own photograph album lately.

The clerk smiled as I paid for my purchase. "Mr. Booth is our best seller," he said. "It's a rare day when I don't sell one of these, and more often two or three. He is a fine-looking man."

"And very pleasant in person too," Anna said. She winked at me. "Or so I am told."

Private Flanagan hardly looked at my photograph when I handed it to him that afternoon. "I'm being discharged, Miss Fitzpatrick. I'll be on the train to New York this time tomorrow."

"I am so glad you are well enough to go home."

Private Flanagan did not look at all glad. He cleared his throat. "I was wondering if I might write to you — when I can write a little better. I mean, to keep practicing."

"Of course you can."

"To write to you as a friend." Private Flanagan stared at my photograph. "I'll speak plainly. I would like to write to you as something more, but I can't ask that just now. Not until I can work and save a little so I can do right by you. I don't know when that will be, if ever, and I don't want you to feel tied to me. Someone's bound to snap you up before then, but that's a chance I'll just have to take. Do you understand me, Miss Fitzpatrick?"

"Yes, I do."

"Then I think we'd better say good-bye now as friends. If you stay longer, I might just go and ask for something more. Will you write down your address for me on your picture?"

I took the picture and wrote on the back: *Miss Nora Fitzpatrick. No. 541 H Street between 6th and 7th Streets, Washington, DC.* "I shall look forward to hearing from you, sir."

"I don't know if I'll have much to say, or if I can spell what I want to say," Private Flanagan said, rising to bid me farewell. He caught my hand and squeezed it in a manner that I can describe only as awkward, and yet both tender and strong. "But I'm going to try my best, miss."

I walked home deep in thought. Was Private Flanagan in love with me? Even as I sternly told myself not to read too much into his words and into his handclasp, I could not see any other logical meaning in them.

And was I in love with Mr. Flanagan? I wasn't spending my every waking moment thinking of him, or writing terrible poetry about him, or scribbling his name. But that didn't mean much, because I doubted I was the sort of person to do such things anyway. What I had been doing was taking his valentine out of its hiding place to look at it and spending more and more time at the hospital. If that wasn't love, I supposed it was awfully close. Two things were certain: I had liked the warmth of Private Flanagan's hand pressing mine, and I was going to be mighty sorry to go to the hospital the next day and see someone else lying in his cot.

When I reached the boardinghouse, I found a note from my father. A friend of his who worked at the Capitol could procure him a good spot on the grounds from which to watch the president make his second inaugural speech. Would I like to come with him? Peter would be coming down from Boston to join us.

Of course I wanted to come. Washington was packed with people hoping to see the inauguration; even the Willard was stowing guests in its hallways and parlors. To witness the event from a fair vantage point, instead of being at the fringes of the crowd, pushed to-and-fro and craning to see past a sea of high hats, was more than I could have ever hoped for.

Anna, of course, was not impressed at my good fortune. "They'll be crowning the ape next." She sniffed.

Undaunted by her attitude, I set off with my father and my brother early on the morning of Saturday, March 4. It was a

thoroughly miserable day, which had announced itself with a hailstorm that had
subsided into a steady, cold rain, turning
the city's mostly unpaved streets to muck.
But no one seemed to care: except for those
who had the privilege of witnessing the
ceremonies inside the Capitol, everyone in
Washington appeared to be on the streets,
either thronging on Pennsylvania Avenue to
watch the inaugural parade or massing on
the Capitol grounds to await the president's
speech to the public. As we trudged to the
Capitol to secure our places, our shoes and
the hem of my dress becoming caked with
mud, the parade moved as colorfully and as
tunefully down Pennsylvania Avenue as it
would have had the sun glowed in the sky.

As we waited for the president to appear
on the platform erected above the Capitol
steps, I asked Father as offhandedly as possible, "What would you think if I married a
man who was poor but who was trying to
better himself?"

Peter and my father both gave me stern
looks. Father said, "You have not engaged
yourself to someone, have you, Nora?"

"No, Father. I was asking only theoreti-
cally. At the hospital I have met some fine
young men who are poor but who want to
improve their lives. Some have been injured

— missing an arm or a leg, for instance — and they will need the help of a wife."

"Well, I was poor when I came here," Father said. "But I held off marrying until I could support your mother. She helped, of course, by being thrifty, and we lived with others, but I was able to keep her and you children on my own."

"But you had both arms, Father. What if a man needed a wife to help run his store or to keep his accounts until he reached the point where he could hire someone to do it?"

Peter chuckled. "*You* keep accounts, Nora?"

"I never overspend my allowance."

"I would have to meet the man, child. If I thought he was worthy of such devotion, as opposed to simply exploiting you while he lay about, then I would be willing to give my blessing. But I would want to know more about the man than I could observe in a short period. I would want to know what his neighbors thought of him, what his priest thought about him —"

"Is this man Catholic, Nora?" Peter asked.

"He is purely hypothetical," I said stiffly. "I have not assigned him a religion."

"I would want to see him over a period of time before I could believe that he was worthy of you." Father sighed. "I know the war has set everything topsy-turvy, but I hope it has not changed things so much that young ladies will marry just anyone without consulting their parents."

"If I marry anyone, it will be with your blessing, Father." I glared at Peter. "And he will be Catholic." I decided a change of topic was in short order. "Remember I told you that Mr. John Wilkes Booth, the actor, would be calling at Mrs. Surratt's house? He did call, and has called several times since. He's very pleasant."

"He calls on you, Nora?" Father asked.

"On all of us, mostly. Sometimes on Mr. Surratt, but he's hardly ever at home. So usually he just sits in the parlor and chats to all of us. Even Mr. Rochester likes him."

"Mr. Rochester?"

"My cat, Peter. Mr. Booth will be here today. The lady he loves gave him a ticket."

With the rain starting to come down heavily again, Father held his umbrella over my head while Peter draped his shawl over my shoulders. As the time wore on, I looked around in the sea of high hats surrounding me. Thousands of people were packed onto the Capitol grounds. The papers had warned of pickpockets come to take advantage of the festivities, but we were massed so tightly together I could not see how any of these people could move about to ply their trade. Yet everyone seemed to be in the best of humor, and I wished Anna, who had made a point of sleeping late this morning, was here to see for herself the mood of the people. But probably the sight of the colored people in the crowd, waiting patiently to hear the man who had liberated them from slavery, would have irritated her more than anything.

At last the platform above us began to fill with dignitaries coming from the interior of the Capitol, where Congress, the justices of the Supreme Court, the press, and a few impostors had heard the president and the vice president take their oath of office. Vice President Johnson came out, looking sheepish and not entirely steady on his feet — later, I would learn that, sick and tired, he had gulped some brandy before speaking and had rambled on before Congress about his humble origins before he could finally be induced to stop talking long enough to take his oath. He was followed by the unmistakable figure of the president, looking so much more gaunt and worn than he did in the picture in my album. I might not have known him but for the roar that came from the spectators.

Then the president stepped to the podium, and at that very same moment, the sun, unseen in Washington for two days, broke through the clouds, making us gasp as its benevolent rays shone over all.

"A sign from God," my brother whispered. "What on earth could be more clear?"

We listened, rapt, until the president spoke the words that, years later, I would listen to my own sons recite for school: "With malice toward none, with charity for all, with firmness in the right as God gives us to see the right, let us strive on to finish the work we are in, to bind up the nation's wounds, to care for him who shall have borne the battle and for his widow and his orphan, to do all which may achieve and cherish a just and lasting peace among ourselves and with all nations."

The crowd erupted into applause, and my father, his cheeks wet with tears, squeezed my hand. "Nora, you have witnessed history."

And then, as the president left the podium, I saw on the balcony above the platform what Mr. Lincoln's tall figure had obscured from me: Mr. Booth, standing. Wearing a high hat instead of the slouch hat he usually wore on his visits to us, he was more elegantly dressed than anyone on the platform, including the president. But it was not his fine clothing or his good looks that made him stand out from the other men on the platform.

He was the only person there not smiling.

13
Mary
MARCH 1865

Though I cannot say I welcomed President Lincoln's second inauguration, it proved a profitable occasion for me, as lodgings were at a premium, and I was able to fill my attic rooms for a few nights — though Anna would have had me leave them vacant out of principle. That I could not do, as principle did not pay my bills, but I did stay inside the day of the ceremony when almost everyone else in Washington was venturing out and returning splattered with both mud and Union sentiment. Miss Fitzpatrick, whom I had begun calling by her Christian name, regaled us for so long with her description of Mr. Lincoln's splendid speech and noble bearing that at dinner, Anna threw a biscuit at her and had to be scolded like a child, after which Nora gathered up her cat and retreated in a huff to my bedroom, where she and Anna had begun sleeping after our recent influx of visitors. Fortunately, Mr.

Booth visited us that evening, and as neither of the young ladies would dream of missing an hour of his presence, he soon had them both laughing with his imitation of the drunken Vice President Johnson delivering his speech while Johnny, playing the role of the outgoing vice president, tugged at his coattails and begged him to stop. Even Mr. Weichmann and I could not help but chuckle, and when Mr. Booth departed, Anna and Nora embraced and soon were poring over Nora's album as the best of friends.

With Mr. Weichmann having gone upstairs to read, and the girls so absorbed, Johnny gestured for me to follow him into the hall. "We may have a visitor in a few days. Your good friend Mrs. Slater. She'll be staying overnight if she comes."

"Johnny, no."

"She has to, Ma. Usually she stops at the National, but they're getting too curious about her, and she's not happy staying there anyway. The men are too impudent, she says."

"I won't have that hussy corrupting your sister or Miss Fitzpatrick."

"She's not a hussy, Ma. She's a charming lady. I promise, she'll be on her best behavior. And how can she corrupt Miss Fitzpatrick? The girl is turning into a flaming Unionist."

"You know what I mean. Where is she going after she leaves Washington?"

"Montreal. I'll be escorting her as far as New York. Now, don't look so horrified, Ma! Separate hotel rooms, I promise, once we get there."

I could have argued more, and perhaps should have argued more, but it all seemed pointless. "Mrs." Slater would have to stay somewhere, and if Johnny wanted to find his way to her bed, he was a grown man and would do so no matter where she slept. "She can stay here, but she must pay for her room. And, Johnny, I repeat: she is a married woman and must act like one around the young ladies."

"Duly noted. So a little romance with Weichmann is out of order, then?" Johnny saw my freezing glare. "Duly noted."

Naturally, our expected visitor had not escaped the attention of Mr. Weichmann. "I have agreed with Johnny to give up my room to this lady," he informed me a day or so later. "He said that you would probably be willing to reduce my rent per diem for my stay in the attic, but I told him that I was quite willing to do it gratis."

"That is very kind of you, Mr. Weichmann. Fortunately, it is only for one night."

"I wonder what brings her north."

What had Johnny told — or not told — Mr. Weichmann? As I had no idea, I could only say, "Family business, I suppose."

Mrs. Slater arrived a day or so after this conversation, wearing her familiar veil. Johnny was not home, so Mr. Weichmann went downstairs to fetch her trunk. "It's a pity we've already eaten," Anna said as we waited for them. "She would have to take off the veil, then."

"We can offer her some refreshments," Nora suggested. "She'll be hungry after her journey, I imagine. At least a cup of tea."

"Let's get the girl to fix something, then."

They were about to hurry downstairs when Mr. Weichmann and Mrs. Slater came upstairs. Mrs. Slater's trunk, like Mrs. Slater herself, was small and neat. She held out her hand and said, in a peculiar accent that was half Northern and half North Carolinian, "Thank you, Mrs. Surratt, for allowing me to stay here. I very much appreciate your hospitality."

"You are quite welcome."

"You will take some refreshment, Mrs. Slater?" Anna asked.

"We had a delicious dinner tonight," Miss

Fitzpatrick added. "There's plenty left over."

Mrs. Slater shook her head. "It is a peculiarity of mine that I have no appetite after I travel."

It was maddening, not only for the young ladies and perhaps even Mr. Weichmann, but for me as well. The veil was just thin enough to suggest that Mrs. Slater was more handsome than otherwise, but one could only guess.

I could, however, see Mrs. Slater's wedding ring, as thin a band of gold as one could buy. "Is your husband fighting, Mrs. Slater?"

"Yes, for the Confederacy," Mrs. Slater said coolly. She gave what I supposed was the North Carolinian equivalent of a French shrug. "It is no secret."

"Then he is fighting for an honorable cause," Anna said. She gave Mrs. Slater a brilliant smile, which unfortunately no one could see if Mrs. Slater returned. "But what are you doing here, then?"

"My mother lives in New York, and I am going to stay with her. I don't care for my in-laws in North Carolina, nor them for me." Mrs. Slater's veil shook vigorously. "They don't care for my husband either. You see, he is — was — a dancing master, and they consider that beneath him."

"Can you make a living from that?" Anna asked.

"Oh, he made a very good living indeed before the war. But after that there was no time for dancing, and my husband had to take a dreary government job. And then he joined the Army." Mrs. Slater rose. She was a very short lady, which I thought with satisfaction would make her look comical next to my tall Johnny. "There is nothing so wearying as travel. Would you mind terribly if I retired?"

"My room is at your service," Mr. Weich-mann said.

"That is very kind of you, sir. I hope it isn't putting you to any great inconvenience. I will disturb nothing."

"Miss Fitzpatrick and I will show you to your room," said Anna.

If Mrs. Slater wondered at the need for this double escort, she hid it and nodded graciously. In a short time, Anna and Nora returned, their faces studies in disappoint-ment. "She never took it off," Nora said. "We were hoping, with no man present, she might."

"I am glad to hear that I was not the obstruction," Mr. Weichmann said.

"What could she be hiding? A dreadful scar?"

"Smallpox," Nora suggested.

"Or maybe just a bad complexion."

"Or a large wen or wart."

"Perhaps she is exceptionally modest," mused Mr. Weichmann.

"How modest can a dancing master's wife be?" Anna put her chin on her hand, a pose I had observed that Mr. Weichmann seemed to find rather fetching. "There must be some way to see her without it. She has to take it off to sleep, doesn't she? Ma, can't you find some excuse to go to her room in the middle of the night?"

"Hardly. I cannot and will not disturb my boarders' privacy like that. And neither will you."

Anna heaved a sigh. "There's always hope for breakfast," she said.

But, alas, there was not. Mrs. Slater preferred to take her little breakfast — coffee and toast — in her room. She was a bear, she explained, before she had properly awakened, and would not inflict her grumpy self upon us.

Mr. Weichmann, somewhat bearish himself after a stay in the attic (which did not have the most comfortable of beds, I must admit) said little at breakfast but lingered at the table longer than was his wont. When it became apparent Mrs. Slater was not going to join us, he consulted his pocket watch, muttered something, and hurried away to work after bidding us a hasty good-bye.

"I am just going to ask her why she wears that veil," Anna hissed to Nora as we walked upstairs to the parlor.

Nora nodded. "It is becoming unbearable, not knowing."

I was getting ready to reprove them when we heard Mrs. Slater's light footstep coming downstairs. "Can I bring you anything else to eat?" I asked her.

"No, indeed, Mrs. Surratt. I am perfectly fine now. I think now that everyone has gone to their offices, I will go for a morning walk. It is such a crisp, clear —"

A key turned in the front door, and Johnny loped into the parlor. "Why, Mrs. Slater! Are you ready for our trip?"

With a flick of her tiny hand, Mrs. Slater swept her veil back. The face revealed was exemplary, without a single mark or scar, except for a tiny, perfectly placed beauty mole. "Mr. Surratt," she cooed in a voice that was suddenly far more Southern than Northern, and with a hint of French, "how lovely to see you!"

14
NORA
MARCH 1865

At first, I did not trouble myself too much about the comings and goings at Mrs. Surratt's. It was a boardinghouse, after all, and — as my father took care to remind me every time I saw him — Washington was teeming with odd sorts of people brought here by the war. One would have to be shut in a nunnery to avoid them. Instead, I rather enjoyed the parade of people so far removed from anyone I'd seen at Georgetown Visitation, or at the Misses Donovan's house.

Then came the lady in the veil, a Mrs. Slater. A lady who could not have been much older than myself, as I learned once I finally saw her features. She stayed for one night, keeping her veil down more determinedly than Esther Summerson after the smallpox. Only when Mr. Surratt ambled in from one of his unexplained absences did she lift the veil, to reveal not the ravages of disease but a very pretty visage. Why had she kept her face hidden all that time?

I was not the only one wondering, I suspected. Almost as soon as Mr. Surratt had come home, he and Mrs. Slater had departed in a buggy — in itself a little odd, I thought, for surely there were more suitable escorts for a pretty young married woman than a young bachelor. But Mrs. Slater must have packed hastily, for soon after Mr. Weichmann came home from work, he appeared in the parlor with a dainty pair of women's slippers in his hand. "I think Cinderella left two slippers behind, Mrs. Surratt."

Perhaps it was because she was tired from cooking that afternoon, but Mrs. Surratt had just scowled, and kept on scowling even after Mr. Weichmann made all of us ladies in the boardinghouse try on Mrs. Slater's slippers. Only Miss Dean could fit into them, and even she would probably not be able to once she became a year or two older.

Where had Mrs. Slater and Mr. Surratt gone? And where did Mr. Surratt go on all of these trips of his? As I sat at church that afternoon with a number of other young ladies, painting china for the upcoming fair, I pondered these questions. Without having any business to attend to that I could tell, he was always coming and going. Furthermore, despite his lack of employment, he dressed well and never seemed short of cash, yet I had gathered Mrs. Surratt did not have much of that to spare. She had once commented, when Father paid my board a little ahead of time, how nice it was to have it; since then, my father had always brought it by early. Anna certainly did not have much spending money; were it not for the piano lessons she gave a couple of little girls from church, I doubted she would have had any at all.

I decided to raise the question with Anna as we walked home from St. Aloysius Church, located over by Swampoodle north of the Capitol. "Anna, where does Johnny go on those trips of his?"

"To Surrattsville, I suppose."

"But he doesn't like it there. I've heard him say so often enough. And doesn't your mother have a tenant there? He surely can't want Johnny interfering. And who is that lady?"

"How should I know? You're as nosy as Mr. Weichmann."

"I am not. I am only curious. And surely, since I am paying to live here, I should be allowed to know something of the people I live with."

"You're not paying, your father is."

"All the more reason. He would not want me to be living with someone who is disreputable." Anna's eyes were flashing, so I hastened to add, "I don't think he is disreputable, of course, but Father might. I want only to make sure that he does not take me away from here because of some misunderstanding."

"I don't think I am at liberty to discuss my brother's affairs."

"Don't you trust me? You have confided in me before, and I have never betrayed your confidence. I even went to the National with you to spy on Miss Hale."

"We were not spying on her. We were merely watching her."

"Regardless, I never said a word to anyone. Did I?"

"I'm not even sure what I think is true. He's never told me anything about what he does, and neither has Ma, though she must know. Ever since Father died and left Johnny as the man of the house with Isaac gone, they treat me like a child, even though I'm older than Johnny." Anna's eyes flashed again, but this time I was not their target. "Why shouldn't I tell you, then? I believe that Johnny runs the blockade, and that he carries messages to Richmond."

"Really?" I wasn't sure what I had been

expecting, but this was certainly more than I had anticipated. "Are you sure?"

"First you ask me to tell you, and then you ask whether I am sure." Anna waved away my apology in what I thought of as her best grand duchess manner. "But yes, I am sure, or as sure as I can be without following Johnny around. I heard him and Ma arguing about it once. Ma wishes he would get a regular job."

"It must be dangerous."

"That's what Ma says to Johnny."

"So is Mrs. Slater a courier too? Or a spy?"

"I imagine she is."

"Do you think they're" — I looked around before saying the word — "lovers?"

Anna nodded in her most worldly manner. "I wouldn't be at all surprised."

I giggled. "No wonder your poor mother was glaring at her so. Maybe she's not even married." I cast my mind back over the other people who had frequented the house lately. "That consumptive Mr. Howell. Do you think he's one of them?"

"Oh, certainly."

"And Port Tobacco?" He had come by the boardinghouse a few times lately, slightly better dressed than when I first met him but somehow not much less grimy looking.

"Lord no, Nora. Johnny just makes use of

him once in a while. Who would trust him with such business?"

"I wonder if Mr. Booth is involved."

Anna stopped so quickly that she nearly lost her balance in her hoop. "How can you even think such a thing? Lumping Mr. Booth in with that Port Tobacco creature, and that strumpet Mrs. Slater?"

"I was just thinking aloud. He and your brother do spend a lot of time together, and you yourself said you thought he supported the South. And isn't Mr. Surratt handling some business for Mr. Booth?"

"Respectable business. Aboveboard business, for Mr. Mudd's estates."

"But no one's mentioned that for weeks."

"Maybe it fell through, and Mr. Booth simply likes my brother's company. Johnny is well bred, after all."

I smiled, remembering Mr. Surratt's drunken duet with Mr. Weichmann. Fortunately, Anna did not catch my smile. "Mr. Booth didn't look happy the day of the inauguration."

"What sensible person would?"

"I should think you'd like to have Mr. Booth on your brother's side."

"I would, but the idea of him sneaking about is too nonsensical. Anyway, I don't really approve of what Johnny's doing. It's dangerous, and it upsets Ma, I know."

"I can't help but wonder."

"I think you read too many novels, Nora."

"Which reminds me," I said. "Let's stop by the bookstore. I have not bought the latest installment of *Our Mutual Friend.*"

Every other day, I stopped in at the post office and called for my mail. I was seldom disappointed, for between my sister in Baltimore, my brother in Boston, some school friends, and some relatives on my mother's side, there was always a chance some correspondence would be there for me. Since Private Flanagan's release from the hospital, however, I had been checking every day, though I felt rather foolish in doing so.

Today, however, underneath a letter written in a school friend's elegant script, was a rather grubby-looking envelope addressed to me in a sprawling hand. I knew it could be from no one else than my hospital friend.

It took me a while to read my letter, between the left-handed penmanship and the spelling, but I smiled the entire time I read. Private Flanagan had kept his promise and not written anything that could be construed as lover-like. Instead, he wrote about his dog, who had been glad to see him, and his younger brothers, who had been as well until they realized he had come to share their bed again. (There, Private Flanagan, considering it indelicate to write the word *bed,* had scratched it out, struggled to find another word, and finally written it again, with "EXCUSE WORD!" written beside it.) He had not found work yet, but his priest and an old friend of his father's were doing the best they could to help him, and perhaps when he wrote me next, he would be "AN EMPLOYED MAN!" Private Flanagan, I gathered, put a great deal of faith in capital letters and exclamation marks. He had signed his letter "YOURS TRULY," amended that to "YOUR FRIEND," and finally settled on "YOUR HUMBEL SERVANT."

I put the letter in my purse — I did not need to fold it, as Private Flanagan had done such a thorough job of that himself — and walked home, lost in thought. I had not entirely expected Private Flanagan to keep his promise to write to me. Now that he had, what did this mean for me? Could I love a poor man, an uneducated man?

But Private Flanagan was educated enough to write an intelligible letter, and as my father often said, no man in America had to remain poor forever. And in any case,

176

I was being a bit presumptuous. New York City had its share of young women, and no doubt one might come across Private Flanagan's way. One whom he didn't have to communicate with by letter. One whom he could court in person, and walk out with wherever people in New York did their walking out.

But in the meantime, I might as well enjoy my new correspondent, which meant I would have to write my own letter to Private Flanagan. I didn't think I could do nearly as good a job as he had.

That very night, we had a familiar guest at the boardinghouse: Mr. Wood.

That wasn't the name he gave us, though. He called himself Mr. Lewis Payne. I could hardly forget his height, however, or his build, or his black hair, as straight as Mr. Booth's was curly. Unlike the last time he had come here, he was elegantly dressed in a gray suit that looked new. I remembered he said he had worked in a china shop, but this evening, he introduced himself as a Baptist preacher. He didn't look like any of the men of the cloth I had known, but admittedly my clerical acquaintance was confined almost entirely to Catholic priests.

Maybe this was what men meant by "muscular Christianity," I thought as I gazed at the burly Mr. Payne.

I had barely seen him during his last visit, as he had spent most of the evening in his room, but this time, he was downright sociable, as a preacher should be. Scarcely after he seated himself in the parlor, he inquired whether any of we ladies were musical, and being told that Anna possessed the talent in that regard, he begged her to favor us with a song. Anna, of course, obliged, and Mr. Payne opened the piano lid for her with a flourish almost worthy of Mr. Booth.

Mr. Weichmann too was giving Mr. Payne a quizzical look, but I was seated too far from him to share my thoughts. When Anna finished, to general applause, Mr. Payne looked at me and said in Mr. Wood's high voice, "Do you play, miss? Or would you like to favor us with a song?"

"I don't play nearly as well as Miss Surratt," I said. "But thank you for asking, Mr. Wood." I had not meant to address him as such — truly — but it had slipped out, and when it did, I saw Mr. Weichmann's face was a study in enlightenment.

No one else took any notice of my slip of the tongue, however, except for Mr. Payne himself, who shot me an imploring look. I supposed he was one of Mr. Surratt's associates, so I said nothing more, and when we sat down to play cards, it was with Mr. Payne and not with Mr. Wood. "Do you have a church, Mr. Payne?" I asked.

"Not at the moment. I preach here and there." Mr. Payne gave a glimmer of a smile. "I don't guess you would want to hear a sermon."

"Maybe on Sunday," I demurred.

"I should be interested in hearing your sermon when you give one," Mr. Weichmann said. "As I am weighing the question of going into the priesthood, it is a subject that interests me, and I have never been in a Baptist church."

"It's different from a Catholic church, I reckon," Mr. Payne said.

"Have you ever been to one of our churches, sir? I would be happy to take you."

"No, I haven't. I'll take you up on that offer sometime, sir."

"Your first convert, Mr. Weichmann," Anna said.

"Oh, I am not attempting to convert Mr. Payne. I only think that it is a good thing to visit churches of another denomination from time to time. It is broadening. Don't you think so, sir?"

"I haven't given it much thought." Mr.

Payne studied his cards. "No harm in it, I reckon."

"Odd preacher," Mrs. Holohan hissed to me later that evening when I went upstairs to repay her for some thread she had given me. "I don't think he will save many souls."

A few days later, the day before I was to go on a visit to Baltimore, Mr. Surratt turned up with a ten-dollar box ticket to see *The Tragedy of Jane Shore* at Ford's Theatre, courtesy of Mr. Booth. As I could not resist such an opportunity, I eagerly assented when Miss Holohan had to decline. She and Miss Dean had been the original recipients of the invitation. It was so typical of Mr. Booth, I thought, that he should ask the littlest two girls in the house, who were the least likely to be included in such an invitation, to enjoy an evening at Ford's.

"Who is going with us?" asked Miss Dean.

"Why, me, of course, and Mr. Payne," Mr. Surratt said, glancing at the latter, who looked less than enthusiastic. Perhaps Baptists did not approve of the theater.

"I have a mind to go myself," Mr. Weichmann said, snatching the ticket out of Mr. Surratt's hand.

Miss Dean, evidently thinking the precious ticket was going to be destroyed, shrieked as Mr. Surratt deftly snatched the ticket back, then gave Mr. Weichmann a good-natured punch in the belly. "Not tonight, old man. Sorry." He cleared his throat. "But perhaps your blue cloak can go. Mr. Payne will strike a more dashing figure with it, and Anna's not here to take umbrage at it."

This struck me as a rather rude request of one who had been left out of the theater party, but Mr. Weichmann merely snorted, said, "Fine by me," and headed upstairs.

"We'll make a bachelor party of it next time, Weichmann," Mr. Surratt promised when Mr. Weichmann returned with his cloak, part of the blue attire he and his fellow War Department employees were occasionally required to wear for drills. "But Booth specifically requested the presence of Mr. Payne, myself, and the ladies, and the box only holds four." He nodded at Miss Dean and me on the sofa. "And their skirts will make it a tight fit at that."

Mr. Surratt had hired a hack for us, which soon arrived. Mr. Payne had me in his charge, and Mr. Surratt had Miss Dean. As we stepped inside the hack, I felt grateful for our respective pairings, as I was still angry with Mr. Surratt for referring to me as an old maid, all the more so because I had not been supposed to see the letter in

181

question and therefore could not take him to task properly. I had not expected the laconic Mr. Payne to be much of an escort, but to my surprise, he roused himself to what for him must have been a veritable fever pitch of conversation. "You said you were going to Baltimore tomorrow, Miss Fitzpatrick. Do you have family there?"

"My sister lives there, and I will probably see her, but she is not the purpose of my visit, as she is a cloistered nun. I will be staying with a school friend."

"I was in Baltimore not long ago. I —"

"Tell me, Mr. Payne. What do you know of this play?"

I frowned at Mr. Surratt for this rather rude interruption, but Mr. Payne appeared indifferent. "Nothing. Who was Jane Shore?"

"Not to be discussed before ladies, Mr. Payne."

"Don't be silly, Mr. Surratt. It's history." I turned to Mr. Payne. "She was a mistress of King Edward IV, sir. Shakespeare wrote about her in his play about Richard III."

"The king with all of the wives?"

"No. The king with the hunchback."

Having set Mr. Payne straight on the English monarchy, I settled myself more comfortably in the hack and gazed down at the theatergoers who were traveling via shank's mare below us. What a pleasure it was, not to have the hem of my best gown dragging in the Washington mud!

When we entered the theater, I saw that Ford's was as elegant as it had been when I saw Mr. Booth play Richard III there back in the fall of 1863. The only thing different was my box seat, in contrast to the twenty-five-cent family circle seats into which Father and I had squeezed ourselves then. Taking my seat and letting my skirts billow around me, I found myself pitying Mr. Weichmann, left out of this excursion.

I did not concern myself with Mr. Weichmann's plight long, however, but settled down to enjoy the first show of the evening. It was a marvelously tragic play, in which the unfortunate Jane Shore, bereft of her royal lover through his death, menaced by Lord Hastings, betrayed by her one female friend, and persecuted by wicked King Richard, finally succumbs to death in the arms of her cast-off husband, arrived too late to save her from the king's clutches. My appreciation of it was unhampered by the occasional soft snores of Miss Dean, who indeed was up past her bedtime, and who fell asleep during the second act, rather to the amusement of the audience, which watched us on the occasions where their attention was diverted by a quiet moment on-stage. Mr. Payne seemed to be hampered by some difficulty in following the plot, and Mr. Surratt watched Mistress Shore's misery unfold with the detached enjoyment of one accustomed to sorrow befalling other people. But I compensated for all of the deficiencies of the rest by dissolving into tears early on, and remaining in that teary state until the curtain finally dropped. I was still sniffling when Mr. Booth poked his curly head into our box. "I see you are liking the play, Miss Fitzpatrick."

"Oh, Mr. Booth, it is magnificent! I have never cried so much in my life. I just wish you had been in it."

"Maybe one of these days, who knows? But it is more of a vehicle for an actress, and Mrs. Phillips is one of the finest. I see you, Miss Apples, have been resting in anticipation of the comedy to come."

"Yes, I have been," Miss Dean said firmly. "I don't care much for kings and queens."

"Spoken like a true American!" Mr. Booth nodded at our escorts. "Mr. Surratt, Mr. Payne, may I have a word?"

The men's conversation was still going on when the curtain rose on the comic fare of the evening, James Sheridan Knowles's *The Love Chase*. It was as humorous as *Jane*

Shore had been tragic, and when the men finally ended their conversation with Mr. Booth and slipped back into our box, they seemed to find it much more to their taste.

Mr. Booth was on hand at the end of the show. He led us through the crowd to our waiting hack — first in line at the stand, in front of several fine carriages — and lifted Miss Dean, who at this point in the evening was all but sleepwalking, into her place. Then he handed me up. "I had a lovely evening, Mr. Booth. Thank you so much."

"My pleasure," Mr. Booth said, and to this day I believe he spoke sincerely.

15
MARY
MARCH 1865

A couple of days after Mr. Payne arrived, Mr. Weichmann hurried into the kitchen, where I was getting dinner together. "I must talk to you, Mrs. Surratt."

My heart sank. Was Mr. Weichmann giving notice? Perhaps he was more irritated than I realized about giving his room to Mrs. Slater. "Of course. Is something amiss, sir?"

"I was in the attic just now, Mrs. Surratt. I came from work, and from the appearance of the room, I knew John was home. So I went upstairs, and what do I see?"

From Mr. Weichmann's tone, I was prepared for just about anything, but all I could do was shake my head.

"Guns," Mr. Weichmann said. "He and Mr. Payne were sitting on a bed surrounded by them. Spurs too. Mrs. Surratt, I do not like this at all."

"Mr. Weichmann, my son rides regularly

into the country. It is necessary that he go armed."

"But why spread them out on the bed like that?"

I shrugged. "Perhaps Mr. Payne is interested in guns. He is a Baptist preacher, remember. Not like the men of the cloth you and I are used to. He seems — rather countrified."

"I still don't like this."

Did Mr. Weichmann expect me to march upstairs and demand that these grown men put their guns away? Even if I had not been suffering from female problems that day, it was not a task I relished. "I see no harm in it as long as they confine them to the attic. But I will take your advice in the kind spirit in which I am sure it is meant, Mr. Weichmann, and will be on my guard. But you must understand that Johnny is a grown man, and one who has been acting as the man of the house for several years. I cannot treat him like a small boy. Now it is time for us to eat."

Mr. Weichmann was right, I feared. Something was going on.

I began to have my doubts when Johnny and Mr. Payne escorted Nora and Miss Dean to the theater and then, having seen the ladies safely home, grabbed a pack of cards from Johnny's room and headed out again into the night. They were not yet home at five in the morning when Mr. Weichmann kindly took it upon himself to accompany Nora to the railroad station. He had just left on this chivalrous mission when Johnny and Mr. Payne at last arrived. They were not precisely drunk, but not precisely sober either, and neither appeared to be in good spirits. They gave me only a few words before heading upstairs to their beds.

It was the first time I had known Johnny to stay out all night, at least when he was under my own roof. What had he done? Gambled, perhaps — but he had hardly anything of value to wager. Consorted with loose women? But surely he would not look so grim if he did so. Perhaps one of them robbed him of the little he had. This seemed to be such a likely possibility that I almost asked Mr. Weichmann, now returned home, to check his trouser pockets before I thought better of it.

And why was Mr. Payne, a Baptist preacher, keeping such late hours? And why did he remind me of someone I had encountered earlier?

I meant to question Johnny when he awakened, but he managed to find a moment when I was distracted and slipped out the door.

I did not get a chance to speak to him over the next day and a half. Father Wiget, who used to teach my sons, called, and there was the usual business of running a boarding-house to attend to. When Johnny and Mr. Payne left that afternoon, shouting a hasty good-bye, I was busy going through the monthly bills and hardly thought anything of it.

The clock struck four, and Mrs. Holohan came downstairs, a peculiar look on her face. "Mrs. Surratt, your son asked me to give this to you." She handed me a letter.

"I do not understand. He saw me just an hour ago."

"Yes. He told me not to deliver the letter until four."

"Why, for heavens' sake?"

"I do not know. Perhaps I should have delivered it sooner, but I assumed he had his reasons, and he specifically asked me not to do so."

I opened the letter. Johnny's graceful handwriting read:

Ma,
I find it necessary to leave town for a while. Mr. Payne is with me. Don't know

when we will be back. It's all for the good.

Your loving son,
John

I stared at this curt letter, then at Mrs. Holohan. "He told you nothing about where he was headed? What his plans were?"

"No, Mrs. Surratt. He said nothing, and I did not press him. I — I assumed you might have quarreled for some reason, and it was none of my business."

"Of course." I stared at the letter, as if doing so would bring some meaning to light. Johnny's absences for a week or so at a time were nothing out of the ordinary, so this absence must be for a longer period. Where was he going? What did Mr. Payne have to do with this? And why had he told me almost nothing about his plans?

Had he left for Europe, as he had threatened to from time to time? Had he enlisted in the Confederate army?

I ran upstairs to the room Johnny and Mr. Weichmann shared and began rummaging in Johnny's table. I found some writing paper (all of it blank), a pen and ink, a bundle of letters from Johnny's cousin Miss Seaman and several other relations, some railway timetables, a couple of cigars, some photographs, and a box where shaving things, a motley collection of cuff links, and a handful of stray buttons (so this was where Johnny's buttons went!) were jumbled together. Nothing provided a clue to where Johnny might be.

Anna, who had come home from giving a piano lesson and was still holding a portfolio of sheet music, came into the room. "What is the matter, Ma?"

"Your brother has gone away."

"Gone away? Where?"

"I don't know! There was a letter, but it told me nothing, and he told Mrs. Holohan nothing." I knew I was beginning to babble, and terrifying Anna, so I took a breath. "It is time for supper. Go downstairs and see to it. Perhaps your brother is just trying to be amusing. You know what an odd sense of humor he has."

"But, Ma —"

"Go. Now."

Anna obeyed, and I turned my attention to Johnny's trunk, but it was even less revealing than the table, containing nothing more than a few articles of clothing. Save for Mr. Weichmann's possessions, there was nothing else in the room to search. Defeated, I slowly made my way downstairs and nearly collided with Mr. Weichmann as he came in from work.

"Mrs. Surratt? Is something wrong?

"No — yes. Make the best of dinner that you can. Anna is getting it. Johnny's gone away."

Mr. Weichmann began to say something, but I pushed past him and into the back parlor that served as my bedroom. Only a set of folding doors separated it from the parlor, but the boarders, even those who shared the room with me, knew it was inviolate when those doors were folded shut. No one was to disturb me.

After I spent a while praying — and fighting back tears — I composed myself and entered the parlor. No one was there except Anna and Miss Dean, Nora being on a visit to friends in Baltimore. I told them Johnny had gone away for a while, probably to look for work, and I was upset because I'd had so little notice, and my companions nodded. Whether they, especially Anna, believed a word of what I said was another matter.

At about half past six, the door banged open, and someone ran upstairs. It could be no one's step but Johnny's, and the voices I heard next — his and Mr. Weichmann's, both agitated — confirmed this. I rose and was just about to enter the hall when another bang of the door revealed Mr.

Payne. He barely tipped his hat to me before hurrying upstairs to Johnny's room.

And then the bell rang. Mr. Booth, carrying a riding whip, stood outside. He looked almost disheveled, and for once he had barely a pleasantry for me. "Ah, Mrs. Surratt. I believe Mr. Surratt just came home. May I see him?" And without waiting for an answer, he too mounted the stairs.

I stood staring upward. Should I follow them? But just as my bedroom was my private preserve, the men's rooms were their own. Besides, if Mr. Booth kept to his usual habits after visiting Johnny, he would join us in the parlor and chat before setting off.

But a half hour later, I heard the footsteps of the three men coming down the stairs. They did not turn into the parlor but went directly down the hall and outside.

I called upstairs. "Mr. Weichmann!"

Mr. Weichmann responded immediately. Having waved Miss Dean out of the parlor and into my room, I asked, "What on earth is going on?"

He shook his head. "I wish I knew, Mrs. Surratt. I was reading when John came upstairs, waving a pistol. He told me his prospects were ruined and he needed me to find him a clerkship immediately. I told him he had thrown away a perfectly good job in the past and he needed to settle down. Then Mr. Payne came in and threw himself into a chair without a word to me. I saw a revolver on his hip when he pulled up his waistcoat. Next, Mr. Booth came in. He just paced about, and he was so agitated he did not even notice I was in the room with the others until I called myself to his attention. Finally, all three of them stormed up to the attic. They had no further conversation with me, but I noticed when they left just now that Mr. Payne had his carpetbag with him." Mr. Weichmann smiled sardonically. "I suppose we will never hear him preach now."

"No."

"There is something very strange going on here, Mrs. Surratt. I have tried to tell you."

"Yes, you have. I will heed what you say more carefully. Good night, Mr. Weichmann."

Mr. Weichmann drifted back upstairs.

Whether Johnny would come home that night I did not know, but if he did, I made sure by chaining the door that he would not evade me. Sure enough, after about an hour, I heard the key turn, then the sound of Johnny pushing at the door. "Ma? It's only me. Open up, please."

I walked to the door and unfastened the

chain. "Johnny, we must talk. Now. In the kitchen, please, where we can have privacy."

He followed me downstairs into the kitchen. "Ma, I'm beat, and I think I'm getting ill."

"I don't care how tired you are. I don't care if you are half-dead with consumption. You will talk to me tonight, and you will tell me what is going on. What is the meaning of this letter? Why did you say you were going away, and why are you here now? Why did you and Mr. Payne and Mr. Booth act so strange tonight? Who is Mr. Payne? Why did he leave tonight, without paying rent?"

"He's good for the rent, Ma."

"I don't care about the rent! I will have no more of this. You are living under my roof — and paying nothing for it, I might add. Even your sister helps! If you do not tell me what went on today, I will have you thrown out into the street. No. I will do better than that. I will denounce you as a spy, and you can rot in Old Capitol Prison."

Johnny's face did not change. Was he going to call my bluff? I would have the greatest of difficulty throwing him out of the house, much less having him thrown into prison, and he must have known this.

A moment passed, and he gave a sharp sigh. "You might as well know, I suppose.

It's all fallen apart anyway. We were going to kidnap the president."

I sank onto the table bench. This was my kind, cheerful Johnny, telling me, without so much as a blink of an eye, like a common criminal, that he planned to kidnap the head of the nation.

"Don't look at me so, Ma! We never intended to harm the man, just to hold him hostage. There would be no point at all in our plan if he were dead."

"What was the point?"

"To force an exchange of prisoners — at least, that was the plan at first. Now that things have become so desperate, to dictate better terms for the South. To destabilize the Union. All sorts of good could have come from having Old Abe in our hands."

"And all sorts of bad, such as you hanging."

"Well, we would have done our best to avoid that. If the government wouldn't come to terms, we were prepared to flee the country. Hence the note I gave you."

"I still don't understand this. What if you failed?"

"It was a chance worth taking. Ma, you haven't been to the South since the war started. It's a wretched sight. You should see Richmond. Women with faces pinched by hunger, children walking around in rags, starving animals. People have rioted over bread, just as in France before the Revolution."

I gazed around at our kitchen, freshly stocked from my last trip to the grocer. From the street, I heard some men laughing together, no doubt coming home from a night on the town. A town that was thriving while the South was in its death throes.

"There's so much misery there, and I wanted to do my part to end it. More than I can do by carrying letters back and forth."

"So this was your idea?"

"No. It was Booth's. I thought it crazy at first, and I told him so. But he convinced me that it could work. It could have — we had the men, the brains, and the equipment. The only thing we didn't have today was the guest of honor. Lincoln was supposed to be attending a play at the Soldiers' Home. We were going to catch him as he rode home. You know that he never has an armed guard if he can help it. Unfortunately, he changed his plans."

"Will you try again?"

"I don't know. Booth's original plan was to kidnap him at the theater — hence our visit to Ford's the other night, to get the lay of the land — but the rest of us thought it too risky. Anyway, I think the government has gotten wind of what we're up to." He glared at me. "And now my own mother is threatening to turn me in."

"You know I would not do that," I said wearily. "And besides . . ."

"Besides what, Ma?"

"I can see the point in this scheme. It is — not unreasonable."

"Exactly!" Johnny began to pace around the room. "Think of that failed raid by Dahlgren last year. Do you remember reading about the papers found on his body? Papers ordering the killing of Jefferson Davis and his entire cabinet. General Meade claimed that Dahlgren was a rash young fool who had come up with the scheme himself, but who believes that? Not me."

I thought about Urlic Dahlgren: young, personable, and handsome, even after he lost a leg in the war, and from an upstanding family in Washington. Mrs. Davis, Johnny told me once, knew him when he was a fair-haired little boy in knee pants. Yet he thought nothing of ordering his men to destroy Richmond and then kill President Davis and his cabinet, a plan that only his own death kept him from carrying out. For months, his old father had been claiming that his darling boy could not have come up with such a plan, that the papers found on him were a forgery by the South. But the rest of the world knew better, and so did I. "Nor I."

"Our plan is nothing like that. It's an honorable one. We seize the president, bring him to Virginia, and force the government to negotiate. What else can they do? No one's forgotten Johnson's performance at the inauguration. They'll have to come to terms." He snorts. "Unless Old Abe decides to drive us mad with his storytelling, in which case we may be begging the government to take him off our hands."

"Who else is involved?"

"Payne, of course. Not a Baptist preacher, by the way, but an ex-Confederate soldier. He's staying at some third-rate hotel tonight before heading to Baltimore tomorrow — thought it was best he get out of town. Port Tobacco — no one calls the poor man by his right name now. Some others who have never been here, and perhaps it's best you don't know who they are, in case someone should ever try to force you to tell."

"Mrs. Slater?"

Johnny grinned at me. "Sorry, Ma, no. She's a fine woman, but she can't ride or shoot or pilot a boat, and those are necessary attributes."

"Does Mr. Weichmann know?"

"Not as much as he would like to. I've kept him in the dark as much as I can, but he's so damn inquisitive. I think he halfway guesses what we're about and would like to be included, but he has the precise disability as Mrs. Slater. He can't ride or shoot — at least, not well enough for us — and he's not at all an attractive figure in crinoline. He's been helpful to us before this, though. Brought home some very useful statistics from his job at the War Department." My son shook his head. "I can't believe I'm telling you all of this, Ma. You're not angry?"

"I don't know what to think. You and the others are taking an enormous risk. But I cannot condemn you for your part in a scheme that could be the South's last hope." I fingered the rosary in my skirt pocket. "If you do pursue this plan further — and I do not give my approval, only my caution — you must be more careful. The boarders here are no fools. Neither is your sister."

Johnny grimaced. "Tell me about it. Miss Fitzpatrick already recognized Mr. Payne as Mr. Wood; he told me. Fortunately, she took it in stride, it appears."

"So that is why he looked familiar to me. Why did he change his name?"

"Neither Wood nor Payne is his real name.

He gave the government a false name when he was taken prisoner once, and the habit stuck. I suppose he felt more at home visiting us the second time as Mr. Payne, the preacher, than as Mr. Wood, the china store clerk. His father's a preacher, I think."

"Son, you must treat Mr. Weichmann more kindly. He is genuinely fond of you, and he is hurt and jealous, as well as suspicious. That is when a man can be his most dangerous."

"I'll sweeten him up." Johnny stretched. "I'm going to bed, Ma. I need to go to the country tomorrow to tie up some loose ends, but I'll be back by evening. Booth is acting tomorrow, and he's given me tickets. I'll take Weichmann."

Johnny kissed me on the forehead and went upstairs to his room. I wondered what he would say to Mr. Weichmann.

Anna was waiting for me in the parlor. "Did Johnny explain what was happening?"

"Yes. A quarrel the men got into with some strangers when they were out the other night. There was talk of a duel, but cooler heads prevailed. It is all mended now, it seems."

I was shocked and more than a little ashamed at how easily the lie came to my lips, but these were dangerous secrets, and I wanted my girl to know nothing of them.

"Oh." Anna yawned. "Men."

The next afternoon, Mr. Booth paid a call. This time, he looked his normal immaculate self, and the house was empty: Miss Dean and the Holohan girl were at school, Mrs. Holohan was visiting her mother, Anna was giving a lesson, and Mr. Holohan and Mr. Weichmann were at work. "My dear lady, please forgive my hasty behavior last night. I was very much agitated."

"Sir —"

"I know what you wish to say. Johnny was with me early this morning — unconscionably early, I must say, for I am a late riser — and told me that he had talked with you."

"Mr. Booth, you must not blame Johnny. He would not have told me, but I threatened to turn him in to the government."

"I do not blame you at all, madam. Indeed, I wish I could make a clean breast of it to my own mother. But she is completely out of sympathy with me on that score, and my dear sister will not allow me to make a confidante of her as to any matter connected with the South — not that I blame her, poor girl, for she is expecting, and married to a fool who does not care for her comfort and happiness in her delicate

202

condition as he should. But I do run on, don't I? If it had been anyone else's mother, I might have been vexed indeed, but I know I can trust you. Johnny speaks so highly of you."

"Does he, sir?"

"He does indeed. And I can speak highly of him. Of the men I have collected, he and Mr. Payne are the ones I value most: Johnny, because he is so committed to the cause, and Mr. Payne, because once one obtains his loyalty, he will never swerve. But we talked last night, and we think it best that we go our separate ways for now, lest we arouse suspicion. I am to act tonight, but after that, I will spend some time in New York. Mr. Payne will remain in Baltimore until he is needed in Washington, at which time Johnny will find a suitable place for him to stay. I would like to ask, though, if you would be willing to aid me in small ways — very small ways — from time to time. No more than what you have been doing all along by letting Johnny's friends come and go freely here and allowing those running the blockade to use your tavern. But if you say no, I will understand."

"I do not wish to bring any harm upon anybody."

"Yet this war of Mr. Lincoln's has harmed

many! It did not have to come to this. But I will tell you, our plan is not to harm the man. One cannot negotiate over a corpse."

"But what if something goes wrong?"

"It shouldn't. I have chosen well. Mr. Payne served with Mosby's Rangers. There is very little he can't deal with. Two of our number, Maryland boys you do not know, have seen combat as well. Your son has a cool head, and Mr. Atzerodt — well, Mr. Atzerodt has his faults, but put him in a boat crossing the Potomac late at night, and he has no equal." He rose. "I must be going. I would not force a sudden decision upon you for the world. You can let me know of your decision through Johnny."

I considered. Mr. Booth had a point: What would I be doing for him that I had not already been doing? Although it was my husband who had made it known that the tavern would welcome those who ran the blockade, it was I who had greeted the travelers, I more often than not who had taken their suspicious packages and stowed them, I who had separated the clandestine mail from the rest and given it to Johnny or one of his fellow couriers. "I need no more time, sir. I will help. With one son fighting for the Confederacy and another carrying messages for it, what else can I do?"

Mr. Booth smiled and pecked me on the cheek. "God bless you, my dear lady. If there were twenty like you in this city! But trust me, I shall not ask you to do the work of twenty. Only a small matter now and then, such as any friend might do for a friend."

Unlike yesterday's dismal dinner, everyone, save for the still absent Nora, was at the table today, and even she was represented by Mr. Rochester. Normally, I would have shooed the cat out of the kitchen, but in my present good humor, I slipped a couple of scraps to him when Anna, who tolerated him only because he was Nora's, was not looking. "What play are you gentlemen seeing tonight?"

"*The Apostate,* about the Duke of Alva. A very unpleasant character. One hopes it doesn't cost Mr. Booth the love of the ladies of Washington." Johnny took a slice of ham. "Sometimes I think of taking to the stage myself, you know. Mr. Booth says I wouldn't be half bad at it."

"Meaning you wouldn't be half good," Anna said.

"All a matter of how you look at it, m'dear."

They bickered cheerfully until it was time

for Johnny and Mr. Weichmann to leave for the play. The entire male population of my boardinghouse would be represented at Ford's tonight, because Mr. Holohan had been given a ticket too. I waited up for the men, partly because it was my habit, partly because I was not quite able to shake off a feeling that every time I saw Johnny would be the last. But he was with Mr. Holohan and Mr. Weichmann as the three of them returned home, sober but reeking of cigars. Johnny and Mr. Holohan bade me good night and headed upstairs, but Mr. Weichmann sat down.

"How was the play?" I asked him.

"It was very well acted. We went for oysters afterward at Kloman's." Mr. Weichmann rubbed his mustache. "It was too well acted, really. When Booth as Pescara dragged in a lady to torture her on the rack, he was terrifying. I was so unnerved, I doubt I will sleep tonight."

"It is only a play," I reassured him gently. "Nothing to lose sleep over at all."

16
NORA
MARCH 1865

I had a wonderful time in Baltimore, where I stayed with Miss Camilla James, an old friend from school. I had taken several copies of my photograph to exchange with her and my other friends, and when I did so, I naturally had to show Mr. Booth's photograph as well, and to mention ever so casually that I was personally acquainted with him. This impressed my friends and acquaintances mightily, except for one young lady who had the nerve to doubt me. If I had been younger, I would have boxed her ears, but instead I settled for smugly pulling out my album, which Mr. Booth had once graciously autographed.

On the subject of Private Flanagan, however, I said nothing. If our correspondence came to nothing, I would feel mighty foolish had I mentioned it to Camilla, Anna, and my other friends. Besides, it was rather nice to have my own little secret.

I also visited my sister, who was known as Sister Michael but whom I still called Hannah from the days when she had mothered me after Mama and her baby died. Father often said Hannah had wanted to be a nun since she was three or four, and she had certainly wanted to enter the church as long as I had known her, but I always thought it was a sad waste, as she had the face of an angel and would have had any number of suitors had she not taken the veil.

I showed her Mr. Booth's picture, and she told me in her best nun's manner that I should not be led astray by the vanities of the world. Then she looked at it again and asked, "Is he this handsome in person?"

"Oh, even more so," I said.

Anna and I had nothing but our photographs of Mr. Booth to look at when I returned home, for Mr. Booth was in New York, Anna told me as I unpacked.

"Did anything interesting happen while I was gone? Did Mr. Weichmann propose?"

Anna swatted me with a fan she picked up just for that purpose. "No. Johnny took some fancy into his head that he had to leave town indefinitely, and scared poor Ma, but it's fine now. He's been practically underfoot for the last few days, in fact. Mr.

Payne is gone, in case you were hoping that he would escort you to the theater again."

"No, thank you. Father would never forgive me if I brought a Baptist home."

My unpacking completed, we adjourned to the parlor, where we were soon joined by Mrs. Surratt. "Mr. Weichmann is past his time today," she said, looking at the mantel clock.

"I hope you won't make the rest of us wait for that man, Ma."

"It is so unlike him to be late. I hope he has not taken ill."

Anna was about to speak again, no doubt in the same vein, when we heard the front door open and Mr. Weichmann, looking his most clerkly self in his high hat, hurried into the parlor. He carried a small parcel in one hand. "I beg your pardon, Mrs. Surratt, for my being late, but I hope you will excuse me. I saw this in a shop window, and I instantly thought of Miss Surratt."

"You have a gift for me, Mr. Weichmann?"

"More for the house as a whole, but I had you in mind."

"Well then, I shall open it." Anna gingerly unwrapped the gift, covered in brown paper, revealing a framed picture. "Why, it's *Morning, Noon, and Night!*"

"I heard you mention it the other day,"

Mr. Weichmann said smugly.

Anna held the picture up as Mrs. Surratt leaned in closer to examine it. It was quite a popular one in those days, and showed a white-haired old gentleman, a pretty young lady who must have been his daughter, and her two children, along with the family dog. All looked rather solemn, except for the little girl, occupied happily with the dog.

Or perhaps the pretty young lady was the old man's wife? If so, I couldn't imagine why he looked so solemn. In any case, she was wearing a beautiful dress, light-colored with flounces. Perhaps if I begged Father hard enough, he would let me have a similar one made for the summer, as it looked deliciously light and airy.

Mr. Weichmann cleared his throat. "Do you like it, Miss Surratt? I distinctly remember you saying you wanted one for your mantel."

I too remembered her saying this, but for a moment I thought she was going to deny it. But Anna said mildly, "Yes, I did indeed. Thank you, Mr. Weichmann. It was very considerate of you."

Mr. Weichmann beamed and kept on beaming all during supper.

The next day, I went to the post office to

call for my mail. There was a letter from a friend of mine, a letter from my brother in Boston — and a letter from New York, thicker than the last one I had received. I casually separated it from the rest and frowned. I knew no one else in New York besides Private Flanagan, yet the envelope was not addressed in his inimitable handwriting.

There were two letters inside. One was from Private Flanagan and said he hadn't been feeling so well but would no doubt be on his feet "SOON!" The second, in the same handwriting as the envelope, was from a priest. Private Flanagan had taken ill about a week or so before, he wrote, and had been too weak from his recent hospitalization to fight off the illness. He had spoken of me fondly to the very end and had asked that I be informed of his death and given a remembrance of him. Wrapped inside a threadbare handkerchief with the initials *H. F.* was a lock of hair, along with the picture I had given to him.

I have no idea how I made it home from the post office alive that day. I walked through crossings without bothering to look around me. Someone yanked a horse to a stop just inches from me, with curses that would have made the Union and Confederate armies combined blush; I stared straight ahead and walked on. Someone greeted me; I said not a word in return. By the time I reached the boardinghouse, my tears were blinding me.

In my eagerness to get to the post office, I had forgotten my house key. I banged on the door, then rang the bell. "Let me in! Let me in, damn it!"

"What on earth is the meaning of this?" Mrs. Surratt opened the door. "Has the devil gotten into you, Nora?"

"He's dead."

"Who?" Getting no intelligible reply, she said, "Come into the bedroom, child, and tell me about this."

She hustled me into the bedroom and forced me into a chair — her favorite chair, in which not even Anna was allowed to sit. Leaving me weeping there, she returned a little while later with a cup of tea. "Drink this. May I see the letter?"

I nodded and handed over the packet I had received.

"Was this your sweetheart, Nora?"

"No." I took a shuddering breath. "He was a young man I met while reading here. We were friends."

"Your father knew you were writing to him? And that you sent him your picture?"

"No, ma'am."

"But you weren't sweethearts?"

"What does it matter now?" I gulped the tea. "We weren't. But we might have been in time."

"Were you in love with him?"

"I don't know." I brushed my hand across my eyes. "I liked him very much. He was kind and amusing. He was poor and not well educated, but he wanted to better himself. I think I could have been happy with him." My tears began to flow anew. "And now I shall never know."

Mrs. Surratt let me have my cry, then poured me some more tea. "Drink this up, and we will go to church and pray for your young man."

I obeyed, and we walked toward St. Patrick's. It was the closest Catholic church to us, although usually Mrs. Surratt favored St. Aloysius. I had been christened at St. Patrick's, though, and it seemed fitting I say my prayers for Private Flanagan there.

Mrs. Surratt served me supper in her room that night, though I barely touched it. When it came time to go to bed, she sent Anna and Miss Dean up to the attic to sleep. "You don't have to do that," I protested. The attic bed was by no means a comfortable one.

"I want to, child. You need a mother to-night."

And I did. I would fall into a sleep and wake up crying, and Mrs. Surratt would hold me tight and stroke my hair until I fell back asleep. When I woke up around midnight, desperately wanting to talk, she made me some tea and sat patiently beside me in her nightgown as I told her about our romance, if it could be called that. She never upbraided me for writing to Private Flanagan, and when I begged her not to tell Father, she promised she never would.

"You must think me very silly, grieving so over a young man I barely knew, when so many women have lost so much more — fathers, husbands, children."

"No, I don't think you silly at all. This war has caused so much misery to everyone. Your poor Private Flanagan is just one more casualty of it."

I was young enough, despite all my sorrow, to cherish those words "*your* Private Flanagan." I settled down to sleep again, curling close to Mrs. Surratt. This time, I slept soundly through the night.

17
MARY
MARCH 1865

There was sorrow in the house: a young man to whom Nora had been writing (and to whom she seemed to have all but engaged herself, without a word to her father) died, leaving the poor child bereft. I should have been keeping a closer eye on her, as her father was trusting me to fill the role of a mother to her, but in the face of her tears, I did not have the heart to scold her for her impropriety, especially since the man's death had put an end to this little romance.

Besides, I had my own secrets.

The day before, while Nora was at the post office fetching her mail, a telegram for Mr. Weichmann — with his name misspelled — arrived from New York. As Mrs. Holohan had to venture out anyway, she offered to take it to Mr. Weichmann at his office. In the wake of Nora's dreadful news, it slipped my mind altogether, but the next morning at breakfast, as Nora picked at her food, I asked Mr. Weichmann. "I believe you received a telegram yesterday. I hope it did not contain bad news."

"No, Mrs. Surratt. It was from Mr. Booth. I actually have no idea why he sent it to me. It merely asked me to tell John to telegraph a number and street at once. It seems he could have sent it directly to John."

I kept my face still, for I knew exactly what Mr. Booth was referring to: Mr. Payne's new lodgings. After some correspondence between Mr. Booth and Johnny — sent, Johnny informed me, to Johnny under an assumed name — the men had deemed it safe that Mr. Payne, known in their correspondence as their invalid friend, return to Washington and board quietly here until needed. Johnny decided the Herndon House, a large boardinghouse on F Street where people came and went constantly, would be the ideal residence for him. "It does seem rather odd," I said lightly, "but theater people are rather impractical, I imagine."

Mr. Weichmann nodded, and Nora sighed as if the weight of the world rested upon her pretty shoulders.

Nora bought a lovely locket in which to keep a bit of her young man's hair — how she was to explain that to her father if he saw it, I did not ask — and was sitting in the parlor braiding the light brown strands together when Johnny came in. "A word, Ma."

I followed Johnny to the bedroom. "Booth and Mrs. Slater will arrive on the early train tomorrow morning. I'll be taking her to Surrattsville, and Howell will get her to Richmond. Would you care to come with us?" He grinned impudently.

"As a matter of fact, I would." I could not help but smile at Johnny's expression. "Your cousin Olivia is coming to stay for a few weeks, and your uncle doesn't want her to travel alone in the stage. We can bring her back to Washington with us."

"Very well," Johnny grumbled, as I thought with satisfaction of Mrs. Slater making the difficult journey to Richmond in the company of Mr. Howell, listening to his hacking cough and trying to drag an affirmative answer to anything from him. It would be a long trip indeed.

Immediately behind the house, as those of us in the back rooms were well aware, there was a stable kept by Brooke Stabler — aptly named, as Johnny liked to point out. Having secured a buggy and horses from there,

217

Johnny left early the next morning for the train station and returned in the buggy with Mrs. Slater dozing on his shoulder. "I was on the train all night," she explained plaintively after Johnny nudged her awake. "I scarcely slept a wink. So you are coming with us, Mrs. Surratt?"

"Yes."

"Delightful!"

This chit was maddening.

Mrs. Slater graciously moved to the back of the carriage so I could ride up front with Johnny, but all this did was encourage Johnny, who, of course, was driving, to keep turning around to speak to her. I kept telling him to watch in front of him, and he obeyed for ten minutes until he remembered something else amusing he wanted to tell Mrs. Slater. He did this so often I almost wished he would run off the road, just so I could have the pleasure of telling him I was right.

Mrs. Slater's nap against my son's shoulder seemed to have refreshed her remarkably. When Johnny was not risking life and limb to gaze into her eyes (for she had lifted that ever-present veil of hers), this hussy was chattering on: about her train ride with Mr. Booth; about the shops she had been to in New York; about her mama, the Frenchwoman; and about the beauties of New Bern, North Carolina (such as they were). The only subject she did not trip her tongue about was that of her husband, except when I asked about him. The little harlot did not even have the decency to be offended: she simply hoped he was safe. Then Johnny, as if to spare her feelings, asked her to speak in French — a language he had learned in school but claimed to speak only passably. How much he could understand of what Mrs. Slater rattled off I did not know, but he looked enthralled, and Mrs. Slater certainly did speak the language prettily.

She had thoroughly ensnared my Johnny.

Not a moment too soon, we arrived at Surrattsville and my tavern. Was it my imagination, or was it looking a little seedy? Before I could give this much thought, Mr. Lloyd lurched out to greet us. It was mid-morning, and if he was not completely in his cups, he was certainly well on his way there. "He's been arrested!"

"Who?" Johnny asked.

"Last night! He had just sat down to play a game of cards when they swooped in and seized him. Carried him off in chains!"

"But who, man?"

"He made a heap amount of fuss about it too."

"He being?"

"Do you mean Mr. Howell?" I asked.

"That's what I said." Mr. Lloyd gave us a look of offended dignity.

"Oh," said Johnny. "Damn." He nodded at me. "Thank you for clearing that up, Ma."

"And I am ruined," Mr. Lloyd said.

"How? You're here, aren't you? Did they arrest anyone else?"

"No."

"Did the card game go on?"

"Yes." Mr. Lloyd strained to remember. "I think I won, actually."

"Well then!" Johnny sighed and stroked his goatee. "But it is a pity about poor Howell. And even more of a pity for the person who tries to get him to talk."

Mrs. Slater had been listening to this from her perch in the carriage. Now she tugged at Johnny's arm. "Mr. Surratt, how am I to travel now?"

"Don't worry, sweetheart. I'll get you across the river, and if there's no one I can trust you with, I'll take you to Richmond myself. To Jeff Davis himself, if you please. Haven't I brought you there safely before?"

"Yes, and beautifully."

"Well then!"

"I wish you would leave," Mr. Lloyd said. "What if they come back?"

"What if they do? They will see your landlady and her son, in company with a fair young lady. Hardly something to send shivers up the federal spine. But I suppose you have a point. Once the horses are rested — they're a handsome pair, aren't they? — I'll take Mrs. Slater on her way, and Ma can fetch my cousin and take the stage back. Is that satisfactory to everyone?"

I nodded, though I could not say I was happy about leaving my son and this hussy together, especially after this "sweetheart" slipped out. But I supposed the Confederacy needed whatever she was carrying.

Mr. Lloyd, however, was still frowning. "Can't you take those damn guns of yours too, Surratt?"

"No," Johnny said crisply. "They must stay here for now."

"What guns was he talking of, Johnny?" I hissed when we were alone, Mr. Lloyd having found agreeable company in the bar and Mrs. Slater having gone to freshen herself for the journey.

"Some things I stowed here after our plan fell through. They're safest here until they're needed. Which reminds me, can you tell Booth that I'll likely be delayed in getting back to Washington?"

I nodded. After bidding good-bye to Johnny and the others, I got one of Mr. Lloyd's men to drive me to my brother's house, where Olivia was rifling through her trunk. "Where is my new brooch? Ma! Help me find my brooch!"

"You're not tying up one of your good rooms, having her to visit, are you?" my brother asked when his daughter was out of earshot.

I shook my head. "Only one of the attic rooms. And don't you worry! Things aren't so bad that I can't have my niece to stay a while."

"But they are bad? Here." Zadock pulled out his wallet. "Let me pay for her."

"I won't have it."

We quarreled over this in a pleasant enough manner and finally reached a compromise: my brother would pay for Olivia's laundry and supply her with ample pocket money. This settled, we drove back to the tavern. "I am so excited," Olivia said as we sat in the parlor awaiting the stage to Washington. "Will I get to meet Mr. Booth?"

"I see no reason why not. He stops by frequently."

"And what in the world will I say to him?"

"Anything. He is a very friendly, approachable man. He makes anyone who speaks with him feel at ease."

Olivia sighed rapturously. "I can hardly wait to meet him. And nearly a whole month to spend in Washington! It will be glorious."

18
NORA

MARCH 1865

The Saturday after I heard of Private Flanagan's death, Mrs. Surratt went to the country with her son. I took advantage of her absence to lie in bed — even missing an opportunity to catch a glimpse of the mysterious Mrs. Slater, whom Mr. Surratt was escorting to the tavern in Surrattsville. Anna was out doing various errands in preparation for a visit from her cousin, and Miss Dean was visiting a friend from school, so I had the room to myself in which to indulge my grief. Only in midafternoon, with the prospect of everyone coming back, did I rouse myself and dress.

As I darned my stockings, a dreary task for my dreary mood, the doorbell gave its usual shattering ring, and I answered it to find Mr. Booth there. "Mrs. Surratt and her son are not home," I said dully. "They went to Maryland."

"Yes, Mr. Surratt told me his mother was

224

accompanying him, but I stopped by on the off chance that she might have changed her mind, or come back early. A fool's errand!"

I nodded.

"Miss Fitzpatrick, you do not seem yourself this afternoon. Are you not well?"

"I am well. It is nothing."

"Nothing? Miss Fitzpatrick, I thought we were friends. Won't you tell me what has upset you?" Mr. Booth's eyes fell to my chest. "Is that a mourning locket, dear girl?"

"Yes."

Mr. Booth pushed his way into the hallway and gently led me to the parlor, sitting beside me on the sofa. "Tell me about it, Miss Fitzpatrick."

And so I did. Mr. Booth nodded patiently as I told him the sad little story — the same type of story so many other women had been telling for the past four years.

"This damnable war," he said when I had finished. "It has cost so many so much, and for what? For that tyrant to bring the South to heel?"

I roused myself to look at him. "You mean the president, sir?"

"Yes, I do — but never mind that for now. You are grieving, and I won't subject you to one of my rants. May I see your locket?"

I passed it to him, and he gently opened

it. Inside was a fragment of Private Flanagan's letter to me and his hair, which I had carefully braided. "Beautiful," he said. "He was your first love, wasn't he? That makes it even sadder."

"Yes, he was." I sniffled and found myself confessing, "And I think he will be my last."

"No, Miss Fitzpatrick. You are very young and will love again. Your young man — I don't know him, but he must have been a fine young fellow — won't expect you to give up on your own happiness."

"It isn't that." I took a deep breath. "It is that no one had ever paid me any attention before — any man, I mean — and now no one ever will. I will die an old maid."

"What makes you think that?"

"Well, look at me!" I tipped my face up and realized it was stained with tears. "I mean, not now. I look worse than I usually do."

"You've a sweet face, Miss Fitzpatrick. It's the first thing I thought when I saw you. You look like my sister Rosalie."

"Is she the pretty one?"

"She's the best person in our entire family."

"You're being evasive, sir." I managed a smile. "But I won't press the point."

Mr. Booth tipped up my chin.

"You're not Helen of Troy," he said very gently. "But you're by no means unattractive. You've bright eyes, pretty hair, a lovely fig— well, it would be improper to list your charms in more detail, but trust me, they are there. What your Private Flanagan, God rest his soul, saw, others will see too. Pluck your eyebrows a little more, and don't duck your head every time a man looks your way. It won't result in your fall from virtue, I promise. Now, I must be going. I am very sorry to hear about this young man. But you're no old maid, Miss Fitzpatrick."

"Mr. Surratt said I would be," I muttered.

"Really?"

"Yes. In a letter I shouldn't have seen. But he still said it."

"Then he is a cad and a fool. Look at me, Miss Fitzpatrick."

I looked him square in the eyes, and he leaned over and kissed me full on the lips.

There are two things a girl can do when one of the most handsome men in the entire country suddenly gets a notion to kiss her. She can squeal like a namby-pamby miss and pull away, or she can kiss back for all she is worth. I kissed back, and Mr. Booth, thus encouraged, kept our kiss going for longer than was strictly necessary. Things I had read about only in the very worst dime novels began to stir in me, and I knew if Mr. Booth had chosen to, he could have ruined me then and there on Mrs. Surratt's sofa, and I would not have let out a squawk of protest.

He didn't, of course. He rose as I sat stunned at what had just happened, and gave me his very best smile.

"You don't kiss like an old maid, Miss Fitzpatrick. Tell Johnny if he ever starts with that idiot talk that he is a prize ass."

Mr. Booth had not been gone ten minutes when Anna, laden with packages, returned home. "I wish you had come along, Nora, to help me. Mr. Booth happened across me in time to help me carry them up the stairs, at least. He said he was just here."

"Yes, he was. He was looking for your mother."

"So I guessed. How long did he stay?"

"Just a few minutes. We talked."

"What on earth did he say? You look as if you've been struck by lightning."

"He kissed me."

Anna sank down on the sofa beside me. "Kissed?"

"It wasn't that sort of kiss. I was telling him about Private Flanagan and grouching that I would be an old maid — and he just kissed me."

"Kissed you? You?"

"Yes."

Anna slapped me hard in the face.

"What on earth was that for?"

"I'll tell you what that's for. You know I like him! You know I have hopes for him. And the minute my back is turned, you start flirting with him!"

"I did no such thing! He was comforting me; that was all. I told him I would die an old maid, and he told me I was wrong. But it meant nothing to him, I am sure of it. He is not in love with you or with me or with anyone else in this house. He is in love with Miss Hale, and never misses an opportunity to say so. It's time you just realized that."

"How can I realize that when you're carrying on like some Irish slattern with him? I should have you thrown out of this house. I've a mind to do it. You've been writing to that Yankee and kissing Mr. Booth. Who knows what other antics you've been up to?"

"Make up anything you please. Your mother won't believe you. She likes me, and she's kind to me."

The door opened, and Mrs. Surratt, accompanied by a pretty blond girl a little younger than myself, came into the parlor.

"Girls, what was the commotion here?" Neither of us answered, and Mrs. Surratt ran a weary hand across her face. "Miss Fitzpatrick, this is my brother's daughter, Miss Olivia Jenkins. She will be staying with us through Easter. Olivia, this is Miss Nora Fitzpatrick. She is a favorite of mine, I own."

Miss Jenkins and I exchanged politenesses while Anna fumed and Mrs. Surratt removed her bonnet. "Have there been any visitors today?"

"Just Mr. Booth, ma'am. He wanted to see you."

"And I need to see him."

"Miss Fitzpatrick will be glad to go to his hotel and fetch him, Ma."

Mrs. Surratt frowned. "Miss Fitzpatrick visit a young man at his hotel? What are you thinking, Anna? That won't do at all. In any case, it can wait until tomorrow, as I am tired from the ride. I will ask Mr. Weichmann to call upon him." She lowered herself to the sofa on which Mr. Booth had kissed me.

"I'll see to dinner, Mrs. Surratt, in a bit."

"Thank you very much, Nora. That is very kind of you."

Sensing the family might want to visit together — and not being in a notion to be in the same room with Anna — I slipped out of the parlor and into the room Anna and I shared with Mrs. Surratt. I had a book I had bought in Baltimore, and I had been planning to read it this afternoon in an effort to fix my mind on something besides Private Flanagan, but instead I sat at the dressing table and took up a pair of tweezers. Slowly, painfully, I began to pluck my eyebrows.

Mr. Booth was right. I did look better when I was through.

19
MARY
MARCH 1865

I came home from Surrattsville to tension at the boardinghouse. Anna and Nora seemed put out at each other about something — I did not know what, and did not ask, as Olivia and Anna were soon chattering together, and Nora had enough sorrow weighing her down at the moment.

Mr. Weichmann, meanwhile, was more inquisitive than ever. "I saw you depart with Mr. Surratt and Mrs. Slater this morning, Mrs. Surratt. Is she going to see her mother in New York again?"

"I believe she is going to try to get word of her husband in Richmond," I said coolly. "And Johnny is going to inquire about a clerkship after he sees her safely to her lodgings." I bit my lip, wondering what on earth had possessed me to mention that Johnny was going to Richmond, but Mr. Weichmann did not seem at all surprised.

"I see" was all he said.

"May I ask a favor of you, Mr. Weich-mann? Before church tomorrow, or after, if you please, would you stop by the National and tell Mr. Booth I wish to see him?"

"Yes, of course."

For lunch, I made certain Mr. Weich-mann's favorite variety of pie was on the table.

I had duly warned Olivia of the probability that Mr. Booth would be our visitor on Sunday afternoon, so when the doorbell rang a few hours later, it was all she could do to restrain herself from rushing to answer it. I did instead, and found not only Mr. Booth, but Port Tobacco — the man, not the town — at the door. Although he was no match for his companion, he appeared to have shaved more recently than usual, and he was clad in a natty suit of salt and pepper.

Before our visitors entered the parlor, I seized the chance for a few words with Mr. Booth. "Johnny may have to go to Rich-mond. Mrs. Slater's expected escort was ar-rested."

Mr. Booth grimaced. "Pity. It would bet-ter to have him here, should the opportunity to carry out our plan present itself. But we must all serve the cause in our own way.

233

Which reminds me, my dear lady, would you be so kind as to bring a note to Mr. Payne from me from time to time? He's known to people in Baltimore as being a Southern man, and even here in Washington I think it best that he not wander about during the day."

"Of course."

We adjourned to the parlor, where Olivia must have been pinching her cheeks madly, for there was a bright color on both of them, soon augmented by a glow of pleasure as Mr. Booth exerted his charms. Soon he had us all — Nora included — laughing and chattering. Port Tobacco too shone in Mr. Booth's company, for he told us some rather amusing stories, even eliciting a grudging chuckle from Anna.

A few days after this, Mr. Booth stopped by my house with a note for Mr. Payne. If I could deliver it to him soon, he said, it would be most welcome, as he was leaving town for New York the next day. "Just stop casually, my dear lady, when you are doing something you ordinarily would be doing, and give him the note."

My ordinary trips in Washington were to church and to the grocer, so I determined to bring the letter to Mr. Payne after church. For once I regretted that my lodgers were such respectable, churchgoing folk, for both Nora and Mr. Weichmann decided to accompany me to Mass, along with my daughter and Olivia, whose presence I had naturally taken for granted. So after church, I had no choice but to stop at the Herndon House with all four of them in tow. "I need to stop in here," I said as we reached the establishment, which called itself a boardinghouse but was to my own modest place as a lion was to a house cat. "I will be but a moment."

Nora, preoccupied with her grief, Olivia, not knowing anything of my usual comings and goings, and Anna, not inclined to question me, merely nodded, but Mr. Weichmann put on his most inquisitive face. "It's a lovely evening," I said before he could open his mouth. "Stroll around the block, and I'll be right back."

The landlady directed me to room number six on the third floor. I knocked and found a glum-looking Mr. Payne watching the streetcars on F Street. He looked so bored in this room, that after handing him the note, I said, "You are welcome to stop by the house some evening, sir, if you think it safe."

"I'd best check with Mr. Booth, ma'am. He's the boss."

20
NORA

After Anna and I had our spat about Mr. Booth, our relationship was decidedly awkward. We were polite to each other, for Mrs. Surratt's sake — and for our own sakes, as this was far too small a house for it to be convenient to be at odds. Fortunately, Miss Jenkins's presence made it unnecessary for Anna and me to have to converse much.

It was rather a lonely time for me, though. Mrs. Surratt seemed preoccupied, as she always was when her son left on one of his trips, and Mr. Weichmann was more aloof than he had been previously. I supposed he had finally decided on the priesthood for sure and thought it unseemly to josh with young ladies. So as I was left to my own devices most of the time, I did my best to stop dwelling on Private Flanagan and to stay busy. I had much to do to help get ready for the church fair to be held in mid-

April, and after having shirked my duties at the hospital for a few days, I went back with my books and my basket in hand. It was not right that the men should lose whatever little diversion I offered them simply because of my own sorrows.

So it came to be that on April 3, 1865, I was sitting by a soldier's bed, reading to him from *Les Misérables* (a great favorite among the men), when one of the doctors, a most dignified and reserved man, ran into the ward, threw his hat into the air, and bellowed, "Richmond has fallen!"

There would be no more reading that day.

Some men cheered, and some men cried. Some began to pray, and others just sat in silence, not yet able to grasp the fact that the war at last was nearly at an end. I had been at school when it had started, and I could still remember the nuns gathering us together and praying for a quick end to it. Now, four Aprils later, their prayers were at last being answered.

I slipped out of the hospital and into a city that was going wild. Men were embracing each other in the street; men in uniform were being hoisted up and carried by cheering crowds. Clerks were abandoning their offices; shops were shutting. Who could sit at a desk or stand behind a counter on a day like this? The only people who seemed to be working were the newsboys, and all they had to do was stand still and pocket the money as the extras they held were snatched from their hands. Even if they had tried to shout, they wouldn't have been heard through the salutes of guns, the ringing of church bells, and the bands that appeared as if out of nowhere to strike up "Yankee Doodle." Without quite knowing how, I found myself marching in perfect time.

Throngs of men and women were streaming into churches, while others were streaming into taverns, which already were beginning to overflow into the street. As I walked past one, a man grabbed me by the hand and waltzed me about for a round or two before releasing me and turning his sights upon another lady.

I could not go home and sit with my embroidery on such a grand day. Instead, I joined the stream of people heading in the direction of the War Department, where an owlish-looking man — Edwin Stanton, the secretary of war — was attempting to speak to the crowd. I say attempting, because between his pauses, when he became choked up with emotion, and the applause every time he took half a breath, he could scarcely say five words at a time. It was a moving speech, giving thanks for our great victory and advising humility and graciousness in our triumph, but the truth was, on this afternoon, the secretary — the most important man in town today, as the president had gone to Virginia to follow the progress of the war — could have been reading from the city directory and still received the same rapturous applause.

In a stronger voice, Stanton read the telegram announcing Richmond had been taken — and was in flames. "Let her burn!" someone yelled happily, and others took up the cry until Stanton waved forward a gangly boy of fifteen or so. "Willie Kettles, the lad who took the telegram!" he called, and the crowd started yelling, "Speech! Speech!"

Willie Kettles blushed and bowed and was about to scurry away when a pretty young woman rushed up and kissed him.

A tall, thin man — William Seward, the secretary of state — came into view and, recognized by the crowd, was promptly dragged over to stand by Mr. Stanton. "All I can tell you is that I have long been in favor of a change in the secretary of war," he said, shaking his finger at Stanton. "Why, I started to go to the front the other day, and when I got to City Point, they told me it was at Hatcher's Run, and when I got there, I was told it was not there but somewhere else, and when I get back, I am told by the secretary that it is at Petersburg, and now I am told that it is at Richmond, and west of that. Now I leave you to judge what I ought to think of such a secretary of war as this!"

The crowd laughed, and Stanton gave Seward a mock punch.

I resumed my wandering in a city that was increasingly turning red, white, and blue as businesses and householders rushed to drape their buildings in bunting. Even the slum of Murder Bay — which I could glimpse from Pennsylvania Avenue but of course would never dare to venture into — was awash with the colors of the flag. I was watching one of the impromptu parades that formed when a dignified figure came into view. "Father!" I ran and tugged on his arm. "Is this not the most wonderful day?"

My father turned and embraced me. "The end is in sight at last, and it has been a long time coming," he said when he released me. He wiped what looked suspiciously like a tear from his eye. "Too, too long! But, child, you should get off these streets. Soon they will be full of drunkards."

240

"Oh, I've met one already. He danced with me."

My father shook his head and gave me his arm. Our progress to H Street was a slow one, for in his own way, he was as caught up in the joy of that afternoon as I was, but at last he landed me safely at Mrs. Surratt's, having promised to take me to dinner the next day when things were calmer.

As he left, Susan, Mrs. Surratt's new servant girl, poked her head out the kitchen door. "I thought that might be the man come back again who was looking for Mr. Surratt," she explained.

"Man?"

"Yes, miss. A man came by and asked for Mr. Surratt."

"Mr. Booth?"

"No, miss. Not him at all. He didn't leave a name. Just hurried off."

Probably one of Mr. Surratt's blockade-running acquaintances, I surmised. Perhaps we were in for another strange visitor. "Well, be sure and tell Mrs. Surratt."

"Oh, I will, miss."

I walked into the parlor, where Anna and Olivia sat knitting as if this were an ordinary day. "Did you hear? Richmond has fallen."

"Yes, well, you needn't be so smug about it. What if Johnny is there? So please keep your crowing to yourself."

"I wasn't crowing, and I hope Mr. Surratt is safe." I grimaced, for I had indeed forgotten that Mr. Weichmann had mentioned Mr. Surratt's escorting Mrs. Slater there. I crossed myself. "God protect him."

The door banged, and I heard Mr. Weichmann's step, followed by his appearance in the parlor. "I thought I would never get through the crowds. You have heard the news?"

"Yes, we have. And if I could get hold of those blue pants of yours, Mr. Weichmann, I would burn them." Anna rose and threw her knitting aside. "Let us go upstairs, Olivia. The atmosphere is too oppressive."

Miss Jenkins shot the offending Mr. Weichmann and me a sympathetic look before following her cousin to the stairs.

After supper, we had settled into our accustomed places in the parlor and I was threading Mrs. Surratt's needle for her when a weary voice called, "It's John, Ma," and Mr. Surratt walked slowly into the room, looking tired and worn. "Is it true? Has Richmond fallen?"

"Yes," Mrs. Surratt said.

"I can't believe it! I saw Judah Benjamin himself while I was there, and he told me it would not be evacuated."

"The secretary of state?" Anna asked. "You saw him in person? Really? What did he look like?"

"What sort of man is he?" I asked.

"What on earth do I care what he looked like or what sort of man he is? I'm not proposing to him."

"Son —"

"Yes, Ma. I'm sorry, ladies. I've a pounding headache, and I'm upset by Richmond falling —"

"As we all are." Anna glanced at me. "Except for Nora, who can't stop chortling."

"I am not —"

"Nora, be a dear and tell the girl to warm up some supper for Johnny. Johnny, come here." He obeyed, and Mrs. Surratt embraced him. "Thank the Lord you are safe. That is all that matters to me at the moment."

I went downstairs and gave the orders. Having set a place for Mr. Surratt and brought some bread and ham while Susan made a pot of tea, I was getting ready to go back upstairs when Mrs. Surratt and her son came down. Mr. Surratt gave me a faint smile. "I'm sorry I was such a bear up there. It's such a grand city, and they say it was put to the torch. Parts of it, anyway."

"I was truly sorry to hear that, whatever your sister thinks. I do not rejoice in anyone's suffering."

"I know you don't."

I went upstairs and was reading in the parlor, Mr. Rochester purring in my lap, when Mrs. Surratt and her son went into her bedroom. Presently, Mrs. Surratt emerged. "Nora, dear, do you have some cologne I can use for Johnny? His head is still pounding."

I nodded and went into the bedroom, where Mr. Surratt was sprawled out on a sofa, looking rather Byronic. My cologne, straight from Paris, had been a Christmas gift from my father. I wore it on special occasions, such as to the theater — and, I confess, on my last few hospital visits to poor Private Flanagan. Once or twice, I had seen him sniff appreciatively.

After I pulled the cologne from my trunk, Mrs. Surratt dabbed some on Mr. Surratt's temples with her handkerchief. "Try to rest a little, Son," she said tenderly. "You have been wearing yourself to rags with your travels."

We left Mr. Surratt alone on the sofa. An hour or so later, he emerged looking much refreshed and bounded upstairs. When he returned, he had Mr. Weichmann, still wearing the blue pants that had so offended Anna, in tow. "Weichmann and I are going for oysters."

"Why, you just ate," Anna said.

"Yes, but there's nothing like destruction and doom to whet a man's appetite for oysters. Don't wait up for us, Ma."

Mrs. Surratt nodded, and we ladies went back to our respective occupations — Mrs. Surratt knitting, me reading, Miss Jenkins putting pictures in her album, and Anna embroidering and throwing out the occasional snide remark about me. The men were not yet back when we retired, but not long afterward, I heard the sound of someone letting himself in. By now, I knew every person's tread in the house fairly well. This was Mr. Weichmann's. I listened again.

No second tread. Mr. Weichmann had come home alone.

21
Mary
APRIL 3, 1865

Richmond had fallen, and I had envisioned just about every horrid fate for Johnny imaginable, when my boy walked into the parlor, weary and dispirited but alive. The sight of him made me forget, for the moment, the news about Richmond.

He was hungry as well as tired from his journey, and I took him downstairs where my servant girl served him the remnants from our supper. "Johnny, the girl says that a man came by today asking for you," I told him in a low voice. "He would not give his name. He could be one of your friends, but —"

"I doubt that, Ma. I heard in Maryland that the feds who captured Howell are looking for me too. I think it's best I disappear for a while. I can't stay here long anyway. Judah Benjamin gave me some papers to take to our men in Montreal. I've got them tucked in *The Life of John Brown,* of all things." He sighed and speared a bit of ham. "Perhaps my last mission for the poor Confederacy."

"When are you leaving?"

"Tomorrow morning. I'll go to a hotel tonight. If there's to be trouble, I'll not drag you and Anna into it."

"Much as I would like to beg you to stay, Canada is probably the best place for you now. Do you need money?"

"No. Benjamin gave me two hundred dollars in gold. I'll see if I can get Holohan to change it before I leave. If I run out of money, I can always work as a clerk, I suppose."

"Promise me you will write."

Johnny nodded. "I'll write to you. Is Booth in town?"

"No. He stopped by the other day and said that he was going north for a while."

"At this rate we'll all be up north." Johnny downed his tea and rose. "Our plan's dead in the water, I suppose. I'll look him up in New York. I'm going to lie down a while. I feel wretched. Then I'll go to dinner with Weichmann, if he's willing. Maybe those blue pants of his will confuse the feds. I'll check into a hotel afterward. So this will be our good-bye, if you want a long one."

"Of course I do," I said and embraced my

son's bony frame.

There were tears in his eyes when he drew back. "Ma, I know we've had our words now and then, and I haven't been much of a support lately. I want to be better when I come back. I promise I will."

"Just protect yourself and come back safely. That is all I ask."

We went upstairs, where Johnny dozed on my bedroom sofa for a while before returning to his room. All too soon, he and Mr. Weichmann came downstairs on their way to dine together. It was like old times: they were laughing together like the school friends they were. As they headed toward the door, I longed to give Johnny yet another farewell embrace, but no one but I knew he would not be coming back to this house tonight. So I had to smile and say, "Goodbye, Johnny," as if he would be crossing the threshold again this very evening.

The door shut, and my son disappeared into the Washington night.

22
Nora
APRIL 1865

With the fall of Richmond and Anna's continuing coolness, I started to think about my future. Despite Mr. Booth's kind words, I held out little hope of marrying, especially since the war had left so many prettier young women bereft of husbands and fiancés. I would be provided for as long as Father and Peter lived, of course, but what would become of me after their deaths? Father had lived frugally, I knew, and had some property to leave me, but I did not know how much. Probably not enough to keep me for more than a few years. I was best off finding something to do, but what?

The most obvious means of supporting myself was to become a teacher. I was certainly well enough qualified in those days. But the possibility filled me with gloom, for I could see myself only too vividly, standing at a chalkboard and getting grayer with each passing year as pert young ladies giggled behind my back at my various peculiarities.

But there was another possibility, one that appealed to me the more I thought about it. Since the war had started, young women had been employed at the Treasury and at the Department of Engraving. Why couldn't I get such a job?

I broached the subject when my father took me to supper the night of April 4 at an establishment that catered to families. "I don't know, child. You have heard of the scandal at the Treasury Department."

Last year, all of Washington had thrilled to the gossip that some of the young women hired as Treasury clerks had become the concubines of their male supervisors. "But they found that was all nonsense, Father. Well, mostly nonsense."

"Still, my dear, it shows the sort of things that can happen when a woman works closely with men."

"Father, there are men coming and going at Mrs. Surratt's all of the time. I have never acted improperly with any of them, or them with me." Except for Mr. Booth, I silently added.

Father frowned. "Men coming and going?"

"I just mean her boarders, Father. Some

stay only for short periods. And of course, Mr. Surratt has friends who visit him there. It's not a house of ill repute, Father."

"Well, I should hope not," Father said dryly.

"Please, Father, can't I try to get an office job? You don't want me on your hands forever."

"Nora, you are not on my hands. You are my dearly beloved daughter."

"I know, Father. But if I am going to be unmarried, I want to at least be able to take care of myself. Why, I could make as much as six hundred dollars per year!"

"At a maximum."

"But that's better than nothing at all."

My father sighed. "Things have changed so much since the war began," he said. "But I suppose I must change with the times. If you can find a respectable office to work in, you may work in one."

"Oh, thank you!" I hugged my father. "I promise, I'll do nothing to disgrace you."

"I know you shall not. Now may I take my daughter to the illumination?"

I smiled. "You certainly can."

What a brilliant night it was! The day before, someone at the State Department had gone back to his desk long enough to issue a proclamation that to celebrate the fall of Richmond, the various government agencies might like to illuminate their buildings. No one wanted his building to be outdone, of course, so in consequence, every workman who was still able to stand after the drinking of the previous day had been enlisted in this great cause. Where the public buildings had led, the private buildings had followed, so all of Washington glowed.

With almost everyone else in the city, it seemed, Father and I strolled about, pointing like children at the splendor around us as the bands struck up one tune after another. The Capitol shone from top to bottom, its newish dome never appearing to such good effect as it did that night. On its western portico was a huge transparency, lit by gas, on which blazed the motto THIS IS THE LORD'S DOING; IT IS MARVELOUS IN OUR EYES. The president was not home, but the White House shimmered. The Patent Office glittered on the city block it had all to itself. The Treasury Department had what I considered the most clever illumination: gas jets arranged in the shape of a ten-dollar note. Grover's Theatre had festooned itself with Chinese lamps, surrounding the single word VICTORY. City Hall, the banks, the newspaper offices, were all aglow. My favorite bookstore, Philp and Solomon's, was so brightly lit one could have read outside of it, while the lights at Dr. Holmes's funeral parlor could have awakened the dead. The dingy prisons on First Street were transformed. Even the lunatic asylum, high on its hill, was a bedazzling sight, and I hoped the poor creatures who were shut up there were able to appreciate it.

Thanks to the brightness, everyone kept spotting acquaintances in the street. I saw a few of my old classmates, my father shook hands with the president of his bank (which was, of course, splendidly illuminated), and Mr. Weichmann ambled toward us with little Miss Dean in tow. She, of course, was agape, and I scolded myself silently for not thinking to take her out. "Are Mrs. Surratt and Anna here somewhere?"

"No. Mrs. Surratt was feeling poorly, and Miss Surratt said that she did not care for such gloating. The Holohans were going, but when I left, they were still fighting about which direction to walk in first."

I laughed, and Miss Dean tugged on Mr. Weichmann's sleeve. "If we stand here talking, they'll shut the lights off!" she wailed.

"A respectable, well-mannered man," Father commented as Mr. Weichmann dutifully allowed Miss Dean to drag him off.

"And kind to children, it seems."

Once again, I laughed. "Don't consider him as a husband for me, Father. He has eyes only for Miss Surratt, and she won't give him the time of day."

"Pity."

Mrs. Surratt was waiting up for me when Father brought me home. As they chatted pleasantly, I found myself wondering: What if they married? Odder things had happened. It was true that my father had two decades over Mrs. Surratt, but he had aged well, and they would be excellent company for each other. Both were regular churchgoers, neither were drinkers, and both liked to live quietly. It would be awkward having Anna as a stepsister, as things stood now, but Mr. Booth was bound to marry Miss Hale sooner or later, and Anna would see how foolish she had been.

While growing up, I had always half longed for, half dreaded a stepmother. But I could not think of anyone better to fill the role than Mrs. Surratt. This — and my office job — was something to work for.

And who knew? If I could bring my father and Mrs. Surratt together, perhaps I could even make a match between Mr. Weichmann and Anna.

■ ■ ■ ■

Between gathering letters of recommendation (I called both Father Wiget and my former headmistress into service) and writing and rewriting my letters of application, I stayed happily busy in the days after Richmond fell. I had not forgotten poor Private Flanagan, of course, but the knowledge that he had not died in vain comforted me as I included him in my nightly prayers.

I prayed for peace as well, and the Lord was listening at last to the many who joined me in that sentiment. Each morning, Washington woke to another encouraging bit of news. Only the tidings that Secretary of State Seward had been in a carriage accident dampened our spirits, and even this report was soon followed by assurances that his injuries, though likely to confine him to his bed for some time, were not expected to cripple him.

The best news of all arrived on April 10, made not the less sweet because of its inevitability: Lee's surrender to Grant at Appomattox Courthouse the day before.

Mr. Weichmann, given a holiday that day, soon came home bearing the newspapers, which I eagerly read before adding them to the pile that still lay yellowing in my trunk. The president was back in town, and as it was hoped he would make a speech, Mr. Weichmann and I decided to walk to the White House. As Miss Dean did not want to miss anything, and Miss Jenkins was heartily in favor of any excuse to stroll around the streets of Washington, we made a party of it. Even Anna reluctantly joined us.

The employees at the Navy Yard, who like everyone else in the city were unable to settle to any work, had decided to march instead, dragging with them two howitzers, the Marine Band, and the Lincoln Hospital Band for good measure. We, and seemingly the rest of Washington, followed in their wake. The streets were as muddy as they had been on inauguration day, and the heavens, unable to quite make up their mind as to whether to stay wet or stay dry, contented themselves by spluttering just enough rain at intervals to keep everyone in a state of perpetual dampness. But no one in the crowd pressing its way down Pennsylvania Avenue to the White House cared. They wanted only to see the man who had brought them safely to victory.

The president was nowhere to be seen when we arrived at the White House, so the crowd — a sea of humanity waving hats, fluttering handkerchiefs, and bobbing umbrellas — determined to tease him out by playing music and shooting the howitzers. To reward us, a figure soon came to the second-story center window, but it was not the tall figure of the president but the small figure of his son, Tad, waving a captured Confederate flag. The crowd shrieked its approval before some anonymous servant tugged the boy back from whence he had come as the band struck up a valedictory tune.

The city bells, all but drowned out by the guns and the band, struck twelve, and the president came to the window. Not before or since have I heard anything like the exultant cheer that greeted him. It was as if the entire crowd — male and female, black and white, military and civilian, old and young, native and immigrant — spoke with one voice. I yelled myself hoarse, and not even Anna, fuming at my side, could stop the happy tears from pouring down my cheeks.

"I am very greatly rejoiced to find that an occasion has occurred so pleasurable that the people cannot restrain themselves," the president said when at last the crowd grew quiet. "I suppose that arrangements are being made for some sort of a formal demonstration, this, or perhaps, tomorrow night."

"We can't wait!"

"We want it now!"

"If there should be such a demonstration, I, of course, will be called upon to respond, and I shall have nothing to say if you dribble it all out of me before," the president protested, to be met by laughter. He looked around. "I see you have a band of music with you."

"We have two or three!"

"I propose closing up this interview by the band performing a particular tune that I will name. Before this is done, however, I wish to mention one or two little circumstances connected with it. I have always thought 'Dixie' one of the best tunes I have ever heard. Our adversaries over the way attempted to appropriate it, but I insisted yesterday that we fairly captured it. I presented the question to the attorney general, and he gave it as his legal opinion that it is our lawful prize. I now request the band to favor me with its performance."

Instantly, the Marine Band struck up "Dixie," and the crowd sang along — Mr. Weichmann next to me looking a little sheepish as he sang, this time fully sober, that he wished he was back in the land of cotton. Anna scowled, though I could not help but notice she was beating time with one of her feet.

The Hospital Band having followed with "Yankee Doodle," the president said, "Now give three good hearty cheers for General Grant and all under his command."

We obeyed, and obeyed once again when the president asked us to cheer for the navy. Bowing a farewell, he departed from the window, and the Marine Band played "Hail Columbia" as the throng went its separate ways.

As we opened the door to the boarding-house, we heard the familiar sound of Mr. Booth's pleasant voice. "So where have all of you been?"

"To see the ape at the zoo," Anna said.

"To see the president," I said firmly. "Except that he had very little to say. He will speak more at length tomorrow."

"And I suppose you will drag us all to that as well."

"No. You were so disrespectful, I shall not."

"Anna, I hope you did not make a spectacle of yourself," Mrs. Surratt said.

"I did nothing of the sort. I merely shut my eyes when he appeared at the window.

He's so ugly it was necessary."

Mr. Weichmann broke in. "What do you think, Mr. Booth? Is it all up with the South?"

"No, indeed." Mr. Booth pulled a little book out of his pocket — a bound map of the war front, which at that time could be found on the person of nearly every self-respecting man in Washington. "General Johnson is still in the field and could head to the mountains and make trouble yet."

"I think it is a forlorn hope," Mr. Weichmann said after Mr. Booth had traced out various routes for General Johnson to take. "Will you be playing in Richmond, now that she is in hands of the Union again?"

Mr. Booth shook his head. "I have no engagements at present, and have been content to be idle. Not a happy state of affairs, I know! But if there is one play that would tempt me to the stage, it would be Otway's *Venice Preserved.* There are some splendid parts."

I was not familiar with the play, and evidently none of the rest were either. As the subject soon changed, I did not think further of it until a day or so later, when I walked to the circulating library I had joined soon after leaving school. "Have you a copy of *Venice Preserved*?" I asked.

"Yes, miss, but it's not your usual sort of play, I think."

"I want only to satisfy my curiosity," I said. "A friend of mine mentioned it."

I took it home and read it that evening. It was a rather gloomy play, in which the entire Venetian cabinet ended up dead. Not one, I thought, that I would see if it were performed in Washington.

Unless, of course, Mr. Booth played in it.

23
MARY

APRIL 10 TO 11, 1865

The day after General Lee surrendered his troops to Grant, I answered the doorbell to find Mr. Booth on the stoop. "A gloomy day in all respects," he said as I showed him into the parlor. "I understand John is in Canada?"

"Yes. At least I believe he is by now. He sent me a letter several days ago from Springfield, Massachusetts. He said that he had overslept and missed his connection but would be catching the next one."

Mr. Booth chuckled wanly. "Well, we must do without him, my dear lady. Are you quite alone?"

"Yes. Everyone is out today. Even Anna."

"If our plan should succeed at all, we must strike soon. That means I will take what opportunity presents itself. I would prefer that John assist me, but we cannot afford to let a chance slip by us. Whatever happens, he will have been of immense help in laying the

262

groundwork. May I ask for your continued help, dear lady?"

"You know you can, pet." The endearment slipped out of its own volition.

Mr. Booth smiled. "I know you go to your tavern on occasion. Could you find some reason to go there — if you do not have one already — and give Mr. Lloyd a message? Tell him the shooting irons may be called for at any time, and that he should have them ready."

"I do have business there. A man, Mr. Nothey, owes me money, and I have heard that he has come into a sum of it. I mean to collect it from him. But even if I did not have business there, I would be glad to help you."

"Bless you, my dear lady."

"But I must ask. You do not believe that it is too late?"

Mr. Booth shakes his head. "If I believed that, I would have no wish to continue on," he said. "I feel today that I have no country."

"I know precisely what you mean."

"You do, don't you? I am so grateful to have met you through Johnny, dear lady. I can tell you things I cannot tell my own dear mother. I cannot even speak of the war with my family now, you know. Do you know what my brother Edwin said when Rich-

263

mond fell? That it was the greatest blessing to mankind that it had fallen. Were it not for the love I bear my mother, I know not what I could have done. But I have digressed. No, I do not believe it is ever too late to strike a blow against tyranny."

That evening, keeping my promise to Mr. Booth, I asked Mr. Weichmann if he would take me to Surrattsville the next day. Too late, I remembered it was a work day for him — Washington's nearly constant state of revelry since Richmond's fall made that all too easy to forget. I was in the midst of apologizing and telling him I could take the stage instead when Mr. Weichmann broke in cheerily, "No, no, Mrs. Surratt, I will be happy to take you. We have a holiday tomorrow, and a drive to the country suits me. Besides, I've never had the chance to drive a buggy before."

"I will see if Mr. Booth can lend us his. It's very smart."

Mr. Weichmann beamed with anticipation.

But when Mr. Weichmann returned from the National Hotel the next morning, he was frowning. "Mr. Booth has just sold his buggy. He gave me ten dollars for you to rent one, though. Why would he sell it?"

I too thought this was odd, as a buggy

would surely come in handy for what he had planned. "Perhaps he is planning to buy a better one."

"Perhaps." Mr. Weichmann sighed. "I certainly wish he had waited, though."

Despite this setback, Mr. Weichmann's good spirits soon returned as he procured a buggy that was as nearly as well turned out as Mr. Booth's. Mr. Weichmann was indeed a novice buggy driver, but he learned quickly, and our horse was so well behaved that he scarcely needed driving anyway.

As we neared Uniontown, just past Washington City, I saw the very man I was to give a message. "Why, it's Mr. Lloyd! Stop the carriage, Mr. Weichmann."

"Whoa!" yelled Mr. Weichmann. The horse stopped calmly and turned its head, clearly wondering why Mr. Weichmann was making so much fuss over the matter.

Seated beside Mr. Lloyd in the carriage was a lady in her thirties — Mrs. Emma Offutt, his sister-in-law, a widow who helped the Lloyds with the tavern occasionally. Rumor (mostly through Olivia, an inveterate gossip) had it that pretty Mrs. Offutt was much too familiar with her sister's husband. Whatever the truth in that, all seemed perfectly respectable at the moment, for the pair was accompanied by a small boy, one of Mrs. Offutt's children, and a neighbor. "Business or pleasure?" I called.

"A little of both," Mr. Lloyd said, climbing out of his carriage. I was pleased to see he appeared reasonably sober. Perhaps he had taken the pledge — and if Mrs. Offutt had inspired this reform, I could not help but think the better of her. "Mr. Griffith and I each have some business in town, and Mrs. Offutt wanted to buy some things for Easter. And I suppose we all wanted to get a little whiff of the excitement."

"There is plenty of that about, and unless the Union finds something else to celebrate, the shops should be open." Mr. Lloyd by now had come to stand beside me, so I said in a low voice, "Please get those things stored at the tavern ready to hand. They will be needed soon."

"Things?" Mr. Lloyd frowned.

"The things that my son brought last month."

"I don't understand, Mrs. Surratt. Mr. Surratt has an extra shirt or two at the tavern, I think, for when he goes to the parties around here."

"The shooting irons, Mr. Lloyd," I hissed.

"Oh, those! I am glad you mentioned them. Ever since they picked up Mr. Howell,

I have been worried about them searching the place. I thought of burying the damned things."

"Please don't, Mr. Lloyd. They will be called for soon, and you will be relieved of your worry."

"Well, that's pleasant news. Is there news of Mr. Howell?"

"None. Perhaps he will take the oath of loyalty so he can go free. I should see if there is anything I can do for him."

"I don't know if you could be of much help, ma'am. Maybe the opposite. I've heard tell that they're still looking for Mr. Surratt after that trip to Richmond of his. They think that he's gone back to Maryland."

The day before, I had a letter from Johnny postmarked Montreal. Knowing my boy was safely out of the country, I laughed. "To Richmond and back in that short a time? The government must think my Johnny a very smart man indeed."

Having bidden Mr. Lloyd and his companions good-bye, we continued into Maryland, passing so many carriages and horsemen heading in the opposite direction that I wondered if there would be anyone in Surrattsville for me to see. Judging from the gay attire of most of the young men, I guessed they were bound for Washington's

267

taverns, music halls, and oyster houses. Those with companions laughed together; those without companions were quick to introduce themselves to each other.

I truly wished I could join in the festive mood. Why should not these young men rejoice? They would not be called away from their loved ones, their professions, and their homes; they would not fall in battle. I could find some cause for celebration as well: as Miss Fitzpatrick had pointed out, the end of the war meant Isaac would likely return to me soon, and perhaps Johnny as well. But I could not help but think of the devastation that had been wrought upon the South, and of Richmond in flames.

24
NORA
APRIL 11, 1865

I received several replies to my inquiries about positions, all amounting to the assurance that although there were no vacancies, I would be given due consideration when one came available. "That's to be expected, child," Father said as we walked to the White House on the Tuesday after Lee's surrender. "Don't let it discourage you."

"I want things to happen now," I said. "I never was very good at waiting."

That night, the president was to give his speech about the future of the nation, and Father, hearing the news during his rounds, had stopped by the house and offered to take me. This would have been an excellent excuse to invite Mrs. Surratt along, but she had gone to the country with Mr. Weichmann on business and had not yet returned by the time we set out, early so as to get a place where we could have a good vantage point.

The buildings, public and private, were again illuminated — probably there were none happier about the end of the war than the town's candle sellers, for in addition to the elaborate gaslight displays in the large buildings, nearly every residence in the city glowed with at least one candle. The White House itself glittered to such effect that one could have confused it with the Crystal Palace.

"Perhaps on Easter Sunday, Father, you could go to church with us," I suggested as we stood there waiting for the president. And perhaps, I thought to myself, Mrs. Surratt could wear her lavender gown, which brought out the color of her eyes.

"I don't see why not."

A misty darkness settled over the city. The crowd stirred, and in the window near the one at which the president would speak appeared a handful of beautifully dressed ladies — Mrs. Lincoln and a few friends, one of whom I later learned was Miss Clara Harris. They looked to be in excellent spirits and seemed to be admiring the size of the crowd as they stood chatting at the open window.

The crowd roared, and Mr. Lincoln, wearing spectacles and clutching a handful of papers, stepped forward, illuminated from behind by a candle that someone held up. "We meet this evening not in sorrow, but in gladness of heart," he began.

It was a quiet, thoughtful speech, one that had my father nodding approvingly but many of the crowd looking somewhat perplexed, having expected the sort of verbal fireworks that would match the real fireworks planned for later in the evening. It was a bit dry for me too, I confess, but at one point, I perked up when Mr. Lincoln mentioned that some had called for giving colored men the vote. He himself, he said, would prefer it be given to the very intelligent and to those who had served in the war.

The excitement of the last few days was beginning to catch up with me. When Mr. Lincoln finished his speech, to vigorous but somewhat restrained applause, I yawned, and my father smiled down at me. "Let me take you home, Nora."

I nodded and let him guide me away. As we made our way out of the crowd onto Lafayette Square, I saw a familiar figure hurry by, talking intently — angrily, even — with a taller, huskier man whose face was averted from me but whose build looked somewhat familiar as well. "Why, that's Mr. Booth," I said to Father. "He must have been here for the speech as well."

"Aren't you going to introduce me to your theatrical acquaintance, my child?"

"Not tonight," I said, glancing back in Mr. Booth's direction. "Somehow he doesn't look as if he wants company at the moment."

25
MARY

On Holy Thursday, Nora and I went to confession, Anna and Olivia having overslept as was their wont.

I did not know what to say. I was a party to something that, if it happened, would certainly be regarded by many as a crime, although others would think differently. And yet nothing had happened yet, and perhaps never would. Was I to ask for forgiveness for something that might never come to fruition?

And in these desperate times, could such a desperate act even be accorded a sin?

In the end, I did not task Father Walter, the kindly priest who heard my confession at St. Patrick's, with such questions. Instead, I confessed my usual sins — pride, sharpness of tongue, envy of those women who were more comfortably situated than me. No doubt Father Walter had heard the same sort of confession from nearly every woman in his congregation, and I distinctly heard him suppress a yawn as he ordered my penance.

The next day, Mr. Weichmann came home from work around noon, just after I heard the mail flutter through its slot. "Secretary Stanton closed the War Department early so that those of us who wanted to attend Good Friday services could do so," he explained. "So I have done so. Wasn't that kind of him?"

"Very kind indeed," I said, frowning at the mail he handed to me. Atop the pile was a letter from George Calvert, the son of my husband's chief creditor. Not only was he pressing me for the money he was owed, but he also had heard I had been attempting to collect the money owed to me. He appeared to have the idea it was only my own recalcitrance that had kept Mr. Nothey, my debtor, from settling with me.

For what had to be half an hour, I paced around the house. Then I made up my mind and knocked on Mr. Weichmann's door. "Mr. Weichmann, do you have plans for today?"

"No, Mrs. Surratt. Merely reading, and perhaps attending services tonight. May I escort you?"

"Yes, but not to church. Mr. Weichmann, that man we saw the other day, Mr. Nothey, has told my husband's old creditor that I am not willing to settle with him — or, at least, I think he has. I must do something about this. I cannot bear having this weigh upon my mind on this holy weekend. Will you take me to Surrattsville again, sir?"

"Why, of course."

"You truly don't mind?" I looked at the book lying on a table. Though not a great reader myself, I knew that those who were — even Nora — could grow testy when one came between them and their books. And I was half beginning to reconsider this journey. What if no one was able to see me? "I do not want to disturb you."

"No, Mrs. Surratt. This book is rather dull, and I am happy enough to be called away from it to try driving another time."

He looked so eager, in fact, that I put my own misgivings aside. At least I could take advice from my brother, who I knew from Olivia would be at home. "Then let me give you the money for the buggy."

Mr. Weichmann was headed out the door when I heard him speaking to someone on the stoop. "Mrs. Surratt, Mr. Booth is here," he called.

"Send him in, please."

Mr. Booth came in, holding a package of some sort. He waited until the door closed behind Mr. Weichmann and we saw his form heading down the steps to the street before he said, "Mrs. Surratt, we are going through with our plans tonight."

Something in me wanted to beg him to reconsider, to tell him it was too late for any good to come of it now. Something else made me want to urge him on. "Tonight" was all I could manage.

"Yes. I have a great favor to ask of you — one last favor. Could you possibly go to Surrattsville this day?"

"Why, I am on my way there on business."

"Such luck, then!" Mr. Booth held up his package. "I would like for you to leave this at your tavern — careful, it is glass — and to tell your tenant, Lloyd, that it and the shooting irons will be called for tonight. Those, and two bottles of whiskey. It will be of immense help, dear lady."

"I will do so."

"I thank you. I have always been able to count on you. I hope this is the last time I shall have to ask for your assistance."

"I fear you are running a great risk. If something should go wrong —"

Mr. Booth shrugged. " 'If it be now, 'tis not to come. If it be not to come, it will be now.' Have you heard these lines, dear lady?"

"Yes, and I understand them. I will have you in my prayers. And I will give you this."

I unfastened my necklace. On it dangled a cross and a couple of medals, including a battered medal of Saint Jude Father Finotti gave me many years ago. Once, in one of his drunken rages, my husband tossed all of my medals into the fire, but I retrieved this one before the flames could reach it. "Take this," I said, sliding it off the chain. "It was given to me by one who was dear to me, and it has seen me through much over the years."

Mr. Booth stared at it as I placed it in his palm. In someone else's hands, it looked much smaller. "I am moved, dear lady. Your husband gave this to you?"

"No. Someone else who holds a special place in my heart." I fastened my necklace again. "God keep you, Mr. Booth. It is all in his hands now."

I could swear I saw tears in Mr. Booth's eyes. He was about to speak when the door opened, and Mr. Weichmann called, "I have the buggy, Mrs. Surratt."

"Then I will wish you a good day, Mrs. Surratt," Mr. Booth said pleasantly, turning around. "And to you too, Mr. Weichmann."

■ ■ ■ ■

I almost forgot the papers I was to take with me to Surrattsville — Mr. Nothey's promissory note and the correspondence we had had on the subject — and I did actually forget the package Mr. Booth gave me and had to hurry back into the house and fetch it while Mr. Weichmann looked on quizzically. "It's glass," I explained as I carefully placed the package by my feet, where it was least likely to be harmed if Mr. Weichmann brought the carriage to one of the sudden stops that seemed to characterize his driving.

Mr. Weichmann nodded. "Giddyap!" he hollered in a voice I feared would send the horse stampeding down H Street. The horse, however, being well accustomed to all sorts of drivers, calmly moved forward, and so we began our second journey in three days to Surrattsville.

My thoughts were busy as we made our way down H Street. How was Mr. Booth going to effect his scheme? Who, if anyone, was going to help him? I thought of what happened in March, when Johnny and the others came home in such states of agitation after their kidnapping plan failed, and in my heart of hearts, I wished something would change Mr. Booth's plans again. And how easy would it be to seize the president? This was not the Washington of a month before: since Richmond fell, the adoring crowds had hardly let the man out of their sight.

And what if the plan was foiled and the men caught? I did not care to dwell on that. To cover my thoughts — which raced through my mind at such a pace I could not imagine why they were not fully visible — I began chattering to Mr. Weichmann. "You are a quick study, Mr. Weichmann. Your driving is much improved over the other day."

Mr. Weichmann preened a little but allowed modestly, "It may just be a better horse. Have you ever driven, Mrs. Surratt?"

"Yes, on occasion. My brother taught me. Of course, it was a necessity in the country. I used to be quite good at it, actually. Let me see if I can still manage it." I reached for the reins.

Mr. Weichmann handed them to me, albeit a little reluctantly, and I urged the horse in a voice I called up from my youth. Back then, I did indeed drive quite often when I was home from my school in Alexandria, but naturally, when I married, I fell out of the habit — save for the occasional time when John was too inebriated to manage the carriage.

I sighed at the memory. To prevent myself from falling into melancholy and back into my worry about Mr. Booth's plan, I began to chatter at Mr. Weichmann once more. "With the war almost over, Mr. Weichmann, will you be able to keep your position, do you think? Or have they said?"

"I daresay there will be something for us to do, Mrs. Surratt, though maybe not of the same nature. In any event, I need only to last until September, when I can resume my studies for the ministry."

So he was still set on that. I considered taking another stab at dissuading him, for it still occurred to me that he might be an eligible husband for Nora. After all, they had been gallivanting around to the festivities in Washington lately and seemed quite happy in each other's company. But Mr. Weichmann was stubborn enough, and male enough, to persist the more I tried to dissuade him. So I said, "That is right. I had forgotten about that. Perhaps you could put in a good word for Miss Fitzpatrick with someone? She wants to work in an office, and I daresay she would be good at it. Unless, of course, you hold the notion that women should not work in offices."

"No, Mrs. Surratt. I believe that ladies can be of great use in an office. And they have certainly put their organizational skills to use through their relief efforts. In a way, the war has been a boon to your sex."

"Well, I imagine most would have preferred the boon come in another way. But I take your meaning."

At the tavern, I sent for Mr. Gwynn, a man of some substance in the county who had helped me with my business affairs occasionally. He obliged me with a few minutes of his time, and I gave him a stern letter, composed by Mr. Weichmann, to hand to Mr. Nothey. I felt somewhat easier about my affairs as we walked to our waiting carriages. Then Mr. Gwynn frowned. "That is your carriage, Mrs. Surratt?"

"Yes."

"Why, it needs a repair, or it will not get you safely to Washington. I could rig up something, but my wife is feeling poorly and will be wanting me home." He turned to Mr. Weichmann. "It's simple to do, really. Are you mechanically minded?"

"I consider myself a quick study, sir."

"Then I think you can manage it. Get a piece of rope . . ."

As Mr. Gwynn gave Mr. Weichmann

directions, I spotted Mr. Booth's package sitting patiently on the floor of the buggy. What if I had come all the way here and forgotten my promise to him? I snatched it up and hurried inside, where Mrs. Offutt was bustling about. "This is for Mr. Lloyd. There are parties who will call for it tonight. Please tell Mr. Lloyd to —"

"I believe I hear him now, ma'am."

Sure enough, Mr. Lloyd had pulled into view. "I was just speaking of you," I said and smiled. "As the saying goes, speak of the devil and his imp will appear."

Mr. Lloyd got out — no, all but fell out — of his carriage. In my short acquaintance with the man, I had seen him in various stages of drunkenness, but this day he was as drunk as a man could be and still be upright. "I am not aware I wash a devil before," he said, glaring at me with a face as red as one.

"A mere saying, Mr. Lloyd. I beg your pardon."

Mr. Lloyd hiccuped.

Years of dealing with my drunken husband had not been entirely wasted on me. "I do have some good news, Mr. Lloyd," I cooed.

"Good news," Mr. Lloyd said.

"Yes. Those guns that have been an annoyance to you will be called for tonight."

"Damn guns. Nuisance. Should have never let that young fool son of yours leave 'em here. Bane of existence."

I passed over this rude comment about Johnny. "They will be called for tonight and will no longer trouble you."

"I know, woman! Stop repeating yourself." Mr. Lloyd glared at me. "Not stupid."

"I know, Mr. Lloyd. Forgive me. Now, I have one more thing to tell you. I left a small package with Mrs. Offutt just now."

As if taking a cue, Mr. Lloyd dropped the package he held, and I give silent thanks I had not entrusted him with Mr. Booth's glass object, whatever it might be. "Just fish," he said, bending over to retrieve it. "No harm. No harm!" He winked at me. "Dead, you know."

"Indeed. Mr. Lloyd, please give the package to the parties who call for the shooting irons. They will require two bottles of whiskey as well." At least, I thought, Mr. Lloyd should be able to remember that part of his instructions.

"Package and shooting irons. Whiskey," Mr. Lloyd repeated. "Got it." His countenance suddenly fell. "I feel sick," he pronounced.

"Fancy that," I muttered under my breath. Mr. Weichmann had spotted the two of us and hurried over, carrying a rope. "Mr. Lloyd," he said plaintively. "Would you be able to lend a hand with a repair?"

I shook my head and mouthed "drunk" to Mr. Weichmann, but Mr. Lloyd, who did indeed appear to be on the verge of sickness, snapped to attention. "Repair! Fix anything if put mind to it." He glared at Mr. Weichmann. "Book learned, aren't you?"

"Well, yes."

"Useless, useless! Fool good-for-nothing schoolboys."

I cast a warning look at Mr. Weichmann — even in Mr. Lloyd's sodden condition, I was not certain he would lose a fight to Mr. Weichmann — and we headed toward the carriage with Mr. Lloyd shambling behind. When he finally reached the carriage, he listened a moment to Mr. Weichmann's explanation, then snapped, "Boysh! Think they know everything. Carriages, playing cards . . ."

"Playing cards?" Mr. Weichmann asked.

Mr. Lloyd ignored the question. Instead, he unceremoniously thrust his packages at me — fish and oysters — and crouched over the fifth wheel, took the rope from Mr. Weichmann, and coiled it around various spots before tying it. "All done!" he pronounced. He attempted to rise but needed some help from Mr. Weichmann. "Thank ye, boy. Stay for supper?" Proving Mr. Weichmann's incompetence appeared to have cheered him up.

"No, thank you," I said. "We must be going back to Washington. I want to try to go to church tonight."

"Each his own," said Mr. Lloyd. He fumbled in the general direction of the pocket where men kept their flasks and nearly lost his footing.

"Perhaps you should lie down, Mr. Lloyd."

"Maybe." He raised his much-abused package in the air as a gesture of farewell and stumbled off, the tail of the fish flapping a good-bye.

Mrs. Offutt hurried toward us as Mr. Weichmann helped me into the carriage. "I am so glad my sister isn't here to see this. It's the reason she stays away so much."

"Has he been like this often lately?"

"Nearly all of the time, to the point of madness, I fear." Mrs. Offutt hesitated. "I will be honest with you, Mrs. Surratt. I have urged him to give up this tavern after the lease runs out. It will be his ruination. He has always tippled a little, but he was never this bad until he had the stuff constantly within reach."

I nodded gloomily. How could I argue? There must be someone who could run this tavern without turning into a drunkard, but I had not yet found him.

Although I did not have much confidence in Mr. Lloyd's repairs, given the circumstances, we met with no mishaps on the road. Our ride was by and large a silent one, however, as the growing darkness required Mr. Weichmann to pay close attention to his driving, and I was brooding over the possibility of having to find another tenant for the tavern. Perhaps I could sell the place . . .

Mr. Weichmann broke the silence. "Do you think Mr. Booth will ever return to the stage, Mrs. Surratt? He seems to be entirely idle now."

"I believe he may be done acting, except for his own amusement. If he marries that Miss Hale, I imagine he will want to find something more acceptable to her father. But if she refuses him, I imagine he will go to New York. There is little else to keep him here, I should think."

"He has spoken of his oil investments."

"Yes, and I fear that he might fall prey to some sort of bubble scheme. He wants to make money other than through acting, I think, to win her family over to him. I think he is a little crazy on the subject, truth be told."

"A man in love." Mr. Weichmann chuckled mirthlessly. "Mrs. Surratt. Do you believe I have any chance with your daughter?"

I shook my head. "No, sir. I am sorry. Anna takes very strong likes and dislikes, and she has never been one to change her mind easily. Her dislikings can be unjust, I confess, and I am sorry you have fallen on the wrong side of her, but there is nothing I can do."

"She is in love with Mr. Booth."

"I believe she is infatuated with him, but he has never given any sign of liking her more than Miss Fitzpatrick or my niece. I do not believe she has met her husband yet, Mr. Weichmann. It is that simple."

Mr. Weichmann gave a piteous sigh, and I patted his hand.

"Mr. Weichmann, I know one thing. You would be unwise to go into the priesthood because you have been disappointed in love. Perhaps you have simply not met your wife either. Or" — I paused to reconsidered but pressed on — "perhaps you have. There are two very pleasant young ladies under my roof, sir, besides my daughter. Both Miss Fitzpatrick and my niece are fine young women."

My lodger made no reply. At least I might have planted a seed.

We came upon a hill about a mile outside the city, and Mr. Weichmann gasped, for the illuminated city shone below us like something out of legend. It was a beautiful sight, but there was a melancholy aspect about it too, which made me say, "I am afraid that all this rejoicing will be turned into mourning, and all this glory into sadness."

"Why, what do you mean?"

"Simply that after sunshine there is always a storm, and that when people are too proud and licentious, God will punish them."

Mr. Weichmann stared below him. "To be honest, Mrs. Surratt, I think we've had enough punishment for the past four years to last a lifetime."

At about half past eight, we arrived home, where a letter from Johnny awaited me, written two days before and dated from Montreal.

As I squinted to read it, I visualized Johnny's lively face with each word. Johnny had bought a new pea jacket for ten dollars in silver — necessary because the cold was going straight through his Washington clothes

— and clad in his new jacket, he had enjoyed wandering around Montreal and was especially taken with the French cathedral. His hotel was fine, but far too expensive, so he would probably be going to a boardinghouse or perhaps to Toronto, if his fancy took him in that direction. It was the most bland and pleasant of missives, but because Johnny had warned me to destroy all of his letters, lest the house ever be searched, I fed it to the fire that burned low on that chilly Good Friday night.

Anna had been sneezing periodically since I got home, and she at last took Mrs. Beeton's recommended remedy — raisins, stick licorice, sugar candy, rum, and a bit of vinegar — and went to the attic room to retire for the night. In her absence, Olivia grew almost flirtatious with Mr. Weichmann, and soon she and Nora were jesting with him. Mr. Weichmann was emboldened enough to do his imitation of the sodden Mr. Lloyd — a rather good one, I am afraid — and all three of them were giggling so hard, I feared Mr. Holohan, who liked his sleep, would start banging on his floor. And the truth is, I was so keyed up, wondering what was happening with Mr. Booth, that I began to pace about.

Nora stopped laughing for a moment. "Are you quite well, Mrs. Surratt?"

"Yes, child. My leg is cramping from the ride to Surrattsville and back."

"You should stay with Grandma overnight next time, Aunt Mary, so you won't have all of that dreary riding back and forth."

"Yes, that is a thought." I paced some more.

The young people resumed their joking. My head was pounding; it was too much. Finally, I clapped my hands. "Shoo! All of you, to your rooms," I said in a light voice. "The Holohans are trying to sleep, and so is Anna."

"Yes, Mrs. Surratt."

"Yes, Aunt Mary."

"Yes, Mrs. Surratt."

And with that, the three of them dutifully trooped off to their three rooms, but not before Mr. Weichmann waved his hand in imitation of Mr. Lloyd's sodden farewell.

It was almost ten. Alone, I said a few prayers before going into my room, where Nora was already in bed. She slept like a little girl, a fist curled under her cheek, and I knew that when I lay down, she would half wake and snuggle closer to me, like she must have done when the mother she hardly remembered was alive. For the first time, it occurred to me how much the child would be grieved if Mr. Booth kidnapped Mr. Lincoln, whose every word she had been hanging on for the past two weeks.

Much as I loved the South, I did not want this to happen. I wanted Johnny and Isaac back, working at steady jobs and looking for respectable wives, and I wanted Mr. Booth to marry Miss Hale and forget about this scheme of his.

For a moment, I considered putting on my shawl and hurrying to St. Patrick's and begging to see a priest — or going to the authorities. But I could not turn in Mr. Booth, who had brought so much light and color into our lives, after he entrusted me with his secrets. And I could not trouble a priest with the heavy burden that lay upon me now.

No, it had gone too far, and we had to see out this play. I was right when I spoke as I did to Mr. Booth this morning. It was all in God's hands.

Stepping quietly so as not to disturb the other boarders, I walked upstairs and knocked on the door of the next best thing this house had to a priest. There was a light shining underneath it; as I had suspected, Mr. Weichmann was likely working or reading. "Come in."

291

Mr. Weichmann was sitting at a desk, a manual of phonography spread out in front of him. He was evidently doing exercises in this art, for a sheet of paper in front of him was covered with the incomprehensible marks of the shorthand reporter. "Mr. Weichmann, may I ask you a favor? Would you pray for my intentions when you say your prayers tonight?"

"I will, but I do not know what they are, Mrs. Surratt."

"It does not matter," I said, withdrawing. "Please pray for them anyway."

26
NORA
APRIL 13 TO 15, 1865

"I don't want to leave," Miss Dean wailed. "There's another illumination planned tonight, and it's going to be the best one ever!"

"Darling, you have to leave," Mrs. Dean said. "It's Easter, and you have a lovely new outfit for church."

"I want to wear it here. Not in Alexandria. Nothing ever happens in Alexandria!"

"This is no way to act, on Holy Thursday of all times! You are getting in this carriage now!" Mrs. Dean looked half apologetically, half accusingly at Mrs. Surratt. "I hope this has not been her normal conduct as of late, ma'am."

"No." I spoke up. "She is normally as good as gold, Mrs. Dean, and Mrs. Surratt is very firm when it is needed. But Washington has been so full of excitement lately . . ."

"That's right." Miss Dean whimpered.

"Be that as it may, we must go," Mrs.

Dean said. "Grandmother is coming to see you."

"Grandma?" Miss Dean perked up.

"She brings her candy," Mrs. Dean said to us sotto voce.

"Miss Fitzpatrick, will you promise to tell me everything about the illumination when I get back?"

"Everything," I promised. "I'll even save the newspapers."

"Then I'll go," Miss Dean said. She hiccuped and let the carriage driver help her to a seat, then blew us kisses as her mother settled in beside her. "Good-bye, house!" she called as the carriage began to pull forward. "Good-bye, Washington!"

"You'll be back on Monday," Mrs. Dean said. "For heaven's sake."

By now we in Washington were becoming rather jaded with illuminations, but Miss Jenkins and I went to this one anyway, escorted by Mr. Weichmann. Mrs. Surratt stayed home, to no one's surprise, and Anna also stayed home, although on this occasion she had a good excuse: the sniffles. "I probably caught this wretched cold from standing in all that rabble watching the gorilla the other day," she said as she settled on the sofa in her wrapper.

"Or from shopping yesterday," I suggested.

Anna sniffed, though whether that was in derision or from her cold I could not tell.

Miss Jenkins and I needed Mr. Weichmann's protection, for the streets were teeming with people, many from out of town and many not quite sober. Still, despite the press of the crowds, I enjoyed myself thoroughly, for the city was a splendid sight. General Grant, newly arrived in town, could have leaned out of his hotel room at Willard's and seen his name in gaslight in any number of places, while one clothing store asked archly in lights, "How are you, Lee?" Some of the visitors were dressed up as garishly as the buildings, and I, used to seeing the sober clothing of the city's clerks, snickered at one young man in particular, resplendent in plaid pantaloons of purple and green.

Even some houses that had been dark before were lit this night, at least by a single candle, and it was touching to see how the poorest colored people had decorated their houses. "It is a little mortifying to live in about the only house on H Street not lit," I admitted to Mr. Weichmann as we turned into our block at last. "I wish I had a front room, so I could have put up a candle. But

Miss Surratt would probably prefer to see the place burn."

"Well, at least it's easy to distinguish it from the rest," Mr. Weichmann said dryly.

On Friday morning, I accompanied Mrs. Surratt, Anna, and Miss Jenkins to St. Patrick's, where we happened to meet my father, who to my delight joined us and sat next to Mrs. Surratt, although he was more engaged in casting approving looks at Mr. Weichmann, who was assisting at the veneration of the cross and admittedly did strike a dignified and pious figure. Afterward, my father returned to the house to join us for breakfast, and I made a point of praising the cooking.

I walked with Father to his bank after breakfast. "Father, have you ever thought of remarrying?" I asked the question in what I hoped was the most casual manner possible.

"Why, what makes you ask that?"

"I have just always wondered, and now seemed a good time to ask. To think, you could live in a nice house like Mrs. Surratt's, instead of in lodgings."

My father gave me an amused look. "Child, are you trying to marry me off to your landlady?"

I scowled at being found so transparent.

"Well, she is a widow, and you a widower, and you are both Catholic."

"Obviously a recipe for future happiness, with so much in common," Father said dryly.

"But she is pretty, you have to admit, Father."

"Yes, she is an attractive woman, and of good character, which is all the more important. But as for my remarrying anybody, I have little enough saved, but there is enough for you to live on, if you are frugal, without having to marry some rascal. I could not provide for your future adequately if I had a wife."

"But that's so dreary a reason not to marry, Father, especially if I find employment, and I fear you are lonely."

"I have friends, child, and I live in congenial lodgings. And I have you children. If it makes you feel better, I am going to the theater tonight with the Misses Donovan."

"Father! Two ladies! And on Good Friday, yet."

"Well, as there is so much rejoicing in the city this week, it seems more permissible than it usually would," my father said a little shamefacedly. "Anyway, the friend who planned to take them discovered that he couldn't go, and they would not go without a man to escort them."

"So it's an act of chivalry, really."

"If it were my party, I would invite you along, my dear. But it is not, of course, and besides, it is only *Our American Cousin.*"

I nodded. This play was an old drawing-room comedy, always a crowd-pleaser, but one I had seen before. Besides, I rather liked the idea of my father having the undivided attention of the two old maids. "Some other time." I kissed my father on the cheek as we parted at his bank. "Enjoy your evening with your ladies, Father."

I spent the afternoon at the hospital and returned home to find that Mrs. Surratt had gone into the country with Mr. Weichmann. Anna was in a foul mood because she had been abed when Mr. Booth called, because she was not in a fit state to see him if he called again, and because he had not called again by the time the clock struck five. "Perhaps he is proposing to Miss Hale," I suggested.

"You're tedious," Anna said.

I started to say, "And you're deluded," but thought better of it. Instead, I said mildly, "Well, I'm sure he has other engagements to attend to," and went out for a walk.

Anna's bad mood continued throughout

the evening, until she at last did herself, and us, a favor and took her sneezing self to bed, leaving Mrs. Surratt, Miss Jenkins, Mr. Weichmann, and myself in possession of the parlor. With her gloomy presence gone, the spirits of the rest of us rose, and soon Miss Jenkins and I were teasing Mr. Weichmann mercilessly about his not knowing his carriage needed repairing. He took it in good humor, though, and we went on in this fashion very well until around ten when Mrs. Surratt decided we were making rather too much noise and shooed us, good-naturedly, to our respective rooms.

It was time to retire anyway. I said my prayers and climbed into bed, wondering as I did how my father was getting on with the Misses Donovan. I didn't think my campaign to have him marry Mrs. Surratt was over yet; he had admitted she was attractive, and wasn't that half the battle? Perhaps once I got a job and he realized I could support myself, he would not feel obliged to remain single for my sake.

Mrs. Surratt came in when I was half-asleep. "Good night," I murmured as she got in bed beside me.

"Nora —"

"What?"

"Nothing." My landlady stroked my hair

as I curled closer to her. "Go to sleep."

And so I did, only to be awoken briefly by some shouts. But I thought nothing of them. Since Richmond's fall, Washington's streets had echoed at night with the sounds of drunken revelers; as the boardinghouse backed up to a stable, we got to hear the sounds of the comings and goings of their horses and carriages as well. I drifted off again, this time into a deep slumber.

Then the doorbell rang.

■ ■ ■ ■

Part II

■ ■ ■ ■

"I was sound asleep when the fatal shot was fired. Thousands of times have I recalled it, for I was as contented as I could be . . . My sleep was peaceful; it was the sleep of innocence and of a clear conscience. I had done no wrong and meditated none. I owed no one a dollar, and as far as I know, in all the world, I had not an enemy."

— Louis J. Weichmann,
*A True History of the Assassination
of Abraham Lincoln and of the
Conspiracy of 1865*

"Here endeth the story of this tragedy upon a tragedy. All are glad that it is done. I am glad particularly. It has cost me how many journeyings to Washington, how many hot midnights at the telegraph office, how many gallops into wild places, and how much revolting familiarity with blood."

— George Alfred Townsend,
The Life, Crime, and Capture
of John Wilkes Booth

27
MARY
APRIL 15, 1865

I was wide-awake when the doorbell shattered the silence of the house. A couple of times since we had moved here, someone had rung our doorbell in the middle of the night — the first time by someone playing a boyish prank, the other time by an inebriate for whom one door on H Street was as good as another — and it had become the unspoken understanding that in such cases, one of the male boarders, in the absence of Johnny, would answer the summons. Sure enough, I heard footsteps come down the stairs and to the door.

Nora emerged from the covers. "What on earth . . . ?"

"The doorbell. Someone has gone to answer it."

Nora sighed. "I am thoroughly tired of drunkards," she announced.

A knock sounded on the bedroom door, and Mr. Weichmann called, "Mrs. Surratt?

Are you awake?"

"Yes."

"There are detectives at the door who want to search the house — and your room."

Nora gasped. I put a hand on her shoulder. "Ask them to wait a few moments, and I will open the door for them. Nora, help me get dressed."

Her hands shaking, Nora obeyed. "What on earth are they searching this house for?"

"We shall find out."

The parlor was already awash with gaslight when I opened the folding doors. Four men were standing there. The one closest to me said, "Ma'am? My name is Detective John Clarvoe. Metropolitan Police Force. Are you Mrs. Mary Surratt?"

"I am."

"Answer me one question, for all the world depends on it. When is the last time you saw John Wilkes Booth?"

So something had happened. Mr. Booth had kidnapped the president — or he had failed and was fleeing. "I saw him at around two this afternoon. I mean, yesterday afternoon."

"And when did you see your son John Surratt?"

"I saw him about two weeks ago, on the

day Richmond fell."

"Where is he?"

"I believe he is in Canada. I received a letter from him on Friday dated from Montreal."

"But you do not know for certain where he is?"

"I told you, the last I heard he was in Canada. This is wartime. There are many mothers who do not know where their sons are. What is the meaning of all this?"

Detective Clarvoe ignored my question and turned to confer with his companions.

Mr. Weichmann, dressed in a half-open nightshirt and pantaloons, pushed his way forward. "They have not told you?"

"No. They have not told me anything, only peppered me with questions about Johnny. What has happened?"

"President Lincoln has been murdered by John Wilkes Booth, and Secretary of State Seward has been attacked in his bed."

Murdered. Not kidnapped. "My God, Mr. Weichmann! You do not tell me so."

Beside me, Nora swayed, and Mr. Weichmann quickly helped her to the sofa. "It can't be true," she whispered.

"It is true, except that I should not have used the word *murdered* just yet. He has been shot, but he still lives. There is no hope of recovery."

A second detective pushed his way past Mr. Weichmann. "Detective James McDevitt. Is this your room, ma'am?"

I nodded.

"I am going to search it."

I stood in my doorway as Detective McDevitt rifled through the wardrobe and Nora's trunk, pulled out the trundle bed, shone his lantern under the big bed, and stepped out onto the sleeping porch. Nora had roused herself enough to stand beside me and watch, tears streaming down her face. There was no Mr. Booth in our room, no Johnny, and his search was soon finished. Detective McDevitt turned to me. "You said your son wrote you a letter from Canada. Where is the letter?"

I would be foolish to say I burned it. "I do not know. I tossed it aside."

"You tossed aside your son's letter?"

"It was a short letter with nothing of consequence. He complained about his lodgings being too expensive and said that he would be moving to a boardinghouse, or even to Toronto." I nodded to Nora. "Child, can you look for the letter?"

Nora started aimlessly searching through the secretary. "I can't find it!" she wailed.

"It is all right, Nora. You did your best."

Mrs. Holohan and Miss Holohan came into the parlor. Miss Holohan was barely awake, but Mrs. Holohan asked, "What in the world is going on here? I heard the doorbell ring and looked out the window and saw all of these men standing on the stairs. What is this I hear about the president being shot? Surely it is a wild rumor?"

Mr. Weichmann shook his head. "Detective Clarvoe showed me the cravat he was wearing when he was shot. It is covered with blood."

Nora shakily made the sign of the cross and began to weep anew. Mr. Weichmann put his arm around her shoulder and stared into space, his face thoughtful.

We heard footsteps coming down the stairs, and Mr. Holohan, Anna, and Olivia, followed by Detective Clarvoe, entered the parlor. If Nora looked ghastly, Anna looked like the face of death itself. She was leaning heavily on Mr. Holohan, but she broke free and ran into my arms. "Is it true what Mr. Holohan said? These men are saying that Mr. Booth shot the president!"

Only if I measured my words in the shortest quantities could I keep from blurting out that I had never agreed to help Mr. Booth do murder; I had never dreamed he would do murder.

"It appears to be so."

Anna sank into a chair, her hand over her eyes, and moaned.

Nora faltered. "Where was he shot? When?"

Detective Clarvoe must have known the answer to this, but he said nothing, and none of us dared to speculate in his presence. The clock struck three, and soon thereafter Susan was brought upstairs by one of the detectives. So now the entire household, white and black, was assembled in the parlor.

One cannot negotiate over a corpse. Had he been deceiving me all along? Or had some devilry caused him to change his plan from kidnapping to killing?

The four detectives conferred in the hall. Then Detective Clarvoe said, "We've found nothing, but we're going to be keeping an eye on this place. If John Wilkes Booth should come here, or John Surratt, you are to notify the police immediately, or the consequences won't be pretty. Understood?"

Everyone nodded.

"Mr. Weichmann, Mr. Holohan, as the men in this house, I'll expect both of you at the station at nine sharp. No later."

The detectives filed out of the house.

When they were gone, Mr. Holohan said, "Clarvoe let drop up there that the president was shot at a theater, but he didn't say which one. I daresay it wasn't the Canterbury, though." He looked sheepish. "Sorry, not a time for a joke."

Nora turned her tear-streaked face toward Mr. Holohan. "A theater! Father was at the theater! I have to go look for him."

"You'll look for no one, Miss Fitzpatrick," Mr. Holohan said. "It's the middle of the night, and from what else the police let drop, the mood out there is ugly. Besides, the police are looking at this place very closely. Bolt out of here, and you'll bring yourself under suspicion."

"We're under suspicion already," Anna said, "with Mr. Booth being here on the very day of the assassination." She turned a terrified face to me. "Ma, they were looking for Johnny too. Why?"

Mr. Weichmann stared at his hands. "I believe he is suspected of attacking Secretary Seward."

Anna managed to glare at Mr. Weichmann. "But he's not even in Washington! How dare they accuse him of this crime! Why are you saying such nonsense?"

"Now, now," Mr. Holohan said soothingly. "We'll all know better what's being said

309

tomorrow. We just need to go to bed and get what sleep we can. Mr. Weichmann and I will have to get an early start."

He took his wife and daughter by the hands and led them away calmly. Susan followed his example, after I nodded permission for her to do so. Mr. Weichmann rose slowly and made his way toward the stairs, and I said to Anna and Olivia, "Go. Mr. Holohan is right. In the morning, all will become clearer." I hesitated. "Nora, be a dear and lie down upstairs with Anna and Olivia. I need to be by myself at the moment. These suspicions about Johnny are upsetting to me."

Nora did not protest. Her head drooping, she trudged out of the parlor.

Alone, I entered my bedroom. It was a shambles, with any space large enough to hide a man having been ransacked. The bedding lay in a heap on the floor, and my gowns had been taken out of the wardrobe and tossed aside. But I was grateful for the disorder; it gave me something to do as I contemplated the unspeakable: the president was dying, Mr. Booth had shot him and gone the Lord knows where, and Johnny — my dear Johnny! — was under suspicion as well.

And with a word to the right people, I could have stopped it all. Why didn't I?

28
NORA

APRIL 15, 1865

You know — everyone knows — what happened on the night of April 14, 1865. You have even perhaps grown hardened to such things, having lived through, or heard of, the shooting of President Garfield as well. Nothing, you might say, can really surprise you anymore.

So how to make you realize how it was to wake that morning of April 15 to learn that the president had been shot? It was as if the world had slipped off its axis, and no one knew whether it could be put back on again.

It was, simply speaking, the bleakest day in American history. And for those of us in Mrs. Surratt's boardinghouse, hearing the crime had been committed by a man we all knew and liked — or loved — it was all the bleaker.

For a solid hour after the doorbell rang in the small hours of the morning, four detec-

312

tives roamed around the boardinghouse, looking for Mr. Booth and Mr. Surratt, and in general, making us feel, in the words of Dickens, that we had committed all of the crimes in the Newgate calendar. Finally they departed, leaving us in the parlor to wonder what was going to happen next. At last, Mr. Holohan said we should all go back to bed. I was following Mrs. Surratt to our bedroom when she said, "Nora, be a dear and lie down upstairs with Anna and Olivia. I need to be by myself at the moment. These suspicions about Johnny are upsetting to me."

I nodded, for what mother wouldn't feel the same, knowing all of Washington was searching for her son? I shuffled upstairs to the room Anna and Miss Jenkins shared and knocked. "May I sleep here tonight?"

There were whispers, and Miss Jenkins opened the door. "Anna's too upset, Miss Fitzpatrick, to be with anyone now. If you don't mind —"

"No," I muttered. This was getting ridiculous. I trudged back down to the second floor. Mr. Weichmann's room was clearly out of the question, but perhaps I could share a bed with the Holohan girl, who had a little room to herself.

Then I heard the not-at-all-unfamiliar

sound of Mr. and Mrs. Holohan quarreling. Mrs. Holohan's voice, soft but clear, came through the door. "I demand that we leave here immediately! Else we could wake up dead in our beds."

I sourly wondered how a person could manage that.

It was clear there would be no hospitality for me there either. Sighing, I descended to the parlor. I pulled someone's shawl from a peg in the hall and, to his no small disgust, rearranged Mr. Rochester on the sofa before curling up on it, wrapping the shawl around me. After some pacing about, Mr. Rochester finally settled himself around my feet.

It wasn't as if I stood much of a chance of getting any more sleep that night anyway.

At half past six, we all filed downstairs for breakfast — all except Mr. Holohan and Mr. Weichmann, who had left the house quietly before dawn in search of news, and Anna, whom Miss Jenkins said was feeling ill and would lie abed a little longer. By the time we had gathered around the table, the men came in, bearing the *Daily Morning Chronicle,* and we sat and listened to Mr. Weichmann read the account of the assassination aloud.

At half past ten o'clock last night, in the front upper left-hand private box in Ford's Theatre, while the second scene of the third act of "Our American Cousin" was being played, a pistol was fired, and Abraham Lincoln shot through the neck and lower part of the head. A second after the shot was fired, a man vaulted over the baluster of the box, saying, *"Sic semper tyrannis!"* and, adding another sentence, which closed with the words "revenge for the South," ran across the stage with a gleaming knife, double-edged and straight, in his right hand. The man was of middle stature, well-built, white-faced, and beardless, save that he wore a black mustache. His hair and eyes were black.

The crowd ascended the stage; the actresses, pale beneath their rouge, ran wildly about. Miss Keene, whose benefit night it was, came forward, endeavoring to quiet the audience. Several gentlemen climbed to the box, and finally the audience was ordered out by some gentlemen.

Mrs. Lincoln, Miss Harris, and Major Rathbone were in the box with the President.

The report of an assassination attempted upon Secretary Seward having reached this office, we set out for the Secretary's house, and there found that he too had been assaulted. We learned also that at ten o'clock, just as the man in charge of Lafayette Square called out that the gates were closed, a man made his way into Secretary Seward's house, representing that he was the bearer of a medicine prescribed by Surgeon General Barnes, and which he was ordered to deliver to Secretary Seward in person.

Pushing into the Secretary's room, he seized the old, suffering statesman with one hand and cut him with a dagger knife on both jaws, then turned and forced his way into the hall, where, meeting with Frederick Seward, the Secretary's son, he attacked him and inflicted three wounds with a dagger knife (probably the same) on the young man's head, breast, and hand. He also attacked Major Clarence Seward, another son of the Secretary of State, and inflicted upon him several serious wounds.

The assassin then rushed out, mounted a bay horse with light mane, and rode off, not at a gallop, but at what is called a "pace."

Doctors Barnes, Norris, and Nutson were soon in attendance and did all in their power for the sufferers.

Secretary Seward was able to speak and swallow, but both caused him much pain, though none of the arteries of the throat were cut. The doctors all agreed that the Secretary was in no immediate danger of losing his life.

Secretaries Stanton and Welles, as soon as they learned the solemn news, repaired to the residence of Mr. Seward, and also to the bedside of the President.

Anna walked into the kitchen and poured herself a cup of coffee. "Go on," she said tonelessly.

"Shall I read ahead a little?"

"Do what you like."

Several persons were called upon to testify, and the evidence, as elicited before an informal tribunal, and not under oath, was conclusive to this point: the murderer of President Lincoln was John Wilkes Booth. His hat was found in the private box and identified by several persons who had seen him within the last two days, and the spur he dropped by accident, after he jumped to the stage, was identified as one of those he obtained from the stable where he hired his horse.

This man Booth has played more than

once at Ford's Theatre and is, of course, acquainted with its exits and entrances, and the facility with which he escaped behind the scenes is easily understood. He is the son of Junius Brutus Booth, the renowned actor, and has, like one of his brothers, in vain attempted to gain a reputation on the stage. His father was an Englishman, and he was born in Baltimore. He has long been a man of intemperate habits and subject to temporary fits of great excitement. His capture is certain, but if he is true to his nature, he will commit suicide and thus appropriately end his career.

"That's quite enough," Anna said. She shoved her toast away.

"May I, Mr. Weichmann?" I took the newspaper he handed to me. After scanning it, I patted Mrs. Surratt's hand. "There's nothing about Mr. Surratt here, ma'am. Perhaps they've given up on that idea."

"Perhaps," Mrs. Surratt said in nearly as toneless a voice as Anna's.

At about half past seven, we heard shouting coming from the street. It was like no shout I have ever heard before or since; it was as if all of Washington had let out a collective cry of anguish. "Dead!"

I threw down the knife with which I had been making a show of buttering my bread and ran out the kitchen door. There on the street, people were standing in the dripping rain with bowed heads, weeping. "The president is dead?" I asked a man.

"Yes, miss. He died at seven twenty-two."

I leaned my head against the door and, for about the fifth time in so many hours, sobbed my heart out.

I have always taken great comfort in newspapers. No matter how horrid an event, there is something in seeing it described in black and white that makes it somehow bearable. So as soon as I calmed myself, I ran upstairs, grabbed some coins, and went outside to buy all of the Washington papers, which I was studying intently as Mr. Holohan and Mr. Weichmann started out the door to go to the police. "What will you tell them, Mr. Weichmann?" Anna asked.

"The truth, Miss Surratt."

The men had been gone for about an hour when the doorbell rang. Before anyone could answer it, in strode my father. Usually the embodiment of courtesy, he did not even say good morning, but he grabbed me by the arm as we all rose. "Mrs. Surratt. Is it true that your son is a suspect in this vile act?"

"I have been told that, sir. But he is innocent."

"And I have no need to ask whether that creature Booth was received here. What have you done, woman, by harboring this serpent? Wasn't it enough to compromise your own reputation and that of your innocent daughter without dragging my own girl's name into the mire as well? What have you done?"

Mrs. Surratt's lips barely moved. "Nothing, sir, gave me any indication that Mr. Booth was capable of such an act. If I had had any inkling, I assure you, he would have never entered this house. I am a parent no less than you."

"It matters not. The damage is done. My daughter shall not stay another moment in this place. Come along, Nora!" When I did not move, he wrenched at my arm so hard I squealed in pain. "Come along! I will send a man for your things later."

"No!" I tore myself from my father's grasp. "It is a mistake, Father. John Surratt is in Canada. He had nothing to do with this." I ran to Mrs. Surratt's side and put my arms about her. "Father, Mrs. Surratt has been like a mother to me. I will not desert her when she most needs friends. You will have to drag me from her house. Bodily! By my hair!"

Father's face turned red, and for a moment, I thought he was going to seize me by my hair. But he dropped to a chair, put his head in his hands, and wept — something I had seen him do only once before, on the day my mother and baby sister died.

I crouched by his side. "Father, please don't cry."

My father raised his head. "I was at the play last night, you know. I didn't know until I arrived there that the president would be coming. I shall never forget when he came in, how delighted the audience was to see him. The play had already started, and the actors stopped it long enough for him and his party to be welcomed, and then it resumed. I couldn't see his box well from where I was sitting, but I could feel his presence — all of us could.

"We all thought the shot, the man jumping to the stage, were part of the show at first. Until we heard a woman's screams — Mrs. Lincoln's screams. I shall never forget those screams. They will haunt me forever.

"All during this cursed war, I have kept silent. It is a necessity, when one's business brings one in contact with people from different sides. But there is no man I have admired more than the president; for me, he embodied all that I came to America for. Of all of the great men in Washington I have encountered, and there have been many, his is the one hand I have always wanted to shake, but I never quite got the courage to do so. Just yesterday morning, I was thinking that perhaps I could at last seize the chance to do so the next time the White House was open. Instead, ever since I saw the Misses Donovan safely to their house, I have been standing outside that miserable boardinghouse by Ford's, keeping vigil with the rest, and this morning I watched as they carried him out. Dead."

He stood slowly, looking every bit his age. "I should have told him that I honored and loved him while I had a chance. I should not have let expedience get in the way of my loyalty. Because of that, I will not force my daughter to go against her own loyalties. She can remain here — unless it should prove that your son was indeed complicit in this crime. Then she must go."

"I promise you, sir, with all my heart, he is innocent. But should every instinct of a mother prove wrong, then I will send her to you."

"Very well." He put on his hat.

I touched his arm. "Won't you stay, Father, for a little while, and take some tea? You look exhausted, and your clothes are wet."

"No. I am going to church to pray for our nation."

"Then I will come with you."

My father and I walked the short distance to St. Patrick's. It was as if we were walking in a different city than the Washington of the day before. Every so often, some late riser would saunter out of his house, clearly anticipating picking up the celebration from the previous night, and would ask a somber-looking passerby what had happened or would buy a paper from one of the grim-faced newsboys, and we would watch as his countenance changed entirely. Each time that happened, it was as if the horrid news had arrived anew.

My father and I said nothing along the way. Even if we had tried to speak, our words would have been blotted out by the sounds of hundreds of church bells ringing a death knell. Already St. Patrick's was packed with the bereaved and the despairing. We squeezed into a pew and knelt for an hour, praying and weeping, before my father finally raised me up and walked slowly back out into the dreary day and to

Mrs. Surratt's. In the short time we had been indoors, Washington had transformed itself. Houses that had been gaily bedecked in bunting were now draped in mourning, and people were streaming out of shops bearing black crepe and mourning ribbons. Even Mrs. Surratt's house had crepe on the lowest windows.

"You remember what I told you, my child. If John Surratt should prove to be Mr. Seward's assassin —"

"I will come to you." I kissed him on the cheek. "Father, please eat and go to bed. You look terrible, and you are at the age where you must take more care."

My father managed just a glimmer of a glare and walked slowly off.

In the parlor, Anna and Miss Jenkins sat side by side, sewing. "Is your father gone? Mercy, I thought he was going to attack us with his shillelagh."

I struck Anna as hard in the face as I could and ran into the bedroom. I must have been there a good half hour, sobbing, when someone knocked. Mrs. Surratt, I surmised, come to kick me out of the house, which would be ironic after I had made such a show of staying just a short time before. "Come in," I said dully.

Anna came in and sat beside me. "I'm

sorry. I shouldn't have said that."

"And I shouldn't have slapped you."

"Mrs. Holohan just gave notice that she is leaving. She's taking her daughter and moving in with her mother. But you chose to stay."

I shrugged. "Your mother's been like a mother to me. How could I run out on her? I like her."

"And you used to like me. I'm sorry we fell out, Nora."

"Over an assassin, no less."

"Is there any way they could be wrong, do you think? Maybe it was someone who looked like Mr. Booth. Some jealous rival trying to ruin his career."

This was an immensely appealing theory, but I had to shake my head. "I doubt it."

"Me too." Anna's eyes filled with tears. "I just can't believe he would do such a thing. God knows I hated Lincoln, but to murder him . . . How could we have loved such a man?"

I forbore from pointing out it was she, not me, who had been in love with Mr. Booth, although I supposed the kissing on my part could make someone rather suspicious. "It could be worse," I said philosophically. "We could be Miss Hale today."

"Everyone knows he came here. I boasted

of it — you boasted of it. We'll be shunned. There is no future for us in this city."

I put an arm around her waist.

"No one will want to board here," Anna continued. "The Holohans are going, and even Mr. Weichmann will go in September for the seminary, if he doesn't leave before that. Mrs. Dean certainly isn't going to let her little girl come back here as long as Johnny is under suspicion. How will we replace them? We'll have to rent the place out, just as we did before. I'll die if we have to move back to that tavern, with all of those crude country bumpkins coming and going. I'll enter a convent first. I swear it!"

"Maybe it won't be as bad as you think," I said. "Mr. Booth knew a lot of people. It's not just us."

"But they're looking for Johnny." Anna shook her head. "Even your father had heard they were. They have to be wrong about him. Johnny couldn't have been involved with this. He's simply not capable of murder."

"Of course he's not," I said. Then I remembered Mr. Booth comforting me after Private Flanagan's death, and putting a bullet into the president's head as Mrs. Lincoln sat next to him, and I decided perhaps it was best to reserve judgment about who was capable of what.

Anna started. "Someone's coming inside the house."

We hurried into the parlor, where Mrs. Surratt and Miss Jenkins were sitting. My mind was racing with optimistic and purely unwarranted thoughts: that John Surratt had come home to explain everything, that Mr. Booth would be standing in the parlor, shaking his handsome head incredulously and chuckling at the bizarre notion that he had killed the president. In my youthful optimism, I even briefly managed to resurrect the president himself; perhaps his death was a false rumor laid as bait to catch his would-be assassin. But it was only Mr. Weichmann and Mr. Holohan, with Detective McDevitt.

Mr. Weichmann looked distinctly unhappy. He said, "Mrs. Surratt, we are going to Maryland to search for Booth. And — and for Mr. Surratt."

Mrs. Surratt nodded. "You won't find my son there. He is in Canada."

"Be that as it may, the officers would like to have a photograph of Mr. Surratt to aid them." Mr. Weichmann gazed at the mantel. "Like that one."

I looked at the photograph as if seeing it for the first time. It had been taken several years back, before Mr. Surratt was capable of growing his present goatee, and was not, I thought, the most flattering image of him. Often, though, I had seen Mrs. Surratt's eyes travel to it wistfully on the many occasions when her son was away from home. "Take it," she said. "Perhaps it will show these people that my boy is not an assassin."

"Precisely what I was thinking," Mr. Weichmann said and tucked the photograph inside his coat.

After the detective and his reluctant companions left, I went out again in search of yet another newspaper. Instead of confining myself to H Street, I walked in the pouring rain to Ford's Theatre. Yesterday evening, this place had been ablaze with light. Now, like the rest of Washington, it was awash with black crepe. Guards stood at every doorway, keeping out the curious and the seekers of souvenirs — and worse. Last night, the crowd outside the theater had threatened to burn it to the ground, and even today, I saw a few men shaking their fists at the place. "I wonder if it will ever reopen," a woman next to me said.

Her companion shook his head. "They will never act a play in there again," he said.

"Bad luck."

Across the street was the boardinghouse to which they'd taken the dying president. The family who owned it had been opening the room in which the president died to the curious — it was either do that or be hounded to death — and after hesitating, I followed a group of people inside. There, inside a tiny bedroom barely large enough to hold a bed and a bureau, the president had died in a bed that was too short for him, his body covered by a patchwork quilt that was already missing a few patches. In front of me, a lady used the tip of her umbrella to peel off a bit of wallpaper and slipped it into her purse.

I wasn't so brazen. Instead, when I left the house, I plucked a flower growing out front to press in my album.

Someone had begun hawking mourning badges in the street, and I bought one and pinned it to my bodice before heading home. As I turned a corner, I screamed.

Two men were beating the life out of a third man as a crowd looked on, some cheering, some indifferent. As I watched, two policemen, wielding clubs, shoved their way through the crowd and managed to rescue the wretch from his attackers. As they dragged him away, using language I had not had occasion to hear before, I saw that his features were barely recognizable.

A man turned me around. "Get away from here, little missy. This isn't a sight for you."

"But what happened?"

"Fool made a joke about the president's murder. He's lucky he got away alive. As it is, he'll be waking up in Old Capitol Prison, I'll wager." The man glanced indifferently at the unconscious man, whose blood was mingling with the mud as the police hauled him along. "And if you think he's an ugly sight, just picture what John Wilkes Booth's handsome mug is going to look like if a crowd can get hold of him."

29
MARY
APRIL 15, 1865

Nora's face had been hidden behind a newspaper almost continually that day since we'd learned the president died. When she was not reading newspapers, she was out buying them, and it was after one of these excursions that she gasped.

"What is it, Nora?"

In a trembling voice, she read: "John Surratt, of Prince George's County, Maryland, is said to be the man who cut Mr. Seward, but as yet no clue to the direction he took, unless he went with Booth, has been obtained."

So it was confirmed; my boy was a suspect in this, the most horrid crime this nation had ever known. I went to my bedroom and prayed: first, that the detectives were wrong about my Johnny, and second, that they would never find him.

Soon after the *Evening Star* appeared, I had

a visitor: Father Wiget. He came on his horse, Jackson, who was a favorite of the local boys, which would ordinarily set off a friendly competition on H Street over who got to hold him but on this day resulted in only one volunteer. After Father Wiget and Nora exchanged some pleasantries about her brother, whom Father Wiget knew as both a pupil and a teacher, and about the upcoming fair to benefit Gonzaga College, she considerately left us alone together.

In a voice that still told of his native Switzerland, Father Wiget said, "Mrs. Surratt, I read the news, and I have come to offer what comfort I can."

"My son did not commit this crime, Father."

Father Wiget fingered the cross he wore around his neck. "Do you know that for certain, Mrs. Surratt?"

I stared out the window. I longed to tell him what Johnny and Mr. Booth did plan — and of my own role in the affair. But this good man might give the advice I most feared, which was to go to the authorities and tell them what I knew. Coming from a man of the church, it was not advice I would dare to ignore, and yet I dreaded what use my information might be put to against my son. Instead, I said, "It is a mother's instinct, no more. But I do know that he wrote me from Canada just a few days before, and I have no reason to believe that he would mislead me."

Father Wiget nodded, though I could not help but see the doubt in his eyes. Whether it was doubt of me or of Johnny, I could not say.

Still, he offered me what help he could. For an hour we prayed and talked together, and when he rose to leave, I felt a little more at peace. "One thing, Mrs. Surratt, and it is a trivial one. The wheelbarrow we at the college lent you some time ago: May we have it back? We have a need for it at present."

"Certainly. I should have returned it long ago. It slipped my mind."

"I will send a boy for it later, then."

The wheelbarrow had the word *Gonzaga* painted on it in large, bright letters. Clearly, it would not do for the school to have it sitting by the house of Mr. Booth's accomplice. The fact that Father Wiget was reluctant to tell me so made me feel a little less guilty about my much greater omission. "I will leave it where he can easily find it."

Father Wiget nodded, and I saw him to the door. He put on his shawl very slowly. "Mr. Booth attended a concert at the church with your son not that long ago," he finally said. "He was quite pleased with the music and gave a generous donation afterward — so very generous that I had been hoping that Mr. Surratt would bring him to our fair. They were laughing and joking together when they left the concert. They appeared to be the best of friends."

"They were close."

"So close, one must wonder if they had any secrets from each other." Father Wiget sighed. "Mrs. Surratt, I have known your son since he was a youngster. I would not like to see his immortal soul in peril. If he puts himself in contact with you, or if you have means of contacting him, tell him to make his confession."

Mr. William Kirby, an officer in the courts who was loosely related to me through his wife, called not long after Father Wiget took his leave. He had always been kind to me, and tonight was no exception, yet even he felt it necessary to advise me to tell the detectives of my son's whereabouts.

"I have told them: he is in Canada. How many times must I say that? He was not in Washington assaulting the secretary of state or helping Mr. Booth kill the president."

"I know. But if there is anything you are

keeping back, you should tell them. It might be something you think is entirely unimportant, after all." He gave me a winning smile, to which I did not respond, and said, "I did come out of concern for you, Mrs. Surratt. Has anyone threatened you or made you fearful for yourself?"

"No. It is only people not speaking to us who used to." I sighed, knowing how much this had hurt Anna. "And people thinking the worst of poor Johnny," I could not help but add pointedly.

Mr. Kirby nodded but stood his ground. "If he comes home, Mrs. Surratt," he said smoothly, "he can clear his name."

Mr. Weichmann and Mr. Holohan did not return for supper. We had taken our meal and retreated upstairs when a weary-looking Mr. Holohan entered the parlor. "Back from chasing wild geese," he informed us with unusual volubility for him.

"Where did you go?"

"First to the Navy Yard. The police had a lead about a young man named Davy Herold who might have been one of Booth's accomplices. No trace of him, but they talked to his mother and sisters, poor ladies."

Davy Herold. A faint memory of a

monkey-faced young man who stopped at our tavern from time to time came to mind. He had a job at a pharmacy in town, I recalled, but seemed to spend most of his time hunting in the Maryland countryside.

"Afterward, they went to your tavern, ma'am. They've learned that Booth passed into Maryland, and they think he might have stopped there. Mr. Lloyd said he never saw the man, though. After that it was in and around south Maryland. No trace." Mr. Holohan yawned. "Pardon me. Anyway, I'm off. Another long day tomorrow with the detectives. They're not through with me yet."

Fleetingly, I wondered if Mr. Lloyd was telling the truth about not having seen Mr. Booth at the tavern — but this was not something about which I could speculate before Mr. Holohan. "Wait. Where is Mr. Weichmann? Is he coming home tonight?"

"Oh," Mr. Holohan said carelessly, "he's under arrest. Not in prison but in custody. Settling down to sleep in the station with a knapsack for a pillow, last I saw him. Young man knows a bit too much, they think."

30
Nora

It being Easter, we naturally went to church — even Mrs. Holohan, who left off her packing long enough to attend early services. In hopes of avoiding attention, Mrs. Surratt and Anna went to the seven o'clock service at St. Patrick's. Father, my plans to match him with Mrs. Surratt in tatters, took me to the next service.

Black Easter, as everyone came to call it, was a strange occasion. Our church was half decorated for the joyous occasion of Our Savior's resurrection, half draped in mourning. The congregation — at least we ladies — was as mixed as the decorations. We at the boardinghouse had decided to leave aside our new Easter finery and dress in quiet colors and our usual bonnets, but others, without our peculiar need for delicacy, flaunted their gay dresses and brightly trimmed bonnets, commemorating the slain president only through the mourning buttons and ribbons that appeared on almost everyone's breast this Sunday. Still other ladies, however, had turned up in mourning, or at least half mourning, and one or two were in such unrelieved black, one would think they were trying to outmourn poor Mrs. Lincoln.

There was another boarder at church that morning: Mr. Weichmann, in company with Detective McDevitt. Father, who appeared to regard all of the men at the boarding-house with suspicion, gave him only a curt nod when he caught sight of us. So much for my father's own matchmaking plans, I supposed.

The manhunt for Mr. Booth and his accomplices had not stood still for this holy day. While we had been praying and singing hymns, Washington's walls had been festooned with wanted posters, which naturally everyone coming from church hastened to read — and to note the thirty-thousand-dollar reward being offered. There were no pictures, only a description of Mr. Booth that pained me to read, for I could so clearly see the jet-black hair that tended to curl and the black eyes described in the poster, could remember him standing in our parlor and inclining his head forward and looking down when he spoke, just as the placard said he did.

Mr. Surratt was not named on the poster, which described poor Secretary Seward's unnamed assailant in minute detail. "Why, this man is nothing like Mr. Surratt," I said as I read it. " 'Hair black, thick, full and straight' — Mr. Surratt's hair is light and thin. Face 'moderately full' and 'rather round' — Mr. Surratt's face is almost gaunt. 'Neck short' — Mr. Surratt is practically all neck. It can't be him, Father." I laughed for the first time since Friday evening. "Mrs. Surratt will be so pleased."

"Child, her son could still be involved in some way. He has been running the blockade, I have been told, and I fear that this plot reaches up to the highest levels of the Confederacy." He sighed. "I hope for Mrs. Surratt's sake that the young man took no part in this, for she seems a kindly woman. But I fear she may be deceived by maternal fondness about this young man's character."

We walked on in silence for a while before I said, "That description on the poster does remind me of someone I know. I just can't think of who."

Father looked at me sharply. "Someone who came to board with Mrs. Surratt?"

"Maybe. Several people passed through and stayed only a few days."

"You must tell the authorities when you remember."

"I know, Father. I will." I frowned. "But first I must think of who it is."

I came home to find Mr. Weichmann hurrying into the house. "You are back home, Mr. Weichmann?"

"Only for a change of shirt, Miss Fitzpatrick. The police are taking Mr. Holohan and me to Baltimore."

"Yes, I heard you were under arrest."

"I am assisting the police, Miss Fitzpatrick. I am a free man." Mr. Weichmann held his wrists in the air. "No irons, you see," he said with a pleasant smile. "Anyway, I must change."

Later that afternoon, I went to St. Matthew's to see a christening. I had gone to school with the child's mother, so the congregation, of course, was full of my classmates, not a few of whom I had managed to tell about my acquaintance with Mr. Booth. They, naturally, had passed this on, so after the service, when we gathered around to congratulate the parents and give our gifts, a little crowd formed around me. Had I known Mr. Booth long? Had I known him well? Did he ever say anything that made me think he would shoot the president?

"Of course I didn't know," I said. "If I had had any inkling, I would have told someone."

I would be saying that quite a bit in the weeks to come.

Mr. Kirby had come to check on Mrs. Surratt when I returned from church, so I left them and the rest of her family in the parlor and went into the bedroom. There, I delved into my trunk and pulled out my album. Holding it, I flipped past the usual keepsakes of a young lady's life — photographs of my family and my friends, school prizes, ticket stubs — until I reached the page where Mr. Booth stared out at me, as handsome as ever.

Why on earth had he done it? How could he have done it? I studied the picture for what must have been a solid hour, as if doing so would conjure up some sort of communication from Mr. Booth. Getting none, I pulled the picture out of the album, intending to feed it to the fire. It was certainly where Mr. Booth deserved to be after such a horrid act.

But whatever the Lord's decision about whether to feed Mr. Booth to the flames of hell, I found I couldn't do the same to his photograph. When had he ever done me an unkindness? I thought of him gently examining my locket with Private Flanagan's hair and comforting me, and my eyes welled with tears. No, even though Mr. Booth had committed the worst sin a man might commit, I couldn't bring myself to cast him out of my life. Instead, I slipped the photograph in between two others and closed the album.

No doubt hundreds of young women across America were looking at their own albums and deciding what to do with Mr. Booth's picture. I wondered what poor Miss Hale was doing with hers.

Mrs. Holohan came back late in the day on Monday to set out some laundry for Susan, who would be doing one more wash for the Holohans. "Guess where the detectives are dragging my husband and Mr. Weichmann now," Mrs. Holohan said to Mrs. Surratt as she came into the parlor. "Canada."

"To search for my son, I suppose."

"Yes. They're taking my husband so he can identify him. The more eyes the better, they say."

Mrs. Surratt stared out the window.

Besides Susan, the servant girl, there were

only four of us in the house now. Soon there would be three: Miss Jenkins was planning to take the coach back to Surrattsville on Tuesday. As Anna had predicted, Miss Dean, who was supposed to have returned that afternoon, had not. "You can sleep in Miss Holohan's room if you'd like a little privacy," Mrs. Surratt offered that night as we sat around knitting — all but Anna, whose cold had become worse. She was lying stretched out on the sofa, thumbing restlessly through *Godey's Lady's Book.*

"I'd rather stay with you, Mrs. Surratt."

She gave me a smile. "Thank you, dear girl."

I turned to Anna. "So what will we be wearing next fall?"

"Who cares?"

I went back to my knitting. "Sorry."

Anna raised herself to a sitting position. "Ma, what will happen if Mr. Weichmann finds Johnny?"

"They will bring him here for trial, I imagine, and he will be found innocent. Don't fret so, dear one."

"And they will hang Mr. Booth if they try him," Anna said. She lay back down listlessly and turned her face to the back of the sofa. Absently, Mrs. Surratt patted her head.

I looked up from my knitting and frowned.

I had never been much for feeling odd sensations, but over the past few minutes, I had been unable to concentrate for the feeling that something was peculiar. With everyone in such dismal spirits over the hunt for Mr. Surratt, though, I said nothing.

Then we all heard it: footsteps, coming up the stairs to the door, followed by the familiar ring. Mrs. Surratt opened the window. "Mr. Kirby?" she called.

"No, but we must come in, if this is Mrs. Surratt's house."

Anna sat up. "Ma, don't go!"

"I must, child. Perhaps they have news of your brother."

I heard voices, too indistinct for me to make out. Mrs. Surratt, trailed by several men, came into the parlor. "Young ladies," she said. "You must hear what I have to say calmly. We are all under arrest."

31
MARY

APRIL 17, 1865

Since Saturday, I had known the police were not done with us — not after they arrested Mr. Weichmann. But I did not expect them to turn up at the door late Monday night, just when most of Washington was going to bed.

As was the case of the night of the assassination, there were four of them, but none had been here before, and two of them wore army uniforms. It was one of these — senior in rank, I supposed, although I was not versed in army insignia — who said, "Mrs. Surratt?"

"I am Mary Surratt, the widow of John Surratt."

"And the mother of John Harrison Surratt?"

"Yes."

The officer held up a piece of paper. "Major Smith, U.S. Army. I have orders, ma'am, from the government to arrest everyone in this house and to search the premises. You will be taken to the headquarters of General Augur, the provost marshal for the district."

So we would not be in the hands of the Washington police, but the military. I took a breath to steady myself. "Everyone, sir?"

"Everyone."

I turned without a word and went in the parlor, where I broke the news to the young ladies. Olivia and Nora took the news quietly, as I had expected, but Anna began crying.

Major Smith glanced at her. "Who is that, Mrs. Surratt?"

"My daughter, Anna. She is sick, sir. Must she —"

"Yes, everyone must go. And the other two?"

"My niece, Miss Jenkins, and one of my boarders, Miss Fitzpatrick."

"Anyone else here?"

"Only a colored servant."

"Where? Abed?"

"No. She is usually in the kitchen at this time of night."

Major Smith nodded to the detectives. "See to her. We don't need her at the general's office at present, but keep her here. She may have information to give us.

Detective DeVoe, get the carriage. Bring it within only a half block. We don't want to scare that Mr. Kirby away."

"Sir, Mr. Kirby is an upstanding man and a native of Washington. He has never been in trouble."

"That may be, ma'am. I don't doubt it. But you called down to us as if you were expecting him, and it's our business to know what business he has here." Major Smith turned back to Detective DeVoe, who had been standing stock still. "The carriage, sir."

"Walking is good enough for this lot."

"It certainly is not. One of the young ladies is sick. I will have her and the rest treated with common courtesy. Now get the carriage."

I squeezed Anna's hand. Major Smith said briskly, "It is a chilly night, ma'am. Come with me and collect what hats and cloaks you and the others need. Captain Wermers-kirch, stay in here with the young ladies. Do not allow them to talk amongst themselves."

With Major Smith trailing behind, I walked to Anna and Olivia's attic room and got their warm things, plus boots for Anna, who had been wearing only a pair of flimsy slippers. In the room Nora and I shared, I reached for Nora's beautiful Kashmir shawl, but Major Smith shook his head. "The

347

young lady won't want that in Old Capitol Prison, ma'am. Get her something plainer, if she has one."

"I thought we were going to General Augur's office, sir."

"We are, but then to Old Capitol Prison."

Old Capitol Prison, where spies, deserters, and miscreants of all stripes went. A memory of my threatening Johnny with it flashed through my mind. I could have never sent him to such a place, and he knew it. "I am ready."

Major Smith nodded. "Very fast you are, ma'am."

I gave Anna her shoes, but she stared at them as blankly as a native of deepest Africa. So I knelt beside her and eased her feet into them as Anna began to weep. "Do not behave yourself so, little one," I said, reverting to my address for Anna when she was still in short skirts. "You are already so worn out with anxiety that you will make yourself sick. The officer who arrested us is in uniform and is a gentlemen and will treat us kindly."

"But, Ma, he told us that we were to go to Old Capital Prison! To be taken there!" Anna began to sob again.

"Hush!" In her ear I whispered, "You must be brave for the South, and for

Johnny."

To my surprise, this actually worked. Anna nodded and sat back quietly.

With all four of us ready to go, I turned to Major Smith. "Sir, I would like to pray before we leave."

"Certainly, madam."

I knelt by the piano, and the girls, while remaining seated, bowed their heads. Silently, I prayed the Lord would keep them safe and give me courage to withstand my coming ordeal. I begged him, as I had every night since Good Friday, for his forgiveness for my role in what had happened. While I acknowledged that Johnny's fate was in his hands, I asked that he keep my boy safe. And finally — although it might not have been entirely right to do so — I asked his help in not saying anything that would get my son into more trouble.

When I was done, I raised my head meekly, knowing everyone had been waiting for me to finish. But Major Smith said, "Have a seat, Mrs. Surratt. I would have thought DeVoe would be here with the carriage by now, but he's not." He paced around a bit before saying to his companions, "Whoever comes here must be kept inside for questioning. If the doorbell rings, let the caller in, then close the door behind him."

Beside me, Nora whispered, "All that for poor Mr. Kirby?"

"I heard that, miss," said Major Smith.

Nora nodded and gestured to Mr. Rochester, who had come into the parlor to give the soldiers a disdainful look. He jumped into her lap, and she cuddled him close to her. Anna leaned against my shoulder, and Olivia wiped a tear from her eye.

And then we all heard footsteps on the stair, followed by the doorbell's peal.

I almost rose to answer it before remembering the circumstances. Instead, Captain Wermerskirch and the one I had heard called Mr. Morgan headed to the door, and Major Smith planted himself in the doorway leading from the parlor to the hall. After a rumble of conversation, he headed into the hallway, and after a few minutes more, he called for me. Standing in the hall was a stranger in a sort of skullcap.

"This man says that he was hired to dig a gutter for you." Major Smith held up a pickax. "He brought this with him. Did you engage him to do so? Do you know him?"

I raised my hand. "Before God, sir, I do not know this man. I have not seen him before, and I did not hire him to come dig a gutter for me."

Major Smith nodded. "Sir, your story does not hang together. I am placing you under arrest. Madam, return to the parlor."

As soon as I took my place in the parlor — occupied only by us ladies at present — Anna asked, "Who was that, Ma?"

"A hard-looking fellow with a skullcap, who came here with a pickax."

Anna began to cry once again. "He must have come to murder us," she wailed. "Had those men not been here —"

Captain Wermerskirch stuck his head inside the door and raised his finger to his lips, and Anna fell silent.

It was nearly midnight when Major Smith finally informed us that our carriage was here. As if Anna were an invalid, Olivia and I helped her to her feet, while Nora gave her cat one last hug. As we walked into the hall, I saw the man with the pickax slumped in a chair opposite the parlor door, guarded by one of the soldiers.

As our carriage rolled through the mist and fog of an April night in Washington, Detective DeVoe, riding in front beside me while the young ladies crowded together in a heap of skirts and hoops in the back, gruffly informed me that I should not expect much of General Augur's headquarters; due to a fire, he had had to relocate to Fourteenth Street. "I am certain they will be adequate," I said inanely.

When we reached our destination, Detective DeVoe hustled us out of the carriage and into a dingy room with a motley collection of chairs, in which he ordered the young ladies to sit and (changing to a more genial tone) to have a catnap if they wished. Leaving them in the company of a young soldier, he led me into a room where a man stood behind a large desk and another one sat behind a stack of paper, inkwells, and ink pens. Waving me to an upholstered chair, considerably more comfortable than those in which the young ladies were sitting, the man behind the desk said, "Colonel Foster. I would like to ask you a few questions. First, tell me where you live, and who lives there with you."

I gave him the information.

"You did not mention your son John Surratt. Does he stay with you?"

"When he is in town he does."

"And when did you last see him?"

"On April 3 of this year. The day Richmond fell."

"He is a friend of John Wilkes Booth?"

"They are acquainted."

"When did they make their acquaintance?"

Wearily, I tried to think back. "I cannot say exactly when."

"Mr. Booth has been a regular visitor to your house?"

"Yes."

"How often did he call? Once a week? Several times a week? Once a day? Twice a day?"

"Sometimes twice a day."

Colonel Foster raised his eyebrows.

"We found him very much of a gentleman."

"Yes, it seems you did. Did your son mention how he came to know Mr. Booth?"

"Not that I recall," I lied tiredly.

"Weren't you at all curious about how your son made the acquaintance of one of the country's most sought-after actors? Did you not find it odd?"

"My son is a country-bred young gentleman. I consider him capable of forming acquaintances in the best society. Besides, Mr. Booth often called when my son was not there. Sometimes he asked for him, sometimes he did not."

"Since the murder, have you not wondered what brought Mr. Booth and your son together?"

353

"Certainly, but I cannot account for it. I do not think anyone was more surprised when we heard that Mr. Booth could be guilty of such an act. He was very clear of politics, and it was a subject that we never indulged in when he visited."

Colonel Foster looked at me intently. "What are your political sentiments?"

"I don't pretend to express my feelings at all. I have often said that I thought that the South acted too hastily. That is about the amount of my feeling." Another lie. How many more would I have to tell?

"Did your son say where he was going when he left you?"

"No. He went out with Mr. Weichmann, who came back without him and said that my son had bid him good-bye. On Wednesday, my son sent me a letter saying that he was laying over in Springfield, Massachusetts, because he had overslept and the conductor neglected to wake him. He did not tell me where he was going, but I think he was going to Canada, because I had heard him say several times that he would leave the country. Last fall he spoke several times of going to Europe. I supposed he had gone to Canada, but I had no particular reasons for so supposing. He had not made any arrangements for going to Europe or

Canada."

"Where is the letter?"

"I have hunted my house over but cannot find the letter he wrote me. I laid it on the windowsill and have not seen it since."

Colonel Foster continued to fire questions at me. How long did it take to cross the Potomac River? How often had Johnny crossed the river? Did I know Mr. Atzerodt? Did he board with me? Who else came to board with me? Who had come to the house since the assassination? Some of his questions simply baffled me, so even when I was not trying to be evasive, I sounded like I was.

Then Colonel Foster asked me a question I understood perfectly well. "Do you think your son was at the theater with Booth?"

I sat up straight. "Not if it was the last word I had to speak."

32
NORA

APRIL 17 TO 18, 1865

After Mrs. Surratt broke the news to us that we were under arrest, we were put into the care of a Captain Wermerskirch and ordered not to talk amongst ourselves while the head of the arresting party, Major Smith, accompanied her to get our wraps. As we had not been ordered not to talk to Captain Wermerskirch, I asked, "Where are they taking us?"

"First to General Augur's office for questioning. Then to Old Capitol Prison."

We all three started up. "But that's for spies and traitors!" I said.

Captain Wermerskirch gave an if-the-shoe-fits-wear-it sort of shrug. "You'll be in good company," he offered. "Belle Boyd was there for a time. So was Rose Greenhow."

"They were spies," I snapped. "We're not." I leaned back and drummed my fingers nervously on a table. "My father! He won't know what has become of me!"

"You can send him a letter from prison, miss."

I settled back and gloomily composed the letter in my head. *Dear Father, You will be surprised to learn that I am at present confined in the Old Capital Prison, among spies and traitors . . .*

For what seemed to be an endless time, we sat there waiting to be transported to General Augur's headquarters, the only relief from the monotony being when a stranger came to the door. A young ruffian was all Mrs. Surratt, who was called to the hallway to get a look at him, would or could say. It was not until around midnight when we were at last filing through the hall on our way to the carriage that I saw him for myself. He had sort of a stocking cap jammed upon his head, and he was far too large for the dainty little chair in which he sat. But it was the look on his face that struck me most. Never had I seen an expression so entirely bereft of hope.

His dejection fed mine as I looked back to see that the men were already beginning to search the house, flinging open doors and yanking out drawers. In an hour, these men would know everything about us that our belongings could tell.

And what would happen when they found

357

my photograph of Mr. Booth?

"Come along, miss. Don't poke."

I looked back one last time. "Someone please feed my cat!" I called as the door closed behind me.

At General Augur's headquarters, Mrs. Surratt was taken away for questioning and the rest of us were put in a sort of waiting room. We were half dozing when the carriage, having made a trip back to the boardinghouse, returned with the man from the hallway. As Mrs. Surratt was still being questioned, they took him to another part of the room, separated from the rest by a railing, and hustled him into a seat. He was in handcuffs and could not remove his cap, so they yanked it off his head.

Mr. Payne!

I looked at him as closely as I could without being downright rude — not that Mr. Payne was in a position to complain. For he indeed *was* Mr. Payne. It was the odd cap that had kept me from recognizing him before, and now that I saw it lying on the floor, it did not appear to be a proper cap at all, but some makeshift one. There was the same black hair, the same muscular build, and those same piercing eyes. With his overcoat removed, I saw he was even wearing the same clothes he had worn when he had escorted me to Ford's Theatre, although they were rumpled and dirty, and he himself was grimy. Had Mrs. Holohan seen him now, she would have been even more certain that he would not save many souls.

I looked harder at Mr. Payne. Suddenly the words of the wanted poster began to run through my head. *Hair black, thick, full and straight. Face moderately full. Nose straight and well formed. Mouth small. Neck short and of medium length.*

Why, this man could be the description come to life. And though I could not say for certain, not having seen the face, I would lay a bet that this was the man I had seen with Mr. Booth in Lafayette Square the night that President Lincoln talked of giving some colored men the vote.

I was surely not the only one who had noticed the resemblance of Mr. Payne to the poster. A trio of soldiers had gathered around Mr. Payne, asking sharp questions, which he appeared completely unequal to answering, judging from his drooping countenance. I could hear only bits and pieces of the interrogation, but one thing became clear: Mr. Payne was giving no clues as to who he might be.

No doubt I should have told someone that I recognized Mr. Payne. Had I recalled his identity under any other circumstances, I probably would have. But we were both here as prisoners, and was it not considered poor form to inform on a fellow prisoner? So I settled back and continued to listen to the soldiers hectoring Mr. Payne.

"You are John Harrison Surratt! Why don't you just tell us that, boy?"

Anna sprang up, her fists clenched. "How dare you say that!"

It was at that instant that Colonel Foster led in Mrs. Surratt, who was walking like a woman twenty years her senior. "Why, what on earth is the matter?" she asked tiredly.

"That man said that ugly creature was my brother. He is no gentleman to say so."

"My daughter speaks the truth, sir. This is not my son."

Unruffled, the soldier motioned to a subordinate. "Take the ladies into the other room. The boy from Seward's house will be here soon to take a look at this fellow. And, ladies — if you do know who this man is, besides his not being John Surratt as you claim, I suggest you tell us."

I pressed my lips together and followed the other ladies out of the room.

I had expected that the rest of us would be questioned, but since Mr. Payne's arrival, no one seemed to be interested in us, save for the bored soldier whose task it was to make sure we did not escape. Perhaps, I began to hope, we might be taken home after all. Anna leaned against Mrs. Surratt's shoulder and dozed off, and soon the rest of us followed suit.

It was nearly dawn when two men came in to blast my hopes. "All right, ladies. Time to go to the Old Capitol."

"How long will we be held?" Miss Jenkins asked.

"Depends on how cooperative you are, miss," said the soldier offhandedly.

We were going through the same waiting area where we had been held, but there was no sign of Mr. Payne. "What happened to that man?" I asked.

"Well, I suppose there's no harm in telling you, as it will be in the papers soon. Taken away in irons." He handed us into the carriage. "That colored boy from Seward's recognized him right away as the man who tried to murder the secretary. Pointed straight at him. Not a doubt in his mind. If he can do that in court, that man will hang."

Occasionally, when walking around the city, I would sometimes pass Old Capitol Prison. I usually avoided it, though, because not only was it a gloomy place to contemplate, but it also stunk to high heaven.

It had not been built as a prison. Congress had met there after the burning of Washington during the War of 1812, giving it its name, and afterward it had served as a boardinghouse before being bought by the government for its present use. Even more elegant had been the nearby Carroll Annex, consisting of five handsome houses in which a number of congressmen, including Abraham Lincoln, had boarded. But they had become run-down over time, and the government had bought the row as well, pressing it into service to house the ever-growing population of prisoners.

So I had learned from my father, before joining this select company.

From the moment our carriage pulled up at First Street and we alighted, I had the sensation of eyes upon me; very soon, I would learn that watching for new arrivals and guessing at what might have brought them here was one of the chief occupations of those residing there. After passing through the entrance guarded by two men with bayonets, we walked down into an office containing a conglomeration of desks and chairs but only one occupant at this early hour: the lieutenant in charge. "Good morning, ladies," he said, suppressing a yawn. "I must ask each of you some questions and search you. I'll start with this young lady, as you're closest."

I sat where he indicated. "First, empty your purse."

I obeyed, spilling its contents on the desk. It yielded only a handkerchief, a few coins, and my house key.

"Is that all the money you have?"

"Yes."

"Pity. You'll want a little spare change for the sutler's. Newspapers and pies and all that."

"If only I had known," I said dryly.

"What is your name?"

"Nora Fitzpatrick."

"Relation to James Fitzpatrick with the Metropolitan National Bank?"

"I am his younger daughter. And he has no idea where I am today."

"You can send him a letter. Age?"

"Nineteen," I lied, partly because in those days no one expected a lady to be entirely forthcoming about her age and partly because I was feeling contrary.

"Residence?"

"Washington. I was born here."

"Why were you arrested?"

I shook my head. "I have no idea."

"Accomplice to murder, I believe it is, like the rest of Booth's associates." My face must have matched the whitewashed prison walls, for he added, "Don't look so scared, miss. They haven't laid formal charges against anyone yet." He scribbled down some notes in a ledger. "All right, miss, you're done. When the others are ready, we'll take you to your room."

I nodded and watched as my companions underwent the same interrogation: Mrs. Surratt calmly, Anna haughtily, Miss Jenkins sleepily. Then the lieutenant whistled, and a guard came in. "Take the ladies to room 41 in the annex."

We followed the guard through the yard, muddy from the night's drizzle, in the direction of the once stately Carroll Annex. From a window, someone yelled, "Fresh fish!"

"Fish?" I asked.

The guard coughed. "That would be you ladies, miss. New prisoners."

"Pretty fish in pink," someone called.

"Nicely shaped fish in gray."

The guard glared and leveled his gun up

at the window. Anna in pink, and I in gray, stared at the ground.

Without further comment upon our persons, we passed up a flight of stairs and into a large room with an elegantly shaped window that looked out over the yard but had doubtlessly not been barred in this house's heyday. Two mice — oh, if only Mr. Rochester had been with me! — scurried into their holes as we entered and gazed around us. Four iron bedsteads, covered with blankets of indeterminate color, a couple of stools, a woodstove, and a table with a jug upon it completed the room's furnishings. Nails, placed at convenient intervals on the wall, would serve as hat and clothes racks.

"This is one of our nicest rooms," the guard said, nodding proprietarily as if this were the Willard. "Make yourself at home. You'll get your breakfast around nine. Oh, and you're free to mingle with the other ladies." He coughed and looked at Mrs. Surratt. "But you might want to take care, ma'am, that the young ladies don't mingle too freely. Some of the ladies here are — er — not ladies."

Left alone in our new surroundings, we looked to Mrs. Surratt for guidance. "Let us try to rest a little before breakfast," she said.

We obeyed, not daring to undress further than to remove our crinolines, lest a guard catch us in our dishabille. The beds we lay down upon were by no means comfortable, and I decided not to give much thought to the cleanliness of the linens and blanket, but soon we were fast asleep.

"Head count," a voice sang out, rousing us from what could not have been more than an hour or two of slumber. The door swung open, and two men, one holding a notebook, stepped into the room as we squealed in horror. "One — two — three — four. All right, ladies. Carry on."

As this seemed the signal to start our day, we began our morning toilettes as best we could. "Do you think they'll let us get some clean things from home?" Miss Jenkins asked.

"Don't count on it," a female voice called from behind the door. "Mrs. Catherine Baxley. May I come in?"

"Yes," Mrs. Surratt said.

A tall lady of about forty or so with light hair and blue eyes, who had somewhat of a masculine air, but who was not unattractive, entered the room. "Welcome to the Yankee hellhole," she said, holding out a shapely hand. "Mrs. Surratt and daughters?"

"One daughter, Anna. Miss Jenkins is my niece, and Miss Fitzpatrick my boarder."

"Quite a haul they got, then. To answer the miss's question, you can ask for a lot of things here, and usually they'll agree, but whether you ever get them is another matter altogether. But you can keep trying." In a softer voice, she asked Mrs. Surratt, "They're looking for your boy, aren't they?"

"They are."

"If you do know where he is, for God's sake, don't let anyone here know, and that includes your fellow prisoners. This place is full of Union spies, planted in amongst the prisoners."

"How do we know you aren't a spy?" Anna asked.

Mrs. Baxley gave her a freezing look. "Because I would throw myself upon the paving stones below before I would give this government a lick of help," she said. "My only child — a lad of but seventeen — is a prisoner here, and ill, and I have not been allowed to see him in days."

"I will pray for him," Mrs. Surratt said. She gave her daughter a rare disapproving look, which made poor Anna bow her head meekly. "We will all pray for the young man."

"How long have you been here?" I asked.

"First time, six months. This time, since January and counting." Mrs. Baxley sighed, then looked through the open door. "Now, these two are safe. Come in, ladies, and introduce yourself."

Mrs. Surratt opened her mouth, then closed it, as the pair obeyed Mrs. Baxley's command, their entry heralded by an overwhelming scent of cologne. Sheltered as I was, I realized straightaway what these ladies did for a living; no person over the age of ten could have been mistaken as to that.

"These are Maggie and Rosie," Mrs. Baxley said as the two, faced with such pillars of respectability such as ourselves, seemed reluctant to open the conversation. "Picked up the Saturday after the assassination, and for what? Just carrying on business as usual."

"Trying to cheer up the men," Maggie said.

"Everyone was so sad," Rosie said.

"We should have worn black ribbons," Maggie said. "I told you we should have been wearing them."

"I was wearing one. Just not on my —"

"Maggie, Rosie," Mrs. Surratt said.

"Please remember there are young ladies here."

"Aw, we're sorry," Maggie said. "We just get carried away."

"Nothing to do but talk here, you see," Rosie added.

"I hope you do not have to spend a long time here for such a trivial matter," Mrs. Surratt said kindly.

"Well, it's a rest," Maggie said philosophically. "They say we'll probably get out when Superintendent Wood gets back here. He has a heart for the working girl. But let's not wear out our welcome, Rosie."

"They're nice girls," Mrs. Baxley said after they had sauntered away. "Not the way I would choose to earn a living, mind you, but it's an honest living. Oh, here comes the slop."

I watched hungrily as two colored women bore in trays, which they set on the table. On the trays were two pots of coffee, four delft mugs, four slabs of bread, and an infinitesimal pat of butter. "Is this it?" Anna asked Mrs. Baxley as the servants went out just as they had come in, without a word.

"I'm afraid so, miss. Mind you, the men have it much worse. They have to go to a mess hall and push and shove to get what we get brought to us."

I poured myself some coffee, noticing as I did so that my cup was still wet, I hoped from washing. Though the sip I took of it was very cautious, I still sputtered as Mrs. Baxley looked on with sympathy. "What on earth is this?"

"Now, that's something no one here has ever figured out. In theory it's coffee, of course, but no one's certain what exactly is in it. It varies, and it hasn't killed anyone here yet. That's the best I can tell you."

I put the coffee down and stared at the bread. Mrs. Surratt reached for it. "Come, girls. We must eat or we will be ill."

"What if eating makes us ill?" Miss Jenkins asked.

Mrs. Surratt ignored this very sensible question and began to chew. We followed suit as Mrs. Baxley looked on. "Dinner will be even worse," she promised us.

33
MARY

I am ashamed to admit that normally I would not have cared to associate with such a woman as Mrs. Baxley. She was separated from her husband, and she spoke of her men friends in such a way that I wondered if they were much more than friends.

But she was a mother also, and her tale broke my heart. She had only one son, a lad of seventeen, and when she was imprisoned here the first time, the boy, then fourteen, was thrown upon his own resources — his father, I gathered, having no use for him. For a time, he found work at the sutler's here so he could be near his mother. When Mrs. Baxley, penniless, was released on the condition that she leave her Baltimore home behind and go south, he followed her, and at age fifteen, he enlisted in the Confederate army. Twice he had been captured and imprisoned by the Yankees. The first time, he was kept at Fort Delaware for nearly eighteen months; the second time, they brought him here.

"He has wasted away so, that when they brought him here with the other prisoners earlier, I did not recognize him, even though I was looking out the window when they came in," Mrs. Baxley told us. "He even called to me, 'All is lost! Our cause is hopeless, and I am badly wounded.' But I merely kissed my hand in sympathy toward him. Then that brute of an assistant superintendent, Wilson, came and told me, 'What do you think, madam? Your precious angel is here, and wounded. Birds of a feather, eh?' In the past, I would have scratched the man's eyes out, but instead I begged to see my boy. I had not seen him for two years. He refused. Superintendent Wood came back — a good man, I must say — and had him brought to the annex where I could nurse him. But Wood has gone away, and Wilson will not allow me to see my boy. And he was growing so weak."

I put my arm around her. "Who is nursing him?"

"A stranger, a colored servant here."

"Then let me ask if I can take your place until Superintendent Wood returns."

Mrs. Baxley whispered, "Thank you."

That afternoon, I sought out Mr. Wilson.

372

"I have a request for you, sir."

"Already?"

"I understand from Mrs. Baxley that her son is ill and that she is unable to see him."

"That woman's a damned nuisance — excuse me, madam, a nuisance. We let her see the lad, even moved him into a room all to himself so she could tend to him. And she started ranting and raving about how we were killing him by not giving him some chicken he begged for when he was out of his head. It's not a hotel we're running here, but we feed the boy well enough. She made her own bed; let her lie in it. She can see him when she can act a little more like a lady."

"I would like, sir, to have permission to nurse him myself. It would comfort her, and comfort him, I believe."

Mr. Wilson pondered this. "Well," he said at last. "I suppose there's no harm in it."

So I went to the garret room where young William Baxley, the pride of his mother's life, lay, and my heart broke for his mother. This boy was dying. The prison doctor told me he might have been saved had his injured leg been amputated, but it was too late for that now. There was little I could do for him but try to keep him comfortable and to calm him when his mind began to wander, as it

373

often did. Except at night and at the times when I went to my room to rest or to check on Anna, at which time the servant took over, I was always by his side.

His uniform was little better than rags, and he was painfully thin — God only knows when the lad last had a good meal. He was quite small for his age too. All in all, he looked more like a street urchin than a soldier.

The funeral procession for President Lincoln, held on Wednesday, terrified him. On the morning after the assassination, he had had a hemorrhage, and it was when he was in that weakened condition that he heard someone say a mob would storm the prison and murder all of the rebels inside. Since then, each time his fever climbed, he begged not to be tormented to death but to be shot quickly. I, at last, was compelled to give him some laudanum, and soon he was resting quietly.

He had a little diary with him, and — telling myself it would make me a better nurse if I knew him better — I could not stop myself from reading through it as he slept. Sadly, he recorded the deaths of various friends. Laconically, without any self-pity, he noted his own imprisonments and hospitalizations. He was no angel; at Fort Delaware, where he was held for a year and a half, he recounted the pranks he and his young friends played on the older prisoners. Once he got hold of some whiskey, and he liked a chew of tobacco. He longed for a real cup of coffee. Most of all, he longed for a sweetheart to write to, a set of whiskers, and a few more inches of height, all of which turned out to be related complaints, for the various young ladies he encountered were kind but treated him as they might their little brother, and even the camp followers shooed him off as too young for their services. He had never kissed a girl, he wrote while being held captive at City Point before being sent here, and he supposed that perhaps he never would.

I put down the diary and wept.

But he was not always delirious or even unhappy. Word had spread around the prison about his condition, so those prisoners who could afford it had the sutler send him delicacies, which he made a gallant effort at devouring. He adored his mother, and the only time I saw him lose his composure when in his senses was when he told me how his father beat her (something Mrs. Baxley had not mentioned) while he stood by, too young and small to come to her aid. I had his bed moved by the window so when he was able to, he could sit propped up against the pillows and watch the passersby. Though his diary led me to believe that in health he was outgoing, nearly as talkative as his mother, in his sickness he was content to be left to his own thoughts while I sat by his side and made what repairs I could to his uniform.

"You know what I'd like to do someday, Mrs. Surratt?" he asked once after several hours of silence.

I followed his eye to a pair of giggling young ladies passing by the prison. "What, dear?"

"Go to the Canterbury here." He blushed. "One of the men told me the girls there are really pretty."

"So I hear." I patted his hand. "When you are better, and when my own sons are back, perhaps you can make a party of it."

I was not at all certain how confident these *whens* sounded. But they seemed to give William hope, for when I next looked up, he was sleeping, a half smile on his face.

Superintendent Wood — a short, rumpled man who looked more like one of the prisoners than our keeper — returned on the day after the procession, and after much cajoling, he released two prostitutes who were imprisoned here, and who often stopped by our room to chatter. I did not believe they were bad girls at heart, but I confess I was glad to see them gone, for while I know Our Savior consorted with thieves and prostitutes, he did not have a daughter to think of.

But most importantly, Superintendent Wood ordered that Mrs. Baxley be admitted to her son's room again. My duties did not cease, however, for it turned out that the boy had grown attached to me, and Mrs. Baxley too needed comfort (and, she confessed to me, wanted a companion lest she again say something that would get her sent away). So a few times a day, I read to them from a little pocket Bible (found in William's uniform, and admittedly not very well thumbed) while Mrs. Baxley sat by her son's bedside, stroking his dark hair as mother and son listened to those words of heavenly comfort.

On Friday, Superintendent Wood came to our room. "I'm going to Maryland to help them look for Booth," he announced. "They've raised the reward to a hundred thousand dollars, and I'll be as happy as any other man to claim it. Fifty thousand for Booth, and twenty-five thousand each for Herold and your son John." He nodded toward Olivia. "And I'm taking you, young lady, with me, and returning you to your father's house. Maybe it might make the good people of Prince George's County a bit more forthcoming."

"Oh, thank the Lord! But can we stop by my aunt's house and get my clothes?"

"Of course." Superintendent Wood winked. "What's catching an assassin to making sure you have gowns? Besides, we'll be going to that neighborhood to pick up Kirby."

"Mr. Kirby?" I asked. "You mean my friend Mr. Kirby?"

"Yes, I've detailed him as part of my search party," Superintendent Wood said offhandedly. "He knows your son, and twenty-five thousand is nothing to sneeze at."

"Sir, is the reward for them dead or alive?"

"It doesn't say. But all in all, I imagine the authorities would prefer to have them taken alive."

I hugged Olivia, too distracted by thoughts of my son being led back here in chains, or carried in lifeless, to bid her a proper good-bye.

Mrs. Baxley cried when she heard of Superintendent Wood's departure, certain it would mean another separation from her boy. But not even Mr. Wilson would be so callous as to part them, for it was apparent that William Baxley had just hours to live.

Mr. Wilson sent for a priest, who heard the young man's confession and gave him the last rites before leaving the boy and his mother alone, with me nearby as requested. William was very weak but generally in his senses, and he listened patiently as Mrs. Baxley apologized to him at great length for everything she had ever done wrong. "I'm the one who's supposed to be repenting, Ma," he said with a faint smile. "Ma, is it my birthday yet?"

"No, my love. A few days off."

"Oh." William Baxley's face contracted. "Kiss me, Ma, like you used to when I was a little fellow, and hold my hand while I sleep."

She obeyed, and just around three in the morning on April 22, her son slipped quietly out of this hard world.

I left Mrs. Baxley alone with her dead son, returning after daylight to help her lay him out in the pine coffin Lieutenant Colonel Colby ordered. We were about to dress him in his tattered gray jacket when Mrs. Baxley shook her head and put the garment aside, folding it tenderly for herself. Other than this, his Bible, his diary, and a ring, which I took off his hand for his mother, the boy had no effects. I cut a lock of his hair for Mrs. Baxley, and with her permission, one for me as well, for it hurt to think how few people would mourn this handsome young boy who, but for this cruel war, would have married a sweet young woman and fathered children.

Superintendent Wood, expecting the worst, had left orders that the young man be taken to Congressional Cemetery and that Mrs. Baxley and anyone of her choice be allowed to attend his funeral. She chose me, and together we rode in the carriage Lieutenant Colonel Colby had hired to the cemetery. It had far too many fresh graves.

I watched as they slid William's coffin into the public vault, where it would rest until Mrs. Baxley could find the means to move it to a place of her own choosing. The coffin held a boy of seventeen who had seen men die horribly, who had experienced hunger and pain and privation, but who had never kissed a girl. The unfairness of it filled me with so much rage that I began to shake.

And then I understood exactly why Mr. Booth did what he did.

34
NORA

Having spent most of my life at boarding schools, I settled into routines naturally, and I soon settled into this one. We had our morning and nightly head counts, our three meals a day, and a couple of exercise periods, and in between all of these regularly scheduled events, we ladies wandered about in each other's quarters and looked out for fresh fish. There was quite a full net of us over those first couple of days, including so many people connected with Ford's Theatre or the acting profession that we might have gotten up private theatricals here, complete with scenery, if anyone had been so inclined.

As fish were concerned, it soon appeared that I was a mere minnow, for on the first Saturday of our captivity, while Mrs. Surratt was at the Baxley boy's funeral, Mr. Wilson came to our room. "Collect your things, Miss Fitzpatrick. You're to be released, and your father is waiting to take you home."

"What about the others, sir?"

"The orders concern only you, miss."

I embraced Anna. "They'll free you and your mother soon, I just know it. They're investigating and realizing that we're innocent of all this."

"I hope so."

Brushing my eyes as I left the dejected Anna behind, I followed Mr. Wilson to the office where I had been searched. There my father was pacing around. "Nora!" He took me into his arms. "My darling child, I have been frantic with worry."

"And she's safe and sound, just as I told you," Mr. Wilson said. "Can we give you a ride in the ambulance? It's a dreary day, as you know."

"Thank you, but I would prefer to take my daughter home myself," my father said stiffly.

"As you wish." He handed me a piece of paper. "Sign this — a loyalty oath — and you are free to go."

I never signed a paper so quickly in my life.

We passed out into the street, I taking one last look at the walls that had held me as my father lifted his umbrella over our heads. "I hope my letter did not alarm you, Father."

"Letter? I got no letter."

"They let me send you one the morning I got here."

"I have seen nothing of the sort, child. I went to Mrs. Surratt's on Tuesday, having heard that a man had been arrested there, and found the place full of detectives, who told me that all of you had been taken here. They detained me for a short time, as they were doing to anyone who happened to stop by there for any reason, and then let me go. Since then, I have been going from pillar to post, begging for your release, but with no success until today."

I looked appreciatively around at the blooming trees, never so beautiful in my eyes as today, even though the rain was falling fast. "Where am I to stay?"

"At the Misses Donovan." Father looked away. "I will be straightforward with you, child. I had already spoken to them about taking you in on the very day you were arrested. The more talk I heard about Booth's being received in that house, and about Mr. Surratt's activities, the more I came to realize that however fond you were of Mrs. Surratt, I could not have you remaining there. Peter himself telegrammed me to urge that you be taken from there, and that decided me."

I was too relieved to be free to complain of Peter's meddling.

As we turned the corner, I saw the placard that had mushroomed around the city: the latest reward poster for Mr. Booth, Mr. Herold, and Mr. Surratt. I'd seen the photograph of Mr. Surratt many times before: it was the one Mr. Weichmann had handed the detectives.

To my joy, Mr. Rochester was comfortably ensconced in the Misses Donovan's best chair when my father brought me to their house. He gave me a bored look and rolled over, clearly content with his new surroundings after all of the inconvenience he had suffered in his old ones.

But if Mr. Rochester took my disappearance and return with perfect equanimity, how the old ladies fussed over me! One would think I had escaped from the Bastille. Nothing but my favorite foods was ever served me, and I am convinced that if I had suddenly announced a taste for porpoise, the ladies would have made every effort to accommodate me.

Pleasant as all this cosseting was, it was also a bit stifling, and I was relieved when Father allowed me to work at my booth at the St. Aloysius fair, as had been arranged

— it seemed decades ago — before the assassination. So, clad in my best Sunday dress that had been liberated from the assassin's den, as the Misses Donovan liked to refer to Mrs. Surratt's boardinghouse, I took my place there at the appointed time on Monday evening.

Normally at church fairs and charity bazaars, I stood forlornly behind a table stacked with plain and fancy goods while men flocked to the tables of prettier young ladies, until, to my utter humiliation, one of the Venuses, her own table empty of goods, would be sent to my table and immediately bolster its appeal. But not this day. As soon as I took my place, a crowd began to flock to my table. I knew why, of course: word traveled fast in this large church, and everyone knew of my arrest and my acquaintance with Mr. Booth. For two straight hours, I pressed my wares on customers while answering the same questions over and over again: Yes, I knew Mr. Booth. No, he did not look to me like an assassin. No, I had not known what he was planning, and if I had, I would most certainly have let someone know. No, I had no idea of where he might be hiding. Yes, I had been in prison. No, I did not know when Mrs. Surratt and Anna would be leaving, but I hoped it was soon, as they had known nothing about Mr. Booth's evil deed. Everyone was so very curious, in fact, they were forgetting to buy my goods.

The first onslaught of questioners had receded when a dark-haired man of about thirty, good-looking in a sort of impudent way, approached, a little girl at each hand. They were Mr. Alexander Whelan and his daughters, who often sat near us at church. Mr. Whelan had a wife, but I had met her only once or twice, as she was an invalid and seldom came to services. The little energy she did have, she expended on her two little girls, six-year-old Mary Catherine and three-year-old Annie, for they always appeared at church in beautiful matching dresses, Mary Catherine's golden curls bouncing, and Annie's duller hair resplendent with a fancy bow. Mr. Whelan raised his hat. "Good afternoon, Miss Fitzpatrick. I'm glad to see you don't look much worse for wear for your stay in the clink."

"It could have been much worse, sir. Really, the most dreadful part about it was the food, and having nothing to read."

"Why were you in jail?" Mary Catherine frowned. "Were you bad?"

"No, no, Mary. Miss Fitzpatrick's a nice young lady."

"Then why did they put her in jail?"

"We'll talk about it at home, princess," Mr. Whelan promised. "And speaking of princesses, look sharp, Miss Fitzpatrick. The queen is coming."

Sure enough, strolling through the hall was St. Aloysius's most prominent parishioner, Mrs. Stephen Douglas, widow of the senator who had lost the 1860 election to President Lincoln. He had been a good thirty years her senior when they married, and he was so enamored of her that he had not only made no fuss about her being a Catholic, but had allowed his own sons by his first marriage to be raised in the church. Every Sunday since I had begun coming here, I had seen her and her stepchildren sitting in Pew No. 1. On the rare Sundays when she was not present, we could still see her, for so lovely was she that she had been the artist's model for the altarpiece showing St. Aloysius with his mother.

Yet as far apart as Mrs. Douglas and I were socially, we did have one thing in common: Georgetown Visitation. She had been a pupil there ten years before me, and after her marriage she had returned on occasion to visit her old teachers and to act as a benefactress. It was there we had met, and as she had the gift of remembering faces that a politician's wife must have, she had remembered me and spoken to me pleasantly on the few times we happened to encounter each other at church.

I watched as Mrs. Douglas, elegantly clad in the lavender she had favored since coming out of full mourning, made her way from booth to booth, at each one asking that something be set aside for delivery to her later. At last she reached my own. Instead of pointing at items with her expensively gloved hand, she said, "Miss Fitzpatrick, I was so sorry to hear of your unfortunate experience. I hope it has not affected your health."

News did indeed travel far. "No, ma'am. I am quite well."

"Are Mrs. Surratt and her daughter still imprisoned?"

"Yes, ma'am, but I hope that they will soon be released."

"I certainly hope so. If I can be of any help, please let me know."

"I will, ma'am."

"Well," Mrs. Douglas said, pointing to a painted cup. "I do believe I'll take this. And this. And this."

I modestly credited myself at least partially for the success of the fair that particular day.

Having bespoken most of what was on my table, Mrs. Douglas bid me good day, and I commenced wrapping her purchases.

"Mrs. Douglas, should you be in need of a painter or a grainer, I'm your man," Mr. Whelan said. "Special rates for parishioners."

"I will remember that, Mr. . . . ."

"Whelan, madam. Mr. Alexander Whelan."

Mrs. Douglas nodded and moved on to the next table. "Pa! Why did you ask her that?" Mary Catherine asked him.

"It never hurts to try, girls." He eyed the remainder of my merchandise. "Now, I bet your ma wants a pincushion."

"She has one, Pa."

"Well, she's going to have another one." Mr. Whelan squinted at the array of pincushions.

"Maybe two," I suggested.

"Pa, what's the man doing?"

"Now, girlie, your ma always tells you it's rude to point."

"Well, they're pointing at us."

Mr. Whelan frowned. "Actually," he said, "they're pointing at you, Miss Fitzpatrick."

"Oh, no," I said. "I've seen him at the provost marshal's."

Mr. Whelan planted himself by my side as

a soldier headed straight in the direction he had been pointed, ignoring even Mrs. Mahoney's famous pound cake, which Father Wiget had pronounced not even Christ himself could have resisted. "Miss Nora Fitzpatrick?"

"Yes."

"There's more we need to talk about, miss. I'd like to see you at the provost marshal's office for a few moments."

"Don't go, Miss Fitzpatrick. It's a trick."

The soldier turned his gaze to Mr. Whelan. "Is this man a relative of yours, Miss Fitzpatrick?"

"A friend," Mr. Whelan said. "What do you want with this young lady?"

"To ask her a few questions, as I said, about some very serious matters. If you know what's good for you, you'll not interfere."

With visions of Mr. Whelan being dragged off in fetters while his poor little girls looked on, I said, "Mr. Whelan, would you please go fetch Father Wiget for me? He is standing over there."

Mr. Whelan muttered something but obeyed. "Is something wrong here?" Father Wiget asked.

"He wants Miss Fitzpatrick to abandon her post and to go the provost marshal's office. I think it's a damned trap."

"Nonsense," the soldier said. "We just need to clarify some things."

"Then why can't you ask about them here?"

"Because the men asking the questions are there. Father, make the fellow see reason."

Father Wiget sighed. "I think you must go, Miss Fitzpatrick. The sooner they catch Booth, the better off we'll all be, and if there is anything you can do to help, you must."

"I'll bring the young lady back here when we're finished," the soldier said. He sniffed. "Maybe even buy some cake."

"Then go along with him, Miss Fitzpatrick."

Mr. Whelan shook his head and glared at the detective.

After fetching my bonnet and shawl from the cloakroom, I walked out to the waiting ambulance, which quickly brought me to the provost marshal's office. There was no waiting this time; I was immediately seated in front of two soldiers. As I never learned their names, I thought of them as Short One and Tall One.

Tall One had an album in front of him, which I recognized as my own. He thrust it in front of me. "Is this yours, Miss Fitzpatrick?"

"Yes, sir."

He pulled out a photograph between two others, and I looked Mr. Booth in the face once more. "This belong to you, miss?"

"It does."

"No need to ask if you recognize it. You've seen the man in person?"

"Yes."

"Many times?"

"Many times."

"When did you hide it?"

"After he killed the president."

Short One said, "You hid it. You didn't destroy it. Why?"

"I didn't have the heart to."

"You were in love with him?"

"Certainly not."

"You say that with a great deal of confidence. Wouldn't it be quite natural for a young lady to be in love with a handsome man like Booth?"

"It may be, but he never showed any interest of that kind in me, and I am not the sort to pine for what I cannot have."

"You knew nothing of his plans?"

"Certainly not."

Tall One jumped back into the questioning. "What did he speak of when he came to visit? Did he talk of politics?"

"No, sir."

"What did he do when he was there?"

"He did the sort of things any well-bred man would do. He made general conversation. He spoke very fondly of his family. He had Miss Surratt play the piano, and had us sing duets. Since he was an actor, he had us read for him."

"Was Miss Surratt attached to him?"

I squirmed.

"Look at these before you answer."

I stared at the paper he showed me. There in Anna's handwriting were a series of jottings. *J. Wilkes Booth. National Hotel. Miss Anna Surratt . . .* "I know nothing of these, sir."

"Aren't they something like a young girl in love might scribble?"

"They could mean about anything, sir."

"So you are telling me that Miss Surratt was not in love with Mr. Booth? Or was she?" Tall One reached down and pulled something from beneath his desk and held it in front of me. "Do you recognize this?"

"Yes. It was on the mantel in the bedroom where I slept. *Morning, Noon, and Night.*"

"Did you ever take a look at the back of the frame?"

"The back of the frame? Why would I do that?"

"Well, someone found a use for it." Tall One turned the picture around. There was a small hole in the frame, from which he pulled out a photograph. "Booth, yet again. Did you hide this back here, miss?"

"No, sir. I had but the one."

"Did Miss Surratt hide it back there?"

"I do not know." Swiftly, I remembered that Anna's photograph of Mr. Booth had suddenly disappeared after the assassination, but I wasn't about to tell this to Tall One.

"She had his photograph?"

"Yes. We each did."

"Why?"

"Because we liked him and were proud of having his acquaintance and wanted to show off to our friends."

"Would you keep a secret for him?"

"Not a secret about killing the president, sir."

Short One stirred restlessly. "When is the last time you saw John Surratt?"

"The day Richmond fell."

"You have not seen him afterward?"

"No, sir."

"He was not in Washington on the night of the assassination?"

"He was not at Mrs. Surratt's house."

Tall One took over. "How many times did

Booth visit Mrs. Surratt on Friday?"

"But once that I heard."

"Don't tell us what you heard. Tell us what you saw."

"I did not see him at all that day."

"Where were you?"

"In the morning, I went to church. In the afternoon, I went to the hospital to visit soldiers."

"What were you doing there, miss? Spying?"

"No," I said. "How can you even say such a horrible thing? I wanted to do something to be useful." For the first time during my interrogation, I dabbed at my eyes with my handkerchief.

"Well, don't cry," Short One said. "It's a fair enough question, given that you were living in a nest of secesh sympathizers, isn't it? Tell us one thing: Has Mrs. Surratt told you to keep quiet? Sworn you to an oath of secrecy? Anything like that?"

"No!"

"You were with her in prison, and she never told you what to say if you were questioned?"

"No. I hardly saw her. She spent most of her time nursing a poor soldier who was sick. Mrs. Baxley's boy."

"The Baxley woman? A notorious spy."

He rose. "Well, we're done."

Short One escorted me to the ambulance, gave the driver a direction, and climbed in beside me. "I'm sorry not to have been of much help," I said politely.

Then I realized we were not going where I expected. "Aren't you taking me back to the fair?"

"No."

"Are you taking me to my boarding-house?"

"No."

"Are you taking me to my father?"

"No."

"Will you let me kneel and say my prayers?"

"Why, certainly."

I knelt in the ambulance, crossed myself, and prayed. When I at last rose, with the help of the detective, I saw the walls of Old Capitol Prison appearing before me. There were the guards with the bayonets, the same walk to the office, the same lieutenant, the same search, the same guard leading me to my same room — but there, I was wrong. "Aren't we going upstairs?"

"No, miss. I have orders to take you here." He flung open the door. "I'm sorry."

I stared inside. With a good imagination, which I possessed, it was possible to make believe that the room upstairs was part of a rundown boardinghouse, no worse. Not this room. Most of the once elegant wallpaper had fallen off, leaving only a few shreds, surmounted with great spots of grease. Cockroaches ambled around merrily, while mice rustled in a corner. There was a log in the fireplace, but I doubted a fire had been lit in years; as it was, it served only as a lounging place for more cockroaches. Every corner held a spiderweb more intricate than the last.

Two large, barred windows looked out into the yard. There were no shades, and the windows could not be completely closed, so not only was I on display to anyone passing in the yard, save for the area where one window was partially boarded, but I also could not shut out the chilly night air. There were no furnishings, save for a bed, a chair, and a table. On the table sat an empty candlestick holder, a water jug, and a tin cup; a basin matching the cup was on the floor. Of the bucket in a corner I say no more than that it had been used before and that it would be used many times again before anyone emptied it.

"I have to stay here? Why can't I stay with Mrs. Surratt and the other ladies? There must be a mistake."

"No mistake, miss. 'To be kept apart from other ladies and to have no communication with them.' Those are the orders with respect to you." He pulled a candle out of his pocket, along with a few matches. "Supper at eight. Roll call at nine. Miss —"

"Yes?"

"If you tell what you know about Booth and Mrs. Surratt, you'll be free in no time."

"Booth and Mrs. Surratt? He was acquainted with her son and visited her house. What more is there to tell?"

The man made no answer but left the room.

At eight, the colored woman who had brought us supper upstairs came in bearing the usual tray. The food was no worse here than what I had been served upstairs, but the utensils and dishes! My knife had no handle; later, I would find that on the occasions when I did get a knife with a handle, my fork was missing a prong, or vice versa. Never did I get a set where all was intact. My cup still bore traces of soap, which actually improved the taste of the coffee somewhat, and my dish had been only partially washed.

I sat in the chair and nibbled the bread, it being the only thing I could bear to eat. Outside, a soldier paced back and forth.

Nine o'clock, and the guard came in and counted. "One!"

Then I was alone, with only my candle and a room of vermin for company.

35
MARY

Since William's death, Mrs. Baxley had sat for hours at her window overlooking the street, clutching his jacket as if hoping he would come claim it. I was sitting beside her one evening, offering what little comfort I could give her, when an ambulance pulled up: an addition to our flock, I supposed. A lady got out, under guard, and Mrs. Baxley roused herself from her misery to say, "Why, it's Miss Fitzpatrick."

I bent forward. My eyes were too poor to make out the lady's features, but Mrs. Baxley was surely right. I had seen Nora wear this pink dress many times to church. "What on earth have they brought her back for?" I rose. "I am sorry, Mrs. Baxley. I should go back to our room so that I can find out what is going on."

Mrs. Baxley nodded dully and resumed her vigil.

But Nora did not come to the room, and

I knew better than to try to extract information from the colored servants who brought us supper. Instead, when head count time came, I asked, "Excuse me, sir. Has Miss Fitzpatrick been brought in?"

"She has."

"Where is she staying?"

"Downstairs, away from the other ladies. She is in close confinement."

"Close confinement?" Anna asked. She stared at me. "Nora?"

"Why, that child has never harmed another person in her life," I said. "What on earth are they thinking?"

The man shrugged. "Two," he sang out before leaving.

Why were there not three? Why were they holding Nora apart from us?

The next day, Anna was sitting at the window, drearily watching the men take their morning exercise, when she started, "Ma! It's Mr. Lloyd."

I hurried to the window to stare at the figure to whom she pointed. The last time I saw Mr. Lloyd, he was shambling drunk. This day, as far as I could tell, he was sober, but his posture was one of utter despair.

"Why have they arrested him?" Anna

asked. "Surely *he* wasn't a friend of Mr. Booth."

"He was our tenant. And Johnny stopped at the tavern while Mr. Lloyd rented it."

And I stopped there, the very day of the assassination, with my message from Mr. Booth about the shooting irons. What would happen when Mr. Lloyd told the detectives about this?

But would he remember what I said, drunk as he was? I knew every drunkard had his own individual peculiarities, but remembering my husband gave me hope. He would play cards in his sodden condition and wake the next morning with no memory of whether he'd won or lost — something his opponents took full advantage of, for as a man of honor, John could not gainsay them when they swore he owed them money. How much that should have been used for the children's educations evaporated in that fashion! Perhaps Mr. Lloyd's memory would prove just as addled.

It was shameful for me, of all people, to be pinning my hopes on a man's dissipation and degradation. Yet I had no choice.

On April 27, Mrs. Baxley came into my room bearing a newspaper. "I wanted to tell you this before our captors do. Booth is dead."

Anna began to weep.

"Are you sure? It's not just a rumor?" I asked.

Mrs. Baxley nodded. "He was shot yesterday in a barn in Virginia. His body was brought to Washington last night." She held up the *Evening Star.* "The sutler's boy knew Willie. He was kind enough to bring me an extra. It's all here."

I took the paper. Accompanied only by David Herold, the monkey-faced boy I remembered from the tavern, Booth had made his way from Maryland to Virginia until a federal cavalry unit finally caught up with him in a tobacco barn, where he had been spending the night. "Anna, can you bear to listen?" I asked.

"No."

I read silently:

The cavalry then surrounded the barn and summoned Booth and his accomplice to surrender. Herold was inclined at first to accede to the request, but Booth accused him of cowardice, then they both peremptorily refused to surrender and made preparations to defend themselves.

In order to take the conspirators alive,

the barn was fired, and the flames getting too hot for Herold, he approached the door of the barn and signified his willingness to be taken prisoner. Herold then came out of the barn and gave himself up and was securely handcuffed.

Booth maintained a defiant attitude, refusing to surrender, and, in braggadocio style, challenged his pursuers to fight him by turns singly. As the roof of the barn was about falling in, and Booth manifested a disposition to make a bolt, he was shot by Sergeant Boston Corbett, of the 16th New York, the ball taking effect in the neck, from the effects of which he died in about three hours.

Booth, before breathing his last, was asked if he had anything to say, when he replied, "Tell my mother that I died for my country."

I put the paper down and gazed into space. Mrs. Baxley awkwardly put an arm around Anna. "Miss Surratt, it is for the best. He might have stayed for weeks in solitary confinement and gone slowly mad. He might have been hanged in front of a jeering crowd. He is past all that."

"I loved him."

Mrs. Baxley sighed and shook her head.

"For God's sake, girl, keep that to yourself."

The next morning, Anna and I were both summoned to the office. After a night spent weeping for Mr. Booth, Anna held her head high. I knew as they led us into separate rooms that she would not lose her composure.

A man in his thirties, with a grave expression and a flourishing beard, seated himself at the desk before me. He introduced himself as Colonel Henry Olcott. Although he did not mention Mr. Booth's death, and neither did I, the fact of it hung uneasily between us.

"You are at liberty to decline answering my questions, Mrs. Surratt, but you will understand any statement you make will be used at your trial."

Trial? I was about to say the word when Colonel Olcott said, "You are a woman of good sense. It is better to refuse to say anything than to not tell the truth."

I assented. Briskly, Colonel Olcott questioned me, as these men always did, about when I last saw Johnny, then about my boarder Port Tobacco. His next question sent a chill down my spine. "A week or two previous to the murder, how many times did you go to the country?"

"Twice."

"Who went with you?"

"The gentleman who boarded with me, Mr. Weichmann. He drove me down in a buggy."

"Where did you stop?"

"At Mr. Lloyd's. He rents my place down there."

"What conversation did you have with Mr. Lloyd?"

I managed to answer in a level tone. "I do not remember any particular conversation. Mr. Lloyd did not return home until I was getting ready to leave."

"What time was that?"

"Friday evening."

"That is, the day of the murder?"

"Yes, sir."

"How long a conversation did you have with Mr. Lloyd?"

"A short one. I did not sit down. I met him only as I was going home."

"Where was Mr. Weichmann?"

"He was there."

"He heard the conversation?"

"I presume he did. I do not remember."

"What did Mr. Lloyd say to you?"

I tried to remember Mr. Lloyd's drunken meanderings. "He spoke of having fish and oysters. He asked me whether I had been to dinner."

"What did you say about having any shooting irons or carbines?"

He remembered, and I, God forgive me, would have to lie. "I said nothing about them."

For the first time in our interview, Colonel Olcott frowned. "Any conversation of that kind? Did you not tell him to have the shooting irons ready, that there would be some people there that night?"

"To my knowledge, no conversation of that kind passed."

"Did you know any shooting irons were there?"

"No, sir, I did not."

What might these men do to wring the truth out of me? I half expected Colonel Olcott to lift a hand and order me dragged to the rack. But he said mildly, "Were Mr. Booth's visits always visits of courtesy?"

"Yes, sir."

"Any business discussed?"

"No, sir, not political affairs. I do not think that his longest stay was over one hour."

"What part of the day did he used to come?"

"Sometimes in the day and sometimes in the evening."

"Did not an attachment spring up between him and your daughter?"

"Not that I knew of."

"He was a handsome man?"

"He was a handsome man and gentlemanly." Had things been different, this might have been Mr. Booth's epitaph. "That is all we knew of him. I did not suppose he had the devil he certainly possessed in his heart."

Colonel Olcott raised a skeptical eyebrow. "I should suppose from the papers and letters that Miss Surratt thought favorably of him?"

Do you know what hurts worst, Ma? Not getting to say good-bye to him that day he stopped by to see you. "If so, she kept it to herself. She never corresponded with him."

"Did he pay attention to any one of the young ladies?"

"No particular attention. We were in the parlor together, and he did not pay particular attention to anyone."

Colonel Olcott scribbled on his paper a little, then asked me about Johnny's acquaintance with Mr. Booth and about my visitors on the day of the murder — and once again asked about Johnny having been at the theater with Mr. Booth. As I knew perfectly well that no such thing happened, despite all of these men dwelling on the subject, I felt a bit less guilty about the lies I had told today.

But only a bit.

Anna was back in our room when I returned. She had flopped wearily upon the bed she could scarcely bear to sit on a few days before. "What did they ask you?" I said when we were alone.

"About the boarders. When we went to bed the night of the assassination. When I last saw Johnny. Who called Saturday and Sunday. How long Johnny was postmaster." Anna sat up. "Ma, do you think they will find Johnny? Kill him?"

"Child, I know in my heart that he had nothing to do with the assassination. If they find him, he will have no reason to force them to shoot him, as did Mr. Booth. They will put him on trial, and they will hear that he left town two weeks before, and he will go free."

"But what if they find him guilty?"

"They will not, because you and I will pray that he stays hidden until it is safe, and that if he is found, he is not convicted. Let us do so now."

Anna looked at me, clearly doubting the efficacy of prayer, but obeyed. As we told our beads, I pondered Colonel Olcott's reference to my own trial. Was he merely using a form of words he used toward everyone he questioned, or was I to be put on trial, and for what? For bringing those shooting irons? Or for something worse?

Whatever was to come, I knew telling Anna would only upset her more. So I stayed quiet.

More familiar faces appeared in the men's exercise yard: Mr. Holohan and — to my horror — my brother. "What has he to do with any of this?" I asked the guard at head count time. "He never met Mr. Booth in his life. He has supported the Union, in fact."

"He's your brother. And John Surratt's uncle."

In these times, that seemed sufficient to send a man to prison.

On April 30, Mr. Weichmann joined my other boarders in their captivity. He caught sight of Anna and me sitting by our window and waved.

"Even in prison I can't get away from that man," Anna muttered.

Mrs. Baxley, who had shown a bit more interest in life as new prisoners were brought in, chuckled. "Not a sweetheart of yours, I gather?"

"No! The horrid creature used to wear blue pantaloons in the house."

Mrs. Baxley shook her head. "Pity my Willie isn't here. The two of you would have been a good match." She looked at the small jacket in her hand. "Except as to height, perhaps," she added grudgingly.

That evening, we lady prisoners were clustered in the once luxurious parlor that served as our gathering place when we heard someone bark, "Double the guard!"

We stared at one another. Since Mr. Booth's death, we no longer lived in fear of our prison being stormed, so what could this mean? Then I realized: they must have Johnny. "No," I murmured. "Not my son."

Mrs. Baxley hurried to her room with its view of the street. "They brought a carriage to the door," she reported in a few minutes, "but there's no one inside it that I can tell."

"They must be about to free someone," Anna said. "Lucky soul."

"But why double the guard?"

We stood there in silence, waiting for something to answer our question, when Superintendent Wood appeared, followed by another man. "Mrs. Surratt, you are wanted. Please get your bonnet and cloak."

It was half past six, well past the usual

time for interrogating anyone. "Wanted where at this time of night?"

"Please do as you are told, madam, quickly."

I turned to obey. Both Anna and Mrs. Baxley tried to follow me. Both were stopped.

Trembling, I slowly walked to my room and took my cloak and hat from their nail. Something told me to bring my purse as well. From the window, I heard Anna's angry voice. "What do you mean, I cannot go with her?"

I hurried back. Anna clutched me. "I will go with her, and you won't stop me!"

"Miss, I will use force only as the last resort, but I will use it if need be. Don't make me cause you pain."

"Anna, do as you are told."

The commanding tone caused Anna to loosen her grip upon me. Instantly, Superintendent Wood moved in and firmly, yet gently, pulled her from me.

I looked at the semicircle of women standing around me. "Pray for me," I said. "Take care of my Anna."

Mrs. Baxley kissed me, and the others followed suit. Then I embraced Anna. "Be brave, child."

"But where are they taking you?"

No one answered. Instead, Superintendent Wood and the other man hustled me away toward the carriage outside. As the door closed, the last sound I heard from the prison was Anna's distant screams.

I slumped in a corner of the carriage. Even if I was disposed to look outside to see where I was being taken, I could not; the curtains were drawn shut.

At last we stopped. My companion, who at some point introduced himself to me as Colonel Lafayette Baker, handed me out. Nothing around me looked the least bit familiar, though the walls surrounding me left no doubt I was in a prison of some sort. "Where am I? Surely you can tell me that much."

"Old Arsenal Penitentiary."

I nodded, having heard of this place. "I didn't think they were using it as a prison anymore."

"They weren't. Now they are again. Come along."

Though I could not see it due to the walls, I knew we were surrounded by water on three sides in this part of the city, and a breeze coming off the river made me shiver as Colonel Baker led me to an office where a man sat behind a desk. "General Hartranft. Your name, madam?"

"Mrs. John Surratt."

"Yes, as expected. A formality we have to go through." He gave a very slight smile, and I sensed a kindness in him. "Please hand me your purse."

I complied. He opened it and neatly laid out the contents, then scribbled on a piece of paper. A gold watch ring. "Very pretty," he commented. A five-dollar note. Three bank bills. A thimble. Some needles attached to a strip of red velvet. My house key. My rosary, which he handed back to me without comment. As he finished writing and placed these items in a little box, it was the disappearance of the house key that pained me most.

"Sir, please tell me. Why was I moved here? Am I to stay here? Am I to be tried, and for what? Why cannot my daughter join me?"

"I cannot answer your questions, madam. I am very sorry. Now, let me take you to your cell."

Unlike Carroll Annex, this place had been built to hold prisoners, and the cell he led me to was exactly that, with iron bars and no furnishings but a straw pallet on the floor. The only light came from General Hartranft's lantern. "Can I not have a candle?"

"No, madam. They are not allowed. I suggest you sleep. I will check on you at seven in the morning."

He nodded a good-bye and locked the door.

I had never been alone like this before. For years, there had always been someone close by — family, servants, boarders. Even when I had not shared my bed, there had always been someone I knew and trusted within call.

Were there other prisoners here? There must have been — surely this place was too large to keep one lone woman — but if there were, they were quiet. I heard only some crickets chirping and the sounds of some night birds.

I knelt and said my prayers, but God seemed very, very far away. Those being done, I lay down on the hard pallet and pulled the blanket around me. What was my poor Anna doing now?

It was the thought of her, motherless, in our room at Carroll Annex that finally, for the first time since my arrest, broke me. I sat up and wept into my hands until I could weep no more.

36
NORA

For days I remained shut up in my solitary room at Carroll Annex, without a soul to talk to. I thought for certain that my captors were trying to drive me mad. But for my two diversions — killing bugs and watching the men exercising in the yard — they might well have succeeded.

What a capital cockroach killer I became! Since then, I have read various memoirs of others, mostly men, imprisoned during the war, and while I cannot pretend to have possessed the military skills my male counterparts brought to their task of ridding themselves of six-legged creatures, I did the best I could, armed with my shoes. At first, it was my greatest regret that I had been arrested at the church fair, to which I had worn my dainty slippers rather than my practical boots, as the latter were, of course, far better suited to my murderous task. As the days passed and I grew more to hate my enemy, however, I found my slipper put less a barrier between it and myself, and therefore was far more satisfying than using a sturdier boot would have been.

But while I could report some success against the cockroaches, I was helpless against the bedbugs. They tormented me so much when I tried to sleep that I finally gave it up and paced around the chamber at night until I dropped at the foot of my bed in exhaustion.

When not engaged in hostilities with the insect world, I sat at my window and watched the men take their exercise. There was a rule at the prison, unwritten but nonetheless most vigorously enforced, that we could not stick our heads or hands outside our windows, which made it almost impossible for me to converse with anyone, but there were a few kind souls, most of whose names I never learned, who would pass by and give me an encouraging smile or a wave, making me feel less alone. Each day, there were more men in the yard to watch: no one seemed to be leaving, only coming.

Despite the fact that my letter to my father during my first captivity had never reached him, I again begged pencil and paper to write to him and to the Misses Donovan,

417

who must have been frantic, poor things, when I failed to return home from the church fair. A pencil was soon brought, but no paper, and when I made the eminently reasonable suggestion that both would be helpful for writing a letter, I received only a blank stare for my pains. I could only hope that Father Wiget had sent word to them and my father. The pencil, however, did afford me a new pastime. Both here and upstairs, the walls were scrawled over with the signatures of my predecessors, along with the occasional scrap of verse, and I dutifully added my own name to the wall:

Miss Nora Fitzpatrick In durance vile
from April 24, 1865, to _____

On Thursday, the fourth day of my captivity (I kept a little calendar on the wall in time-honored style), a guard pushed open the door and thrust in a basket, for which the roaches and I all scrambled. It was a selection of little cakes from my favorite bakery and could have been brought to me by none other than my father. I pictured him standing at the counter, worried to death about me, yet making certain all of my favorites were well represented, and my heart ached. Why had I ever brought all of this trouble

418

upon him by wanting to leave the Misses Donovan in the first place?

The next day, toward dusk, my door banged open again. This time, it was a woman who was unceremoniously pushed into my cell by the guard, who muttered something about bringing in another bed and left her staring around in horror.

She was a maiden in her midthirties, and I shortly learned that her name was Miss Mattie Virginia Lomax and that she was a schoolteacher from Baltimore. "I was put in here merely for inquiring about my relations, the Greens, who are in here simply for having a nodding acquaintance with Mr. Surratt," she said. "And you?"

I hesitated, having heeded Mrs. Baxley's warning about spies. "I was Mrs. Surratt's boarder."

This seemed enough for Miss Lomax. "Yes, I've read about the arrests. I believe I met your father in the office. He is an older gentleman with white hair that hangs to his shoulders?"

I nodded. "That's Father."

"He said that he had been coming here every day, asking to see you, and bringing you food and other gifts."

My eyes filled with tears. "I have never been allowed to see him, and have received only one basket of cakes from him." I pointed to my shawl hanging from a nail on the wall. "I keep them tied up in there to keep them from the roaches. We can share them."

"That is kind of you, but is the food really that bad here?"

"Indeed it is," I said with all of the relish of a boarding school pupil introducing a new girl to the place. "The food is awful and the place is full of bugs and there is a guard in front of our room at all times. You will see his eye at the door from time to time, especially when he thinks we might be in a state of undress. I stop up the keyhole with my handkerchief, but he pushes it right out."

"Mercy," Miss Lomax said faintly.

"We must never stick our head out of the window, or we will be shot — at least that is what they told me when I tried." I was fairly chattering away, for the relief of having a human being with me, even one who was a complete stranger and who might be a spy, was almost too great to bear.

I began giving her a rundown of our schedule — breakfast at eight, dinner at three, supper at eight, morning and evening head counts. Poor Miss Lomax was looking rather overwhelmed and in need of a bed to

420

sink upon when that very article arrived, carried in by two men who dropped it in the corner with a grunt. "No blanket?"

I looked out at the yard, where one of the women who brought us our meals was vigorously shaking a brown blanket. Miss Lomax's eyes followed mine. "Oh," she said faintly.

I decided not to dishearten Miss Lomax by mentioning the blood on her sheet (which at least had had a chance to dry), but she noticed it presently, just as the woman bore in the blanket, on which my experienced eye soon detected the omnipresent bedbugs. "You can have the stool," I offered.

"Thank you, but where on earth can I hang my things?'

I pointed to an unoccupied nail on the wall, which, like the one on which my own things hung, clearly had been intended for a more Amazonian creature than either Miss Lomax or me. "You'll have to stand on the stool as I do."

Grimly, Miss Lomax complied, and I looked at the keyhole. Sure enough, the eye was pressed against it. I rather doubted the guard could get much of a peep up her skirts from this point, but as our sex had to stick together, I stood and blocked his view.

"I suppose you have heard the news," she said when she had accomplished her task and dismounted.

"No. I have heard nothing."

"Booth is dead."

All of the pleasure I had been taking in inducting this fresh fish into our company vanished. I took the newspaper she offered me, and as I read the account of Mr. Booth's last hours on earth, I began to cry.

I should not have cried for him, knowing what he had done and how many lives he had devastated — but I did. I cried for his poor mother, of whom he'd spoken in his dying hours, and of whom he had spoken so fondly in Mrs. Surratt's parlor. I cried for poor Miss Hale, who would soon be whisked off to Spain by her father, not to set foot in America for many years. I cried for poor Anna, who had loved him. I cried for the sheer waste of Mr. Booth's finer qualities in the pursuance of a mad idea that hadn't saved a single life or made a single person the happier for it.

Most of all, I cried because he had given me my first kiss, and I couldn't forget that special bond between us even though he had shot the president. And that night, I prayed for his soul with all of my might.

■ ■ ■ ■

Despite the assurance that all I had to do was to tell all I knew about Mr. Booth and Mrs. Surratt, there had been no opportunity for me to tell, for I had not been questioned since my return here. This all changed on the day after Miss Lomax's arrival and the news of Mr. Booth's death, when I was summoned to the office. I was greeted by Tall One, my interrogator from the other day. "Good morning, Miss Fitzpatrick," he said genially. "I trust you will be more co-operative than you have been in the past?"

"I have not been uncooperative in the past, sir. I simply do not know what you seem to think I do."

"We'll be the judge of that."

He started out by asking me to name Mrs. Surratt's boarders. When I came to Port Tobacco, it seemed to please him very much. Then he began to fire questions at me. When did Port Tobacco come? How long did he stay? Did he come alone? Did he ask for Mr. Surratt? Had they been previously acquainted? Had Mr. Surratt been out of town before Port Tobacco came? Was Mr. Booth with him? When I gave what appeared to be the wrong answer, I trembled

423

under his steely gaze, as if I were a private he was getting ready to send to the stocks, and when I gave an answer that appeared to suit him, I trembled to think of the consequences to Port Tobacco or Mr. Surratt, if they ever found him.

The subject of Port Tobacco being exhausted, Tall One turned to Mr. Payne. He had not, I admitted, looked like much of a Baptist preacher to me, and yes, he did have a bit of a fierce look to him, I supposed. Then why had I not recognized him the night of my arrest?

"I was frightened that night," I said quite truthfully, "and he had a thing on his head."

"Would you have told anybody that night if they had asked you whether you recognized him?"

As I had recognized him at the provost marshal's office but had not said a thing to anybody, I said only, "I was frightened when they arrested me."

"When did you last see John H. Surratt?"

This was a familiar question, though I could answer it to no one's satisfaction. "Three weeks ago last Monday."

"Did you never have any suspicion that all these men were contriving something? Did you never hear them talking as though they were?"

424

"No, sir. I never heard them say anything of the sort."

"When was it that Mr. Surratt burned some papers, do you remember?"

"If he burned any, I didn't know that he did it."

"You were not there at the time?"

My head began to throb. "I never saw him burn any papers," I snapped. "What he did when I was not around I cannot say."

Tall One seemed to concede my point. After questioning me about my whereabouts on Easter Sunday (church, which he seemed to find vaguely sinister), he terminated our interview. I followed the guard dejectedly back to my quarters, which after my visit to the comparative luxury of the office looked worse than ever. Miss Lomax was perched upon the stool, reading. "The oddest gift has arrived for us, Miss Fitzpatrick. *Harper's Weekly,* and a perfectly dreadful dime novel."

"From whom?"

"The guard would not or could not say, of course." She glanced at the keyhole. "The magazine could have come from just about anyone, I suppose, but no one of my acquaintance reads this trash." She held up the dime novel gingerly.

"Mine neither. Maybe one of the other

prisoners sent it."

"Yes, that must be it." Ever the school-teacher, she frowned as I took it from her hand. "I really wonder if you should be reading this, Miss Fitzpatrick. It is hardly suitable for a young lady."

"Neither is this room," I pointed out and opened the book. It was titled *The Trapper's Bride* and contained a great deal of fighting between the white men and the Indians, all ending happily with a series of engagements worthy of a Jane Austen novel. It was quite improbable, but it got me through those dreary days, and for that I was heartily grateful to the donor — whoever he or she might be.

Since my return to prison, I had not caught a glimpse of either Mrs. Surratt or Anna. As they were in the room above ours, I could hear them moving about, which gave me a certain comfort, and I had even investigated the ceiling for holes in the hope of opening communication with them. Had I been equipped with a broom, I often thought, I could have tapped out some sort of message, though how I might code one was another matter altogether. Before I could devote much more thought to this, however, Miss Lomax arrived, and her presence meant I could simply pass messages through her to my friends, as for reasons known best to Superintendent Wood and God (in that order), she had liberties I did not and could mingle freely with the other women. I dared not send a written message, as that would have perhaps been disastrous for all of us, but I frequently sent oral messages of love and affection, which were reciprocated. From Miss Lomax I learned that Mrs. Surratt was bearing her imprisonment calmly but that poor Anna had taken the death of Mr. Booth very hard, although she had enough sense to conceal her emotions from our jailers.

On April 30, Miss Lomax told me Mrs. Surratt had been taken away from prison, to where she did not know. After discussing the matter, we came to the conclusion that she had been sent to the provost marshal's, or perhaps even the War Department for questioning, and would soon return. We even took turns sitting up that night, watching the yard for Mrs. Surratt. But daylight came with no sign of my landlady, only the sound of Anna endlessly pacing overhead, waiting in vain for her mother.

37
MARY

MAY 8 TO 13, 1865

During my first few days at the Old Arsenal, they shifted me back and forth between two cells: 157 and 200. Except in my walks from one to another, I did not see anything else. The food at the Arsenal, while of the most simple type, was more wholesome than that at the Old Capitol Prison, but all I could consume was tea and toast, and for the first few days at my new prison, I could not even manage to eat the toast. I recoiled from food altogether until Dr. Porter, who saw me daily, told me kindly that, as the government did not want me to starve to death, he would have to feed me by force if I did not take some sustenance.

They were not unkind to me. At the doctor's recommendation, they supplied me with warm slippers; when the doctor decided 157 was unwholesome, they moved me to 200, to return to 157 only when 200 was being aired. My one complaint was they

428

would not tell me for what I would be tried.

There was to be a trial; I knew that much. Who was to be tried with me and where the trial was to be held were as unknown to me as what charges I would face. Would my Anna be tried? Would Nora? Had Johnny been captured?

No one told me a thing, but they were perfectly polite about it.

The days were monotonous, but the nights were far worse. With no company and nothing to relieve the darkness, I had nothing to occupy my mind but the memory of Anna's screams as they dragged us apart.

Nothing else, that is, besides regrets. How could I have been so foolish?

Darkness had fallen upon the prison on the evening of May 8, a Monday, and I was preparing for another miserable night with my own thoughts when General Hartranft came to my cell, bearing a lantern and some papers. "Mrs. Surratt, I have the charges against you. I can allow you to read them while I wait, or I can read them to you, if you wish."

I looked at the papers with their small type. "I cannot read that in this light. Please read them to me."

"As you like." General Hartranft cleared

his throat. "The charge and specification against David E. Herold, George A. Atzerodt, Lewis Payne, Michael O'Laughlin, Edward Spangler, Samuel Arnold, Mary E. Surratt, and Samuel A. Mudd. For maliciously, unlawfully, and traitorously, and in aid of the existing armed rebellion against the United States of America, on or before the sixth day of March 1865, and on diverse other days between that day and the fifteenth day of April 1865, combining, confederating, and conspiring together with one John H. Surratt, John Wilkes Booth, Jefferson Davis —"

"Jefferson Davis? Sir, I have never seen the man, much less conspired with him."

"Madam, please let me read the specification. It is my duty, and it is necessary that you know with what you are charged."

I nodded, and the major read on. An Edward Spangler was accused of helping Mr. Booth gain entrance to the presidential box of Ford's Theatre and of assisting his flight from the theater. David Herold was accused of helping Mr. Booth evade capture. Lewis Payne was accused of attempting to murder Secretary of State Seward. George Atzerodt was accused of lying in wait to murder Vice President Johnson. Michael O'Laughlin — whoever he was — was accused of plotting to murder General Grant. Samuel Arnold, another name that meant nothing to me, was accused of plotting with Mr. Booth and others.

General Hartranft paused for breath. Then, in a particularly clear voice, he read, "And in further prosecution of said conspiracy, Mary E. Surratt did, at Washington City, and within the military department and military lines aforesaid, receive, entertain, harbor and conceal, aid and assist the said John Wilkes Booth, David E. Herold, Lewis Payne, John H. Surratt, Michael O'Laughlin, George Atzerodt, Samuel Arnold, and their confederates, with the knowledge of the murderous and traitorous conspiracy aforesaid, and with intent to aid, abet, and assist them in the execution thereof, and in escaping from justice after the murder of the said Abraham Lincoln."

I shook my head. General Hartranft continued on to detail the charges against Samuel Mudd, a doctor who treated Mr. Booth's injuries and sheltered him within his house for a short time after the assassination. A memory stirred, and I heard Johnny's voice. *You must walk through the Mudd to get to the Booth . . .*

"Sir, I do not understand. Why all of this language about military lines?"

"Your lawyer — when you get one — can explain it to you, madam. But I expect the language is there because it is to be a military trial."

"A military trial? Why on earth will be there be a military trial?"

"Your lawyer —"

"Can explain it. When will I have a chance to ask for one?"

"You will be brought before the commission tomorrow and may ask for one then. Have you any more questions?"

"No, sir."

"While I am here, are you finding room 200 more agreeable than room 157?"

"Yes, sir."

"Then I will take my leave. I have several more of these to deliver this evening."

He bustled off, and I lay back down on my pallet. How was I to find a lawyer? How was I to pay for one? I supposed I would have to give the H Street house as security — an irony, seeing as it was moving to that house that had brought me where I was.

I sifted through the names of the various lawyers of whom I had heard. Most were country lawyers dealing with country cases, such as land disputes — the very sort of lawyer I would have called upon when my worst trouble was trying to collect my debt from Mr. Nothey. None I knew had handled a murder case, much less a murder case of a civilian being tried by a military commission.

One name finally came to mind: Senator Reverdy Johnson, one of the most prominent lawyers in Maryland. He had tried the Dred Scott case before the Supreme Court and was certainly capable of standing up before this military commission. But would he take the case? And could I afford his fee? At least worrying about my lawyer distracted me from the scene that otherwise haunted my waking moments: Anna screaming as I was led away.

The next morning, I was told to prepare for court, although there was not anything I could do except to wash myself with the water brought for that purpose daily and put on my bonnet. "Where is the court?" I asked the young guard as he began to lead me from my cell. "Is it far from here?"

He chuckled. "No, ma'am. It's right next door. They've rigged up a special entrance for the prisoners to pass from the cell block to the courtroom."

"There was a courtroom here?"

"There is now. It's been made into one, especially for this trial. They did it right fast

— oh, damn — pardon me, ma'am. I thought they were already in there."

Shuffling down the hall, each led by his keeper like a bear being taken to his baiting, were six men, their hands cuffed, their ankles shackled — and each man's head covered with a black linen hood, save for a slit through which his mouth and part of his nose were visible. Several had an iron ball, carried by a guard, chained to one leg. A seventh man, hoodless but shackled and under guard, followed the rest, his pale face alight with horror.

It was almost as if their fate had been preordained, and they were being led to the hangman. I shuddered.

We stepped back into my cell while the men shambled past us. "Am I to wear a hood?" I whispered.

"No, ma'am. Only the men wear them, except for Dr. Mudd."

"They are to wear them while they go to the courtroom? How horrid!"

"No, ma'am. They wear them all of the —" My young guard stopped himself. "I've said too much, ma'am."

My guard led me down the hall and into a whitewashed room, where an empty seat immediately by the door awaited me. The hooded men were being pushed into their seats when I took my place.

Seated at a table on my far left, close to the room's only windows, were a group of men in uniform. I heard one look at me and whisper, "A woman? Here on trial?" The others' eyes were riveted on the hooded men.

"Unhood them," said one of the uniformed men.

The guards complied, revealing six puffy, unnaturally pale faces topped with tousled, damp hair. As the men, reacting to the sudden burst of daylight, shook their heads and blinked, I recognized only three of them beneath their swollen features: Mr. Payne, Mr. Atzerodt, and Mr. Herold.

"Is that all of them?"

"Yes, sir."

"Then let us begin."

For an hour or so, the commissioners talked and argued amongst themselves while the eight of us sat silently, the men glancing from time to time out of the windows. At last, a stern-looking man rose and introduced himself as Judge Advocate Burnett. One by one, he asked whether we wished to secure counsel and if so, whom. Mr. Herold named three men; Dr. Mudd, the unhooded prisoner next to me, named one. The other men wanted counsel but required more

435

time to think about the matter.

"Very well. Mrs. Surratt?"

"I wish to retain Senator Reverdy Johnson, sir. And I would like to consult with Mr. William Wallace Kirby as well. He is not a lawyer, but I would like to take what advice he can offer me."

There was a murmur, suggesting Senator Johnson was too prominent to want to bother representing me. But Judge Advocate Burnett said, as he did to Mr. Herold and Dr. Mudd, "Very well, I will write to them today. Guards, take the prisoners back to their cells."

The guards started to replace the hoods on the men's heads, but a man who I had learned during the proceedings was Judge Advocate General Holt, who would be our chief prosecutor, stood. "Leave those damn things off them until they're out of this courtroom."

The next day, General Hartranft came to my cell with a message: Senator Johnson regretted that a scheduling conflict might prevent him from representing me, but asked two younger lawyers, Frederick Aiken and John Clampitt, who had a partnership here in Washington, to appear for me. "I have never heard of them."

"They have been in practice together for less than six months, I understand."

Dear God, two fledgling lawyers. But Senator Johnson must have had some faith in their abilities to recommend them to me, so I simply nodded. "Thank you, sir."

On Thursday, my lawyers appeared in court. They were not quite as young as I feared — in their late twenties or early thirties — and they brought, in the very brief consultation we had, the encouraging news that Senator Johnson would likely appear for me after all, and perhaps even without a fee. They would be doing the drudge work, they assured me, and merely assisting their more experienced colleague. My heart, though it could hardly be called light, was somewhat less heavy as I was led back to my cell.

I also met with Mr. Kirby. "Mrs. Surratt, if you would tell all you know about your son and Mr. Booth, I believe with all my heart that you would be set free. At the very least, why do you not ask that he give himself up? Say the word, and I will speak to every newspaper editor in Washington. His mother's plea, printed in the papers, will bring him back. I am certain of it."

"I do not know what he discussed with Mr. Booth, and if I did, I would never tell.

And I will not ask that he return to Washington to be hooded and shackled with these men who sit beside me."

"Well, I tried." Mr. Kirby sighed. "In any event, Mrs. Surratt, I am ill positioned to advise you, because it is possible that I might be called as a witness. I helped search for Dr. Mudd, and I have helped search for your son as well. For your sake," he added, "I do not want to see you sacrificed for him."

It occurred to me, as it had fleetingly occurred to me before when Superintendent Wood informed me he had included Mr. Kirby in his search party, that Mr. Kirby was as eager as anyone else to collect the reward for capturing my son — the only reward anyone could aspire to now that Mr. Booth was dead and Mr. Herold hooded and shackled in the prisoners' dock. "Do you know anything of Mr. Clampitt and Mr. Aiken?"

"Mr. Aiken served in the Union army for a while, was a newspaperman for a while, then got back into law." Mr. Kirby shrugged. "Strange, it's usually law to journalism, rather than the other way around. Both he and Mr. Clampitt are Democrats. How they are as lawyers I can't say, but you'll be in good hands with Mr. Johnson." He rose.

"And now I fear I must be going, Mrs. Surratt."

I had better be in his good hands, because you are washing yours of me. I did not say this, of course. "Thank you for stopping by, sir."

The next day, Friday, was the first day of testimony, although the public was not allowed inside. The gentlemen of the press were here, though, staring hard at us defendants. I was grateful General Hartranft had procured some clothing from the boardinghouse for me, so not only could I change my garments for the first time in weeks, but I could also hide myself behind a veil from the reporters' scrutiny. The men came into the courtroom without their hoods but still in manacles and shackles.

The government was determined to link this mad scheme of Mr. Booth's to the upper reaches of the Confederacy. There was a great deal of testimony about Mr. Booth's travels and his oil investments. General Grant himself appeared as a witness, chiefly to discuss the jurisdiction of the Military Department of Washington, and the commissioners promptly assumed their best posture and gazed at the victorious general like moonstruck privates. General and Mrs. Grant, I had learned, were to have accompanied President and Mrs. Lincoln to the theater on Good Friday but changed their plans, and as the general testified, I wondered whether his presence might have thwarted Booth's plans — or whether he might have shared the president's fate.

An actor friend of Mr. Booth's, a handsome man who identified himself as Samuel Knapp Chester, took the stand — more, I thought, as if he were taking the stage. Even we defendants listened in fascination as he detailed Mr. Booth's futile attempts to get him to join his plan to kidnap the president. If only Johnny — and I — had been as wary . . .

"Did he have any conversation with you at a later period, after the inauguration, as to the opportunity he had for the assassination of the president? Did he speak of that?"

Mr. Chester nodded. "Yes, sir. On Friday, one week previous to the assassination, he was in New York. We were in the House of Lords at the time, sitting at a table, and had not been there long before he exclaimed, striking the table, 'What an excellent chance I had to kill the president, if I had wished, on inauguration day!' "

If he had wished. Had he still been planning only to kidnap at that point? When, and why, had he changed his mind? If only

I could drag him back from the dead and force him to go to this stand and tell us all.

And had he not considered the consequences his act would bring upon the innocent — his family, his friends, his fellow actors, the young ladies, like my daughter and Nora, who had enjoyed his company so much?

But, I reflected behind the shield of my veil, I had not considered them all that well myself.

As the men, preparing to go back to their cells, cast a last wistful look out the window, an older man entered the room. After conferring with my attorneys, he said, "Mrs. Surratt? I am Senator Reverdy Johnson, and I will be serving as your counsel."

Close to seventy, Reverdy Johnson was a stately figure with a resonant voice. Whatever other mistakes I had made over the last few months, I had at least chosen my lawyer wisely. I pushed back my veil — thinking, as I did, of little Mrs. Slater and Johnny. "Senator Johnson, I am so grateful you have agreed to represent me."

"I could not refuse a Southern Maryland lady, Mrs. Surratt. Now, do you have any questions for me?"

"Why is there to be a military trial?"

Senator Johnson shook his head. "The

explanation is that the assassination of President Lincoln was a wartime act, and that Booth and his accomplices violated the laws of war, and that you and the rest should therefore be tried by a military court instead of a civilian one. All that is balderdash. The truth is, there are still so many Confederate sympathizers in Washington, Secretary Stanton fears that he could not obtain a conviction by a jury were you to be tried by a civilian court. I am preparing an argument against the jurisdiction of this court, but for the time being, we must proceed here."

"Will I be allowed to testify?"

"No, but in that one respect, it makes no difference what sort of trial you have. Except in the state of Maine, a defendant in a criminal case cannot testify in his own defense."

"Sir, what do you think will happen to me? I know that we are on trial for our lives."

"No woman has been hanged by the federal government, Mrs. Surratt, and I cannot imagine they would dare to do it now. It would be against all notions of chivalry, all that we hold dear. Besides, there are enough desperate-looking characters in that lot to hang. I would not like to be Mr.

Atzerodt's counsel, for instance, and that Payne fellow, having actually attempted the murder of Secretary Seward, doesn't stand a chance."

"But will they imprison me? What will become of my daughter?"

"I cannot assure you at this time that you will not be imprisoned, Mrs. Surratt. I must hear the evidence — and yes, I will hear it as you hear it. Even so, I have the best of hopes that your imprisonment will not be long or harsh. They will have their pound of flesh in the men here, and then they can make a great show of pardoning you and sending you, suitably chastised, back to your home and family."

"I will trust in your judgment, Senator Johnson."

"I believe that our greatest hope lies in challenging the jurisdiction of the court," Senator Johnson said briskly. "It is something that I will bend all of my energies to. And with that, Mrs. Surratt, I will bid you good day."

On Saturday, the spectators came.

The trial was the best show in town, I heard the lawyers telling each other as everyone settled into their places. The general public could not attend, but those who had the connections to get a pass could, and judging from the fine attire of the spectators, these were very well-connected people indeed. Some of the men brought their ladies and courteously gave them the best seats.

The ladies pointed and squealed like children visiting a menagerie. "There's Payne! There's that horrid Atzerodt! There's Mrs. Surratt!" Mr. Herold seemed to find this attention diverting, and he admired the younger and prettier of the ladies. Mr. Payne stared straight ahead, his face never changing expression, which fascinated the ladies all the more. With his strong build and chiseled features, he was their clear favorite; presentable but unexceptional Mr. Arnold and Mr. O'Laughlin, scruffy Mr. Spangler, disreputable Mr. Atzerodt, hobble-dehoyish Mr. Herold, and dejected Dr. Mudd barely merited a second glance from them.

After Mr. Payne, I was the second most popular attraction. "There is the horrid creature!" "Look how demure she pretends to be!" "Look how bold she looks!" Two pretty ladies got into a spirited argument about whether I looked sufficiently wicked to have plotted to kill the president, and they were still arguing the point when

General Hunter, the president of the commission, called the court to order.

Senator Johnson entered the courtroom. Catching sight of him as a murmur went about, General Hunter asked, "Do I understand Mr. Johnson is appearing for any of these prisoners?"

"I do not know whether I shall be able to appear or not. I have taken no part in the case thus far, except to speak to the counsel. Whether I shall appear or not will depend on whether I can find that I can stay as long as may be necessary. I have no objection to appearing if the court will permit me to leave it at any time."

Leave?

I was frowning over this when the commissioners and Senator Johnson began arguing over whether he recognized the oath of loyalty to the government. Their exchange was so spirited at one point that my co-defendants sensed a fight, for all seven of them sat up straighter, their manacled hands balling instinctively into fists.

But after a great deal more talk, during which the ladies drooped with boredom, everyone was mollified, and the first witness of the day was called. He was a detective, who gave evidence against Mr. Atzerodt.

Then the second witness was called. I

heard the name, but only when the witness walked to the stand did I believe what I was hearing. He raised his hand and swore to tell the truth and nothing but the truth.

He was Mr. Weichmann. And he was testifying for the prosecution.

38
NORA

I could get no information about what had happened to Mrs. Surratt after she was taken away. Even Miss Lomax, who continued to enjoy privileges I did not, was unable to obtain any word as to her fate.

During this period, I had my own tribulations, although in retrospect, they hardly seem worthy of mention. One night, Miss Lomax and I were awakened by an unearthly howling, which we were convinced could only be the anguished noises of some poor prisoner in torment. Only a few days later did we learn the truth: the large gray feline who was the prison's chief mouser had disappeared for a day or two, only to be found locked in the cellar, from which it emerged with a vigor that proved to be the terror of the Old Capitol's rodent population. Another time, just before lights-out, two drunken male prisoners found their way to our cell "just to visit the ladies!" It was

one of the few times during our imprisonment when we were grateful for the man
pacing back and forth outside our door, for
we could hear him threatening to blow their
brains out if they did not make a quick
retreat, an order they tipsily obeyed.

After a week or so of durance, Miss
Lomax was released. Later, she wrote a
memoir of her time here — anonymously
and with most of the names disguised,
though any lady who was at the Old Capitol
at the time would have no difficulty recognizing her or her fellow inmates in its pages.
I was rather disappointed — as I suppose
those who find themselves put into books
are destined to be — to find myself en-
shrined, under the uninspired name of
"Mary," as a rather timid miss, five years
younger than my true age (although perhaps
this was a politeness), and without an
overabundance of spirit. I was also amused
to see that Miss Lomax added weeks onto
her own imprisonment. Still, she painted a
kind portrait of Mrs. Surratt, who along
with Anna was the only person in the book
to appear under her true name, and for that
I could forgive Miss Lomax any of her
deficiencies.

I was not alone after Miss Lomax was
freed. A third lady, whom Miss Lomax

named in her book as Mrs. Thomas and whom I shall call the same, had been placed in our cell. Her story did not hang together well, and I suspected, and still suspect, she had been placed with us as a spy. Certainly she ate the prison food with gusto and slept on the bed without a bit of squeamishness, which made me believe she was not all that sorry to be here and that prison might indeed be a step up for her. But she was such a talkative lady that, even if I had been so foolish as to say anything compromising, I doubt I would have been allowed to get enough words in edgewise to do so.

In the meantime, I had heard nothing from my father, although another basket of cakes had finally been delivered to me. With Mrs. Surratt's departure, however, I was allowed the privilege of seeing some other prisoners' cast-off newspapers, and it was from them I learned the horrid news that Mrs. Surratt and seven men were to go on trial for their lives at the Old Arsenal Penitentiary here in Washington.

The Old Arsenal was located at the very tip of a poor part of Washington known as the Island. A number of young women from the neighborhood, most of them poor Irish, had worked packing cartridges at the arsenal, and the previous summer, there had been a dreadful explosion that had killed twenty-one of them and burned a few others horribly. I had read of the tragedy, and the mass funeral for the victims (which President Lincoln had attended), from the comfortable confines of Georgetown Visitation. There I had guiltily contemplated how similar I was to those girls, in age and background, and yet how entirely different, being blessed with a father who could provide for me instead of having to provide for myself.

How could anyone on trial in such a sad place come to any good end?

39
MARY

Everyone in the courtroom, even the ladies, fell silent when Mr. Weichmann took his oath. The very first question Judge Advocate Holt asked was whether he knew my Johnny, to which Mr. Weichmann gave a firm yes.

"When did you begin to board at the house of his mother, Mrs. Surratt, a prisoner here?"

"The first of November, 1864."

"Mrs. Surratt, who is sitting near you there?"

An officer motioned for me to remove my veil, and Mr. Weichmann, who had his back to me, turned and looked at me for the first time since he had left my boardinghouse to look for Johnny. I could not see his face well enough to read his emotions, and perhaps I could not have read them even if my sight were better. "Yes, sir, she is the lady."

As Judge Holt briskly examined Mr. Weichmann, who gave his replies in a more firm, confident tone than I ever remembered hearing him use in my boardinghouse, I discovered there was simply nothing this man did not remember. Mr. Booth's comings and goings. The mysterious Mrs. Slater. Mr. Payne's visits, first in his guise as Mr. Wood and then as Mr. Payne. Our two carriage drives to the country. The young ladies calling Mr. Atzerodt "Port Tobacco." Dates, times, places, clothing — Mr. Weichmann had it all perfectly, to the point where I wondered if he had been keeping a pocket diary of all this.

Judge Holt moved on relentlessly as I leaned my head on my arm. Since being moved here, I had been suffering off and on from female problems, and Mr. Weichmann's testimony was making me no better. "Will you state whether, on the afternoon of the fourteenth of April, the day of the assassination, Mr. Booth did not call and have a private interview with Mrs. Surratt at her house?"

"I will state that about half past two o'clock, when I was going to the door, I saw Mr. Booth. He was in the parlor, and Mrs. Surratt was speaking to him."

"Were they alone?"

"Yes, sir, they were alone in the parlor."

The lady spectators tittered.

"How long was it after that before you drove to the country with Mrs. Surratt?"

"He did not remain in the parlor more than three or four minutes."

"And was it immediately after that you and Mrs. Surratt set out for the country?"

"Yes, sir."

During this conversation, my counsel and his associates had been scribbling on paper, their faces impassive. Senator Johnson rose for the cross-examination. "Were you upon intimate terms with Mr. Surratt?"

"Very intimate, indeed."

"Did he ever intimate to you or anybody else, to your knowledge, that there was a purpose to assassinate the president?"

"No, sir."

"Were you in the habit of seeing John H. Surratt almost every day when he was at home, at his mother's?"

"Yes, sir, he would be seated at the same table."

"Was he frequently in your room, and you in his?"

"He partook of the same room, shared my bed with me, slept with me."

And got drunk with you, shared oysters with you, laughed with you, Mr. Weichmann . . .

"And during the whole of that period you never heard him intimate that it was his

453

purpose, or that there was a purpose, to assassinate the president?"

"No, sir. At one time he mentioned to me that he was going on the stage with Booth, that he was going to be an actor, and that they were going to play in Richmond."

For some time, Senator Johnson shot questions at Mr. Weichmann, who answered them all in an unruffled voice. I wondered how many interrogations he had undergone since being sent to Old Capitol Prison.

"You have known Mrs. Surratt ever since November, and before that?"

"I have known her since 1863."

"You have been living at her house since November?"

"Since November."

"During the whole of that time, as far as you could judge, was her character apparently good and amiable?"

"Her character was exemplary and ladylike in every particular."

"Have you been to church with her?"

"I generally accompanied her to church every Sunday."

"As far as you could judge, her conduct, in a religious and in a moral sense, was altogether exemplary?"

"Yes, sir. She went to her religious duties at least every two weeks."

"Did she go early in the morning?"

"Sometimes early in the morning, and sometimes at late Mass."

"Was that the case during the whole period up to the assassination?"

"Yes, sir."

"Then, if I understand you, from November up to the fourteenth of April, whenever she was here, she was regular in her attendance at her own church, and apparently, as far as you could judge, doing all her duties to God and to man?"

"Yes, sir."

Senator Johnson nodded and took his seat with an air of satisfaction. Gamely, my other two lawyers cross-examined my boarder, as did all of the other defendants' lawyers. By the time Mr. Weichmann finally left the stand, his voice was hoarse.

The commissioners called a recess, and my counsel gathered around me. "Well," Senator Johnson said. "That was certainly an observant young man."

"Sir, do you think he did us damage?"

Senator Johnson gathered some papers together. "The jurisdictional question will be our best defense, as I said earlier. Now, I must be going, but of course Mr. Clampitt and Mr. Aiken will remain here for the afternoon session."

He bustled off. My codefendants' lawyers, busy conferring with their own clients, looked at him, puzzled, as he left.

After the recess, I heard a second familiar name called to the stand. "John Lloyd." His imprisonment, and I guess enforced sobriety, had on the whole had a beneficial effect on him, for he looked healthier and thinner as he made his way to the stand.

Did he know he held my fate in his hands?

Mr. Aiken seemed to know so. He rose. "Sirs, I would request that in the absence of my senior counsel, and its importance to my client Mrs. Surratt's case, that Mr. Lloyd's testimony be postponed until Monday next, when Senator Johnson will be present."

Judge Holt rose. "I object, sir. Mrs. Surratt has two perfectly competent lawyers present. She does not need three."

"Overruled."

As Mr. Aiken sat down, defeated, Judge Holt asked Mr. Lloyd whether he knew my son, Mr. Herold, and Mr. Atzerodt, and was met with a series of affirmatives. "Will you state whether or not, some five or six weeks before the assassination of the president, any or all of these men about whom I have inquired came to your house?"

456

"They were there."

"All three together?"

"Yes: John H. Surratt, Herold, and Atzerodt were there together."

"What did they bring to your house? And what did they do there?"

"When they drove up there in the morning, John H. Surratt and Atzerodt came first. They went from my house and went toward T. B., a town about five miles below there. They had not been gone more than half an hour when they returned with Herold. Then the three were together — Herold, Surratt, and Atzerodt."

"What did they bring to your house?"

"I saw nothing until they all three came into the bar room. All three of them drank, I think, and then John Surratt called me into the front parlor, and on the sofa were two guns with ammunition. I think he told me they were carbines."

"A sort of a shorter rifle," one of the gentleman spectators explained in an undertone to his lady, who was looking baffled.

"Anything besides the carbines and ammunition?"

"There was a rope, and also a monkey wrench. Surratt asked me to take care of them, to conceal the carbines. I told him there was no place there to conceal them, and I did not wish to keep such things in the house."

"You say that he asked you to conceal those articles for him?"

"Yes, sir, he asked me to conceal them. I told him there was no place to conceal them. He then showed me where I could put them underneath the joists of the house — the joists of the second floor of the main building. This little unfinished room will admit of anything between the joists."

I almost nodded in agreement before I caught myself. Johnny had hidden things for himself and his courier friends there many a time; I had watched him do it.

"Were they put in that place?"

"They were put in there according to his directions."

"For what purpose, and for how long, did he ask you to keep those articles?"

"I am very positive that he said he would call for them in a few days. He said he just wanted them to stay for a few days, and he would call for them."

"Will you state whether or not, on the Monday or Tuesday preceding the assassination of the president, Mrs. Surratt came to your home?"

"I was coming to Washington, and I met Mrs. Surratt at Uniontown on the Tuesday previous."

"Did she say anything to you in regard to those carbines?"

I closed my eyes.

"When she first broached the subject to me, I did not know what she had reference to, then she came out plainer, and I am quite positive she asked me about the 'shooting irons.' I am quite positive about that, but not altogether positive. Think she named 'shooting irons,' or something to call my attention to those things, for I had almost forgotten about their being there. I told her that they were hid far back, that I was afraid the house would be searched, and they were shoved far back. She told me to get them out ready; they would be wanted soon."

Mr. Herold, who seemed to find our trial rather entertaining on the whole, looked in my direction to see how I was reacting to all of this. I sat up straighter.

"Will you state now, whether or not, on the evening of the night on which the president was assassinated, Mrs. Surratt came to your house with Mr. Weichmann?"

"I went to Marlboro on that day to attend a trial there in court, and in the evening it was probably late when I got home. I found Mrs. Surratt there when I got home. I should judge it was about five o'clock."

"What did she say to you?"

"She met me out by the woodpile as I drove in, having fish and oysters in the buggy, and she told me to have those shooting irons ready that night. There would be some parties calling for them."

"Did she ask you to get anything else ready for those parties besides the shooting irons?"

"She gave me something wrapped up in a piece of paper. I did not know what it was till I took it upstairs, and I found it to be a field glass."

"Did she ask you to have any whiskey prepared for those parties?"

"She did."

"What did she say about that?"

"She said to get two bottles of whiskey also."

"And said they were to be called for that night?"

"Yes. They were to be called for that night."

"State now whether they were called for that night by Booth and Herold."

Mr. Lloyd swept the air with his hand. "Booth told me, 'Lloyd, for God's sake, make haste and get those things!' "

"Did he not seem, from the manner of his

language, to suppose that you already understood what he called for?"

"From the way he spoke, he must have been apprised that I already knew what I was to give him."

"What did you say?"

"I did not make any reply but went upstairs and got them."

"Did they take one or both of the carbines?"

"Only one."

"Did they explain why the other was not taken?"

"Booth said that he could not take his, because his leg was broken."

"Did he take a drink also?"

"He drank while he was sitting out on his horse."

"Did Herold carry the bottle out to him?"

"Yes, sir."

"Did they say anything in regard to the assassination as they rode away?"

"Just as they were about leaving, Booth said, 'I will tell you some news if you want to hear it' or something to that effect. I said, 'I am not particular. Use your own choice about telling news.' 'Well,' said he, 'I am pretty certain that we have assassinated the president and Secretary Seward.'"

Even in my present state, I could imagine

461

Mr. Booth, injured and fleeing for his life, sitting on his horse and telling my tenant in his pleasant voice that he had committed the crime of the century.

As the days passed, more and more ladies made their way to the court, encouraged, I suppose, by the reports of their friends who had attended early on. There were so many of them, they overflowed into the spaces occupied by the press and by the defense counsel. Sometimes they forgot where they were and began to chatter among themselves as if they were leaving church after a particularly interesting sermon. The commissioners, who would surely have dealt with them swiftly if they were men, appeared to be completely intimidated by these pretty women in their finery, and when they were forced to shush them, did so in the mildest way possible.

The ladies' greatest occupations were gazing at Mr. Payne and at me. Mr. Payne seemed to overawe them, so they kept their thoughts about him to themselves, but they had no such compunctions when it came to me. Each day before court started, they got within mere feet of me and debated whether I was ugly or pretty, whether my proportions were stout or mannish, whether I had an evil face or a benevolent one. If it were not for Mr. Payne, a look from whom quailed them, they would probably have tried to lift my veil.

It hurt me to the very bone. When had I ever done a sister woman an unkindness? Could not they think how it pained me to sit every day and hear my Johnny spoken of as a criminal? Did they know how I longed to see my poor Anna, of whom I had not had a word since being brought here?

I had sinned, and perhaps I deserved this pointing and giggling, but that still made it no easier to bear.

On a hot morning in mid-May, the ladies subsided into their seats, whispering that they hoped there would be some interesting witnesses today and not a bunch of dreary bores. They got their wish, for soon Mr. Weichmann emerged from the room where the witnesses waited their turn to be called.

Mr. Weichmann started by identifying the telegram he received from Mr. Booth, telling him to ask Johnny to telegraph an address to Mr. Booth. Judge Holt asked, "Did you or did you not deliver to Mr. Surratt the message contained in the dispatch?"

"I delivered it to him the same day."

"What did he say?"

"I asked him what particular number and

street was meant, and he said, 'Don't be so damned inquisitive!' "

Sourly, I thought Mr. Weichmann had never in his life had so many women hanging on his every word.

Mr. Weichmann told the court about the day Johnny, Mr. Payne, and Mr. Booth returned to the house after the failed kidnapping. No one asked him what we had for dinner that night, but I had no doubt that if someone had, he would remember it to the last biscuit.

Rising to cross-examine Mr. Weichmann, Mr. Aiken asked him about my meeting with Mr. Lloyd at Uniontown, and Senator Johnson — here in court for the first time in several days — joined in, albeit to no account I could see. He made matters even worse by asking my boarder about Mrs. Slater. As Mr. Weichmann prepared to answer — never in this trial had I heard him utter the words "I don't know" — I wondered what had become of that pert young woman. Although her name had come up from time to time before at the trial as Johnny's companion and a guest at the boardinghouse, no one had accused her of plotting to kill the president, and no one seemed to know what she was doing now or where she was doing it. Was she back with her inconvenient husband, warming my Johnny's bed somewhere in Canada, or locked up in some Yankee prison? For all I disliked the chit, I hoped she was free. She ought to be: not even Mr. Weichmann knew her Christian name, and she had certainly kept herself well hidden with that veil of hers.

"Mrs. Surratt told me that she was a North Carolinian, I believe, and that she spoke French, and that she was a blockade runner, or bearer of dispatches."

"When, if ever, had I told Mr. Weichmann those things?"

Echoing my doubts, Mr. Aiken asked, "Are you certain, beyond all doubt, that Mrs. Surratt told you Mrs. Slater was a blockade runner?"

Mr. Weichmann said resoundingly, "Yes, sir," and the ladies clucked their tongues comfortably, assured beyond all doubt that I was on the best of terms with the spy Mrs. Slater.

Mr. Aiken asked Mr. Weichmann whether, while employed at the War Department, he had agreed to share any of its information with those of us in the prisoners' dock. I tensed with attention, for Johnny had told me he did precisely that. But Mr. Weichmann batted back his question with a firm "No, sir," lying with a conviction I doubted

I would have been able to muster.

Left with no choice but to move on, Mr. Aiken asked, "You state that all the prisoners at the bar were free and unreserved in your presence in their conversation?"

"They spoke in my presence on general topics, and so on, but, on their private business, they never spoke to me."

"In all your conversation with them, you never learned of any intended treasonable purpose or act or conspiracy of theirs?"

"No, sir."

"You never did?"

"No, sir."

"And you were not suspicious of anything of the sort?"

Mr. Weichmann raised his right hand. "I would have been the last man in the world to suspect John Surratt, my schoolmate, of the murder of the president of the United States."

"You state that your suspicions were aroused at one time by something you saw at Mrs. Surratt's?"

"My suspicions were aroused by John Surratt and this man Payne and Booth coming to the house. My suspicions again were aroused by their frequent private conversations. My suspicions were aroused by seeing Payne and Surratt playing on the bed with

466

bowie knives."

"Then, if your suspicions were aroused on all these different occasions that you have mentioned, and you had reason to believe that something was in the wind that was improper, did you communicate any of them to the War Department?"

"My suspicions were not of a fixed or settled character," Mr. Weichmann said a little sulkily. "I did not know what they intended to do. I made a confidant of Captain Gleason in the War Department. I told him that Booth was a secesh sympathizer: I mentioned snatches of conversation that I would hear from these parties, and I asked him, 'Captain, what do you think of all this?' We even talked over several things they could do. I asked him whether they could be bearers of dispatches or blockade runners. At one time I saw in the paper the capture of President Lincoln fully discussed, and I remarked to Captain Gleason, 'Captain, do you think any party could attempt the capture of President Lincoln?' He laughed and hooted at the idea."

"You were a roommate of Surratt's?"

"John Surratt has been my companion for seven years now."

"And did you still profess to be a friend and confidant of his at the time you were giving this information that you speak of to the War Department?"

"I was a friend so far as he was concerned, but when my suspicions were aroused as to the danger to the government in particular, I preferred the government to John Surratt. I did not know what he was contemplating. He said he was going to engage in cotton speculations. He was going to engage in oil."

"If you did not know what he was contemplating, how could you forfeit your friendship to him? What is the rationale of that proceeding?"

"I never forfeited my friendship to him. He forfeited his friendship to me."

"Not by engaging in the cotton speculation?"

"No, sir. By placing me in the position in which I now am — testifying against him."

The commissioners, along with the lady spectators, all nodded sympathetically at poor Mr. Weichmann's plight.

40
NORA

Soon after the trial began, my friend Tall One visited me in Mr. Wood's office. "You are on the list of witnesses to testify for the prosecution," he informed me. "Testify satisfactorily, and you will find yourself safe at home."

"What do you call testifying satisfactorily?"

"I call it testifying to the points you've been cooperative on, which haven't been all that many. You saw Booth, Payne, and Atzerodt at Mrs. Surratt's house. Are you prepared to admit to that?"

"I can hardly deny it."

"Then don't try. Second point: you went to Ford's Theatre with John Surratt and Payne, sat in a box there, and saw Mr. Booth pay the men a visit. Are you prepared to admit to that?"

"I am."

"Then just don't make any unpleasant

469

surprises for us, miss, and testify as you just promised me."

"I will not have to testify against Mrs. Surratt?"

Tall One eyed me. "Is there something you know against her?"

"Nothing."

"And if you did, I doubt you'd tell it," Tall One remarked. He rang for my guard. "Women," he muttered.

With the start of the trial, I soon became accustomed to a new routine. Each morning, a group of us prisoners would be herded into ambulances, which took us to the Old Arsenal. There, we were crowded into a small room adjoining the courtroom, waiting to be called to testify if needed that day. Usually we were not needed but would sit there for hours under guard, listening to the day's proceedings.

Mr. Weichmann often shared the ambulance with me. Over the first few days of the trial, he took the stand no fewer than four times, and I listened as he testified about Port Tobacco and Mr. Payne, about Mr. Surratt's meeting with Mr. Booth and Dr. Mudd, about Mrs. Slater and Mr. Howell, about Mr. Booth's comings and goings, about Mrs. Surratt's trips to the tavern with him, even about my own visit to Ford's Theatre. All of it made a nice little package of conspiracy, which Mr. Weichmann tied up with a pretty bow and handed to the government. Whether he did so out of fear of being placed in the prisoner's dock himself or out of a genuine desire to see the guilty punished, I cannot say, but when he left the stand and went to sit with the rest of us, awaiting the drive back to Old Capitol Prison, he left off the fine posture he exhibited on the witness stand and sat slumped in a chair, toying with a pocket watch.

We never spoke in the room or in the ambulance, as we were under guard the entire time. Only once, as we stood waiting our turn to climb into the ambulance, did I get a chance to hiss to him, "Since you volunteer testimony from time to time, I wish you would tell the rest, Mr. Weichmann."

"The rest?"

"Yes. About Mrs. Surratt comforting me when Private Flanagan died. About you and Mr. Surratt singing 'Dixie.' About the time we went to see the election results. About the readings we did for Mr. Booth. The times when we were amusing ourselves and no one was plotting anything."

Mr. Weichmann gazed at me rather sadly.

"It's not relevant, Miss Fitzpatrick."

"Maybe," I said just as the guard came into view. "But it's part of the story, isn't it?"

On Monday, May 22, an officer said, "You'll be first today, Miss Fitzpatrick," as we were led to our usual gathering place.

I gulped.

As my name was called and I walked to the stand, I glimpsed Mrs. Surratt sitting in a chair in a corner. Clad in black, she held a fan in her hand. I could not see her expression through her veil, and I could only pray that she realized I had not chosen to testify for the prosecution.

I had learned through the chattering of our guards to one another and the newspapers that the trial had attracted many spectators, women as well as men, and the former were especially well represented this morning. Their titters followed me to the stand, and I could see why, for I was a shabby-looking creature. Although Father had been allowed to send in a change of undergarments for me, I was still wearing the dress I had worn when I was arrested at the church fair, and after nearly a month it was none too fresh. After much fuss, I'd finally been given a towel to wash with in the morning, but as the towel was seldom replaced, my face felt nearly as grimy as my dress.

At least I was free of lice, I consoled myself. Each morning, I sat down and coolly checked myself for them, and sometimes Mrs. Thomas and I checked each other for them, like a pair of monkeys. (Even Mrs. Thomas's lack of squeamishness stopped at lice.) I had been imprisoned long enough to no longer find this particularly odd.

I stepped as far as I could into the witness box — there was a little chuckle when the audience noted it was not built to accommodate a lady's crinoline — and gazed at the commissioners as I took my oath. Then rose Judge Advocate Bingham, a thin, stern-looking man of about fifty. "State, if you please, to the court your name and residence."

"My name is Honora Fitzpatrick. I am a resident of Washington."

"At whose house did you reside during the month of March last in Washington?"

"At Mrs. Surratt's."

"The house of the prisoner at the bar?"

It was such a cold appellation. "Yes, sir."

"State to the court whether, during the time of your residence at her house last winter, you saw John H. Surratt and other men in company with him there."

"I saw John Surratt there."

Judge Bingham nodded approvingly. "State what other men you saw there during the time of your stay last winter."

"I saw Mr. Booth there."

"John Wilkes Booth?"

"Yes, sir."

"State whether you saw any of the prisoners at the bar there during your stay last winter."

"Yes, sir."

Judge Bingham snapped, "Who are they?"

Seven men with irons on their wrists and I looked at one another. "There is one, Mr. Payne there, and another, Port — I mean, Mr. Atzerodt."

"How often did you see this Mr. Payne at Mrs. Surratt's house? And when?"

"I never saw him there but twice."

"How often did you see this Mr. Atzerodt that you speak of there?"

"He was there for a short time."

"Do you understand whether he stayed there overnight once?"

"Yes, sir, he did."

Judge Bingham gestured. "Look at the other prisoners at the bar — that one at the bar talking." He pointed to a young man, whom I recognized from the wanted posters as Mr. Herold, who was conversing with a man I supposed was his lawyer.

"I do not know him. I never saw him."

This seemed to disappoint Judge Bingham. "State to the court whether you accompanied Surratt and this Payne to Ford's Theatre one night last March," he said curtly.

"Yes, sir."

"State whether you occupied a box in the theater that night with them."

"Yes, sir."

"Which box was it that you occupied?"

"I do not know."

"On which side of the theater was it, as you went in?"

"I did not pay attention which side it was on."

"And cannot tell now which side it was on?"

"No, sir."

"Was it the upper or lower box?"

"I think it was the upper."

"State whether John Wilkes Booth came into that box that night while you and Surratt and Payne were in there."

"Yes, sir, he did." For the first time, it occurred to me that I'd likely been watching *Jane Shore* in the same box where the president had been murdered a month later. I shivered at the thought.

"What other lady accompanied you?"

I hoped they did not intend to make the little girl testify. "Miss Dean."

"When did you leave Mrs. Surratt's after going to the theater?"

"I went on a visit to Baltimore."

The commissioners murmured at the word *Baltimore,* and I wondered if I should have mentioned that I had paid a visit to my sister, the nun.

"When did you start on that visit?"

"In the six o'clock train the next day after going to the theater."

"How long were you absent?"

"I was absent a week."

Judge Bingham nodded toward the commissioners. "Have you any questions of the young lady?"

Someone asked, "Do you recollect, on entering the theater, whether you turned to the right or to the left to get to the box you occupied?"

"No, sir, I do not know which side I turned to."

"You may step down," said Judge Bingham.

I obeyed, managing to smile at Mrs. Surratt as I turned to walk back to the waiting room. I doubted she could see my expression, but at least I had made the effort.

I had returned to my cell — I almost said "to my home" — only for a few minutes when Superintendent Wood entered. "You're free, Miss Fitzpatrick."

"Free?"

"Orders of General Augur. Gather your things, and I'll take you to your father. He just arrived to escort you home."

Numbly, I obeyed. I had little to gather but my shawl and my bonnet, which I had but just hung in their places, and my change of undergarments, which Mr. Wood gallantly pretended not to see. I snatched up *The Trapper's Bride* as well. I was on my way out when I turned. "Wait, sir."

I still had the stub of a pencil I'd been given when I'd asked to write to my father. I took it out of my pocket and turned to the wall. When I had finished, the inscription there read:

Miss Nora Fitzpatrick, In durance vile from April 24, 1865, to May 22, 1865

Mr. Wood watched me indulgently. "All done, miss?"

I nodded. "Done."

I followed Superintendent Wood, taking one last glance at my handiwork. It and the wall on which I wrote are dust now, smashed to smithereens like the rest of Carroll Annex to make room for the new Library of Congress building. I passed by it not long after it was knocked down and pondered whether it was a good thing that a place where so many people had suffered should be gone for good, or an ill thing that it and all those who suffered inside should be forgotten.

Father was pacing around Superintendent Wood's office when I came in. He gathered me into his arms and embraced me. "My dear child," he whispered. "How I have worried about you." He stepped back and stared at me, then at my keeper. "What have you done to my daughter? She's skin and bones! I sent her a basket of food every day. Why was she kept here so long?"

Superintendent Wood decided to answer the easiest question. "Secretary Stanton wished to keep her here until she testified satisfactorily, sir."

My father launched into a description of the secretary of war so vivid, colorful, and completely obscene that it was miraculous

478

he wasn't thrown into prison straightaway. I had never heard him use such language in my life and could do nothing but stand and wonder where on earth he had acquired it. Superintendent Wood seemed equally impressed. "Good day, sir," he said when my father had at last finished his tirade. "I wish you and your daughter well."

Father muttered something less colorful and ushered me out the door.

"Goodness, Father!" I said.

My father said nothing but walked beside me as I pretended not to notice the tears pouring down his face. Finally, he regained his composure. "It is hard, child, not to have been able to do anything to free you. I have never felt so helpless in my life. And what if they take a whim and decide to put you back?"

"I doubt they will, Father. I told them what they wanted."

"Then I would like to send you North to recover your health, child. Peter suggests the mountains of Vermont."

"My health is fine, Father," I said. "I just need a bath. The Misses Donovan will fatten me up in no time. Besides, I can't leave while the trial is going on."

"There were no conditions upon your

release. That Superintendent Wood told me that."

"I meant I can't leave while Mrs. Surratt's fate is being decided."

"I find your loyalty to that woman unaccountable, Nora, after she dragged you into this."

"She didn't drag me into it. Mr. Booth did that." I looked at my father. "I could never enjoy myself in the Vermont mountains worrying about what's happening here. I would pine away."

My father sighed, but it was the familiar sigh indicating that he was about to give way. "Very well. If your health does not appear to be in danger, you can stay here. I confess, I would miss you anyway."

We proceeded to the Misses Donovan, who wept over me for a decent interval before drawing back and ordering their servant to prepare a bath. In as short order as possible, I was luxuriating in a warm tub in the kitchen. My grime at last removed, I sat down to eat. It was a simple meal, as the old ladies usually prepared, but it tasted infinitely delicious. By the time it was finished, the nearly thirty nights of poor sleep I had had were beginning to tell on me, and I was nodding over my plate.

The servant girl led me upstairs into my

chintz-covered room, where Mr. Rochester was dozing. Although it was still light outside, I undressed, then said my prayers and climbed into bed.

But I had forgotten something. Sitting up, I checked myself for lice, inspected the coverlet and sheets for bedbugs, and looked through the keyhole to see if anyone might be spying on me as I slept. These preparations concluded, I settled into bed next to Mr. Rochester once more and slept a good twelve hours.

I probably could have slept far longer on my first morning home from prison, but it would have been impossible, for while I had been incarcerated, Washington had at last shed its funeral attire and draped itself again in bunting. That day and the next, there was a grand review of the armies of the republic, and the bands began striking up at nine sharp.

Washington had never been so crowded — not even for the second inaugural, not even for the illuminations. Even the Misses Donovan, although they had faithfully kept my own room waiting for me, had given into temptation and rented out a few rooms and the attic to a couple of parties of ladies.

I was less strong than I had admitted to

my father and was not inclined to push my way through the throngs, much less stand for hours watching the spectacle, so after eating the breakfast of Brobdingnagian proportions pressed on me by the misses, I returned to my room and sat by the window, listening to the bands. It was good to see the city of my birth with flags flying and with spirits high again, even though I could not forget my friends languishing in prison. Nor did I omit to shed a tear for poor Private Flanagan, who should have been marching with his regiment this fine day, or for all of the other young men who would not be returning home when this grand review ended.

The sound of the bands had begun to die away and I was dozing in my armchair when the servant girl knocked. "A man for you, Miss Fitzpatrick."

Was I about to be hauled to prison a third time? Shakily, I read the card she handed me.

Frederick Aiken, Attorney at Law. Mrs. Surratt's attorney.

"Is the parlor empty?"

"Yes, miss. The misses are napping" — the misses napped a great deal — "and the other ladies are at the review."

"Then send him in there. I will be down

straightaway."

Mr. Aiken was studying the bookshelves when I arrived. He smiled at me. "Miss Fitzpatrick? I am glad to see you in comfortable quarters after your imprisonment. Mrs. Surratt spoke very highly of you."

"Sir, how is she bearing up?"

"She is feeling the effects of close confinement, and I believe has a complaint of a female nature as well, but she is bearing up."

I felt tears come to my eyes. "I wish I could do something to help her."

"You can, Miss Fitzpatrick, and that is why I am here. You can testify in her defense. I know that you have been waiting around in the courtroom for days, and I do not like to ask you to do so again, but —"

"I will gladly testify, sir, to anything you want me to. What do they call them, character witnesses? I can be one. When do you need me?"

Mr. Aiken smiled. "It is pleasant to see an eager witness. Most have been reluctant. We will call some priests as character witnesses, but there are a few things you can help establish. Much has been made of the fact that Mrs. Surratt did not recognize Mr. Payne when he appeared at her house the night of her arrest, the implication being that she knew who he was but concealed it.

Is her eyesight poor?"

"It is indeed, sir, especially in gaslight."

"And you can testify that John Surratt did not come to the boardinghouse since Richmond fell?"

"I can."

"Good. The court is adjourned until Thursday for the grand review, but I will send a carriage for you first thing that morning to take you to court. I can't promise you will be called that day, though, because the prosecution has not yet rested its case."

"I have nothing to do, sir. I can go there as often as needed."

Mr. Aiken nodded and picked up his hat.

"Sir, tell me: What if . . . what if Mrs. Surratt is found guilty?"

"We are doing everything to ensure that does not happen," Mr. Aiken said a little touchily.

I supposed it was bad form to ask a lawyer what would happen if he lost, but my worries over Mrs. Surratt took precedence over Mr. Aiken's professional pride, so I persisted. "Say just in case. She could not possibly hang, could she?"

Mr. Aiken shook his head. "It would be a perversion of justice. But let us put up our defense before we start worrying about the punishment."

My father was not happy when he learned I would be testifying on Mrs. Surratt's behalf, but as he knew I could be subpoenaed if the defense chose, and I told him priests would be testifying as well, he said no more on the subject.

At nine sharp on Thursday, as Washington busied itself cleaning up from the masses who had flocked to town for the grand review, I climbed into my waiting carriage. Inside it, I found Mrs. Holohan.

"Will this never end?" she asked without even bothering to greet me as the driver helped me in. "First my husband gets thrown in prison, when he scarcely exchanged two words with that man Booth, and now I have to testify. I told him all along there was a nicer boardinghouse we could have gone to, for only a little more money, but he wouldn't hear of it. So he saved a little money, and for what? I tell you . . ."

For the entire time of our drive to the Arsenal, Mrs. Holohan kept up her litany of grievances against her husband, Mrs. Surratt, Mr. Booth, Secretary Stanton, and even President Lincoln for being so careless as to get shot. I was content enough to sit back and listen to her complain, as it took my mind off the question of what might happen to Mrs. Surratt if her defense failed.

The prosecution did not wrap up its case until late in the afternoon, at which time the defense called several priests to the stand, followed by Mrs. Holohan. As she made her huffy way to the stand, I hoped she at least did not say anything to harm Mrs. Surratt.

Nothing untoward happened, however, and in due course Mrs. Holohan returned. "Well, that's over," she muttered. "And we have to stay in case one side wants us back on the stand? Botheration."

I wondered what it would have been like to have to share a cell with Mrs. Holohan at Old Capitol Prison. Then the guard said, "Miss Fitzpatrick, you're next."

Following the now-familiar path to the witness stand, I took my place. Clad in a fresh summer gown and a newly trimmed bonnet, with my hair arranged with the benefit of a mirror, I looked quite a different young lady from a few days before, and there was no tittering this time from the female spectators.

I was facing the commissioners, as before, but I could not see Mr. Aiken and the rest of the defense attorneys without turning my head, as they were sitting at a table next to

Mrs. Surratt.

"When did you first commence to board at Mrs. Surratt's?" came Mr. Aiken's voice from the table.

I turned to look at him. "On the sixth of October last."

"Face the court," a judge barked.

"How long did you board there?"

With the greatest of difficulty, I avoided turning around and continued to face the court. "I boarded there from the sixth of October until the time I was arrested."

"When did you first meet at Mrs. Surratt's the prisoner at the bar, Mr. Payne? Was it in March or April?"

I wondered why I was being asked about Mr. Payne. "I do not know when it was. I know it was during the winter."

"How many times did you meet him there?"

"I have seen him there only twice."

"When was the last time you saw him there?"

"The last time was in March."

"How long did he stay there that time?"

"I do not know. I started for Baltimore the next morning."

"How long did you stay in Baltimore?"

"I remained in Baltimore a week."

"Was Payne gone when you returned?"

"Yes, sir."

"Do you know the prisoner at the bar, Atzerodt?"

So we were done with Mr. Payne, at least. But when would he ask me about Mrs. Surratt? "Yes, sir."

"When did he first come to Mrs. Surratt's?"

"I do not know. I do not know the month, nor the date of the month, when he came."

"Did you learn whether he was welcome at Mrs. Surratt's or not, or whether he was disagreeable?"

"I object," snapped Judge Advocate Bingham.

The prosecutors objected frequently to the defense's questions, I later learned, and their objections were almost always sustained. Mr. Aiken said, "Are you acquainted with the fact of his being sent away at any time, or that he was to be sent away?"

"I object to any question of that sort," Judge Bingham said.

To my left, I heard the sound of Mr. Aiken and Mr. Clampitt conferring. Then Mr. Aiken asked, "How long did Atzerodt stay there?"

"He stayed there only for a short time."

"Can you state any of the circumstances of his leaving, or under what circumstances he left?"

"I suppose that Mrs. Surratt sent him away."

Judge Bingham broke in. "You need not state suppositions."

My questioner audibly sighed. "Do you know anything of the circumstances of his going away?"

"No, I do not know anything about his leaving."

"Are you aware that he got drunk in the house and made a disturbance?"

I awaited Judge Bingham's objection to this, but he remained silent. "No, sir," I said. "I heard that he had bottles up there, but I do not know anything about his getting drunk."

"What room did you occupy in the house?"

"I slept in the same room with Mrs. Surratt."

"And with her daughter, Miss Surratt?"

"Yes, sir, we all three slept in there for a time."

"Was the photograph of Booth in that room?"

I supposed he meant Anna's. "Yes, sir."

"Was it your photograph?"

"No, sir, the one in that room was not mine."

Mr. Aiken left his seat. Walking into my line of vision, he held up *Morning, Noon, and Night,* which by now I detested. "Have you ever seen this before?"

"Yes, sir."

"Was that yours?"

"No, sir, it did not belong to me."

"To whom did it belong?"

"It belonged to Mrs. Surratt's daughter."

"Did you know anything of a photograph being placed behind this?"

"No, sir, I do not know anything about that at all. I think the frame was on the mantelpiece, but I do not know anything about it."

"Did you yourself own many of the photographs that were there?"

"No, sir."

"Did you own any of them?"

"Yes, sir, I owned some that were in an album."

"Were there photographs of Union generals in the house?"

"I saw one there of McClellan, I think."

One of the male spectators muttered, "Next best thing to a rebel."

"While you were in the house, did you learn anything of defective eyesight on the part of Mrs. Surratt?"

On safe ground at last, I replied, "I heard

490

Mrs. Surratt talking about it herself."

"Do not state what Mrs. Surratt stated, but what you know."

"I know she could not read at night, or sew, on account of her sight."

"Are you acquainted with Louis J. Weichmann?"

"Yes, sir."

"Was he treated as a friend in the house?"

"I think he was treated more like a son," I said firmly.

"What was the last time you saw Mr. Booth there?"

"The last time I saw Mr. Booth there was on a Monday."

"On the Monday before the assassination?"

"Yes, sir, I think it was the Monday before."

"What time did you see John Surratt there last?"

"I saw John Surratt the night he left home."

"When did he leave?

"He was gone two weeks before the assassination. He had been gone two weeks when that happened."

"Did you ever see him anywhere in the city during those two weeks?"

"I never saw him after that night."

"Did you ever buy any photographs of Booth?"

"Yes, sir," I said softly, thinking not of Mr. Booth but of poor Mr. Flanagan.

"Did you take them to the house?"

"I bought one."

"And took one there?"

"Yes, sir."

"Did you give one to Anna?"

I grimaced. "She bought one herself."

Mr. Aiken nodded and passed me, as they say in court, to Judge Holt, who frowned at me and asked, "Did you ever know Mrs. Surratt to have any difficulty in recognizing her friends in the parlor by gaslight? Did she always recognize you?"

"Yes, sir."

"You spoke of owning some of the photographs. Did you own the photographs of Stephens and Beauregard and Davis?"

"No, sir, they did not belong to me."

"You may step down."

I obeyed and went back to the witness room rather dejectedly. I had answered all of the questions put to me — but had I really helped my landlady any?

The Misses Donovan, knowing my fondness for newspapers, had been so kind as to buy them for me while I was in prison, and I of course had bought them for myself once

I was free. As the trial wore on, I read them all, back and current issues, Washington and out-of-town papers, and I came to realize that several things were damning to Mrs. Surratt: she had spoken to Mr. Booth in private in her home; she had seen him the very day of the assassination; she had delivered a package to Mr. Lloyd that day, along with a message about shooting irons (so said Mr. Lloyd); and Mr. Booth had come by that night to pick up those shooting irons. Nothing I could say about Mrs. Surratt's eyesight, or really nothing else I could say, could change those facts.

Yet nothing in those facts showed she had known about a plot to kill the president. To kidnap, maybe, especially given that day in March when Mr. Surratt had said he was going away, and he, Mr. Payne, and Mr. Booth had all stormed into the house waving guns around while I had been happily visiting friends in Baltimore. Then again, what lies might Mr. Surratt have told her about all of these things? What might she not have known about his life? I certainly had a few secrets from my father, sheltered as I was. A man like Mr. Surratt, roaming between Richmond and Canada, might have plenty more from his mother.

There was only one thing, I decided as

the newspapers piled up in my room, that would solve Mrs. Surratt's troubles: Mr. Surratt coming home and taking her place on the prisoner's dock.

But the trial dragged on, and the days grew hotter and more humid, with no appearance by Mr. Surratt. He seemed to have vanished off the very face of the earth.

41
MARY

MAY 25 TO JUNE 6, 1865

At last, my defense began. Mr. Aiken and
Mr. Clampitt — Mr. Johnson had disappeared from the courtroom altogether —
called a series of priests to the stand, each
attesting to my good character, each attesting to the fact that I had never uttered
disloyal sentiments to them. It was quite
true; I had never spoken of politics with
men of the cloth. The trouble was, except
for Father Wiget, the first priest they called,
I had hardly spoken to any of these priests
at all, except for a few pleasant words after
church from time to time. They could have
been testifying about any pious and discreet
woman in their congregation, and the commissioners knew it.

Mrs. Holohan took the stand on my
behalf, and so did Nora. Poor Nora! She
testified for the prosecution several days
before, and I could tell the child had no
desire to be there. She answered the ques-

tions in a flat, dreary voice, and she looked bedraggled and thin. If her late mother could have seen her little girl thus, it would have broken her heart.

But this Thursday, she came to court wearing a crisp dress and a smart bonnet, and she testified in my defense in a clear, firm voice. There was, admittedly, not too much she could do to help me, but I could see she was pleased to be trying to.

Over the next few days, other witnesses took the stand on my behalf. Mr. Gwynn testified to my difficulty collecting the debt owed to me by Mr. Nothey. Mr. Calvert came forth to confirm that he wrote a letter demanding his money from me. Mr. Nothey himself acknowledged that he owed me money.

As he left the stand, I wondered if he would ever pay it to me.

I had not seen Mr. Howell since he dashed off from my boardinghouse that day with Mrs. Slater, although when I was still at the Old Capitol, Anna saw him exercising in the yard there on occasion. Ragged and thinner than ever, he coughed no fewer than five times as he approached the witness stand, and it occurred to me that he had every incentive to shorten his stay in prison by giving testimony that favored the government.

But he did not, and I felt more than a twinge of guilt when I recalled that I did not warm to him during his brief stay with me. Mr. Weichmann, he told the court, was no loyal unionist, but a secesh sympathizer who longed to pack up and move to the South. He showed Mr. Weichmann how to make a cipher — obtained from a magic book — and Mr. Weichmann in turn gave him information, culled from his employment in the War Department, about the number of Southern prisoners the North had in its custody. There were some mutterings among the commissioners when he gave that testimony, and for a moment it seemed that the halo around Mr. Weichmann's head had begun to slip a little.

But not for long. Soon the government was questioning Mr. Howell about his stint in the Confederate army, his trips to Richmond, and his association with Mrs. Slater, and after a great deal of effort on the government's part, he was forced to admit my Johnny traveled with the woman. Moreover, Mr. Howell acknowledged, he had never taken the oath of allegiance to the United States.

Still, I had to give Mr. Aiken credit for

trying with him.

My brother came to the stand on May 30. It was good to see a friendly face there — even though my lawyers failed to have him state his relationship to me, leaving that to the government to point out, as if it were something we were trying to hide.

Would they call Olivia? I was pondering this when the next witness was called. "Miss Anna Surratt."

I had not seen my dear child in a month, and now because of the spectators sitting close to me and a guard standing in front of me, I could only hear her voice as she gave her testimony. In a haughty tone, she admitted to owning photographs of Davis, Stephens, Beauregard, and Stonewall Jackson; she treasured them because they were given to her by her father, and she also owned photographs of General McClellan, General Grant, and General Joe Hooker.

And then she unraveled.

"Did you ever hear it discussed by any member of the family to capture the president of the United States?"

"No, sir, I did not. Where's Ma?" Anna's voice climbed. "Where's Mama?"

"Anna!" But I spoke so little, my voice came out as a croak.

None of these men were prepared to deal with this situation. Near me, one of the lady spectators rose to her feet, as if to help, and one of the other defense attorneys rose. In a paternal voice, he said, "What year did your brother leave college?"

"In 1861 or 1862, the year my father died. Where is Mama?"

"What years were you at school in Bryantown?"

"From 1851 to 1861. The sixteenth of July was the day I left."

"Did you ever see Dr. Mudd at your mother's house at Washington?"

"No, sir." The courtroom was silent but for the sound of Anna's foot tapping. She had never had a fit, but I feared she was on the verge of one.

"Is Surrattsville on the road between Washington and Bryantown?"

"Yes. Oh, where is Mama?"

A man hurried through the crowd and took Anna by her arm. Mr. Aiken followed. "You shall soon see your mama, Miss Surratt," he promised her as they headed back toward the witness room.

It was too much, at last, for me to bear. As my daughter passed close to me, allowing me to glimpse only the sweep of her black silk dress and her pretty jockey hat, I leaned my head on the railing and wept.

Two days later, as General Hartranft led me into court, he smiled and nodded over in the direction of the press table. There, seated at a discreet distance from the lady spectators, was my daughter.

Her own guard nodded in my direction, and Anna gave me a tremulous smile. We were not allowed to speak to each other, but for that whole blissful day in court, we could look at each other all we pleased. When we were not trading glances, she put her hands under her chin in her most endearing fashion and listened to Judge Bingham and a Mr. Craig, one of Mr. Lloyd's drinking companions, square off over who was more drunk on the afternoon of April 14: Mr. Craig or Mr. Lloyd.

There were no church services here, of course, so on Sunday, the only day court was not in session, I performed my own devotions as best I could. I had just finished when General Hartranft entered.

"Mrs. Surratt, your daughter has obtained a pass to see you and is waiting for you in the courtroom."

Anna threw herself into my arms, weeping, as soon as I stepped inside the courtroom. "I have missed you so much," she whispered at last. "I thought those horrid Yankees would never let us meet."

I looked around for the horrid Yankees who were supposed to be guarding us, but they had all quietly left the room to Anna and me. "Child, it was General Hartranft who made it possible for you to be in the courtroom with me."

"He is still a Yankee beast. He confessed to me that he stationed a guard in front of you that day to keep me from getting distracted on the stand."

"Well, that didn't exactly work."

"No indeed," Anna said with a slight grin. "I have been released from prison, Ma."

"Where are you staying?"

"Father Walter found me a boardinghouse, but I have been told that the government is willing to let me move back into our house."

"You will be lonely there, child."

"It's home, Ma. And the Holohans told me they would come back to stay if I was there. It's too crowded at Mrs. Holohan's mother's house, and besides, I think Mr. Holohan wants to help me. I wish Nora would come, but her father won't let her. She's back living with those old maids she lived with before."

For two heavenly hours, Anna and I sat

and talked, undisturbed by the guards. She did not ask what would happen if I was sent to prison, and I dared not bring it up. Instead, Anna told me the news of our friends and family, and I assured her that I was not being ill-used. Of our friends in prison, she informed me that Miss Lomax had been long since released, and even Mrs. Baxley had finally given in and signed the oath of loyalty and returned to Baltimore, where I hoped she would soon be able to move her son's remains.

A guard scratched at the door and called, "Time!"

I embraced Anna, who broke down weeping again. "Child, this won't do," I said. "We will see each other in the courtroom tomorrow — General Hartranft said so — and I am sure you will get another pass soon. You must be brave."

Anna nodded as the guards came to lead her off. "All right, Ma."

"God be with you, child," I said calmly, watching as she passed out of sight.

Whether it was the heat, the strain, or what, I cannot say, but I found myself swaying on my feet. Before I could call for help, I fainted.

One day, we had a diversion in court — a

Bloomerite resplendent in short skirt and trousers. The male prisoners, so used to being stared at themselves, fixed their eyes upon her and grinned, and Mr. Herold snickered outright. The Bloomerite ignored them but sat down calmly amid her hoop-skirted sister women. With the bloomers on, she took up much less space than they did, which I heard one lady noting as a relief.

"Who was that?" I asked Mr. Aiken as we conferred during the recess.

"Dr. Mary Walker, a surgeon. Now, I have a matter of business to discuss." Mr. Aiken pushed a paper toward me. "Read this carefully, please, and sign it. It concerns my fee."

"Again? I signed something not that long ago."

"Yes, but there are some points that need to be clarified. Read it very carefully, please."

How like a lawyer; however the world might roll along, they must get paid. I fought through a thicket of "hereafters" and "party of the first parts" and "party of the second parts."

"Let me clarify something for you." Mr. Aiken bent close to me. He whispered, "Your son is safe and secure, and sends his love. He wishes to know whether he should give himself up. If you wish it, say so, and he will surrender himself immediately."

I stared at the paper.

So he has not forgotten me, was my first thought. My second thought was of him hooded and shackled, possibly swinging on the gallows. "No," I whispered. "Keep him away from here."

"Mrs. Surratt, as your attorney, I must tell you that if he were to turn himself in, there is a strong chance that you would be set free."

"Perhaps, but I will not trade my chances for his. Tell him he can do no good by coming here. Tell him I will be acquitted. Tell him anything — just keep him from coming to Washington."

"I promise, Mrs. Surratt, I will." Mr. Aiken resumed his normal tone. "If these terms are satisfactory to you, Mrs. Surratt, please sign."

I frowned. "You lawyers bleed your clients to death with your fees," I snapped. "But I suppose I have no choice."

As the trial resumed — Anna was sitting in the courtroom — I thought of Johnny. I wished I could have asked Mr. Aiken where he was and how he was living — if, indeed, Mr. Aiken even knew these things — but at least I knew he was safe and, I hoped, far from here. With God's help, he would stay there.

42
NORA
JUNE 1865

I was called once more to give testimony for Mrs. Surratt in early June. I told the court that Anna and Mrs. Surratt had never denied seeing Mr. Payne before, only that Anna had emphatically denied that that man was her brother. I did not know whether my testimony would do any good, but at least it would do no harm.

In the meantime, Anna had been released from prison, and on the same day I gave my testimony, she was allowed to return to her house. Father had flat-out refused, when he heard of this, to allow me to move back in as a boarder, but he had not forbade me from visiting Anna (at least not in so many words), so a few days later, I called at my old lodgings.

How sad they looked! It was not just seeing the mess the government had left behind, but the emptiness — the deserted room where Mr. Weichmann and Mr. Surratt had shared a bed, the bare attic, Miss Dean's unused trundle bed, and, most of all, Mrs. Surratt's favorite chair, in which Anna studiously avoided sitting. And though he lay rotting goodness knew where, I could almost fancy that Mr. Booth might walk in at any moment and ask Anna to play on the forlorn pianoforte, the keys of which had not been uncovered in weeks.

Anna followed my glance around the place. "It's not so bad now that the Holohans are here," she said bravely. "Though I don't know how long they'll be willing to stay. Besides there being no servant, I spend most of my time in court with Mama. They'll have to get their board elsewhere until . . ."

As her sentence trailed off, the doorbell rang. Seeing Anna's pale face, I hastened to answer it myself. A man in his early twenties stood on the doorstep. In a voice that like my father's bore traces of time in Ireland, he said, "I am Mr. John Brophy, miss, here to see Miss Surratt."

"Let him in, Nora."

I obeyed. "Mr. Brophy went to school with Johnny and that creature Weichmann," Anna said after introducing us. "He has been taking an interest in Ma's case."

"Meddling, some might say," Mr. Brophy

said with a smile. "But I believe Mrs. Surratt to be innocent, even though I fear the press has already convicted her. They have said the most vicious things about her. So I have taken the liberty of distributing this."

He handed each of us a little pamphlet. "*The Trial of Mrs. Surratt*," I read. I turned to the last page. "By Amator Justitiae. Lover of Justice."

"I didn't deem it wise to publish it under my own name, as I am employed by a school here," Mr. Brophy explained. "But I have distributed it all over the city — at the railway station, at the circulating libraries, even in some of the taverns — and I hope one of the newspapers will print it."

I scanned the pamphlet. Written in high-flown language, with numerous literary allusions, it passionately argued for Mrs. Surratt's innocence.

Anna said, "Sir, I cannot tell you how grateful I am for this, but I hope you are not putting yourself in danger."

"No, Miss Surratt, but even if I were, I cannot just sit back and do nothing. It is not in my nature."

"Pity my brother didn't have you boarding with us instead of that creature Weichmann," Anna muttered.

Mr. Brophy smiled. "And now I must be going, Miss Surratt. I have a few more places to leave my pamphlets."

As he left, I took Anna's hand. "There's hope, Anna. If one man feels this strongly, perhaps others do too."

Anna nodded. "That is what I have been telling myself."

I couldn't resist asking. "This Mr. Brophy, is he unmarried?"

"Nora! Yes, he is, but he is courting a young lady here in Washington. And he has rather too many freckles for my liking anyway. But he certainly has been kind."

I grinned and took my own leave. As I walked home, I passed a newsstand piled high with out-of-town papers. Casually, I put my copy of Mr. Brophy's pamphlet in their midst.

If Mr. Brophy could do his part to help Mrs. Surratt, I could certainly do my own.

43
MARY

The last of the witnesses — there had been close to three hundred of them, Major Hartranft told me — had testified, and there was nothing to do but for the lawyers to sum up their cases. I had not seen Senator Johnson in weeks, and I no longer even looked for him in the courtroom. So I was not surprised when Mr. Clampitt announced to the court that Senator Johnson had prepared a closing argument, but had delegated Mr. Clampitt to read it.

It was, as far as I could comprehend, a repetition of Senator Johnson's earlier jurisdictional argument. It was full of fine words, and Mr. Clampitt tried his best to put some fire into his reading, but either he was falling short, or I could not focus on what he was saying. Soon even his figure began to blur and dance before me, and I shut my eyes to make it stop.

There was a crash and some cries, and

suddenly men were gathered around me, lifting me in their arms.

"I have never been prone to fainting," I told Dr. Porter, the physician appointed to minister to us, as we sat in the anteroom previously used for witnesses waiting their turn to testify. Just a day before, he and a colleague had examined all of us, and the result in my case had been the appearance of a soft armchair in my cell and a selection of books for me to read. "But it is so close in the courtroom, and — and over the past several days I have had female problems, which have troubled me from time to time over the past few months," I added in a low tone. "Forgive me, Doctor, it is not easy for me to discuss these things."

"I know, madam. I am going to recommend that you be allowed to stay in this room, where it is cooler and fresher. In the meantime, just sit here and rest."

I obeyed, thinking that this trial was turning me into a feeble old woman.

That evening, my few possessions were brought from cell 200 to my new lodgings, along with the armchair, in which I drank in the sight of a summer sunset in Washington. During court the next day, I sat in the armchair in the doorway, allowing me to see and hear the proceedings — and, I confess, to doze in my comfortable chair.

After court, two featherbeds made their appearance in my new room. "Two?"

"Yes, madam," General Hartranft said. "I have been given permission to allow you a female attendant in light of" — he coughed — "your peculiar difficulties."

"That is very kind of you, sir." Silently, I hoped it was not some pert little Irish girl from the surrounding neighborhood.

"She will be here shortly."

I nodded and thumbed through the *The Pickwick Papers,* having been given a choice between that and *The Last of the Mohicans.* Evidently General Hartranft, who confided to me that he had been given liberty to bring us books, provided they had not been published within the last thirty years and were not otherwise unsuitable for us, had forgotten about Mr. Pickwick's imprisonment for debt.

"Your attendant is here, Mrs. Surratt."

I looked up and there, holding a basket of food, was my daughter.

Anna could come and go as she pleased, and each day she brought me a treat — some buttered scones, my goose-down pillow from home, the prayer book that Father Finotti gave me. "How are you paying for this?" I asked as she presented me with some candy for my sweet tooth. I looked at her ears and found to my relief that her favorite earrings were hanging there. "You have not been pawning your nice things, have you?"

"No, Ma. Uncle Zadock and Grandma have both sent me money." She winced. "Actually, I asked Grandma for it. I told her we would pay her back when we were able."

"Did she send any message to me?"

"Only that she was praying for you."

This was about as much comfort as I was likely to receive from my mother, especially now that I had brought the family into disgrace. At least she had the goodness to lend my daughter money.

I looked at my own precious girl, darning my stockings. "Anna. Have I ever told you that you are very dear to me, and that I love you?"

"Why, of course, Mama."

"Good. I just wanted to make sure."

For two solid days, Mr. Bingham made his closing argument for the government as I watched from my doorway and the male

513

prisoners watched from their dock. In his black frock coat, which reached almost to his shoe tops and seemed in danger of tripping him, the small Mr. Bingham should have cut a faintly ridiculous figure, but instead he gave the impression of being a much taller man as he denounced each of us in turn, as well as my Johnny, whom he even accused of having been present in the city on that dreadful Good Friday. "Nothing but his conscious coward guilt could possibly induce him to absent himself from his mother, as he does, upon her trial!"

I clenched my fists.

"That Mary E. Surratt is as guilty as her son at having thus conspired, combined, and confederated to do this murder, in aid of this rebellion, is clear," Mr. Bingham continued, making a flourish in my direction.

At this point, I could almost sum up the evidence for him. I kept a tally in my head as he neatly reached each point. I received Mr. Booth and the other men in my home, and met privately with Mr. Booth. I drove twice to Surrattsville, ostensibly on my own business but in reality that of Mr. Booth. I gave Mr. Lloyd the messages about the shooting irons.

"But there is one other fact in this case

that puts forever at rest the question of the guilty participation of the prisoner, Mrs. Surratt, in this conspiracy and murder, and that is, that Payne, who had lodged four days in her house, who during all that time had sat at her table, and who had often conversed with her, when the guilt of his great crime was upon him, and he knew not where else he could so safely go to find a co-conspirator, and he could trust none that was not, like himself, guilty with even the knowledge of his presence, under cover of darkness, after wandering for three days and nights, skulking before the pursuing officers of justice, at the hour of midnight, found his way to the door of Mrs. Surratt, rang the bell, was admitted, and upon being asked, 'Whom do you want to see?' replied, 'Mrs. Surratt.' "

Mr. Payne looked in my direction, then hung his head.

It was over. Mr. Bingham had concluded his argument. Now our fates were in the hands of the nine commissioners.

Mr. Aiken and Mr. Clampitt, meeting with me in the courtroom after Mr. Bingham departed, mopping his forehead, were optimistic. "The case against you depends on a coward and a drunkard," Mr. Aiken told me. "Mr. Weichmann is Secretary Stanton's puppet, and would be on the dock with the other men if he hadn't been bullied into testifying against you, and Mr. Lloyd wouldn't have known if you said 'shooting iron' or 'curling iron' after his day swilling at Marlboro."

"Do you think the commissioners will see them in that light?"

Mr. Clampitt said, "How can they not? I have spoken with some of my older colleagues, who have been closely following the case, and they are confident of your acquittal."

"And if I am not acquitted? Senator Johnson thought I might get a short imprisonment, followed by a pardon. Do you agree?"

Mr. Aiken nodded. "Yes, I do. I imagine you would be sent back to the Old Capitol for a while."

"And how am I to live? There is your fee to pay, and the money I owe to Mr. Calvert that led me to go on that trip in the first place. And after all that has happened, I cannot see Mr. Lloyd continuing at the tavern — not that I want him there either. I suppose I must sell it, which would not be a bad thing, for it has brought me nothing but grief. Unless Isaac wants to run it. And

I do not even know if he is still alive. And Johnny . . ."

"He is safe, Mrs. Surratt, and we have followed your wishes in keeping him away," Mr. Aiken said in the lowest of tones. "Let that be a comfort to you for now. The rest will fall into place."

"Yes, I suppose you are right. It hurt so to hear him being called a coward, though." I sighed. "When do you think we will know the verdicts?"

Mr. Clampitt shook his head. "That I cannot say. The commissioners do not have to be unanimous, as a civil jury does, so a decision could come quickly. But they have a huge amount of evidence to sift through, and eight cases to consider, some clear-cut like Payne's, others less so. I promise that when we hear the news, you shall hear it immediately."

We bade one another good-bye, and I thanked them for their representation of me, for with all their blunders, they had perhaps done as best they could, thrown into the case as junior counsel and then virtually abandoned by Senator Johnson. Whether their optimism was well founded or the product of their inexperience I could not say.

■ ■ ■ ■

For two days, the commissioners met in the courtroom; with my door shut, I could hear only the drone of their voices. Their second session, on the last day of June, did not last long, and when General Hartranft came to visit that afternoon, I saw the courtroom was deserted, with only some crumpled papers and full spittoons to indicate its recent occupation. "Are they finished?"

"I believe so, madam."

Anna clutched my hand. "Then we shall hear soon."

But we did not. June rolled into July without a word of our fates.

The delay, General Hartranft told me with the sheepish air of a man who knew he should probably not be giving me this information, was due to the illness of President Johnson, who had to approve the commission's recommendation. My keeper wished the president would soon recover, he confided, because he sorely missed his wife and children in Pennsylvania and knew his wife would be particularly sad about spending the Fourth of July alone.

The delay was wearing on all of us. In early June, the male prisoners had been relieved of their hoods, Anna told me, and they were allowed to exercise in the yard each day, two or three at a time. From my window I could see them wandering about, their shoulders slumped. Only Mr. Payne, pitching quoits with his guards, seemed unperturbed by the wait. "I wonder why," I told Anna.

"They say he doesn't care what happens to him," Anna said, staring down as Mr. Payne yelled in triumph. "In fact, he wants to die."

On the Fourth of July, Anna and I stood at the window and watched the fireworks going off across the river. Poor Major General Hartranft, I thought as the last burst of colored light faded away.

Another day passed with no word. Then on the sixth, around noon, soon after Anna had left to go to the post office, General Hartranft, accompanied by another man, entered my room. In a tone of voice I had never heard him use before, he said, "Madam, the commission has issued its findings and sentences, and they have been approved by President Johnson. This is Major General Hancock. He is here to witness me reading you the findings and sentence."

"Just tell me, sir, without reading me that lawyer's prose. Am I to go to prison? For how long?"

Major General Hartranft shook his head and held up a paper with a trembling hand. "After mature consideration of the evidence adduced in the case of the accused, Mary E. Surratt, the commission find the said accused of the specification guilty. And the commission do, therefore, sentence her, the said Mary E. Surratt, to be hanged by the neck until she be dead, at such time and place as the president of the United States shall direct." He looked up. "That will take place here. Tomorrow, between the hours of ten and two."

"Tomorrow," I mumbled.

"Madam, I cannot tell you how sorry I am to give you this news. It is not what I expected, not what I had hoped. Whom do you wish me to send for, to stay with you in your last hours? Your daughter, I suppose? A priest, a friend, a relation?"

I was shaking from head to toe. "Sir, I did not plot to kill the president. I knew nothing of any such plot. No one at that trial testified that I did. No one could testify that I did. I am innocent! For God's sake, I have done wrong in my life, but I have not done murder, and I do not deserve to die for this!"

"Mrs. Surratt, please tell me whom you wish me to send for. There is no time to be lost."

"I am innocent!" I could barely speak through my sobs. "I am innocent!"

General Hartranft put his arm around me as I wept. Finally, when I stopped to catch a breath, he said again, "You want Anna, don't you?"

"Yes." I wiped my eyes. "Try to have them find her before she hears the news from someone else. She was on her way to the post office."

"I will. What priest do you wish to see?"

"Father Jacob Walter from St. Patrick's, and Father Bernardine Wiget from St. Aloysius." I had worshiped at both of their churches; surely at least one of these men would attend me.

"And is there anyone else you wish to see?"

"Mr. John Brophy." He was a friend of Johnny's whom Anna told me had taken an interest in my case. If he could not help me, at least perhaps he could help my child, so soon to be alone.

"I will get them all here as soon as possible. Now I am going to send Dr. Porter to give you something to ease you. Try to rest. I am so very sorry." His own voice broke, and Major General Hancock, who had stared gloomily out the window throughout his visit, clapped him on the shoulder and steered him to the door.

I lay on my bed. Even though the temperature had to be close to ninety degrees, I was shivering. *Hanged by the neck until she be dead. Tomorrow.*

44
NORA

"Extra! Mrs. Surratt to be hanged tomorrow!"

My blood still runs cold to recall those words.

Throwing down the novel I had been leafing through, I ran out of the bookstore and snatched a paper from the newsboy's hands. "Hey, miss! You forgot to pay!"

I tossed a coin in his general direction and read the paper, praying that the newsboy was barely literate and had misunderstood what the paper was saying. He had not. There in the cruelest black and white the *Evening Star* could muster were the headlines: MRS. SURRATT, PAYNE, HEROLD, AND ATZERODT TO BE HUNG! THE SENTENCE TO BE EXECUTED TOMORROW!

In a daze, I walked to the house on H Street and knocked on the door. No one answered.

I turned my steps toward the Misses Donovan's house, where I found my father sitting in the parlor. "Come here, child. You have heard?"

I nodded, and he took me into his arms while I sobbed. "I know you were fond of this lady. I am very sorry that it has ended thus."

He was speaking of Mrs. Surratt, I realized, as if she were already cold in the grave. I pulled back. "Father, I have to do something."

"Do what, Nora?"

"I don't know," I admitted. "But I can't just let her hang, and do nothing. There must be something I can do."

"She has lawyers, Nora, and her daughter. No doubt her family in Surrattsville will come to her aid as well. She is not without help, although what good it will do I do not know."

"She is innocent, Father. She would never have plotted the death of the president."

"The commission does not share your view of her. Nora, I have hesitated in saying this, but I do not think you are aware of what your association with her has done. I have heard from several people, well-informed ones, that you have lost your chance for the government jobs you hoped to obtain. You are tainted, and it is her fault, and only hers, that you are. She should have known the damage that her doings could inflict upon you, her daughter, and any other young person in her household."

"She did not know what Mr. Booth planned, Father."

"I cannot believe that she was ignorant of his doings. At the very least, she must have known of the kidnapping, and that is enough to hang her. I am sorry for it, but my concern is with you and not with her. And that is why I am sending you to Baltimore today."

"Baltimore?" I asked as if I had never heard of the place.

"Yes, to stay with your friend Camilla."

"Today?"

"Yes. It is short notice, but I know you have a standing invitation, and it is best to get you out of here, when all of the talk will be of the execution. I have telegraphed her mother."

"How long am I to impose upon her hospitality?"

"As long as she wishes. Child, don't glare at me so! I know you are grieving for this lady. But you can do her no good by staying here, and you are doing yourself no good by staying here. Now, please go and pack."

Obeying, I threw some things into a

carpetbag, not bothering to look if they were suitable for summer or winter. "I'm ready," I said flatly when I returned.

My father smiled and offered me his arm. I yanked it away rudely, relishing the hurt expression on his face, and together we made our way to the station in silence.

Our train ride was every bit as miserable as our trip to the station. I snatched a book out of my carpetbag and held it to my nose for the duration of the ride, although I wasn't comprehending a single word, while my father sat there wearing a face of stony misery. It didn't help that all around us the talk was of the execution.

At last, we pulled into Baltimore's Camden Station, where I hoped no one would be there to meet us. Then wouldn't my father have to take me back to Washington? But Camilla and her mama were there in their fine carriage, beaming at us. My father fairly shone with relief. "I thank you very much, Mrs. James, for receiving my daughter on such short notice," he said. "The circumstances —"

"I understand perfectly, Mr. Fitzpatrick. We'll take good care of her." Mrs. James smiled, though I detected a look of worry in her eyes. Entertaining someone whose landlady was on the verge of execution was not something dealt with in the conduct books.

My father shoved some bills into my hand and patted me on the cheek. "Try to enjoy yourself, Nora," he said very gently. "Child, I truly mean well, though you don't realize it."

I nodded and let him hand me into the carriage. He lifted his hand in farewell as I stared stonily ahead.

"Well!" said Mrs. James brightly. "Shall we do a little shopping?"

How Camilla and I had become friends I never quite understood, for she was pretty and blond, with hair that fell in perfect ringlets. She was also the most talkative girl at Georgetown Visitation, and I had always been on the quiet side. Maybe that was my appeal — I made a most admirable listener.

After our shopping trip — I had refused to spend my father's money, but Mrs. James had thwarted me by purchasing a new bonnet for me — Camilla and I adjourned to her room, where she pulled out her album and gave me a report on what every girl at Visitation pictured in it had done over the past year. "Do you remember Miss Turner? She married a merchant and moved to Philadelphia. She has a lovely little baby but gained an enormous amount of weight. I do hope she can get it off, because she had a lovely figure. Do you remember how the men used to stare when we walked about with her? Oh, and here's Miss Gray — such a pity, her father lost his money, and she's had to teach school. Of course, she'll probably marry soon. And here's Miss Butler — I don't mind saying at this point that I thought she was dreadfully snobbish, and for what? So what if her father had fifty slaves — they're all free now." Camilla took a breath and turned a page. "And here's — oh, dear, I'm sorry." Camilla ruefully gazed at a photograph of Mr. Booth in side view. "I'd forgotten he was here. He was a handsome devil, wasn't he? Well, this is most awkward —"

But I wasn't thinking of poor Camilla's faux pas, I was gazing at the *carte de visite* of the beautiful lady next to him. "Mrs. Douglas," I said.

"Yes. Don't you go to the same church with her? Is she as lovely still as she is there?"

"Yes." *If I can be of any help, please let me know.* "Camilla, I'm begging you. Please do me a favor. It's the most I'll ever ask of you, ever."

"Goodness, Nora, what?"

"Lie for me. I have to go back to Washington, and I have to go back tonight."

"Nora —"

"Please! You're my only hope. I have to see my friend Anna Surratt. And I have to see Mrs. Douglas. She might be able to save Mrs. Surratt. If I leave now for the train station, I can get to Washington by nine."

Camilla hesitated. "All right," she said finally. "But what do I tell Mother? She'll be expecting you for dinner."

"You'll think of something. You're smart, and you know it." It was true, for all her rattle-brained conversation and her even more rattle-brained letters, Camilla had always been one of the best students at Visitation.

"It's your time of the month," Camilla said slowly. "You're having dreadful cramps — no, Mother will be up with that concoction she makes me when it's my time of the month. It really works, though, you know. I'll give you some. Oh, I have it. You're at church! You're at church praying for Mrs. Surratt's reprieve! And you are perfectly prostrated with grief and don't want to see anyone, not even Mother. And —"

"I'll leave the details to you," I said, kissing Camilla on the cheek. "Now, help me sneak out of here."

"And that's another thing," Camilla said cheerfully. "Our servants are *eminently* bribable."

45
MARY
JULY 6, 1865

It took General Hartranft's men very little time to catch up with my daughter, for not an hour after I was told of my impending death, she was at my side. Wordlessly, we wept in each other's arms until Father Walter entered the room, soon followed by Father Wiget and a young man I dimly recognized as Mr. Brophy. Johnny had brought him home to dinner a couple of times in those quiet days before Mr. Booth entered our lives.

They gave me wine of valerian, and its effect allowed me to lie back on my bed and watch calmly as the two priests, who had surely never been called upon to assist on such an occasion as this, consulted with each other about their respective duties. Finally, Father Walter turned. "Mrs. Surratt, I will give you communion tomorrow morning at seven, but for now, I suggest that I take your daughter and attempt to see the president and move him to pardon you, or at least to give you more time to prepare for your death."

"I want to stay with my mother," Anna said fiercely.

"Miss Surratt, your presence may mean the difference between life and death for your mother. It may move the president in a way that my words could not."

"Go, child. I wish to speak to these men alone anyway."

Anna obeyed instantly, and she and Father Walter departed, leaving me with the other two men. "Shall I leave?" Mr. Brophy asked. "If you wish to make your confession . . ."

"No. I first wish to talk to you about my Anna. You have been a friend to her, and I hope you will continue to be. She will need help with the most practical things of life, and I fear she will be taken advantage of."

"I will do everything I can for her, Mrs. Surratt. Mr. Holohan has said to me that he and his wife will look after her as well."

"Thank you, sir. Now let me speak to Father Wiget privately for a moment."

Father Wiget took Mr. Brophy's place in the chair nearest my bed. "What do you wish to tell me, madam?"

"That I am innocent of plotting the president's murder. That I am guilty of aiding

Mr. Booth." It was the first time I said this to anyone, and my breath came more easily when I said it. "I did not know murder was planned, and I had no inkling of it. But I assisted him in what I thought was his plan to kidnap, and for that I must seek forgiveness. I also did nothing to alert the authorities, and for that I must repent as well.

"And there is Johnny. I told him through my lawyers not to come here. But there is a bitterness in my heart now that he has obeyed and that he has not come back to be by my side, even though I know that he would probably hang if he returned. I cannot stop thinking that in his place, Anna would have returned. You must help me, sir. I do not want to die with this bitterness. I do not want him to come back and hang."

"Could he save you by coming back?"

"I doubt it, and even if he could, I do not want him to die in my place." I closed my eyes. "I am so muddled with all this happening, and the stuff they have given me."

"Your son will have a very heavy burden to bear when he learns of your death, Mrs. Surratt," Father Wiget said gently. "Remember, it was he who brought Mr. Booth into your house, bringing all of your present troubles upon you. He will carry the weight of that for as long as he lives — and he is barely into his majority, is he not? Let me tell him, if he ever stands face-to-face with me, that you died in charity with him. I know him, and I believe he will need that comfort in days to come."

"I will try, Father."

Father Wiget smiled, as if relishing the challenge. "I will help you, madam."

That afternoon, about the same time the Washington sun grew hottest in the sky, I began to hear a commotion in the prison yard — objects being dragged, hammering, men barking orders. Father Wiget heard it too, of course, and I saw him exchange sad looks with Mr. Brophy, who had returned. Only then did it dawn on me what was being built, and the courage I had been striving so hard to attain failed me utterly. I broke down weeping again.

It was at that time that General Hartranft came into the room. "Mrs. Surratt, I am sorry, but I must move you downstairs in preparation for tomorrow. Please take what things you will need for tonight."

I took a carpetbag Anna had brought me from our house and stuffed a few items in it: a prayer book, my rosary, a brush and comb, a toothbrush and tooth powder, my goose-down pillow.

A person needed very little for the last night of her life, I found.

The cell I was taken to on the first floor was small and gloomy, without the creature comforts of the room I had been occupying upstairs — only a mattress on the floor and a couple of stools. Its one merit was that the sound of the scaffold being built was not as distinct. The three men who were to die with me had also been moved to nearby cells, for I could hear the comings and goings of their own visitors.

Soon after I was moved, Anna returned, her face wet with tears. "The president wouldn't see us. Judge Holt did, but he told us that there was nothing he could do, that only the president could commute your sentence." The tears splashed from her eyes. "I can't do anything to help you, Ma."

"Anna, you tried." I stroked her hair, damp from the sweltering Washington heat. "My good girl, let that be a comfort to you in the years to come."

My daughter looked around her. "This is a horrid cell. Why did they move you here? Why are they treating you so? How can they be so cruel?"

"Anna! They have moved us all down here. Come sit beside me. There are some practical matters I must talk to you about."

Anna hesitated but obeyed. For a short while, I talked to her about the things that had to be talked about: the money I owed, the few debts that were owed me, the lease on the tavern, my lawyer's fees. "It is a great deal to put on you, but you are stronger than you realize. These last few weeks have shown that. And you will have help. Mr. Brophy has proven to be a good friend to you."

Speaking of these ordinary affairs seemed to steady Anna's nerves, but not for long. As the evening fell, she became more unstrung, so much so that I began to fear for her reason. This death watch was no place for this child. "Mr. Brophy, please take Anna home to spend the night."

"Mother!"

"Anna, it is best. I need to compose myself for tomorrow, and we are only upsetting each other here. I want you to get some rest and get out of this place."

"It is best," Father Wiget joined in. "Your mother needs some time for prayer and reflection, with which your presence, however welcome, can only interfere."

"Your mother is right," Mr. Brophy said. "Besides, if you wish to visit the White House again tomorrow, you will be better placed to do so if you stay at H Street. Here, you will have a long walk, and half a dozen things could prevent you from going."

Anna listened drearily to my counsel and Father Wiget's, but Mr. Brophy's words made her nod and accept his proffered hand. She hugged me fiercely and followed Mr. Brophy down the corridor, her shoulders sagging.

I watched her go, and it was all I could do to keep from calling her back.

46
NORA

JULY 6 TO 7, 1865

I made it to Washington undetected, with the help of a little veil I'd borrowed from Camilla. Mrs. Slater would have been proud of me, I thought as I boarded the F Street car heading toward the boardinghouse. There was no point in seeing Mrs. Douglas until I got news of Mrs. Surratt, and the Holohans, assuming they were there, would be the best placed to tell me.

The news wouldn't be good, I surmised as I approached my old lodgings. There was a crowd surrounding the boardinghouse. "John Wilkes Booth stood on those very stairs," a man told his family, "and plotted the killing with Mrs. Surratt. In that very parlor."

"Where did Payne sleep?" his son asked him.

"Up there," the father said confidently. "Or maybe in back."

"Well, that narrows it down, darling," said

538

his wife.

A lady said to her companion, "You heard that her daughter came here tonight."

"No. My word, she's in there now?"

"Yes, the poor child got out of a carriage not two hours before, almost prostrate with grief. Whatever you can say about that fiend, she has a lov—"

I shoved my way through the crowd and to the policeman guarding the place. "You can't have a souvenir, miss," he said wearily. "People are living here, and they'd like to be left alone."

"I know, sir. *I* live here. See?" I opened my purse and took out my key. "It fits, you'll find. Tell them that Miss Nora Fitzpatrick is here."

The detective sighed but obliged. After a brief conference with someone inside, he returned. "Go ahead in."

I scurried through the door, supplying the crowd with enough fodder to fill a good half hour of conversation.

Inside, I found Mr. and Mrs. Holohan. "Where is Anna?"

"Trying to get some sleep."

I rushed into the back room where Anna was sprawled on the bed. "Nora?" She began crying. "I heard the knock and thought it might be a reprieve."

"No," I said. "I'm so very sorry."

Anna sat up. "I went to Mama, then Father Walter and I went to the White House to beg the president for a pardon," she said in a flat voice. "He wouldn't see us. Someone sent us to Judge Holt instead, and he couldn't do anything either. He said that he pitied me, but it was all in the president's hands. So I'm going back tomorrow. I should be with Ma, but we only make each other grieve, and it's such a long way from there to the White House . . ." She trembled. "I can't bear to think of her dying, Nora. She's so good, so kind . . ."

"Me neither. Anna, I have one idea. Mrs. Douglas — Senator Douglas's wife. She's beautiful, and she's society. The president can't exactly throw her out on her ear. If she begs for your mother's life, he's bound to listen."

"But what makes you think she will?"

"She asked about your mother when Mrs. Surratt was still at the Old Capitol, and told me to tell her if she could do anything to help. And she's a devout Catholic. She'll want to help another Catholic."

Anna sniffled. "But is she even in town?"

I hadn't thought of that. "There's only one way to find out," I said. "I'm going to her house."

"Now?"

"Now." I kissed her on the cheek, grateful she was too weary and sad to talk some sense into me. "I'll be back later tonight."

Although a police officer was still stationed outside the house, the curious gazers had dispersed, a sure sign that it was too late for me to be out. "I'll be back," I called.

"Miss —"

I ignored him and hurried on my way.

The path I trod was a familiar one, for this was the way I walked to St. Aloysius Church, only two blocks from Mrs. Douglas's mansion. It was not a terribly long walk — from H Street between Sixth and Seventh Streets to New Jersey Avenue and I Street — but at this late hour, it began to get lonely very quickly. First I prayed that my father would not somehow spot me and haul me off to Baltimore — and then, when I saw two men ambling down West Fourth Street from the direction of Pennsylvania Avenue, right into my path, I began to pray that he would.

"Little lady, where are you going? Would you like some company?"

I shook my head.

"Little lady, don't be cruel! Let us walk with you."

"Damn it, Jack. Leave her alone."

"Maybe she doesn't want to be left alone." The man seized my arm. "Want some company tonight, missy?"

My scream could have awakened the dead, but their assistance proved entirely unnecessary, for in a matter of seconds, Jack lay in a heap at my feet, dispatched by a single punch from his companion, Mr. Alexander Whelan. "Miss Fitzpatrick? What in the name of God are you doing out at this hour, and alone?"

"Is he dead?"

Mr. Whelan snorted, then waved at a couple of householders who had poked their heads out the window. "All's well," he called. "Just a fellow getting fresh with this lady here." As the onlookers disappeared from view, Mr. Whelan said, "No, Miss Fitzpatrick, he's not dead, although I hope his head will make him wish he was next morning."

"Thank you, sir." I began to walk on.

Mr. Whelan stayed beside me. "To get back to my question, miss, what are you doing out this late at night?"

I sniffed. Mr. Whelan, though not obviously drunk, was decidedly redolent of spirits. "I could ask what you are doing out drinking with a wife and children at home."

"It's a man's constitutional right to drink, I'll have you know, Miss Fitzpatrick."

I mentally reviewed the various provisions of the Constitution and found none that quite fit Mr. Whelan's claim. But standing here arguing fine points of constitutional law with Mr. Whelan wouldn't help Mrs. Surratt. "Sir, I must be going."

"And I have to ask you again, where are you going this time of night alone?"

"It's none of your concern, sir."

"It is my concern, miss." There was an odd catch in his voice when he said that, and I wonder to this day how much of my future was decided with those five short words. He cleared his throat. "It's my concern because if you wander around the city at night by yourself, you're going to be robbed or ravished, as you should have figured out from what just happened, and I'm not going to let either happen to you. You can go where you like — but I'm going with you to keep you from harm. Agreed?"

"Agreed. It's not far from here."

"Then will you tell me where we're going, miss?"

"You heard that Mrs. Surratt is going to die tomorrow."

"Yes." Mr. Whelan looked rather sheepish. "We were toasting her over at the Marble

Saloon."

"For shame, sir!"

"Well, it's a hot night, miss. We toasted the other three first."

I sighed. "In any case, sir, I want to enlist the aid of Mrs. Douglas in begging for Mrs. Surratt's life. So I am going to her house."

Mr. Whelan nodded. "Go straight to the top, that's my motto. Now, does your father know about this, miss?"

"No. You won't take me back to him, will you, sir?"

"Take you back? Have you run away from him?"

"No, but I'm supposed to be in Baltimore."

Mr. Whelan considered this. "I ran away from my old man, miss. Nothing to be ashamed of. Sometimes I think that everyone should run away from their old man."

"For heaven's sake, Mr. Whelan! I have not run away. I just disobeyed him."

"Well, that's how it starts, you know. First you disobey your old man, then you run away from him."

"Why did you run away, sir?"

"Because he was a right proper bastard — excuse the language. Beat me and took my wages. One payday, I grabbed up my money and left him, and Canada, behind. Haven't

544

seen either of them since."

"That's sad, sir."

"Yes," Mr. Whelan said reflectively. "Sometimes I miss Canada. Not the old man, though."

As we made our way down the street, Mr. Whelan taking my arm to guide me, it occurred to me that I was traipsing around close to midnight arm-in-arm with a married man I barely knew, who was perhaps not entirely sober, in a city where I wasn't supposed to be. It was an impressive list of accomplishments in one evening for a girl who had spent most of her life in convent schools. I cleared my throat. "Mr. Whelan, I hope your wife won't be worried about you."

"No, miss. She understands me." Mr. Whelan pointed at a wall emblazed with an advertisement for soda crackers. "See that, miss? My work."

"Very nice."

"Did you get a book in prison called *The Trapper's Bride,* miss?"

I stared up at him. "Why, yes, I did. How did you know that?"

"Because I sent it."

"You?"

"Yes. A friend of mine passed it on to me. I'm not much of a reader, but I remembered what you had said about not having anything to read the first time you were in prison, so I gave one of the guards there a chaw of tobacco and asked him to pass it and a *Harper's Weekly* on to you. The book, I mean, not the chaw. Probably not your type of book, though."

"It kept me very well entertained, sir, and I thank you."

"Well, here we are, miss."

I stared at the Douglas mansion. I had passed by it before, but seeing it shut up for the night, and having business there, made it a daunting sight.

"Aren't you going to knock, miss?"

"I don't know. Maybe it is too late after all —"

Mr. Whelan banged on the door. "Police!"

In no time at all, a colored servant appeared at the door as Mr. Whelan disappeared into the shadows. "Where's the police, missy?"

"There are no police. My companion thought —" I opened my purse. "Is Mrs. Douglas home?"

"She's long in bed, missy."

"I must see her. Or at least give her this letter."

The servant looked at me kindly. "Are you in a family way, miss? Mrs. Douglas gets a lot of girls in a family way coming here.

Young cads promise them all the world, then leave them high and dry. Happens all the time. It does. Nice girls too."

"I am not in a family way. This is a matter of life and death. Please, may I see her? It will take only a few minutes. Tell her that I am Miss Nora Fitzpatrick, from church. And from Georgetown Visitation as well." I handed him the letter I had composed on the train. "And give her this."

"I'll ask, missy. But it sure is late, if you ask me."

"Family way." Mr. Whelan chuckled from his hiding place.

"Why are you hiding, sir?"

"Thought after what happened to Mr. Seward, they might be a little reluctant to open the door to a man."

"Well, that makes sense," I said grudgingly.

To my immense relief, the stately figure of Mrs. Douglas soon appeared in the hall, lit by gaslight. "Miss Fitzpatrick, surely you are not alone this time of night."

"No, ma'am. I have a companion. For heaven's sake, come out, Mr. Whelan."

Mrs. Douglas lifted her eyebrows, then said in her usual serene tone, "I have read your letter, Miss Fitzpatrick, and I will gladly go on the errand you urged of me, but I do not want to give you false hope. My friends tell me that the president is adamant that Mrs. Surratt must die."

My heart sank, but I said, "False hope is better than none at all. Thank you, Mrs. Douglas."

"I will be there early tomorrow. Now let me have my driver take you home."

"That's not necessary, ma'am."

"I rather think it is," Mrs. Douglas said dryly and went to give the orders.

I turned to Mr. Whelan. "Thank you, sir, for helping me."

"Any time, miss. I hope they save her."

I watched him disappear down New Jersey Avenue. As I settled into Mrs. Douglas's fine carriage a little while later, I found myself wishing he was still with me.

Just a little.

47
MARY

Much as I hated to send Anna away, I was soon grateful that she was gone, for I was seized by cramps and congestive chills, necessitating a visit by the physician. It was not in this condition, groaning and crying out, that I wanted my daughter to remember me. Indeed, I was so ill at one point that it occurred to me that if the government waited a few days, it would not have to hang me at all.

Through all, Father Wiget prayed with me and endeavored to comfort me, but I was still base enough to wish there was another priest at my side — Father Finotti, who could always cheer me. He could be in no doubt I was the same person as his congregant of old: the press had seen to that. Once I even thought of writing to him, but enough people had suffered through their association with me, and I would not drag another unwitting soul into this web.

549

Yet for all that, I had hoped he might write to me anyway — a simple letter of solace — but nothing had come. Perhaps he had forgotten me. Perhaps he was never the man I thought he was. I could hear the mocking voice of my husband, telling me it was about time I realized that.

I had not judged men well. Mr. Booth, hiding his murderous plan under the kindest of facades. Mr. Weichmann, testifying against me and Johnny. Senator Johnson, offering high-flown words and little practical help at my trial. My Johnny — yes, even my Johnny, who had not come to stand trial with me. It was those I had barely known — Mr. Brophy and this patient man whose voice was getting hoarse, General Hartranft and his unfailing kindness to Anna and me — who in their different ways had proven to be the best of friends to me.

And here I was, ignoring the gospel because it was not being read by a man I had not seen in years. "Father Wiget? If I do not remember to say so tomorrow, thank you for your kind care of me."

Father Wiget smiled and, in a firm voice, resumed his reading. " 'My Father,' he said, 'if it is possible, let this cup pass me by. Nevertheless, let it be as you, not I, would have it.' "

■ ■ ■ ■

Deep in the night, I told Father Wiget I would try to sleep, more for his benefit than for mine. I stretched out on my mattress and shut my eyes.

It had grown very quiet. The commotion of the scaffold being built had ceased hours ago, but throughout the evening I had heard the sounds from the other cells — Mr. Payne's stoic murmur of conversation with his minister, Mr. Herold's bevy of sisters, some weeping and some calmly reading aloud, Mr. Atzerodt's deep sighs. Now, only the footsteps of the guards broke the silence of this place.

Somewhere in this prison, I heard from Anna, who saw it in the newspapers, lay the body of Mr. Booth, safe from those who might desecrate it and hidden from those who might make its burial place a sort of shrine. His poor mother!

"Does she have a favorite, Mr. Booth?"

"Anna! No mother admits to such things."

"No, she does not mention it, as you say, Mrs. Surratt, but I believe my brothers and sisters, if pressed, would say that I was the favorite."

I struggled to a sitting position. "Father

Wiget?" I said in a low voice.

Evidently, my priest had been no more successful at finding sleep than I had, for he raised his head and answered immediately, "Yes, Mrs. Surratt?"

"Would you say a prayer for the repose of a soul?"

"Certainly. Whose?"

"Mr. Booth's."

Father Wiget looked surprised, but in a very low tone, dutifully prayed for the soul of Mr. Booth.

Morning. The prison was awake, and my life was now measured in hours.

I asked for pencil and paper and managed to compose a short letter to each of my absent sons, giving them my love and asking them to take good care of their sister. As I wrote Isaac's, I considered the irony that my farewell to him should be by letter, for that was how he had bid me farewell one spring day in 1861: leaving a letter on the mantelpiece and making the impossible request that I should not worry about him. As the war ground on, and especially during the last few months, he had been pushed to the back of my mind, but I had never ceased to love him or to remember him in my prayers. As I folded the letter, I silently pleaded for the Lord to bring him home safely, both for his own sake and Anna's.

Just after I wrote the letters, someone brought me breakfast, which I could not touch, even though I had scarcely eaten the previous day. No sooner did I push it away when Father Walter came bearing the Holy Communion, which I was able to take. As I lifted the wafer to my mouth, I saw my hands were shaking.

Then Mr. Brophy hastened in. "There is good news, Mrs. Surratt! Overnight, Mr. Clampitt and Mr. Aiken got Judge Wylie from the Washington Supreme Court to issue a writ of habeas corpus, directed to General Hancock."

"What does that mean, sir?"

"It means that General Hancock must produce you before the court — the hour given is ten o'clock. Your lawyers argued — on Mr. Reverdy Johnson's advice — that the military trial was illegal and that you should be tried, if at all, before a civilian court. Payne's lawyer is seeking the writ as well."

As I absorbed all this, Mr. Brophy continued, "I have been by your house and notified Miss Surratt, who was gratified to hear the news. She and Miss Fitzpatrick are on their way to the White House to beg an audience with President Johnson, whom I have written as well to dispute the testimony of Mr. Weichmann. And that is not all! Mr. Payne has declared several times that you were not involved in the assassination plot. It is weighing on him very heavily. I plan to get something in writing and take it to the president myself."

A man with a cause, with all of the energy and passion of the young, he barely gave me time to thank him before he hurried off.

48
NORA

JULY 7, 1865

Anna and I made an odd pair as we left the boardinghouse that morning. I was still in the light, flowery summer frock I'd been wearing when I got the news at the bookstore, whereas she was clad in the same black silk she had worn to the trial, which, as it was unrelieved by any accessories, gave her the unfortunate appearance of being in mourning before the fact. Her friend Mr. Brophy had come by with the encouraging news of the granting of Mrs. Surratt's habeas corpus petition, however, so she was more hopeful than she had been the day before.

At Mr. Brophy's suggestion, our first stop was the Metropolitan Hotel, where General Hancock was staying. Anna sent her card up to General Hancock, who promptly appeared in response. "Sir, what can I do to save my mother?"

"Miss Surratt, I do not wish to see your

mother — or any lady — hang, but it is beyond my power to stop it. Your one hope is to go to the president, to go on your knees before him and beg for her life."

"I am on my way there, but I was there yesterday, and he offered me no solace."

"It cannot hurt to go back. His health has been poor of late, and much depends on how he is feeling from day to day. I wish you the best of luck, Miss Surratt."

He bowed and showed us out the door. "Well," said Anna as we stepped onto Pennsylvania Avenue, already baking in the heat, "he was cold enough."

"He was courteous, Anna, and honest at least."

As we made our way down Pennsylvania Avenue to the White House, we passed through a crowd of people streaming in the direction of the Old Arsenal, hoping to catch something of the executions, or at least to share in the pervading excitement. I glared at them all, but with no effect, as I was wearing my veil. Camilla was a late riser, and it was entirely possible that my absence wouldn't be discovered until nine or so, but I could hardly be sure of that, so each time an aging man approached us, I quailed lest he be my father. I could only pray that if I did encounter him, he wouldn't recognize my dress, as he was one of those men who paid little attention to such matters.

All one had to do to get into the White House was open the door and walk in. Seeing the president, of course, was a different matter, depending on who was in office, but in Mr. Lincoln's day, it had not been hard.

As soon as Anna and I entered at the North Portico — I staring around me in curiosity despite the gravity of our mission — an usher approached us. "Your business, misses?"

"I am Miss Anna Surratt."

The man's expression instantly turned gloomy.

"I was here yesterday to talk to the president about my mother and was told to see General Holt. He said that he could do nothing but refer me to the president. So I have come back."

"Miss Surratt, the president is indisposed and will see no one today."

"Sir, I want only five minutes of his time. It is literally a matter of life and death. Please!"

"Madam, I know well what errand you have come on. The president knows of the event that is to happen today, but he nonetheless left the firmest orders not to be

557

disturbed."

"Please! Do you not have a mother? Is she not everything to you?"

"I sympathize with your plight, Miss Surratt. But I cannot let you up to see the president."

For a moment, I thought Anna was going to make a run for the stairs or faint — I could not guess which. Instead, she commanded herself to say calmly, "Then please let me see General Mussey."

"I will tell him you are here, miss."

"Who's General Mussey?" I hissed as the usher disappeared from sight.

"The president's private secretary. I saw him briefly yesterday."

A man of about thirty, with a kindly face and tired eyes, entered the hall. "Miss Surratt? What I can do for you?"

"Sir, I must see the president. Just one word, sir. One little word!"

General Mussey sighed. "The president has made it utterly clear that he will see no one about the trial, Miss Surratt."

"I can change his mind, sir, if he would only see me!" Anna knelt at the general's feet and raised her hands in supplication. "Please, sir, let me see him! Take me up and leave me alone with him, for just a minute. Surely he will relent when he sees me."

"The president is not that sort of man, Miss Surratt. If I were to bring you to him, against his explicit orders and while he is ill, it would do neither you nor your mother any good."

"She is too kind and good to die, and she is innocent!" Anna pulled on the hem of General Mussey's jacket. "Take me to him, sir!"

"I cannot, miss."

Anna rose and tottered toward the staircase, which two guards had moved to block. She dropped, weeping, upon the stairs and said, "If Ma is put to death, I wish to die myself."

I sat on the staircase and held Anna while she sobbed. The hall was full of people by now, all moved by Anna's plight, all unable to do anything to help her. "Sir, may Miss Surratt at least stay here for a while, in case the president does relent?"

General Mussey, his face wet with tears, nodded. "Take her into the East Room when she recovers. But I tell you, miss, there is little hope if any. The president said yesterday, in my hearing, that Mrs. Surratt had kept the nest where the egg was hatched, and that if he pardoned her, it would only encourage women to commit treason."

At last, I managed to coax Anna into the East Room. Not three months before, President Lincoln's body had lain in state here, and I tried to picture the large room draped in black from ceiling to floor.

Each time a newcomer appeared in the hall, Anna would leap up and run to the door, in hopes of seeing the one person who could touch the president's stony heart. Instead, we saw two of Mr. Herold's sisters, begging that the president pardon their brother for the sake of their dead father, who had served the government loyally as an official in the Navy Yard. "He was but a foolish boy, whom Mr. Booth made use of," the eldest young lady urged. "Our father died last year, and without his guidance, my brother went astray."

"Prison will be punishment enough for him," pleaded the second. "He will be utterly miserable there, never being able to hunt, doing hard labor. He hates to labor, sir."

"I am sorry," General Mussey said. "He will not see you."

As the Herold girls left, dejectedly but quietly, a distinguished-looking man hurried into the hall. "Charles Mason," he said, handing his card to the general. "Please allow me to see the president. I've known him for years."

"On what business, sir?"

"On this business of executing the woman, sir. I know no one in this affair, have been sent for by no one, but it disturbs me deeply. I have seen no evidence that shows she was more deeply involved than O'Laughlin and Arnold, who were part of the kidnapping plot — yet they will go to prison, along with Spangler and Dr. Mudd, and she will die upon the gallows. Is that just, sir?"

"No, sir, it is not!" Anna ran forward and clasped his hand. "Please, sir, let this man see the president!"

"You are her child?" Mr. Mason said. "Dear me." He patted Anna, who was clinging to him like a long-lost daughter.

The door flew open, and Mr. Brophy rushed in, bearing papers aloft. "General Hartranft provided me with his carriage and horses so I could get here as soon as possible," he said, handing them to General Mussey triumphantly. "Father Walter has signed them as well. Mr. Payne — the conspirator who was more trusted by Booth than any of them — has repeatedly stated that Mrs. Surratt was guiltless of conspiring to murder the president. Except for Booth himself, who would be better placed to

561

know that than Payne? And I have added my own observations, to the effect that Louis Weichmann was a lying wretch desperate to save his own skin."

"I will take the papers to him," General Mussey said and retreated to the stairs.

I turned to Mr. Brophy. "Sir, what about the writ of habeas corpus?"

He shook his head. "President Johnson has issued an order suspending it. This is our last hope."

As if in answer to our prayers, the doors opened, and Mrs. Douglas swept into the room. "I am here to see the president."

The usher made his now-familiar refusal. Mrs. Douglas nodded graciously, then brushed past him and ascended the stairs. "There is no need to give me directions, sir. I know my way around this house quite well."

Openmouthed, the two soldiers standing on the stairs lowered their bayonets and let Mrs. Douglas past them. "A deus ex machina," whispered Mr. Brophy.

Clutching one another, the four of us gazed at the stairs as Mrs. Douglas's skirts disappeared from view. As the minutes passed and others congregated in the hall to join our vigil, Anna whispered, "Surely she would have been back by now if she had failed."

Mrs. Douglas, her head drooping, soon returned. "I am sorry," she said. "The president is obdurate on the matter. There is no hope."

Anna let out a shriek. Mr. Brophy said, "Madam, has he seen the papers that I sent?"

"That I do not know, sir."

"Then please go back, madam, and ask him if he has."

Mrs. Douglas nodded and again made her way upstairs. This time, her absence was much briefer. "He has seen the papers, sir, and says there is nothing in them to change his mind. He has seen a petition by Mr. John Ford on Mrs. Surratt's behalf as well." She passed into the East Room, where we trailed behind her. "The man is as stubborn as a mule, and about as kind." Mrs. Douglas touched Anna's cheek. "I am sorry I could be of such poor assistance to you, Miss Surratt. You and your mother will be in my prayers tonight." She glanced at Mr. Brophy, Mr. Mason, and me. "You have devoted friends, Miss Surratt. Let that be some comfort to you."

We watched in silence as Mrs. Douglas

left the East Room, and our hopes, behind her.

Mr. Mason whispered "God bless you, Miss Surratt" and followed Mrs. Douglas.

"We have done all that we could, Miss Surratt. Let us leave now if you wish to see your mother while she lives," Mr. Brophy said.

Anna nodded and let Mr. Brophy lead her out of the White House and into the carriage he had procured from General Hartranft. I followed, batting back tears. All along, I realized, I'd been hoping Mrs. Douglas and President Johnson would have reenacted the scene I'd devoured so many times in Miss Strickland's *Lives of the Queens of England:* Edward III giving into Queen Philippa's pleadings and releasing the Burghers of Calais. *"Ah, lady, I wish you had been anywhere else than here; you have entreated in such a manner that I cannot refuse you. I therefore give them you — do as you please with them."*

But there were no knights in shining armor in Washington. Only poor Mr. Brophy and Mr. Mason, doing the best they could for a woman they barely knew or didn't know at all. And they had failed. All of us had.

Yet there was one man who would have

listened to Anna's pleas, I thought as I wearily sank into my seat. He would have let her into his office, heard her out, and perhaps told her a story. He would have signed Mrs. Surratt's pardon. He might even have taken it to the prison himself.

Yes, there was one man who would have saved Mrs. Surratt. And Booth had shot him dead.

49
MARY

Ten o'clock passed, and I was still here when Mr. Holohan came to my cell and stood in front of me awkwardly, hat in hand. "I don't know what to say, Mrs. Surratt, except that I'm sorry that this happened, and I'll do my best to help your daughter. Mrs. Holohan too. She feels for the girl, for all her grumbling."

"Thank you, Mr. Holohan." The doctor had given me doses of wine of valerian throughout the night, and it had slowed my thoughts somewhat, but I managed to tell Mr. Holohan what he needed to know to help Anna get through the difficult months ahead, while Fathers Walter and Wiget took the welcome opportunity to stretch their legs outside my cell.

He jotted down some notes, then rose to go. "God grant you courage, Mrs. Surratt," he said, taking my hand.

■ ■ ■ ■

Mr. Aiken and Mr. Clampitt — I knew better than to expect Reverdy Johnson — arrived next. President Johnson, they told me, had suspended the writ of habeas corpus.

"So there is no hope?"

The two lawyers considered, clearly not wanting to admit defeat. "Very little," Mr. Clampitt finally conceded. "Not unless the president relents." He brightened. "General Hancock has stationed couriers along the route from the White House to here, in case of a last-minute pardon."

"Sir, is the president a man to give one?"

Mr. Clampitt's sad eyes answered my question. He took my hand. "I will bid you farewell, Mrs. Surratt. I wish with all my heart that the outcome had been different."

"And I too," said Mr. Aiken.

"You did your best," I said, and thanked them once more before they departed, shoulders slumped. I wished the president would issue me a pardon, but almost more for their sake than for mine, for the long night with Father Wiget had resigned me to death. It was not the fact of death I feared now, but its manner — the fall into space, the possibility of not dying quickly, the chance of mortifying myself in front of the onlookers.

So I thought, at least, until the next visitors came in: Mr. Brophy and my dear Anna.

I thanked Mr. Brophy for his kindness to me and to my daughter, and he left the cell with streaming eyes, followed by the two priests. Then Anna and I fell into each other's arms, oblivious of the young guard required to keep an eye on us so Anna did not slip me poison.

We had so much to say, and so very little time to say it. She did not waste her time telling me her trip to the White House was in vain — I knew it as soon as the pair of them walked in. Instead, she told me of her regrets, and I of mine. She wished she had been less prone to bad temper; I wished I had made her home a happier one.

But it was not all regrets. She recalled the new pianoforte I purchased especially for her (none of the rest of us being at all musical); I recalled her playing songs she never cared for, only because I liked them. She remembered that no matter how hard times were, I saw to it that she was beautifully dressed; I remembered how she had lovingly nursed me through my time here.

"I know you loved your father very dearly,"

I told her gently. "But our marriage was not happy, and perhaps it would have been better if we had married other people. Don't marry hastily. Get to know a man's character — and his habits — very well first. I know it will be lonely for you, but in the long run, when you are contented and happy, it will have been worth it."

"I will." Anna settled against me, and we spent a few minutes in silence.

I knew from the increasing commotion outside that we would not have much more time together. I reached in my bag. "Anna, I have written letters to each of your brothers. Give them to them if — when they come back, and give them my love."

Anna nodded and took them, but I saw her give Johnny's a hard look. "What is wrong, Anna?"

"Ma, why has he not come? Why has he not come to sacrifice himself for you?" She stared at the letter. "It is what a man should do." She turned her face from me. "I don't know if I can ever forgive him."

I laid my hands on her shoulders. "You must forgive him, Anna, for my sake. He is but young, and life is very sweet. He will need your love when he returns, for he will have much to bear. Can you promise me that you will forgive him? It will make my last moments easier."

"I will, Mama."

"Good." I embraced her again, and in that moment, I too forgave my son.

As footsteps came near the door, I pulled off my wedding ring and my earrings and placed them in Anna's hand. "I wish I had more to give you, my girl."

"Mrs. Surratt." General Hartranft pushed open the door. "Madam, I am deeply sorry, but you must part now."

Anna clung to me. "I won't let you go!"

General Hartranft stood there, unable to bring himself to pull my daughter away. It finally fell to Mr. Brophy to gently pry her from me.

"Miss Surratt, it is time."

"Ma, are you resigned to death?"

"Yes, I am, Anna."

"Father Walter, ask her if she is resigned to death."

"I am, Anna. Please obey the general now."

"Wait." Anna pulled a pin, in the shape of an arrow, from her bonnet, and pinned it to the top of my dress. "So it doesn't fly open."

"God bless you, Anna," I whispered as we embraced one last time. "Take care of her, Mr. Brophy."

"I will, Mrs. Surratt."

One last worldly thought entered my mind as Anna exited, weeping into Mr. Brophy's handkerchief: it was a pity Mr. Brophy had a fiancée.

Now that my life was to be measured in minutes, they moved quickly. Two soldiers, Lieutenant Colonel McCall and Sergeant Kenney, entered the cell and, after apologizing, proceeded to chain my feet and fasten my hands behind my back. "Her bonnet," prompted Lieutenant Colonel McCall.

Sergeant Kenney gingerly took my bonnet from the windowsill and held it on a level with my head, then removed my manacles. "Maybe you had best put it on, Mrs. Surratt."

I tied the ribbons and arranged my veil with shaking hands before Sergeant Kenney refastened the manacles. Then he and his companion led me to a chair outside my cell, telling me General Hartranft would give the word when we were to start.

Father Walter knelt beside me, holding a cross to my lips. "Father, may I say something on the — on the scaffold?"

"What, my child?"

"That I am innocent of conspiring to kill the president."

"No, my child. The world and all that is

571

in it has now receded forever. It would do no good, and it might disturb the serenity of your last moments."

From the prison yard, a drum sounded. My escorts gently raised me to my feet, on which I suddenly had trouble standing, and half led, half carried me toward the prison yard. Murmuring prayers, the two priests followed behind.

As soon as my feet landed outside, I was overwhelmed by the heat, brutal even for Washington in July, and by the smell of the freshly cut wood of the new-made scaffold that loomed in front of me. I came to a halt. Behind me, Father Wiget said, "Pray with us, Mrs. Surratt."

I obeyed, keeping my head down to avoid the sight of the scaffold and the crowd of soldiers, newspapermen, and spectators who filled the usually empty prison yard. Only when I saw, not far from the steps of the scaffold, four yawning graves and four crude coffins piled next to them did my knees give way. The soldiers kept me from falling in a heap. "Steady, Mrs. Surratt."

With the chains on my feet clinking, the men lifted me, stair by stair, up to the scaffold platform. Four wooden armchairs, against which rested umbrellas, had been placed upon it. The soldiers seated me in the armchair on the far right and gave their places to the priests as I stared at the noose dangling in front of me. "No," I moaned.

"Don't look at it, child," Father Walter said as Father Wiget snapped open an umbrella and lifted it above my head. "Pray."

As I muttered familiar words that no longer made much sense to me, I closed my eyes and slumped against Father Wiget. To the priests' prayers I added my own petition, the final thing with which I would ever trouble the Lord. *Please don't let my Anna see me die.*

50
NORA

After our futile trip to the White House, the street leading to the Old Arsenal was so crowded with the curious that only General Hancock's spotting our carriage and ordering the way to be cleared brought us to the prison gates in time. "Lemonade!" a vendor shouted as we passed through the gates. "Last chance for lem-o-nade!"

"Cakes! Get your delicious *cakes*!"

"Barbarians," muttered Anna. It was the first word she'd spoken since we left the White House.

General Hancock's permission to pass through the gates having enveloped all three of us, I followed Mr. Brophy and Anna into the cell area. Instead of accompanying them into Mrs. Surratt's cell, I sat in an anteroom, for I had no pass to see her and did not want to take any precious minutes from her last time with Anna. Mr. Brophy, pale and red-eyed, soon joined me, and we sat in silence, listening to the wailings of loved ones parting for good. Mr. Herold's mother could not bear the strain of coming to see her condemned son, but his sisters were here, dressed in black like Anna. Even Mr. Atzerodt had company, some relations of his and the lady with whom he resided. Only Mr. Payne had no visitors, save for a minister and his lawyer. Later, I would learn that he was actually named Mr. Powell, the son of a Baptist preacher, and that his family in far-off Florida had received the news too late to make the journey to see him.

At about half past twelve, soldiers came to the cells for the grim task of sending the visitors away — a task scarcely less enviable, I thought as I heard Anna and the Herold sisters sobbing, than that of the hangman himself. As they emerged from the cells, Mr. Brophy having hurried in to support Anna, a clerk stepped forward. "There are places upstairs where the ladies can rest."

We followed him, Mr. Brophy half carrying poor Anna, to the second floor, where he guided each dismal little group to a different room, sending Mr. Brophy, Anna, and I to a little chamber with a cot and a chair — his room, he volunteered with some pride. Anna collapsed by the cot, sobbing wildly, while I stroked her hair helplessly, powerless to do anything to ease her grief. To my relief, she soon fell into an exhausted sleep — aided, I suspected, by something in the restorative Dr. Porter, the prison physician, sent upstairs.

Once Anna was asleep, Mr. Brophy raised the window shade, revealing a view of the scaffold that made me gasp. With four nooses hanging still on the windless, scorching day, it stood in perfect readiness for its awful task, the armchairs and umbrellas on its platform giving it a bizarrely homey look. On the wall overlooking it stood a line of soldiers, clearly prepared for any trouble. "Miss Fitzpatrick, perhaps you should go to another room."

"No. Anna might need me." As Mr. Brophy seemed disinclined to accept this rather feeble excuse, I added, "I'm here, sir. I want to see this to the end."

Mr. Brophy sighed but did not protest further.

"How will they fall, sir?"

Even at a moment of deepest sorrow, a man can derive some comfort by explaining something, especially if the party in need of the explanation is a woman. In a voice barely above a whisper, Mr. Brophy said, "There are two traps on which the prisoners will stand that are held up by props. Those soldiers you see standing underneath the gallows will knock the props out when they are given a signal. And then . . ."

I did not ask him to elaborate.

At a distance, I heard a clock strike one, and Mrs. Surratt, flanked by two soldiers and followed by Father Wiget and Father Walter, tottered out of the building toward the scaffold. She was dressed as I'd seen her at the trial, except that her gown, bereft of its usual crinoline, dragged along wearily behind her. "She can barely walk," I whispered. "Why have they bothered to tie her hands?"

Mr. Brophy looked down grimly as Mrs. Surratt made her painful progress. "They're not only hanging an innocent woman; they're hanging a sick one as well."

Behind Mrs. Surratt came Mr. Atzerodt, Mr. Herold, and Mr. Payne, who, like Mrs. Surratt, had their hands bound behind their backs and their feet shackled. All — except Mrs. Surratt, who wore the old shoes I'd often seen her work in around the house — were in stocking feet or slippers. No one had thought to provide Mr. Atzerodt with a hat, but Mr. Payne looked incongruously jaunty in a sailor hat I later learned had been procured by his minister. Only his shackled feet impeded his cool march to the scaffold.

Anna slept on beside us, mercifully unaware of her mother's painful progress up the stairs of the scaffold and into a seat at its far right, where the two priests quietly prayed with her, Father Wiget holding the cross and Father Walter holding a prayer book. As the three men settled into their seats — Mr. Payne to the left of Mrs. Surratt, Mr. Atzerodt on the far left, and Mr. Herold to his right — I took out my rosary.

But I could not keep my eyes off the scaffold. As I cautiously poked my head out (a holdover from my stay at Old Capitol) to get a better view, I saw something else poking out from a nearby building: the nose of Alexander Gardner's camera, here to capture the execution for generations to come. It occurred to me that I was seeing history in the making, although it was far from a pretty process.

General Hartranft, shielded by an umbrella, came to the center of the scaffold and read the death warrants, with the two priests continuing to minister quietly to Mrs. Surratt. I turned my eye to the men. Mr. Atzerodt, his head shielded from the blazing sun by a handkerchief provided by a sympathetic soldier, listened quietly and attentively to the general, while poor Mr. Herold squirmed in his chair and looked desperately around him — whether in search of an escape or of someone to speak to him, I could not say. At last, his minister bent over him and murmured a few words, which seemed to calm him.

Mr. Payne stared impassively at the sky, a puff of wind blowing his hat away. Someone caught it and began to replace it but was met with a slight smile and a shrug. He wouldn't be needing it much longer.

General Hartranft finished reading and stepped back. Now would have been the perfect time for a horseman to gallop into the yard, waving Mrs. Surratt's pardon, but no one obliged. Instead, Mr. Payne's minister, Mr. Herold's minister, and Mr. Atzerodt's minister each stood and offered prayers on his prisoner's behalf. Mrs. Surratt, seemingly oblivious to the speeches, murmured prayers while the priests stood over her. Only once, during the prayer for Mr. Atzerodt, did she let out a faint groan.

"Stand here, please," General Hartranft said softly.

Mr. Payne rose immediately and walked to the edge of the scaffold, followed by Mr. Herold and Mr. Atzerodt, both of whom trembled so badly it was impossible to say which of the pair was more unnerved. Father Walter and Father Wiget helped Mrs. Surratt to a standing position and relinquished her to her two escorts, who gently guided her to the hinged area of the drop. Quickly, the soldiers bound the men's arms, knees, and ankles with strips of white cloth.

Mrs. Surratt stood with her head drooping, half shielded from the gaze of the crowd by the soldier who supported her. My eyes filled with tears when a second soldier bent to deal with her bindings. She was a modest woman. Surely he wouldn't yank her skirt up and reveal her legs, would he? I sighed as he settled for tying a large strip around her skirts near the knees.

Next to Mrs. Surratt, Mr. Payne stood pinioned. He gazed forward expressionlessly as his attendant placed the noose behind his left ear, adjusted it, and fastened a white hood atop his head. I got my last look at the face of the man who had sat beside me at Ford's Theatre and had asked me about Jane Shore.

Mr. Herold, plainly batting back tears, received his noose and hood, then Mr. Atzerodt. There was a long pause before Colonel McCall carefully untied Mrs. Surratt's bonnet and took it off her head.

As she blinked in the sunlight, he murmured something only she could hear and slipped the noose over her head.

"Gentlemen!" A man standing in the yard threw up his hands and turned to face the crowd. "I tell you this is murder. Can you stand and see it done?"

51
MARY

Fathers Wiget and Walter kept me so securely in a protective cocoon of prayer that I hardly noticed the arrival of my fellow prisoners on the scaffold until Mr. Payne took his seat in the chair next to mine and said despairingly to his minister, "Can't anyone save her?"

The minister murmured some reply, and Mr. Payne sighed.

What if he had not come to my house that night? What if I had not made those trips to Surrattsville? What if I had sold my tavern instead of leasing it to Mr. Lloyd? What if that mad scheme to kidnap the president in March had succeeded? So many what-ifs I could not help but wonder about, even as I tried to heed the priests' words that it was God's will that I die on the scaffold instead of as an old woman in a bed surrounded by my grandchildren.

I hoped it was also God's will that death

come quickly to me.

There were rituals to be gone through at a hanging, I learned — the reading of the death warrant, the prayers offered on behalf of the condemned. The priests ministered to me throughout them, preparing me for the moment to which all this ritual tended. "Lord Jesus," I whispered with them. "Into thy hands I commit my spirit."

At the other end of the scaffold, Mr. Atzerodt's priest ended his own prayer with a fervent amen. There was a long silence, broken by General Hartranft's solemn voice ordering us to stand.

Slowly, Fathers Wiget and Walter lifted me to my feet. "God bless you," I managed to say before they relinquished their hold on me to those who would prepare me in another way for execution. "Look after my poor girl."

Colonel McCall, who had always been kind to me during my imprisonment, gently took over. "A couple of necessary preparations," he said as Sergeant Kenney bound me with white strips of cloth. The sergeant was clearly ill at ease in trussing a lady in this manner and, in his eagerness to be done, tied my arms much too tight. "It hurts," I complained weakly.

"It won't hurt for long," he snapped, and I could tell before he finished the words that he regretted them. Gently, he loosened my bonds. "Is this better?" he asked softly.

"Yes."

With a sigh, Sergeant Kenney stooped to bind me below the knees as I bent my head, grateful for the veil hiding my flush of humiliation as he drew my heavy woolen skirts tight with his ribbon. When they balked at being constricted, I remembered the Bloomerite at my trial, and it occurred to me that in her odd style of dress she just might have had a point.

My trussing was over. Gently Colonel Mc-Call guided me forward, just beyond the hinge of the platform from which we would plunge to eternity. "I think you would prefer me to do the next myself. Would you, madam?"

I nodded. Delicately, the colonel removed my bonnet, which he handed to someone near him as I blinked in the blaze of sunlight revealed by the absence of my veil. He took the noose dangling in front of me and slipped it around my neck, nudging it against my left ear. Someone on the ground shouted something about murder, but I could not look down to see the commotion even if I dared. Instead, I stared ahead as

Colonel McCall adjusted the noose. "You will most likely lose consciousness very quickly," he told me. "Perhaps as soon as the trap is sprung, given your weak condition."

"Thank you, sir."

I turned my head slightly to see Captain Rath make a final adjustment to Mr. Payne's noose. "I want you to die quick," he explained.

"You know best, Captain," Mr. Payne said matter-of-factly.

My noose in place, Colonel McCall said, "Don't be frightened by this. It is only to hide your face," as he slipped a white hood over my head, blotting out all earthly sights. "Courage, madam," he said as he fastened it. "God be with you."

In the darkness, I felt him step back a little. "Please don't let me fall!" I begged.

A hand — earthly or heavenly — steadied me. Then a muffled clap, like that of a weary playgoer, sounded from the ground below.

A second clap.

And then a third.

52
NORA

JULY 7, 1865

The man who had shouted, failing to gain any response, turned his back to the crowd and, weeping, pressed his palm to his bowed head. Beneath the scaffold, one of the four men detailed to knock out the props wearily leaned against a support. Atop the scaffold, Mr. Payne, Mr. Herold, and Mr. Atzerodt stood noosed and hooded as Colonel Mc-Call carefully slipped a hood over Mrs. Surratt's head.

And in our room, Anna slept on, and I thanked God for this one small mercy.

Captain Rath, who had been overseeing the final preparations on the scaffold, descended the stairs, his face set. As the weary prop knocker pulled himself upright, the captain looked toward the building as if expecting a signal. Receiving it, he looked up at the gallows. Everyone but the prisoners had stepped back. Only Colonel McCall's outstretched arm kept Mrs. Surratt upright.

Slowly, Captain Rath brought his hands together three times as Mr. Atzerodt cried out, "Good-bye, gentlemen who are before me now. May we all meet in the other world! God help me now!" Then the props crashed to the ground, and four human beings plummeted to their deaths.

Mrs. Surratt, who had pitched forward when she fell, wildly swung back and forth like a ghastly pendulum, one hand making a slight clenching motion, before the rope subsided to a gentle spin. Mr. Atzerodt hung motionless, save for a heaving of his belly. Mr. Herold writhed as urine stained his pants, his body finally going limp after five minutes. And Mr. Payne — poor Mr. Payne! Even after Mr. Herold had ceased to fight for life, Mr. Payne struggled on, even pulling himself into a sitting position before death finally claimed him.

All this time, the crowd had remained frozen and silent. Even Mr. Brophy, who had made toward the window shade as if to shield me from watching Mr. Payne's grisly exertions, had paused, rooted to the spot. The bodies growing still, however, was the crowd's cue to come to life. The men of the press resumed scribbling in their notebooks, while some spectators, clearly shaken, left the yard, probably in search of something stronger than the lemonade waiting outside the gates. Others began to debate who had given up life the hardest, Mr. Payne or Mr. Herold, while a few began a furtive search for relics.

The clergymen gathered up their Bibles and crosses and slowly walked down the gallows stairs, followed by soldiers carrying the seats in which the four condemned had sat. At last, nothing remained on the gallows but the dead, hanging there listlessly while a young boy — surely too young to be watching a scene like this — stared at them in awe.

Anna stirred, and Mr. Brophy quickly drew down the window shade. Unwilling to wake Anna and numb with what we had just witnessed, Mr. Brophy and I sat there in utter silence until Father Walter, holding a bonnet, entered the room. "I'll take Miss Surratt home. I have a carriage here somewhere."

Anna blinked and rubbed her head. "Is Mama — ?"

"Yes, child. It is all over." To Mr. Brophy, he said, "The doctor has pronounced them dead."

When Anna — still too groggy to grieve — had finally been roused enough to walk, the men supported her out of the room. I started to follow, then said, "Excuse me. I forgot something."

I had to take one last look at her.

Returning to the room, I opened the shade. The four bodies, still wearing their white hoods, were lying atop the crude boxes that would serve as their coffins. Up on the scaffold, soldiers were cutting down the ropes and tossing bits of them to their friends, who were scrambling for the souvenirs. When one of two men, competing for a bit of Mr. Atzerodt's rope, stumbled backward and fell into one of the open graves, his friend seized a shovel and gleefully began throwing dirt on his flailing companion.

I pulled down the shade and hurried away.

At the boardinghouse, its door covered with black crepe I supposed the Holohans must have put there, a crowd had again gathered. As I followed Father Walter and Anna out of the carriage, and a policeman yelled at the crowd to stand back, I saw my father. I walked over to him, and I saw another familiar face: Alexander Whelan. He gave me a sad little salute and disappeared into the crowd.

I put my arms around my father. "I'm

sorry, Father. I had to try to help her. And I had to see her."

He shook his head and led me out of the crowd. "You have the look of death upon your face, child. You saw the executions?"

"Yes."

"I saw a hanging many years ago, and I have never been able to forget it. You saw four. I have not been able to protect you from anything this summer."

We walked on in silence. "What are your plans?" he inquired politely.

They must have been developing at the back of my mind all along. "I want to move in with Miss Surratt and be of what help to her I can. And I want to find work. If no one in the government will have me, perhaps I can find a teaching job. But first — first, I want to go back to Baltimore and get away from here for a while."

"As you wish."

I squeezed his hand. "And I would like you to take me there, Father."

We got to the station just in time for the next train, crowded full of people talking excitedly about the executions, a few clutching bits of fake souvenir ropes that were already being sold to the gullible. This time it was my father who sat stiffly beside me until the train started to move and I began to nod off.

"You're exhausted, child. Rest here."

I leaned my head against my father's shoulder, then opened my eyes wide.

You don't forget the sight of a woman who treated you like a daughter swinging at the end of a rope. That night, and many long nights afterward, I would be haunted by the sight. I would never be the same, just as I knew the men in blue who had walked in triumph down Pennsylvania Avenue and the men in gray making their way in defeat to their homes would never be the same. Maybe someday the memory would beat me down. If the past few months had taught me anything, it was that everything could change in the blink of an eye.

But I was sick of death. It was life that was calling out to me, and I wanted to make the best of mine.

I closed my eyes again. This time, amid the gabbling of the crowd clutching their ersatz ropes, the train lulled me straight to sleep.

Epilogue:
Nora
JUNE 1869

Four years after her mother's hanging, Anna married William Tonry, an Irishman who had spent much of his childhood in Boston and who worked as a chemist for the army.

In other words, he was a certified Yankee.

What singular quality in Mr. Tonry possessed Anna to abandon her most cherished prejudice, I cannot say, but when (with President Johnson's permission) Mrs. Surratt was finally laid to rest in February 1869 with a proper funeral service at Mount Olivet Cemetery in Washington, Mr. Tonry was there, and it was plain to everyone, even the members of the press who stood at a discreet distance from the mourners, that he adored Anna, which certainly helped. All that was needed was a decent interval from the funeral to pass so they could marry, and that interval having passed, the party that had gathered at Mrs. Surratt's graveside gathered at St. Patrick's Church for a very different occasion. I knew if Mrs. Surratt's soul had been uneasy, it surely was at peace now, knowing Anna was in the hands of a good man who would cherish her.

The day before, Anna had gotten all of her crying done over the fact that her mother wasn't there to see her married (I had shed some tears myself), so as she dressed the morning of the ceremony, she was dry-eyed and beautiful, if not exactly calm.

I adjusted her headdress for perhaps the fifteenth time. "Is this better?" I asked.

"No!"

You don't argue with a bride. Sighing, I tried again, moving it forward just a fraction. "This?"

I held my breath as Anna, her mother's earrings sparkling, surveyed herself in the mirror. "Perfect," she pronounced.

"Then don't you dare move your head until after the ceremony is over."

The press still took a certain interest in Anna, so this was to be a private, quite wedding with no bridesmaids or groomsmen, save for her oldest brother, Isaac, to lead her to the altar. He had finally made his way back east in the fall of 1865, having been held in Texas along with the rest of his regiment.

Having dressed Anna to her satisfaction, I left her in the charge of Isaac (whose resemblance to his mother still startled me at times) and slipped into the pew that Mrs. Surratt had favored when I was living in her boardinghouse. It was a tribute I'd paid to her on many a Sunday since her hanging.

At the front of the church sat John Surratt, lost in his own thoughts. Having learned from the newspapers of his mother's execution, Mr. Surratt, then hiding in a remote part of Canada, had fled to Europe and had finally ended up in Egypt, where he was caught and brought back to Washington to be tried for the president's death. I had reprised my testimony from the conspiracy trial, as had many others, including Mr. Weichmann, whose memory, I thought bitterly as I read the newspapers each morning, seemed only to have sharpened with time.

But although the government had trotted out witnesses swearing Mr. Surratt had been in Washington on the night of April 14, other, more convincing witnesses claimed to have seen him elsewhere, and the civilian jury had been unable to reach a verdict. So he had gone free. But many shunned him now, some because they believed he'd had a hand in the president's murder, and others because they believed he could have saved his mother by returning to Washington. Still, Anna and Isaac had remained loyal to him — Anna visiting him in prison, taking him delicacies, and procuring a first-rate lawyer for him, Isaac sitting in the courtroom and glaring at whoever glared at John — and I hoped he would take comfort in that in the lonely days to come.

Anna, looking as pretty and rosy in her wedding dress as when I first saw her, glided down the aisle on Isaac's arm, and the small congregation, John Surratt included, broke into a collective smile. Father Walter, presiding as he had at Mrs. Surratt's reburial, had tears in his eyes as he pronounced the couple man and wife.

We had a little wedding breakfast before Anna changed into a cream-colored traveling dress, her mourning dresses having been packed away, not to be needed again, I hoped, for years to come.

"Write to me," I said, hugging her goodbye as the carriage that would take her and her husband to the railway station appeared at the church door. "And you had better bring me a souvenir from Niagara Falls, do you hear?"

"I will," Anna said. She kissed me on the cheek, then took Mr. Tonry's arm. "Nora!"

she called when she reached her carriage. "Catch."

I held out my hands, and Anna tossed her wedding bouquet straight at me.

As the couple settled into the carriage, someone coughed, and I turned to see the now-widowed Mr. Whelan, who had lately gotten into the habit of walking me from work to the house where I resided with the other teachers. "How was the wedding, miss?"

"Beautiful."

"Are you going back to school?"

"No, sir. I have the day off. A substitute is boring my girls to death."

"Then maybe you'd like to get some ice cream?"

I smiled and took his arm. "That would be lovely," I said, cradling the bouquet in my free arm as the wedding carriage clattered away.

AUTHOR'S NOTE

Nora married Alexander Whelan in January 1870 and bore him three sons: James, Bernard, and John. Unfortunately, the marriage broke down, partly due to Alexander's alcoholism and perhaps partly due to Nora's deteriorating physical and mental health. After separating from Alexander in 1882, Nora was in and out of hospitals until August 1885, when her brother committed her to the Government Hospital for the Insane (known informally then, and officially now, as St. Elizabeths). Whether Nora's mental health problems were in any way connected with the events of 1865 can only be guessed at. Her brother, who wrote a detailed account of her troubles at the time of her admission to St. Elizabeths, blamed her misfortune on her husband and made no mention of the war years at all.

Nora's slender file tells us little about her life at the asylum, but she appears to have stayed in contact with her sons and step-daughters and was allowed occasionally to visit her sister in Baltimore. She died of tuberculosis at St. Elizabeths on January 7, 1896, at age fifty. Her death certificate describes her as having suffered from "chronic melancholia." Nora was buried in Mount Olivet Cemetery in Washington next to her parents, in a plot not far from Mary Surratt's grave. Her husband, Alexander, died in 1916, at age eighty, and was buried in the same cemetery at some distance from Nora. If anyone at the time of her passing remembered the brief part Nora had played in history, it went unremarked.

Days after he married Anna, William Tonry was dismissed from his government job in what the press believed was an act of petty retaliation for his marrying the daughter of Mary Surratt. Despite this setback, Tonry went on to become a prominent chemist who was often called upon as an expert witness at trials. He and Anna settled in Baltimore and had five children. Anna stayed far out of the public eye following her marriage, letting her husband speak for her about the events of 1865 on the rare occasion that it was necessary. She died in 1904 and was buried next to her mother at Mount Olivet; the following year, her husband was laid to rest beside her. Although the *Cincinnati Commercial* made the sensationalist claim in 1882 that Anna was a "wreck, both mentally and physically, with hair as white as the driven snow," this is likely a gross exaggeration.

In 1870, a financially strapped John Surratt began a speaking tour in which he acknowledged plotting to kidnap President Lincoln but denied knowing of any plan to assassinate him; he also denied the involvement of the Confederate government in the kidnapping scheme. As for his mother, John claimed that he had made contact with her lawyers and was told to stay away; not until the day his mother was hanged did he realize that her life had been at stake. Victorian audiences, however, found his lectures both unseemly and insufficiently revealing. When a furor erupted over his plan to speak in Washington, John canceled his lecture and retired from the public eye. After a few unhappy years working as a teacher, he moved to Baltimore and found work at the Old Bay Line steamship company, where he spent the rest of his career, rising eventually to the position of auditor. In 1872, he married Mary Victorine Hunter, with whom he had seven children. He died in 1916, reportedly having burned a memoir, and was buried in Baltimore.

Isaac Surratt never married. He also worked at the Old Bay Line. Following his death in 1907, he was laid to rest in Mount Olivet by his mother and his sister, in accordance with his dying request.

After the conspiracy trial, Louis Weichmann abandoned his plans to become a priest. Instead, he worked for the government in Philadelphia. His brief marriage to Annie Johnson, a temperance activist, ended in a separation. In 1886, after a change in administration cost him his government job, he moved to Anderson, Indiana, where some of his family lived, and opened a business college. Weichmann died in 1902, swearing on his deathbed that he had told the truth at the conspiracy trial. Unlike his erstwhile friend John Surratt, he did leave behind a memoir, which was finally published in 1975.

Olivia Jenkins testified on behalf of her cousin John Surratt at his trial in 1867. The following year, she married Robert Thorn, by whom she had a daughter and a son. In 1879, the widowed Olivia married James Donohoe, whose two brothers were married to two of her sisters. She died in 1898 of influenza at her home in Capitol Hill. Her son served as a pallbearer for both Isaac and Anna Surratt and for Anna's husband.

Mary Apollonia Dean married Napoleon Bonaparte Grant, a railroad engineer who died in a train wreck in 1894, a few months before Mary's own death. John T. Holohan died in 1877; his wife, Eliza, who had been working as a "sewer of books," followed in 1899.

Catherine Virginia Baxley returned to Baltimore after being released from prison. While at Old Capitol Prison, she kept a diary in the pages of Tennyson's *Enoch Arden,* in which she recounted the death of her son. The diary eventually passed into the hands of her niece, who gave it to the New York Public Library. I have not found out when she died; the last trace I have found of her is in 1867, when she wrote to Robert E. Lee about some funds he had donated to benefit Southern orphans.

John Brophy continued to proclaim Mary Surratt's innocence after her execution. He married the blue-blooded Elizabeth Warren Tyler, a relative of President Tyler, in 1866 and eventually moved to New York City, where he was the president of St. Louis College, a small Catholic school in Manhattan, and later a clerk of court. The father of a large family, he died in 1914. His diverse interests included the Fenian movement and his wife's genealogy, on which he and his sons published an endearingly snobbish little book.

Mr. Howell was released from prison shortly after the executions of Mary Surratt and her codefendants. He died in 1869 of typhoid fever and was buried in Washington's Congressional Cemetery under the name of Gustavus Howell.

Mary Surratt's tenant John Lloyd gave up his ill-fated career as a tavern keeper and returned to Washington, where he worked as a bricklayer and a contractor. He was fatally injured on the job after falling from a scaffold in 1892. Writing of his role in the Surratt trial, the *Washington Post* claimed that despite the importance of his testimony in sending Mary to the gallows, he believed her to have been an innocent victim of circumstance.

Although Mrs. Slater was brought up frequently during both the conspiracy trial of 1865 and John Surratt's trial in 1867, she was never linked to the assassination plot and never seems to have been arrested or even questioned. One paper, the *Hartford Courant,* identified her during the conspiracy trial as the former Sarah Gilbert, an erstwhile resident of Connecticut. But no one followed up on this scoop for over a hundred years, until in the 1980s, famed assassination researcher James O. Hall painstakingly traced her history from birth through April 1865, after which she disappeared into obscurity. Further research by John Stanton shows that she surfaced briefly in Manhattan in 1866 as Nettie Slater to divorce her husband, Rowan Slater. She remarried twice and died in Poughkeepsie, New York, as Sarah A. Spencer in 1920. Eschewing the lecture circuit and leaving no memoir behind, Sarah took her secrets to the grave, the marker of which shaves some ten years off her age. (Ironically, her third husband was a Union veteran.)

Those who study the Lincoln assassination in depth will have noticed the absence of some of the minor players in the events of that terrible Good Friday of 1865. Indispensable as they may have been in life, they proved dispensable in fiction! In the same vein, although Mary Surratt had two female servants toward the end of her stay in Washington, for simplicity's sake, I have combined them into one person: Susan. Otherwise, in telling Mary's story, I have stayed as closely to known facts as possible. For the trial testimony I used Ben Perley Poore's transcript and adhered closely to the original, although it has been heavily condensed and in some cases altered slightly for the sake of readability. The letter Johnny gives to his mother prior to the failed kidnapping attempt is my own invention.

While Adele Douglas did come to the White House to beg President Johnson for clemency for Mary Surratt, there is nothing to suggest that she did so at Nora's request, although there was indeed a connection between Adele and Nora in that both were alumnae of Georgetown Visitation. Likewise, although press accounts record that an unidentified lady accompanied Anna to the White House and the Old Arsenal Prison on the day of Mary Surratt's death, there is no evidence that this lady was Nora or that she watched the execution. Nora, however, seemed to me to be the likeliest candidate to have been Anna's companion, especially since Nora was one of the select company present at Mrs. Surratt's reburial in 1869, by one account riding in the first carriage with Anna. As for whether Anna herself saw her mother's execution, recollections given years after the fact vary. Lewis Powell's lawyer claimed in 1915 that Anna watched until fainting at the sight of the noose around Mary's neck; John Brophy, on the other hand, recalled in 1880 being told by General Hancock that he should on no account permit Anna to witness the hanging. Given Anna's near-breakdown at her mother's trial, I found Brophy's account more likely.

In 1881, George A. Townsend, a prominent reporter of the day, noted rumors that Father Joseph Finotti "got into such a flirtation with Mrs. Surratt that it raised a commotion, and he had to be sent to Boston to get him out of the scandal." While it seems unlikely that either party misbehaved, it is a fact that Father Finotti was transferred from Maryland to Massachusetts, and Mary's surviving letters to Father Finotti suggest that she was aware that the two had been the subject of gossip. Her letters also make it clear that she sorely missed the company of the priest, to whom she confided her worries about her children's futures and her dismay and disgust at her husband's alcoholism.

Nora's romance with Private Flanagan is fictional, as are Private Flanagan himself, the Misses Donovan, and Nora's friend Camilla, although a young lady by that first name is mentioned in passing in a surviving letter to Nora. Her kiss by Booth is fictional as well. Nora was indeed arrested twice in April 1865 and was ordered to be held apart from the rest of the ladies following her second arrest. She gave testimony for both sides at the conspiracy trial and at John Surratt's trial.

Within a few years after Mary Surratt's execution, both her boardinghouse and her tavern were lost to creditors. Both buildings survive, but their fates have been quite different. Renumbered as 604 H Street NW and missing the front staircase that led to Mary's parlor story, the boardinghouse now houses a Chinese restaurant: if you eat there, you will be sitting in the dining room where Mary and her boarders took their meals. As for the tavern in Prince George's County, the house gradually fell into disrepair and seemed destined for the wrecking ball until it was saved by historical preservationists in the 1970s. Restored and filled with period furnishings, it now is known as the Surratt House Museum and can be toured by the public. A modern building behind the house hosts the James O. Hall Research Center, an indispensable resource for those researching the Lincoln assassination. Surrattsville itself was renamed Clinton some years after Mary's death.

Although most of the Old Arsenal Prison, where Mary and her codefendants were imprisoned and executed, has been destroyed, the building in which the trial was held has survived. Located in Grant Hall on what is now the Fort McNair Army Base, the courtroom has been reconstructed and is periodically open for tours. As Nora noted in her narrative, the Library of Congress now occupies the site of the Carroll Annex, while the United States Supreme Court perches on the site of the main Old Capitol Prison. The National Hotel, where John Wilkes Booth resided, was destroyed in 1942; the Newseum stands in its place. The post office where Nora got her mail (not to be confused with the Old Post Office from a later decade) still stands and has been converted into the Hotel Monaco.

In the 150 years since Mary Surratt's execution, the question of her guilt has continuously been debated by passionate advocates on both sides. Equally debatable is when John Wilkes Booth changed his plan from kidnapping to murder and whether his mission had the approval of Confederate leaders. Rather than give you my thoughts, I suggest you read some of the books and publications I list below, which represent only a tiny fraction of those that have been written, and continue to be written, about the tragic events of April 14, 1865, and the people caught up in them. One caveat: the subject is addictive, and having delved into it, you may never have an empty space on your bookshelf again.

Alford, Terry. *Fortune's Fool: The Life of John Wilkes Booth.*

Kauffmann, Michael W. *American Brutus: John Wilkes Booth and the Lincoln Conspiracies.*

Larson, Kate Clifford. *The Assassin's Accomplice: Mary Surratt and the Plot to Kill Abraham Lincoln.*

Loux, Arthur F. *John Wilkes Booth: Day by Day.*

Ownsbey, Betty J. *Alias "Paine": Lewis Thornton Powell, the Mystery Man of the Lincoln Conspiracy.*

Pitch, Anthony S. *"They Have Killed Papa Dead!": The Road to Ford's Theatre, Abraham Lincoln's Murder, and the Rage for Vengeance.*

Steers, Edward, Jr., ed. *The Trial: The Assassination of President Lincoln and the Trial of the Conspirators.*

Surratt Courier. Monthly newsletter by the Surratt Society, based at the Surratt House Museum.

Swanson, James L. *Manhunt: The 12-Day Chase for Lincoln's Killer.*

Tidewell, William A., James O. Hall, and

David Winfred Gaddy. *Come Retribution: The Confederate Secret Service and the Assassination of Lincoln.*

Trindal, Elizabeth Steger. *Mary Surratt: An American Tragedy.*

Weichmann, Louis J. *A True History of the Assassination of Abraham Lincoln and of the Conspiracy of 1865.*

READING GROUP GUIDE

1. Even though Mary's role in the conspiracy puts Nora in jail twice and ruins her prospects of getting a government job, and despite Nora's high regard for President Lincoln, Nora remains loyal to Mary. Would you have been?

2. In a lecture given in 1870, John Surratt claimed that while hiding out in Canada, he sent an agent to confer with his mother's attorneys and was advised that Mary was in no danger and that any action on his part would only make matters worse. Many have speculated that if he had come to Washington, Mary would have been spared and John would have been hanged. Would you have returned in his position? Whose death do you believe Mary could have borne better, John's or her own?

3. As John Surratt reminds Mary, following

Ulric Dahlgren's failed raid on Richmond, papers were found on his body detailing a plan to kill Jefferson Davis and his cabinet. Assuming the papers were genuine, do you think such a plan, if carried out, would be regarded as an atrocity or as an act of war?

4. Mary Surratt maintained until the very last that she was innocent of the charges against her. Do you believe that she was innocent of conspiring to kill the president? Of conspiring to kidnap him?

5. In prison, Mary tells Anna that she is stronger than she realizes. Is she right? How do Anna and Nora change over the course of the novel?

6. Defending his kidnapping plot in his lecture, John Surratt said that his motives were honorable and that any young man in the North would have gladly entered into a plan to kidnap Jefferson Davis. Do you agree? What if John and his accomplices had succeeded in kidnapping President Lincoln in March 1865?

7. President Johnson believed that if he pardoned Mary Surratt, it would only

encourage women to commit treason. Do you agree with him? Would you have pardoned Mary? What about Powell, who failed to kill Secretary Seward? Atzerodt, who lost his nerve and never tried to kill Vice President Johnson? Herold, who assisted Booth's escape but shed no blood? What of the fact that each of the four, had he or she alerted the authorities, could have saved President Lincoln's life?

8. Bearing in mind that under the law of the time, Mary would have not been allowed to testify, but a jury would have had to reach a unanimous verdict, do you believe she would have met the same fate had she been tried in a civilian criminal court?

9. While on the run, John Wilkes Booth wrote in his pocket calendar that his assassination of the president "was not a wrong, unless God deems it so." Few would agree with him in President Lincoln's case, but can assassination ever be justified? What if one of the numerous plots to assassinate Hitler had succeeded? What about the assassination of a terrorist leader?

10. The two leading witnesses against Mary Surratt were her boarder, Louis Weichmann, and her tenant, John Lloyd. If Weichmann had refused to cooperate with the government, do you believe Mary could have been convicted on Lloyd's testimony alone? What if only Weichmann had testified?

11. In his lecture, John Surratt emphatically denied plotting to assassinate President Lincoln. Do you believe him?

12. At trial, Louis Weichmann claimed that he had confided his suspicions about John Surratt and his companions to a colleague at the War Department. If your close friend was involved in criminal activity, would you notify the authorities? What if the offense was a relatively minor one? What if your friend's activities were treasonous? Do you believe that Weichmann knew more about John Surratt's activities than he admitted?

A CONVERSATION
WITH THE AUTHOR

What drew you to Mary Surratt's story?

I've always been interested in the Lincoln assassination, but I'd never read about it in depth. A few years ago, I read James Swanson's *Manhunt,* and it rekindled my interest. I picked up Kate Clifford Larson's book about Mary Surratt's role in the conspiracy, *The Assassin's Accomplice,* and it occurred to me that Mary would make an excellent subject for a novel. The fact that I lived just a few hours away from the setting of the novel made the idea even more appealing.

How did you research *Hanging Mary*?

There's a wealth of material related to the Lincoln assassination, including witness statements and transcripts of the conspiracy trial, so that part of the book wasn't at all difficult to research — it was more a matter of accumulating all of the sources and sifting through them. What was a bit more challenging was researching the character of Nora Fitzpatrick. I knew nothing about her life after 1869 when I began researching the novel, so to get started, I put a query into the Lincoln Discussion Symposium, a discussion board where there's almost no question relating to Abraham Lincoln or the assassination that someone can't answer. Sure enough, someone was able to provide me with some basic genealogical information about Nora — as well as the shocking fact that she had died in an insane asylum. Fortunately, St. Elizabeths's records from the nineteenth century are available to the public, so I was able to obtain her file. Even better, her brother had written a long letter to the superintendent detailing her history. From that, I learned where Nora had gone to school, and I also got some insight into her character.

I also made use of both the National Archives and the District of Columbia Archives, where I looked through prison records, wills, guardianship reports — everything I could that was connected with Nora or her family. Much of what I learned never made it into the book, but it was great fun finding it out. My dream now is to be locked in the vaults of the National Archives for a weekend.

One source I found tremendously helpful was newspapers from the period. Not only did they publish detailed accounts of major events such as the president's assassination, the conspiracy trial, and the executions, but they published what we would consider the most minor of human interest stories — such as an article about the retirement of Nora's father from his bank, which gave me not only a little history of him, but some keys to his personality.

Did you change your mind about any of your characters?

I started the novel thinking of Anna Surratt as a high-strung bigot — I really didn't like her much. But as the novel progressed, I began to like her more, and I developed a great deal of respect for her. It took a strong character, much more than she's usually given credit for, to get through those horrible weeks culminating in her mother's execution with her sanity intact.

John Surratt is another character I warmed to. He didn't exactly play a heroic role in history — staying away from his mother in her hour of need — but I found it hard to dislike him. His letters to his cousin, including the one Nora sneaks a peek at, are lively and winning, and he speaks of his mother with warmth. A letter from his grand-daughter in the files of the James O. Hall Research Center speaks of him as a loving husband and father who was haunted by his mistakes in 1865.

Nora's brother called Alexander Whelan a worthless drunkard, and I was inclined to agree until I did some further research on him. He patented three inventions; he took the pledge occasionally; and when Nora died, he had the good sense to put his youngest son's small inheritance from her in the hands of a guardian. So he turned out to be quite likable in the final draft of my novel.

Louis Weichmann is a different story. While he was in an unenviable position at the trial, which cast a shadow over the rest of his life, it also brought out some of the most unattractive aspects of his personality. He never let anyone associated with the prosecution forget the role he had played in securing Mary's conviction, and in one particularly off-putting letter written in 1896, he told the aging Judge Bingham that the judge might not have many years left to him and asked him to contribute a letter to Weichmann's book about the "mead of praise" to which Weichmann was entitled for testifying!

Did you find it difficult to write John Wilkes Booth's character?

Actually, he was one of the easiest characters to write. Most people found him charming and engaging, so it wasn't hard to bring out those qualities in him. I think it is a pity he didn't enlist in the Confederate army and die a valiant death on the battlefield — many people, and the nation, would have been a lot better off for it.

Is there something you wish you had been able to find out?

Although she's a minor character, it really annoys me that I haven't been able to find out what happened to Catherine Baxley, who shares the ladies' imprisonment for a brief time. Her trail grows cold in 1867, when she and Robert E. Lee corresponded about a donation he had made to a charity in which she was involved. I check the various newspaper archive sites from time to time in hopes that one day I'll run across a mention of her. It's difficult for me to imagine that she simply vanished into quiet obscurity, because she wasn't a quiet lady.

Would you like to have lived in 1860's America?

As interesting as it would have been, no

— I like antibiotics and our other modern conveniences. Especially air conditioning, having spent summers in Washington, DC! But I would like to wear the clothes from the period. For author appearances, I got together a period ensemble, complete with corset, drawers, and hoop skirt, and I felt downright shabby after changing back into my usual sweater and jeans. I wish I could find more occasions to wear my gown, but the neighbors might think it a bit odd to see me walking the dogs in it.

All of your previous novels were set in medieval or Tudor England. Was it difficult for you to make the transition to nineteenth-century America?
Once I stopped typing "1565" for "1865" it was fine! Actually, it did take a little adjustment going from the high nobility in England to the middle class in America. I had to remember not to have my characters address each other as "my lord" and "my lady," and to have them do for themselves instead of having servants waiting on them. And my nineteenth-century characters were more buttoned up — in every sense of the word — than my characters from centuries before.

Would you write another novel set during this period?

Certainly! I have some ideas percolating. And doing archival research is addictive.

ACKNOWLEDGMENTS

Having previously written about medieval and Tudor England, I thoroughly enjoyed researching and writing *Hanging Mary,* set a mere five-hour drive away from my home. The American setting allowed me to enlist some homegrown assistance, first and foremost that of my husband, Don Coomes, who generously drove me to and from Washington, DC, altered his schedule to accommodate mine, and put up with our dogs while I sat in a padded library chair and delved through documents to my heart's content. I thank him and my children, Thad and Bethany Coomes, for putting up with me.

I am grateful to Cliff Roberts on the Lincoln Discussion Symposium forum for supplying the information that allowed me to begin my research on Nora Fitzpatrick, which saved me countless hours of genealogical inquiry. I would also like to thank

Laurie Verge, director of the Surratt House Museum, and Sandra Walia, its former research librarian, for their assistance. Author Betty Ownsbey generously shared some of her newspaper clippings with me.

Thomas Otto, who has written an excellent book on St. Elizabeths, was kind enough to give me much-needed pointers on research at the U.S. National Archives. I also received helpful assistance from staff at the District of Columbia Archives, Duke University's Rubenstein Library, the Georgetown University Library, the Library of Congress, Rice University's Papers of Jefferson Davis project, and the Virginia Historical Society.

My editors at Sourcebooks, editorial director Shana Drehs and editor Anna Michels, did a marvelous job of whipping my manuscript into shape. They and my agent, Nicholas Croce, bore a very long interval between books with great patience and understanding. I also have to thank production editor Heather Hall and copy editor Gail Foreman for their thoroughness.

Finally, for entering (and winning) my contest to name Nora's cat, I congratulate Evelyn Dangerfield, Libby Hunt, Jayne Smith, Julia Strouse, and Cyndi Williamson. Nora's cat no doubt could have told the government quite a bit about what went on at Mary Surratt's boardinghouse in the spring of 1865. But, as the late P. D. James's Inspector Dalgliesh observed in a similar context, would he have told the truth?

ABOUT THE AUTHOR

Susan Higginbotham has worked as an attorney and an editor. *Hanging Mary,* the first of her historical novels to be set in the United States, is her sixth novel. Her first novel, *The Traitor's Wife,* won the gold medal for historical/military fiction in the 2008 Independent Publisher Book Awards. For more information about her novels and the history behind them, visit her website and blog at www.susanhigginbotham.com and her Facebook page.

LARGE TYPE
Higginbotham, Susan
Hanging Mary

JUN   2016